BLOOD GORGONS

THE DROP-POD'S SIDE hatches unfolded like flower petals.
There was an exhalation of pressurised air. The outside
rushed in towards them as if a flood gate had burst.

Barsabbas crouched and shot on instinct. His first
shot punched through a human chest. The body had no
chance to fall as others pushed in from behind. It
remained upright – jammed by the press of people. The
freshly killed man seemed to writhe. Barsabbas thought
he saw its arms raise but he dismissed it as a ghost
image. He took aim for a second shot – and paused.

The body continued to walk towards him, lurching
with blind, drunken steps. This time Barsabbas
removed its head with a clean shot and it dropped.
Only then did he realise that they were surrounded by
the dead.

Hundreds of dead. Their arms were outstretched
and their faces waxy. Corpses swarmed over the drop-
pod, climbing the chassis and being pushed by
thousands more from the rear.

Recoiling in physical disgust, the Blood Gorgons
opened fire with a whittling, sustained volley that
fanned out in all directions.

In the same series

EMPEROR'S MERCY
FLESH AND IRON

More Warhammer 40,000 from the Black Library

EISENHORN
Dan Abnett
(Contains *Xenos, Malleus* and *Hereticus*)

RAVENOR: THE OMNIBUS
Dan Abnett
(Contains *Ravenor, Ravenor Returned* and *Ravenor Rogue*)

HAMMER OF THE EMPEROR
An Imperial Guard Omnibus
Steve Parker, Steve Lyons and Lucien Soulban
(Contains the novels *Gunheads,*
Ice Guard and *Desert Raiders*)

BLOOD GORGONS

Henry Zou

BLACK LIBRARY

he told her, 'I will make you something of warmth and living wood.'
'that's silly,' she said, 'for you are neither carver nor carpenter.'
rebuked, he borrowed the paper of a tree and wrote a book instead.

A BLACK LIBRARY PUBLICATION

First published in Great Britain in 2011 by
The Black Library,
Games Workshop Ltd.,
Willow Road, Nottingham,
NG7 2WS, UK.

10 9 8 7 6 5 4 3 2 1

Cover illustration by Raymond Swanland.

A CIP record for this book is available from the British Library.

UK ISBN: 978 1 84970 006 1
US ISBN: 978 1 84970 007 8

See the Black Library on the Internet at
blacklibrary.com

Find out more about Games Workshop
and the world of Warhammer 40,000 at
www.games-workshop.com

Printed and bound in the UK.

IT IS THE 41st millennium. For more than a hundred centuries the Emperor has sat immobile on the Golden Throne of Earth. He is the master of mankind by the will of the gods, and master of a million worlds by the might of his inexhaustible armies. He is a rotting carcass writhing invisibly with power from the Dark Age of Technology. He is the Carrion Lord of the Imperium for whom a thousand souls are sacrificed every day, so that he may never truly die.

YET EVEN IN his deathless state, the Emperor continues his eternal vigilance. Mighty battlefleets cross the daemon-infested miasma of the warp, the only route between distant stars, their way lit by the Astronomican, the psychic manifestation of the Emperor's will. Vast armies give battle in His name on uncounted worlds. Greatest amongst his soldiers are the Adeptus Astartes, the Space Marines, bio-engineered super-warriors. Their comrades in arms are legion: the Imperial Guard and countless planetary defence forces, the ever-vigilant Inquisition and the tech-priests of the Adeptus Mechanicus to name only a few. But for all their multitudes, they are barely enough to hold off the ever-present threat from aliens, heretics, mutants - and worse.

TO BE A man in such times is to be one amongst untold billions. It is to live in the cruellest and most bloody regime imaginable. These are the tales of those times. Forget the power of technology and science, for so much has been forgotten, never to be re-learned. Forget the promise of progress and understanding, for in the grim dark future there is only war. There is no peace amongst the stars, only an eternity of carnage and slaughter, and the laughter of thirsting gods.

CHAPTER ONE

COME DAWN, THE small craft settled on a disused runway sixteen kilometres east of the Belasian capital. The landing struts sought purchase on the broken rockcrete and Gammadin of the Blood Gorgons emerged purposefully. His men followed him, stepping down the landing ramp into the quiet morning. He led the way, parting the tall weeds that choked the landing strip as they threaded west towards the distant city lights.

The sun was rising, spilling a weak light over the disrepair of Belasia. Along the way, rockcrete blockhouses struggled out from the bushes. Their windows were broken, their roofs collapsed, and they had been abandoned long ago. The wind moved amongst the yellowing plant life, rustling the dead grass and shuddering the knotted, leafless brambles. In the distance, the rusting frame of an air mill lay on its side, its skeleton scorched white by bomb blasts.

Gammadin and his Blood Gorgons scanned the broken panes of glass, their helmet arrays searching for thermal heat. There was none to be found except the tiny, skittering signatures of rodent life.

'All clear,' reported one of Gammadin's companions.

'Remain alert and adjust your auspexes,' replied Gammadin. 'They may mean to deceive us yet.'

Heeding his words, Gammadin's men spaced themselves out into a wide echelon. They bent low, the butts of their guns locked tight against their shoulders. At the fore, Gammadin walked upright, almost nonchalantly, as he led them to the Belasian capital. He held out his palm, skimming the tall grass with one hand as he walked. In the other hand, held tight behind his back, he gripped the handle of a heavy tulwar blade.

They were large, these men, and some would say they were not men at all. They were post-humans – living constructs that evolved the human form into a singular purpose of warfare. They were mortal things, but most whispered their names with a superstitious fear reserved for phantoms and daemons.

There were nine such warriors following Gammadin. Encased in plate and horn, they moved slowly and deliberately, as if they lived by their own rhythm and the world simply orbited their presence. Like their lord, each Traitor Marine wore power armour the colour of burnt umber. Barnacles and fossilised organisms spread across the sweeping surface of each plate. There was an organic element to their regalia, accentuated by the mutant growth of dorsal fins, quills and hard, segmented shells. Shambling ancients, slow and terrible, the eight Impassives appeared not to move at all as the landscape glided beneath their feet.

Behind them, almost as an afterthought, ghosted the witch, Anko Muhr, following behind in a tower of rigid armour with curtains of black silk trailing from his shoulders. Unlike his brethren, Muhr was pensive, his fists clenching and unclenching. Unhelmed, his equine face was painted white but the war markings could not mask the agitation in his eyes. He watched the still grass and blinked against the rising sun. Nearby, leafhoppers chirped, promising a hot, quiet day. There was a still tension in the dawn, a fragile peace that could not last. Muhr could feel the taut energy on the wind.

Picking up speed, Gammadin and his warriors cut through the yellowing hills that bordered the capital. They stopped every now and again, trying to catch the scent of a human; a pack of blackened hunters, crashing through dry branches, lifting their heads to taste the air. Belasia lay ahead, a shoulder of rock-crete that surfaced above the flatlands and pastures. In the distance, yet clearly audible, the early morning was accompanied by the waking screams of thousands.

THE WEATHER WAS unusually fine in the Capital State of Belasia. The sun shone lime-bright on the highways and gridded, austere buildings. Such temperate weather only contrasted with the depressive state of each precinct. The air was hazed with heat and summer dust. There was not a single window within the rectangular ministry blocks and tenements that remained intact. Life still dwelled there, but it was sporadic and rare. The long silence of the day was interrupted only by sudden and intense swells of gunfire.

Belasia had once been a stable world of the Imperium. High density city blocks dotted efficient highways that traversed the wide plains of chemically wilted flora. It was neither a metropolis nor a thriving port of trade, but its governance had been effective. A modest export of coal and non-ferrous metals to the domestic subsector maintained a reasonable standard of living for its large labouring populace. Like their plain proto-Imperial architecture, Belasians were an uninspired group. Austerity, order and economic prudence were the prevailing ideology, alongside honest work for the Emperor's glory.

But this stability had been undone by the discovery of rich mineral seams along the Belasian Shelf and the civil war that followed. As with all civil wars, it became a battle of interests. The wealthy collared the poor and the poor fought amongst themselves.

The military chieftains of the Belasian PDF were quick to declare their interests in the mineral wealth, mobilising Belasia's 'Red Collar' regiments to forcefully secure mining sites. In reaction, the Imperial administration levied a conscript force and transformed their modest primary production sectors into industries of war. The ensuing conflict wiped out thirty per cent of adult males in Belasia within a decade. When the number of able-bodied young men dwindled, both factions turned to recruiting boy soldiers to continue their campaigns.

Rebels, looters and activists added to the degeneration of society. The entire infrastructure of Belasia deteriorated as her people descended into violent madness. It was not long before boy soldiers roamed the streets, proclaiming themselves rulers, brandishing lasguns. With the sudden proliferation of arms, no one argued with them.

By virtue of their obscurity within the star system, the Belasians fought a vicious war amongst themselves for seventeen years. Neither PDF militants nor the local government requested aid from Holy Terra, for neither wanted to share the spoils of victory. By 855.M41, entire cities were held by local warlords and their gangs. The Red Collar regiments became mere mobs of heavily armed children fighting for food and ammunition.

That was when the dark eldar chose to strike.

Not much can be remembered of the invasion, for nothing was recorded. Although the xenos were small in number, the population of Belasia possessed no means to repel them. The Red Collars and child rebels, soft from plundering unarmed civilians, fled at the advance of the dark eldar. In the days following the xenos landings, the remaining military vox-channels spread tales of alien raiders and mass murders. People hid in their public shelters or fled from the cities.

In the years that followed, the dark eldar cultivated Belasia as a farmer tends an orchard. They harvested slaves from the pockets of life, never taking more than the population could replenish. They indulged in orgies of bloodletting to keep the humans fragmented and fearful, but never pushed a region into extinction. These slaves were sold on to other dark eldar kabals, to Chaos cults in neighbouring subsectors and even to Chaos Space Marine warbands such as the Blood Gorgons.

IT WAS THE first meal Jonah had eaten in three days. That in itself was not uncommon on Belasia. Not many dared to forage wild cabbage in the city outskirts when pressured constantly by the fear of being hunted.

But finally Jonah had succumbed to hunger, and under the cover of darkness he left the shelter of his basement. From the local chemical mills, he would gather fungi that spored in the rubble and rust of demolition. Over where the highways led out to the district outskirts, he knew of a spot where string vines grew in patches, between the cracked pavement slits. They were palatable enough if boiled with salt.

Travelling light, Jonah tucked the scavenged vegetables into a plastek bag and stole his way through the darkest lanes and drainage pipes. At all times, he watched his back carefully, looking for a glimpse of the stick-men. Jonah remembered a time when it had only been a brisk stroll from his hab to the outer townships. Now the creeping, hiding and constant panic took him hours.

Back home in his basement, his family waited for him – his daughter, Meisha, and his wife in the corner, looking mousy and long suffering.

They ate in silence, concentrating on the task of spooning, chewing and savouring. It made the food last longer that way. Quietly they ate, hidden from the outside world.

It was not until they finished that Jonah heard a cracking on the floorboards above. A low groaning of the wood, soft at first but growing persistent as it crept close. It sounded, quite dreadfully, as if someone was treading across the abandoned rail station above them.

Had he been followed? He had never been careless when foraging for food or water in the city.

They held their breaths. A shadow glided across the boarded up windows, rippling through the tiny slits between the planks.

The fear in him was so great. Jonah knew very well what those stick-men did to people. Pushing the sinking fear from his mind, Jonah closed his eyes and began to count. Slowly, with his breath still and taut in his chest.

The footsteps faded.

Meisha hissed a low wheezing breath. It was too soon.

Suddenly and without reason, the lone candle flickered out.

The door buckled with a sudden crack. Jonah screamed in shock without meaning to. The door warped under the pressure before popping uselessly off its hinges. Meisha began screaming because he was screaming. Soon his wife followed suit and they were all shrieking in terror as the stick-men skittered into their shelter.

Their limbs shot through the door first, long and fluted like finely carved lengths of ebony. This was followed by the uncurling spindle of their torsos as they swooped beneath the door frame. They moved so fast that they seemed to flicker.

Jonah fumbled for the shotgun beneath the blanket trunk. He had once been an enforcement officer, when Imperial law had still been relevant on Belasia, and that weapon was the last remaining vestige of his pride. It had pained him when his wife had insisted he keep it locked away from the children. Now it was too late. Jonah never got to the shotgun.

They came to him with such speed, kicking him in the jaw with a finely pointed boot and sprawling him onto the floor. In a daze, Jonah could not see how many there were, he only saw the whirl of tall thin bodies. In the dark, their armour matched the hue of a midnight sky and their faces were enclosed in tusk-shaped helmets.

'Pa!' shrieked Meisha. 'The ghosts are here! The ghosts are here!'

A stick-man aimed his rifle at her, the razorblades that edged the weapon flashing with his movement. It was said by some that their guns spat poison. Jonah leapt to his feet, his fear suddenly forgotten, and lunged for his daughter. But the stick-men were too quick. An armoured fist punched him on the chin and blackened his vision entirely. The last thing he remembered was the shrieking.

JONAH AWAKENED SLOWLY to pounding pain in the back of his head. He was groggy and it took him a moment to realise he was not in his own home any more. He panicked with a start and began to fight against the paralysis of sleep. With a thrust of conscious effort he forced his eyes to open.

He lay in an old armoury of some kind, likely the PDF staging station in St Orlus Precinct. The tin shed was unlit except for the bay of small windows that let in hazy shafts of sunlight. A thick patina of blackened soot covered the inside of the corrugated tin shed while old tools still hung from the roof racks in cocoons of dust and spider webs.

The place had been stripped of its equipment during the civil war, likely many years before the coming of the stick-men. Civilian vehicles, uparmoured and customised, replaced the old tanks and carriers of the Red Collar regiments. Jonah could make out a road hauler with a heavy bolter mounted on its bonnet and a Chimera, its hull sprayed with skull motifs in the manner of the child soldiers.

As his vision began to focus, Jonah realised there were others with him. There were bodies shifting under the scant light, packed into the armoury. Jonah recoiled in fright, but hands pushed back at him, intruding on his space. In such tight confines, he smelt sweat and the oiliness of human hair.

There was a man of middle years next to him, his shoulders pressed together. Squinting, Jonah saw the silhouette of a beard and matted hair. The man said nothing, but Jonah could feel his shoulders tremble softly as he cried. Jonah looked away, suddenly ashamed. There were many others around, moaning and babbling.

The noise rose as more captives regained consciousness. The nonsense sounds of human misery grew louder until suddenly Jonah heard a stinging crack. The moans turned into howls.

Something was amongst the writhing captives. A

tall figure, standing above them, lashing a whip into the mound of bodies. Following each snap of the whip came a protest of humiliated pain. Jonah tried to move away as the stick-man picked his way through the captives, thrashing his whip. There was a final, sinking pain in Jonah's chest as his fears became real. He had been captured by the stick-men; there was no denying that reality any more.

The stick-man's face had the pallor of the dead and his eyes were large and almost entirely black, their pupils seeming to swallow up the whites. Narrow and vulpine, his features had a wicked upward slant that were locked in a darkly comedic grin.

Jonah started to yell. He did not mean to, but he became caught up in the panic around him. It was the deep, bawling cry of a terrified human adult, equal parts a sound of distress and the loud roar of an animal trying to frighten away its tormentors.

The armoury erupted with shrill, maddening laughter. Jonah realised there were more stick-men watching him than he had realised. The laughter came from behind him, and even seemed to drift down from the darkened rafters and furthest corners. Bladder muscles loosening, Jonah sank back into the floor as the whip crashed against his back.

THE WATER WAS an unctuous yellow. It was so heavy with pollutant that the liquid sat with an unmoving viscosity. Stringy, grassy vegetation scummed its surface, collecting in progressively larger bales towards the centre of the lake, gathering into a morass of dark, hairy fibres.

Standing on the banks, Lord Gammadin watched

as Captain Hammurabi descended shin-deep into the water. The still surface rippled awkwardly, bubbling and frothing in fits. With one mighty stroke of his broadsword, Hammurabi collapsed an entire copse of small bushes.

Gammadin had a great admiration for the captain of his personal guard, the eight Impassives. Hammurabi had a good sword arm, and was loyal as far as a worshipper of Chaos can be termed so. He followed his duties as Gammadin's first blade strictly. He executed those duties well now as he sloshed deeper into the water, parting reeds with heavy blows of his sword.

Gammadin waded into the water. The disturbance rocked the water grasses and they rustled a collective sigh, swaying gently back and forth. The sun caught the water and flickered. For a moment, Gammadin thought he saw a face, but then it was gone.

Blinking his hooded eyelids, Gammadin studied the grasses but found nothing. His hand slithered over the hilt of his tulwar and there it stayed. The air was hot and still, the sun steaming off the lake's surface. The water seemed to murmur, furtive with secrets. Suddenly, Gammadin sensed a presence. He felt a chill in the base of his neck.

He advanced waist-deep into the water, the ancient servos of his power armour whirring as they churned his legs through the muddy bottom. Yet still that feeling would not leave him.

'My Khorsaad,' Hammurabi said, gesturing respectfully for Gammadin to follow. The captain had already advanced several dozen paces ahead, cutting a swathe through the bog.

Gammadin raised his ceramite palm. 'Wait.'

Despite the stillness, there was a restless quality to the atmosphere, beneath the surface. Long ago, the gods had gifted Gammadin with enlightenment, and his psychic abilities had matured into a fearsome prospect ever since. Gammadin could see the arcs and mathematic patterns in the air that modelled the space and materium of this world. He could channel his will into displays of physical force. But above all, he could sense the consciousness of the world around him – the rocks, the soil, the trees. He sensed, now, there was a hidden danger. The lake seemed to tremble with anticipation and the air was coarse with a lively, barely contained static. Hidden energy surrounded him everywhere.

The water stirred behind Gammadin. The lord turned slowly to see Anko Muhr enter the lake with Gammadin's retinue, an elite core of venerated seniors bonded in the ritual way of the Blood Gorgons. There were four pairs in all, each pair having shared organs and tissue to produce a symbiosis of shared battlefield experience.

What manner of beast or man could ever overwhelm the eight Impassives?

Gammadin quelled the troubling instinct and began to walk across the lake. Together they fanned out into a staggered formation, waist-deep. The lake was wide, but drought had evaporated its depth. Heavy minerals crunched underfoot, feeding the floating water grasses that obscured the distant shoreline from view. They did not travel far before Gammadin felt it again. Stronger this time, a palpable warning that drummed with percussive urgency in his temple.

'Halt!' Gammadin called. He spied movement in the water to his immediate left. The grass parted softly, tentacle roots bobbing listlessly away in the water. Their steps had disturbed the soil. Something dark and round bubbled to the surface.

Gammadin gnashed the spined pincer of his right arm with a loud click. The Impassives dropped low, their bolter barrels chasing the grass for a target. Sliding his tulwar from his waist, Gammadin slapped the flat of its blade against the mottled shell of his right arm.

The object burped to the surface with one final pop of oily water. A black hat. It sat still on the surface. A black felt hat with a round crown and wide brim.

Hammurabi slid through the water and flipped it over. It turned, floating like a high-sided boat, revealing blood and hair on the underside. The blood was still fresh and soaked into the felt like an ink stain.

'How curious,' Muhr observed. He seemed to drift. His dark brown cloak, sagging with charms and fetishes, clung to his power armour wetly as he waded closer.

Gammadin eyed the witch warily. He did not trust Muhr. Not only because he was a sorcerer, but also because Gammadin could sense a jealous ambition in Muhr's black heart. Muhr was the Chapter's senior Chirurgeon and high priest of the witch coven, and Gammadin was aware of his power lust.

'Leave that,' Gammadin commanded.

''Tis truly a gods-damned omen,' Muhr said theatrically, rubbing the wreaths of knuckle bone necklaces that coiled down his breast. 'A dead man's hat, drifting in the current.'

The troubling fear still weighed heavily on Gammadin's brow. He was not one to listen to the witch's superstitious meanderings, but there was something in the air.

'Let us beseech the protection of the gods,' Muhr said. 'Only they can convert ill-luck to fortune.'

Gammadin scanned the lake, motionless now. He agreed reluctantly and signalled for the witch to go ahead.

As the chanting began, Muhr's black craft unsettled even the eight Impassives. He swayed, rocking gently at the waist. A monotonous prayer rasped from his vox-grille. It had a steady, hypnotic cadence. With the raising of his voice, a light wind picked up which brought grit and dry leaves on its draught.

The Impassives grew ever more restless. They breathed heavily. The Blood Gorgons were renegades but they had not been lured into depths of arcane lore like the warbands of their more superstitious brethren. They considered themselves a warrior band first and foremost. Despite their worship of the Sects Undivided, sorcery was a fickle and dangerous thing to be feared and respected from a distance.

Muhr finished his chant and began to splash oil from a ceramic gourd. He splashed some against Gammadin. The droplets felt like intrusive hammer blows, and Gammadin immediately felt drowsy, as if his eyes were blinking through the haze of half-sleep.

'What have you done, witch?' Gammadin asked brusquely. He felt his muscles unknot involuntarily as the ominous urgings dissipated. Yet it did not quell his instincts. He simply felt blinded now. The trouble did not seem to go away, it felt to Gammadin that he simply could not feel it any more. As if it were hidden from him now, just out of reach, as if someone had hooded his psychic abilities.

'The gods, they have dampened our souls against the daemons that watch us.'

'I feel–' Gammadin took a deep, clattering breath. 'I feel like a dull razor.'

'A mere blessing of the gods' gaze. They watch over you now, so you do not need to watch for yourself,' Muhr replied.

'Khorsaad, there is movement,' Blood-Sergeant Makai announced, pointing his boltgun warily.

As Makai spoke, the reeds to their immediate left parted and a man hurtled through the water. He was dazed and bleeding, running wild. He did not even seem to register the presence of the Traitor Marines. He simply tried to churn his legs wildly through the sluggish water.

Makai cut down the man with a burst of his bolter.

'No!' Gammadin said, his voice rising slightly in anger. The man was already dead, bobbing softly over a dark patch of aquatic weed. It was not like Makai to be spooked so easily. Something was irritating all of them.

'I acted hastily, Khorsaad,' Makai replied.

Hammurabi interjected, shaking his head as if to clear it. 'Be still, Makai. We came here to test this world for genestock. This is not a kill-raid.' As Hammurabi spoke, he flipped the dead man onto his back.

For a brief moment, Gammadin's flesh tensed. He

thought he saw fear in the man's rigid features. The man had been running and frightened before he had even seen them. As Gammadin studied the corpse, he began to wonder if the Impassives stood on the same soil as something even more terrifying to these humans than an Astartes. Perhaps there was more on Belasia than the topographic scans had revealed. From orbit, the planet had appeared to be a prime slave colony, but now they were on-world, he was not so sure. There was just something in the air…

'This is a lawless world and this human's suffering is no uncommon thing,' Muhr said, pointing at the dead man. 'We should make haste and think nothing of it.'

Gammadin slapped his thigh decisively. 'Come then. We go,' he said, resuming his steady wade.

STANDING AMONGST THE chemical-churned mud and dead reeds of the shoal, Jonah was stripped of his clothing. There was no dignity, no modesty. The captives stood close together, each trying to hide behind the person in front. A cold draught blew across the lake's surface, drawing goose bumps across Jonah's forearms.

The stick-men surrounded them. Perhaps two hundred slaves, shepherded by tall, thin shapes. Jonah dared not look at them directly but he felt them in the corners of his vision. Stick-men enslavers hauled against the straining leashes of their hounds. Further behind them, Jonah could hear the high-pitched machine hum of their war engines. A fleet of four or five craft hovered metres above the ground, their long ship-like chassis sharp and narrow. Poised for speed, they rocked gently under the gravitational pull as the stick-men clung to the running boards, shouting and keening in anticipation.

When it finally happened, the stick-men gave them no instructions. They simply pointed across the lake with long, clawed fingers. The meaning was clear enough. Slaves were to run, make a break for freedom across the lake.

And then the stick-men unleashed their animals.

Jonah could not avert his gaze any more. He looked up and saw a hound pounce on a man at the edge of the mob. They were not like any canines that Jonah had handled in his enforcement days. These were hairless things, all naked flesh and gristle. Teeth with jagged regularity snapped closed as the creature began to savage the man into the mud, grinding the man down with its weight and mauling him.

Jonah ran. They all ran, a stampede that crashed into the water and moved as one. Blinding fear forced them to stay together.

Flanking them, running parallel, the warp hounds chased the slaves, forcing them to run in the same direction. The animals did not bark, but they laughed with a shrill yapping as the pack communicated to each other, herding the running humans along the lake bank.

A slave went over, tackled from behind by a hound and nailed into the mud face first. On impact, the hound flipped over its victim, hurtling through the air with its legs upturned and twisting. Before the captive could rise, the other hounds were snapping all over him.

* * *

GAMMADIN STOPPED MID-STRIDE, his boot sinking into a mud crater. He raised his hand.

The shore grass swayed beneath a sudden bar of wind. He could smell the scent of humans on the gust, but there was something else too. More than the gamey, mammalian oil of human skin, there was something organic that stung Gammadin's olfactory glands.

He realised that they were not here simply hunting for slave samples any more. Without a doubt, there was something purposeful manifesting itself. Something knew of the Blood Gorgon presence and was prepared for it, this Gammadin could feel. He knew.

Gammadin's helmet optics were already scanning the surrounding area for danger. The banks of the lake were wide and flat, covered in clumps of dry grass and semi-aquatic rushes. There could be danger there. A fluid stream of information was filtered from his helmet's sensors into his neural relays – wind current, visibility and metallic resonance.

Hammurabi sank into a squat beside Gammadin, leaning on his sword. 'I feel it too, Khorsaad. There is a background roar in my ears.'

Probing psychically, Gammadin attempted to expand his consciousness into the surrounding environs, but he found himself mentally disorientated. The air and slight buzzing of insects made him listless, almost distracted. He had felt the same way ever since Muhr had invoked his black arts.

Muhr. Gammadin growled deep within his blackened hearts. What did he know of the events here?

'Khorsaad!' Hammurabi began, rising suddenly.

They came over the crest, hugging the line where

the water met the earth. Slashing, frothing and flailing as they went, a stampede of people.

It was unclear who fired the first shot. A bolt-round exploded in the midst of the rapidly advancing human tide, but they ran undeterred. Closer now, Gammadin could see their faces, contorted in fright and utterly unaware of the Blood Gorgons in their path of flight.

'Formation!' Gammadin shouted at his Impassives.

The Impassives tightened into a defensive shell around Gammadin. In a circle, they fired into the oncoming avalanche of thrashing limbs, flashing bursts of ammunition into the mob. The horde rushed into and directly over the Blood Gorgons. Naked bodies collided against the anchored warriors, bouncing off their solid weight and swarming around them like an estuary.

'We are being fired upon,' voxed Bond-Brother Carcosa as he placed a hand to his suddenly bleeding neck.

'We are receiving fire,' Khadath affirmed as panicked bodies drummed and bumped against him.

From the distant slopes, a high-pitched whistling could be heard as high-velocity missiles whipped through the grass. They came from every direction at once, slicing into the enamel of his armour. It was an indiscriminate volley, slicing down the fleeing humans as it ricocheted against their plate.

Gammadin magnified his vision threefold towards the slopes. He saw thin humanoids in dark blue carapace standing up from the grass, darting from position to position. They raised long rifles and moved with the fluid coordination of trained marksmen. Gammadin recognised their attackers as dark eldar and knew there was treachery on this world.

He threw the tulwar blade in his palm underhand; the heavy dagger shot out in a wide arc before meeting a dark eldar almost forty metres away, sending it sprawling into the grass. Before his blade had found its target, Gammadin had already picked out several shots with his combi-bolter. The mag scope of his vision lens spun and whirled as it tracked multiple targets before seeking a new one as Gammadin put them down. His rage was building. A xenos round, a crystallised shard of poison, sliced through the back of his knee joint. The toxin tingled in the wound, potent enough to have immediately paralysed any normal human being. The wound only enraged Gammadin further, his killing becoming methodical as he picked target after target.

The eight Impassives fanned out to lay down a curtain of fire. Like Gammadin, they were not pressured to shoot wild. Even as a constant shred of dark eldar weaponry hummed through the air, they picked their shots. The Blood Gorgons refused to give ground, despite the fleeing humans who were adding to the confusion. Growing bold, the dark eldar emerged from the grass to charge down the sandy gradient in a ragged line. A grenade went off at close range, shaking the world and jetting up sheets of mud.

Gammadin's withdrawal was being cut off. The dark eldar hooked around their flanks as the stampede of captives blocked and hemmed in the Impassives. Gammadin nearly lost his footing in the treacherous mud as the storm of xenos weaponry thickened considerably. Splinter rifles rippled shots across the mud flat, steaming up a fog of dirt particles. The airborne mud hung in swirls and lazy drifts, choking the Blood Gorgons' targeting systems.

'We must withdraw,' Gammadin voxed over the squad link.

As they fell back, the dark eldar pressured them, staying in their pocket and exchanging a blizzard of shots. Blood-Sergeant Abasilis and his bond, Bond-Brother Gharne, moved to intercept the dark eldar flanking pincer on their left, banging off crisp, precise shots. Gharne had been blinded in the firefight, his helmet discarded and his eyes shorn by shrapnel. Abasilis called out coordinates to the sightless Gharne, directing his bolter wherever the enemy gathered to return fire.

Movement was the only thing that prevented the Blood Gorgons from being pinned in the open. Gammadin, still facing the enemy, moved backwards into the lake. His combi-bolter was spent of bolt shells. The dark eldar chased him, daring to rush so close that Gammadin could see into the vision slits of their helmets. Easily excited, the dark eldar were growing careless in their pursuit. Gammadin raised his right arm, the monstrous chitin of his pincer, and caught them as they lunged in. With his left he expelled the last of his flamer.

The dark eldar caught in the high pressure stream shrieked and died loudly, their inferior carapaces charring under the chemical flame. Capable of stripping paint off a tank-hide in its raw form, when ignited the palmitic acid burned to a glowing white two thousand degrees. Within seconds the dark eldar were melted into stumps of fused plating and flesh.

Corrosive fumes billowed out in a thick, cloying raft, driving back those dark eldar who were hounding Gammadin too closely.

Behind Gammadin, Blood-Sergeant Khadath, Carcosa and Blood-Captain Hammurabi escorted Muhr, who was extracting Nagael's gene-seed with his scissor hands. The trio surrounded the witch-chirurgeon, firing outwards as they fought their way towards Gammadin. A dark eldar raider, too confident in his abilities, darted low at Hammurabi, twin blades trailing. The ancient captain dismissed him with a back-handed slap, breaking the dark eldar's neck while he continued to cycle through his bolter. Khadath suddenly fell, his neck ruptured. Carcosa caught him by his bolter sling and dragged him backwards.

Gammadin milked the last of his flame chambers as he watched the dark eldar close in. How many of them were there? Hundreds? Certainly, judging by the bodies that were beached on the shores.

The remaining Impassives, their bolters now slung, slaughtered their way deep into the lake with mace, axe and hammer. They drove a path through the dark eldar who tried to engage them hand to hand. For all the speed and deft blade-skill of the xenos raiders, the Impassives crushed them with brute strength. Bond-Brother Gemistos led the way, sprinting at full speed, all three hundred kilos of him. An ironclad juggernaut crashed through the dark eldar, swinging his antlered helmet from side to side.

Together the Impassives clustered around Gammadin like a shield wall. They became a solid phalanx of ceramite. The dark eldar could not manoeuvre close enough to surround them. Bolt shells whistled and spat through the water grass.

And that was when Muhr revealed his hand.

Trailing behind, the witch moved away from his lord. The dark eldar around him did not strike nor fire upon him, even as he raised his arms to summon his powers. A sudden wind gusted across the river, flattening the grass on the banks as it reached a high-pitched crescendo.

'Witch!' shouted Gammadin. 'What manner of–'

Gammadin was cut short as Muhr clapped his hands. The air pressure dropped as if in a vacuum. Shadows began to rise out of the boiling current, humanoid in shape, with multiple reaching hands.

The water frothed violently around the Impassives. Shadowy apparitions bubbled forth from the river and began to swarm over them. The mud beneath the Chaos Space Marines' feet gurgled wetly, slipping and sliding as if falling away.

'Muhr. You are not worthy of the Blood Gorgon title,' Gammadin whispered on the squad link.

The lake bottom suddenly imploded with a thunderous gurgle. It yawned like a sinkhole, thirstily draining water into its aqueous abyss. Four Impassives were carried down by the crashing flood of water. Gammadin sank down on one knee, fighting for purchase in the mud. Warning lights flashed across his vision as the spirit of his armour began to babble nonsense in his ears. The ground beneath him continued to give way. Sensing his weakness, warp hounds began to paddle across the lake towards him.

'I have plenty left for you!' he roared, drawing a

scimitar from his back scabbard. The pitted blade was almost two metres in length, scarred and nicked from centuries of service. It resembled a tool rather than a blade, a piece of metal stripped of any elegance in favour of the utility of killing. Dragging it to his left he met the charging hounds with three horizontal strikes, rushing past them as they leapt into the air and leaving severed corpses in his wake.

He turned to meet Muhr the betrayer. The sorcerer was wise to keep his distance, stepping away even as his hands throbbed with black, sorcerous fire.

'Witch. What have you done here?' Gammadin demanded.

'You're a tiresome one,' Muhr replied. 'The Blood Gorgons need leadership. I tire of roving like vagabonds, adrift in space with no purpose.'

'We are raiders, Muhr. That's our way of doing things,' growled Gammadin. He tried to rise to his feet, but the lake bottom sucked and slurped. The waterline lowered visibly as the Champion Ascendant planted his foot into solid mud, but it yielded completely. The gushing water pushed against him and suddenly Gammadin was going over.

'You're going to die now,' Muhr said.

It was the last thing Lord Gammadin heard as the lake opened up to swallow him whole.

CHAPTER TWO

GAMMADIN WAS DEAD.

Those were the words that echoed aboard the *Cauldron Born*. From the fortress-ship's hammerhead prow, word spread quickly of their champion's death. Cries of alarm could be heard in the ship's temple bowels, and sorrow radiated out into thousands of chambers and connective corridors of the floating fortress. The daemon bells were tolled and the ship fired broadsides in salute. Many did not believe the news. It should not, nay, it *could* not have happened and some refused to accept it.

Lord Gammadin had been their master when the Gorgons were first created in the 21st founding. He had been their shepherd when the Imperium declared them renegade – *Excommunicate Traitoris* – mere centuries later, and it was he who parted the warp-sea to lead them into the Eye of Terror. The

Blood Gorgons knew no other commander.

Even the ship itself strained in mourning. As an artefact of Blood Gorgons biological experimentation – pseudo-surgery and daemonology – all eight kilometres of the vessel seemed to tremble. It was said that the floating fortress had been grafted with the flesh of a daemon prince and that organic matter had been cultivated to merge with the ship's engines, spawning a spirit that inhabited the circuitry. Gammadin was its master and the ship was his steed.

Panic and disturbance accompanied the news of his passing. The captains of the companies, nine in all, retreated to their lairs within the labyrinthine depths, drawing around them their most trusted warriors. None knew what the following days would bring, but they knew well enough not to act in haste.

Sabtah the Older, Chapter Veteran, slipped into a berserk rage. He had been Gammadin's blood bond, having exchanged excised organs and blood with him in the Rituals of Binding. The death of his bond drove Sabtah insensate with grief and fury.

It was recorded in history that when Gammadin had first begun to experiment in daemonology and the rituals that would form Blood Gorgons custom, Gammadin had been bound to his most trusted lieutenant, Monomachus. Utilising the superhuman constitution of an Astartes, Chirurgeons had transfused blood and nurtured organs from excised tissue into prospective bonds. Using Gammadin's knowledge of arcane lore, rituals of the forgotten text were followed, creating an almost supernatural connection between those who survived the procedure.

Together, Gammadin and Monomachus led the Blood Gorgons to raid and terrorise the shipping lines of the Segmentum Obscurus. So attuned were they, that in battle the pair could orchestrate intuitive tactical decisions without communication. During the War of the Wire, Gammadin had sensed Monomachus's beleaguered disposition and sent reinforcements from two star systems away, despite the oceanic gulf of distance.

For four centuries they fought as parallel twins until Monomachus angered the gods and his form was corrupted into that of a spawn. It was said that Gammadin was greatly shamed by this and slew Monomachus himself, an act that would have caused him considerable physical pain. By now, Gammadin was a warrior so great, with blood so rich and vibrant with the power of Chaos, that no mere aspirant could hope to be blooded to him.

Following Monomachus, numerous unsuitable aspirants were killed by the rich blood of Gammadin. Rituals of Binding were dangerous, both through the traumatic shock of surgery and the whims of daemonic spirits. Although Gammadin's experience was vast, he could not share it, for dozens of aspirants died or went mad in the rituals of transfusion and excise.

It was not until Sabtah – an inductee from the legion plains of Symeon – that a bond showed promise. The aspirant endured months of torture on the operating slabs, his body sent into shock by the process of plasma binding, until he emerged as a young charge of the great Gammadin. For the next three thousand, six hundred and fifty-one years,

Henry Zou

Sabtah the Older had become Gammadin's brother, growing stronger and wiser through their synergy.

And now Gammadin was dead.

THE MAZE OF Acts Martial, a sixty-hectare section of interior combat facilities set beneath the engine decks of the *Cauldron Born*, was littered with corpses. Narrow ossuaries meandered into charnel houses where the bones of slain 'training prey' filled the walls. These macabre displays formed neat lattices, while bare skulls of all species formed low pyramids. Even the floors were snowy with a build-up of bone powder. Each time prey was released into the maze, the Blood Gorgons interred them where they fell, and in the preceding centuries, the Blood Gorgons trained often.

'Push to the left. The prey is on your left, at thirty degrees,' Sargaul whispered into his vox-link.

But Barsabbas didn't need to hear the command. He could already judge by the way Sargaul stood, the angle of his helmet and the urgency in his voice, that their prey was on his left. Such was the shared experience of a blood bond that Barsabbas fired before he took aim through his bolter scope, so sure was he of Sargaul's warning.

The termagant was shredded by the salvo of shots. The plates on its forehead crumbled away as its frontal lobe exploded. Its bulbous hind legs loosened out from underneath it and the creature collapsed, its thick tail straightening. As it died, its thigh muscles continued to work, twitching and kicking the last of its life away.

A kill counter chimed in the corridor, signalling a successful training shot. 'Perfect,' Sargaul said, slapping the back of Barsabbas's bulky power pack. 'But next time, do not wait. Aim your shot if you can spot it. Our blood bond allows us to kill efficiently together, not through some rigid singularity.'

Barsabbas nodded intently as his blood bond spoke. Bond-Brother Sargaul was an experienced warrior with almost six decades of service to his trophy racks and although Barsabbas had been bonded to him since his early days as a neophyte, they were markedly different. Barsabbas was young, at least for a Traitor Marine. He had been plucked from his family as a child and survived the test and ordeals required to become a neophyte. At the cusp of adulthood he had been selected to bond with Sargaul and survived the ritual of excise that transplanted their major organs and homogenised their blood. Since then, he had only served as a fully fledged bond-brother on two major tours and a dozen minor raids.

Physically too, Barsabbas differed from his bond. Where Sargaul reached almost two hundred and fifty centimetres tall in bare feet, Barsabbas was short for a Traitor Marine, topping out at two metres thirty in plated height. While Sargaul was long in the hamstrings and forearms, Barsabbas was wide and thick in the legs. Although their differences would go unnoticed among humans, who viewed all Astartes as uniform giants, a Space Marine perceived such subtle differences in stature and interpreted accordingly. Theirs was a martial culture and Barsabbas had often felt the lesser of the bond. The pair were anything but the same.

'That was sharp, brothers,' said Sergeant Sica. 'Gather on me for post-training evaluation.'

The six Traitor Marines of Squad Besheba took a knee and began to break down the entire training session, from movement formations and firing patterns down to the finite details of xenos psychology and communications theory.

As the youngest of the squad, Barsabbas scribbled notes on a data-slate while the others listened with the casual confidence of experience. There was the pair Hadius and Cython, impetuous and helmet-less, both displaying knife scars on their cheeks and nose bridges, mirror images that perfectly aligned. There was stern Sergeant Sica with his chainaxe slung across his shoulders. Crouched next to him was Sica's bond, Bael-Shura, clacking his metal jaw, an augmetic replacement that had been purposely left jagged and rough-cut. The downward point of his stalactite chin cemented Bael-Shura's face into a morose, forlorn grimace.

The sirens in the ossuary blared again, signalling the end of the session. Having dispatched the last of their prey, the six members of Squad Besheba picked their way down the corridor towards the caged exits.

They followed the trail of dead, the remains of those they had felled that day. Most had been lower organisms of the tyranid genus, smaller wiry animals that had been herded from the slave pens into the maze. The Chapter had recently procured a large quantity of such creatures from xenos slave drivers on the Edge Rift Worlds, and it seemed as if every training drill since then had involved using the captured tyranids. In truth, Barsabbas had grown bored of killing them. At first, the flocks of skittering, agitated little creatures had been a challenge. They leapt and bounced in defiance of the ship's artificial gravity, running vertically up walls and racing across the ceilings like paper debris ejected from a venting pipe. But it had not taken Barsabbas long to recognise their patterns of movement and adapt his bolter drills accordingly. Soon, the challenge of shooting them became a chore, a mere series of 'trajectory calculations' to be hard-wired into Barsabbas's muscle memory through repetition.

The trail of dead was kilometres-long. The Maze of Acts Martial needed to be large in order to accommodate the training requirements of the Blood Gorgons Chapter. Only in these rambling tunnels could the Blood Gorgons simulate the violent claustrophobia of a ship boarding action. A system of concentric corridors, murder holes and dead ends, it was perfectly adapted for the ship boarding actions of the piratical renegades.

The maze was so vast that slaves released into the labyrinth could hide for days, if not months, before Blood Gorgons squads found them again. At times, the slaves would be supplied with weapons and rations, so they could better mimic enemy action. It was not uncommon for slaves of higher intelligence to survive for periods of time, subsisting on fungus and condensation. They often converged into groups for survival, leaving behind the unmistakable remains of food scraps and refuse. Some lost their sanity and were driven to cannibalism. Humans and orks were especially susceptible to such madness, prowling the maze in ghoulish packs.

* * *

BARSABBAS LED THE way as the maze sirens barked again, more urgently this time. The corridors were unlit and lined with porous granite that seemed to soak up light as well as it did blood. Relying only on the dimmest vision setting, Barsabbas probed the way with his chainsword. The persistent tolling of the bell swelled into an imperious clanging. This was no longer a signal that the training drills were over, Barsabbas realised. Somewhere, deep within the Temple Heart of their ship, a call had been issued for Chapter formation. Barsabbas did not know why, but he knew Sargaul echoed his confusion. The temple bells were never rung, except in the event of Chapter-scale war or calamity.

Quickening his pace, Barsabbas slashed away at a solid, gossamer curtain of spider webs through a passage that had been disused for centuries. Barsabbas was not sure what was happening. Stomping through the carcass of a termagant, he threaded his way towards the ship's Temple Heart.

DEEP WITHIN THE ship's core, the bells were sounding again and again. The twin bells swayed ponderously in their chancel arches, pounding out Gammadin's swansong. Carved from ore stone, each bell was fifty metres from crown to lip and their echo could be heard clearly in the furthest points of the fortress-ship. The Blood Gorgons knew the sound as the *Apocalypse Toll* – a herald of calamity.

For the past several days, the bells had been sounded at the passing of each ship cycle. Now they were hauled with a climactic urgency to mark the Summoning. Gammadin's death song would end only with the invocation of the Chapter's patron daemon – Yetsugei.

Their peal woke the Dreadnoughts from their rusting slumber. The sixteen Dreadnoughts of the Blood Gorgons shifted sleepily as servitors anointed their machine joints. They were old bondsmen – some four thousand years old – locked in their coffins of war. They had earned their rest and did not wake for petty foibles, but even they recognised the apocalypse tolls.

The knells radiated outwards and down to the ship's bowels, where the Blood Gorgons berthed the few rare armoured machines they still maintained. These Rhinos and Land Raiders from the ancient past were now hollow shells inhabited by dormant spirits. At the crack of the bells, the engine daemons started, their motors throaty with promethium-phlegm. Some of the armoured carriers jolted forwards, pulling against the shipping chains that lashed them to the decking. They growled and revved, suddenly excited, like leashed dogs straining towards bait. The *Cog's Teeth*, a Rhino-pattern armoured carrier, broke free of its moorings and crashed into a far wall, crumpling the bulkhead. Servitors rushed forwards to calm the daemon spirit within, splashing its tracks with blood to satiate its rage.

All throughout the *Cauldron Born*, from the central barracks to the most crooked of forgotten passages, all were summoned to the temple at the core of the cruising leviathan. The temple matched the bells in their size and grandeur. The ribcage of a dead beast ridged the domed ceiling; intercostal spaces were filled with personal shrines, each maintained daily by one of the nine hundred Blood Gorgons. Some were tall and narrow, like grandfather clocks, while others were squat cubbies brimming with offerings of spent bolter casings, ears, teeth and baubles.

THE TEMPLE. THE Pit. Daemon's cage.

Muhr and his coven were painting the geometrics onto the marble floor with careful strokes of their ash brushes. The Chirurgeon-witches, nine in number, were barefoot and clad in loose black robes. They appeared as ants against the wide, featureless expanse of the marble dais, yet they painted with tiny brushes, tracing precise triangles and interconnected pentagrams. These wards had been inscribed on the domed walls too, painted via scaffolding that swayed gently in the gravitational lurch.

The pit smelled of sorcery – incense, braziers, oil and acidic paint. Of slow, focussed intensity. Muhr and his witches could make no mistake. The slightest error in the wards would be unthinkable.

Elusive and ever clandestine, the Chapter knew to leave the witches to their own rituals. The coven were not blood bonded like their brethren, and from this there grew a rift between the witches and the companies. It was a respectful rift but a rift nonetheless.

Unseen by others, the witches had cleaned themselves first, a ritual cleansing that washed away all their scent. The skin files and dermabrasion had left them pink and newborn, which would not give away their musk to the warp ghosts, or so the ritual claimed.

Once the last wards were laid, and the bells

finished tolling, the Chapter would gather for summoning.

YETSUGEI WAS AN old daemon. Older than the Imperium, than Terra, old even when men still fought with sword and shield. He was known by many names, and had appeared under many guises throughout the history of man.

But he was not strong. Not strong in the way a greater daemon, or even a warlike daemon prince, was strong. He was a mischievous daemon, a trickster.

He was also a patron. He had chosen the Blood Gorgons, for they, much like him, were rogues. They came to him for his prophecies and his knowledge, and he chose to humour them for he yearned for human company. Yetsugei enjoyed the petty foibles and insignificant dramas of their short lives.

When they summoned him, as they had done so for the past three thousand, six hundred and fifty-one years, Yetsugei roared. As his avatar materialised on the prime worlds, Yetsugei spread his arms and shrieked. In truth he would have preferred a quiet summoning, but the humans responded well to theatrics.

There was a maelstrom of warp fire, coalescing into a spiralling column. With a clap of crashing air it disappeared and Yetsugei found himself in the familiar Temple Heart. Pentagrammic wards criss-crossed his vision like the interlaced bars of a cage. They sprouted from the wide marble floors and lanced down from the domed ceiling. Beyond the dais he could see the souls of the assembled Blood Gorgons.

or not, Yetsugei could not deny his daemon
r. Given the chance, he would devour them all.

'You intrude upon my slumber again?' Yetsugei
cawed, feigning shrill indignity. In truth, he had
grown tired of the warp and a glimpse of the prime
worlds was a welcome respite.

The Blood Gorgons psyker he knew as 'Muhr'
stepped forwards and onto the dais, stopping shy of
the external pentagram. 'Yetsugei – the most grave
and reverend. Baron of the Reef of Terror, what deeds
you soon must hear! What sorrow you must behold,
for we mourn the passing of our Great Champion.'

Yetsugei rolled his ropey shoulders. 'Most dreadful
to hear and even more so to see. But first, loosen my
bonds, they are too tight.' Yetsugei pretended to con-
tort his daemonic form in discomfort.

Muhr crouched down and brushed a line with his
hand. Pigment came away from the marble onto his
palm. On his hands was a tiny smear, almost imperceptible considering the immense size of the
marking, but it broke an external seal. It was a calculated risk, and a dangerous one at that, but Yetsugei
knew the humans needed something from him and
Muhr did not dare to antagonise him. He had other
plans.

Yetsugei felt his confines loosen ever so slightly.
Their souls grew brighter to him.

The daemon stretched languidly. 'Ah. How these
bonds make me weary.' He yawned and opened one
eyelid coyly. 'Perhaps you can loosen another?'

'So you say,' Muhr replied coldly. He stepped back
from the dais.

The witch was no fool, and he knew better than to

trust a daemon. Although Yetsugei was their chosen patron, he was a deity and they his mere humans. He appeared to Muhr as a leaping shade, narrow-waisted and smoky, with horns that formed an intricate crown atop his head – a towering pillar of unreality – a thing from another existence. They trusted him for his prophetic knowledge but not with their lives.

'Amuse me, then. What favour would you crave of me?'

Muhr cleared his throat. 'Lord Gammadin is dead.'

Yetsugei yawned. 'How did Gammadin die?'

Muhr lowered his head solemnly. 'Lord Gammadin and his warrior few embarked across the warp-sea to claim a new slave world for harvest. But the pirates of the eldarkind had long ago colonised this world in secret. They were prepared and the battle was their theatre, their stage. We were ambushed and fought on their grounds. I was the only survivor.'

Yetsugei steepled his fingers and fixed his eyes on the witch. Muhr was a good liar, and it was clearly a story he had rehearsed and no doubt recounted many times. But a daemon could see deception against the fabric of reality. Although this was the story Muhr had told the Chapter, Yetsugei knew the witch was hiding his own involvement.

'Yes, so you spake of his demise, that is not your present plight,' the daemon purred. 'It matters not the death of an old champion. Merely that you present a new one to the gods.'

'Gammadin has appointed me sole guardian in his stead,' Muhr recited.

The daemon knew this to be a lie too. There were

other factions at play here and Muhr was simply one such cog in the machine. But Yetsugei did not reveal Muhr's lie. He would enjoy whatever plot was to unfold.

'Tell me, witch. How did he die?' the daemon asked, baiting the witch to reveal more.

'Slain by treachery,' Muhr responded.

That was the truth this time. Yetsugei smiled.

'I challenge that claim!' said a low voice. 'The witch has no proof.'

Yetsugei knew that voice. Sabtah! The daemon clapped with glee. 'The bond of Gammadin! Come forth! Come forth!'

Sabtah stepped onto the dais from the audience. Yetsugei could see raw aggression rippling from the old warrior. 'The wardship is mine to hold,' he stated boldly.

'So it should be!' Yetsugei agreed eagerly, straining against the circle of ash and paint. As he writhed, paint faded from the walls and several of the wards disappeared from the marble. His constraints were breaking. Souls grew closer, brighter.

'Then denounce this man as a liar,' Sabtah said, stabbing his forefinger at Muhr.

Yetsugei cocked his head. 'I sense this witch has some power. A foreign power. Perhaps Gammadin has given you this power... or perhaps another...?'

Yetsugei could tell Muhr was beginning to wither under his attention. The witch was being influenced by greater powers, a rival patron perhaps? There was something more to this tale. Gammadin had not simply been slain by the dark eldar in an accident, leaving the witch a sole survivor.

Muhr's eyes narrowed defiantly, as if sensing Yetsugei's intent. 'Gammadin chose me.'

Biding his time, the daemon leaned forwards and smiled at the witch and the old wolf. 'You must enthrone an Ascendant Champion. Hear me this – do not displease the gods or there will come bad spirits. They will snatch good fortune from your grasp.'

Yetsugei was cracking the seals now. He strained against his weakening confines. He hungered for their souls. Reaching out with his hand, Yetsugei beckoned Muhr closer.

'Daemon, begone!' Muhr shouted suddenly, as if angered. He dispelled the coven's bindings and unravelled the daemon back into the warp. There was a swirl of cold and the wards blackened to ash.

CHAPTER THREE

ON THE FIRST day of Swelter, in the Central Territory of Hauts Bassiq, herdsmen of the plains were mustering their caprid for the early morning drove. When they looked up, they saw a dark ochre cloud hidden amongst the swells of the light dawn cumulus. It was the colour of powdered groundnut and seemed to have the same grainy texture. Heavy and brooding, the strange cloud spread out and descended to cap the distant ridges.

The herdsmen thought little of it, rushed as they were to return to their kinships with caprid milk for breakfast. Yet there was something about the cloud that troubled them. The season of Swelter brought with it brutally clear skies, bathed almost white by the harsh suns. By morning, the red rocks of the plains would be hot enough to curdle lizard eggs. Seldom did the storms come until evening, and even then only briefly.

When the cloud landed, far away from their eyes, it began to kill. More clouds like it soon followed and the microfauna began to die first. Across the plains and dunes of Bassiq, beneath the layer of red iron oxide dust, ore beetles shrivelled up into husks and died. The microscopic filing worms that inhabited the top layer of ferric sand writhed in toxic pain, burrowing deeper to no avail.

The cloud savaged the earth. Distant Ur, the sealed city, cocooned its gates and weather-shields against the encroaching clouds. For as long as Ur had stood, it had been sealed and silent against the outside, opening only intermittently to trade with the plains nomads. Now it sealed itself permanently.

A light southerly carried the fumes across the dry clay seas and dispersed the poison across the lower part of the continent. Ancient boab trees whose swollen trunks and leafless branches had survived centuries of remorseless sun and drought sickened visibly, their silver bark peeling like wet skin. Amongst sheltered gorges that had resisted the climate, patches of coral brush and cacti wilted upon contact.

Only when the clouds began to affect the caprid herds did the plainsmen become concerned. The leaping caprid was the lifeblood of the Bassiq kinships. In ages past, when the mining colonies of distant Terra had harvested the ferrous-rich planet of Hauts Bassiq, these goat-antelopes had been brought with them as a hardy food source. It had been a wise choice, for the horned bovids proved remarkably resilient in the scorching desert, surviving off runt flora while providing the settlers with milk and meat.

Even when the colonists began to leave Bassiq, abandoning its ultraviolet heat and its isolation from the Imperium, the caprid flourished. With their musterers gone, they escaped their pens and became wild, their numbers multiplying. The industrial mines fell silent and the colonists who remained were too few to operate the earthmovers or tectonic drills. Some retreated to the walled city of Ur and sealed themselves within against the heat, drought and radiation. Their fates became unknown, their envoys only emerging from their sealed city to trade. An isolationist Imperial cult, Ur became a forgotten bastion of the early colonists.

Many others wandered the plains in loose familial bands known as kinships, gathering petrochemicals in a vain attempt to keep their machines running and resist their decline into savagery. Soon the Imperium had forgotten that scorched, thermal planet of Hauts Bassiq and Bassiq, in turn, forgot the Imperium.

Even then, the caprid remained a key factor of their survival. From their shaggy long hair sheared in the Swelter Seasons the colonists-turned-plainsmen wove their fabrics, and from their curved horns they crafted tools. Although official history had largely been forgotten, it was said, by word of mouth from kinship to kinship, that the caprid were the true settlers of Hauts Bassiq.

The animals' death was of great concern to the plainsmen. Affected caprid refused to eat, wasting away within a matter of days. The herdsmen could not bear to watch the caprids shrink away until they could barely lift the thick horns on their heads, stooped and bent as they stumbled about. Before succumbing to the disease, the caprid would become aggressive, their eyes rolling white as they bit and kicked in a frenzy. The herdsmen soon realised it was better, and safer, to kill any caprid they suspected of being ill before they could become 'possessed by the ghost' as the plainsmen coined it.

In due time, the sickness spread from the caprid to the plainsmen. At first there was panic amongst the nomadic kinships. They sent emissaries to the north, to the only permanent settlement on the continent, to the Mounds of Ur. But the city hid behind its walls, blind to the fate of wandering nomads. The denizens of Ur had never considered the plainsmen worthy of anything more than infrequent trade.

Although the nomads had no central king, an elder named Suluwei gathered all the wisest elders of the North Territory to discuss this great catastrophe that had befallen them. Suluwei was not a king, but he was the elder of the Ganda Kinship and he owned a great many head of caprid. His possession of so many herds earned him a respected place among the leaders of other kinships and they acknowledged his word.

At his request, the wisest men of the Northern Kinships gathered to discuss the disease that was spreading so rapidly. As was custom for the plainsmen, stories were abundant. Some spoke of black skies in the extremities of the north, dark clouds that besmeared the sky even during the hottest midday. Others spoke of famine and entire kinships disappearing. Others still muttered of ghosts and the restless dead. It was difficult to separate fact from fiction amongst a nomad's word of mouth, but it was clear that strange and frightful things were occurring.

Suluwei spoke briefly of summoning the Godspawn, but the elders, grave though the situation, dared not resort to such measures. In the end, nothing came to fruition from the meeting and the elders returned to their kinships. Within two days, Suluwei was sick, his brain wracked by fever and his eyes rolling white as he succumbed to a sickness he had likely contracted during the meeting of elders. He died soon after, not remembering his own name or where he was. Within a tenday, fully half of his kinship fell ill. Even Suluwei's slight exchange with the other kinships had been enough to infect them all.

Yet most frightening of all was the story of Suluwei after his death. It was passed, from word of mouth, by kinless herdsmen to the Southern Territories, and there were many variations of the tale, but the core of it always remained the same. It was said that Suluwei's kin buried him in the hollowed bole of a boab tree, as custom required, and sealed the hole with many heavy rocks. They performed the ceremonial dances to calm his spirit into the plains and buried him with his warbow, hatchet and saddle so he would not need to seek his possessions in the afterlife.

Yet despite their precautions, Suluwei returned many days later. Here the tale differed, for some said Suluwei returned to his kin with his eyes white and a smile on his face, asking them for one last meal. Others spoke of Suluwei returning at dusk, a flesh-hungry ghoul who tapped on the carriages of his kin, pleading to be let in with a beguilingly sweet voice. Whatever the truth, the story spread as rapidly as the sickness.

When this story reached the ears of Suluwei's brother-in-law, Chetsu, an elder of the Zhosa Kinship, it was decided that they could wait idle no more. Although Chetsu did not own many caprid, nor did his kinship boast many young men, the Zhosa were a brave family. There was evil in the northern tip and Chetsu was resolved to ride out and find those kinships that had fallen silent there.

Chetsu chose five of his kinship's most robust men, all of them his own blood cousins. He made sure they groomed and saddled their talon squalls properly, preening the black feathers of the flightless sprint-birds with oil until they were glossed against the sun and hooding their beaks in sheaths of leather. As usual, young Hantu neglected to oil the bare legs and long neck of his bird, featherless parts which were especially susceptible to sunburn, and Chetsu had berated him furiously, dashing a clay bowl onto the ground in anger. Chetsu was in no mood for slothfulness at a time such as this.

The riders were dispatched in the dawn before the suns could grow thermal. Each man wore a *shuka* of brilliant red wool, a loose sarong worn by all the plainsmen across the territories. Red was a favoured dye and it would give Chetsu and his riders much bravery and aggression. They rode with bows across their saddles and weighted hatchets at their hips. The kinship saw them off with dancing and singing, jumping up and down on the spot to clatter their wrist bangles and necklace wreaths. The plainsmen were not a warlike people and the departure of five warrior braves was a momentous occasion for the Zhosa.

Chetsu rode to the north and that was the last time his kinship saw him. The days passed and the riders did not come back. Chetsu's wife waited for his return, watching the horizon. For as long as she watched, the sky in the distance was ominously dark, contrasting with the harsh white everywhere else. Some of the clouds were pileus, rolling like caps of toxic amber; others were low stratus clouds, coating the horizon in a flat, featureless black rind. They uncurled ponderously, boiling themselves into monstrous shapes that resembled faces, always creeping closer. It would not be long, she thought, until they blocked out the many suns.

THE TEMPLE HAD no name. It had no name because it was the only temple they knew. From outside, it resembled a pylon of uncarved red rock, like a ridged tooth that rose from the flat ground around it. If one were to carve away the exterior, to tear away the rust storms and ferric build-up that cocooned its outside surface, one would find a cathedral of grand design, an edifice built to worship the double-headed eagle from another era. Within its cool interior was a vaulted ceiling of coloured glass, arches and columns – designs that the plainsmen of Bassiq had forgotten how to construct.

By the time the elders of the various northern kinships met in this temple, only three weeks after Suluwei's first summons, there were very few of them left.

Many of the kinships had never responded to the

ageing hand-wound vox-casters, nor had they responded to the secondary smoke signals. Although it had not been spoken, they were already counted among the dead.

All the elders waited in reverential quiet, sometimes expressing their concern in hushed tones. The temple was dark and only pinpricks of sunlight managed to pierce gaps in the rocky crust that covered the windows. The darkness did not matter, for the attention of the assembled elders was centred solely on the single shaft of light at the centre of the temple.

Captured beneath the beam of an open skylight above was a curious machine piece. All the elders had seen it before; some had even prayed to it, but never had they seen it used. There had never, in all their collective memories, been a time that required it.

It just lay there, on the ground, an oblong of tin no larger than a block of compacted nut flour. It was inert, like a sleeping beast, with a thick skin of dust that covered its dials and press pads. In all the time it had been there, no one had dared to touch it. A cranking shaft, delicate and small, protruded from one end of the machine, as if waiting to be turned.

Around the machine, a wide circle had been marked in the stone and simple illustrations of armoured warriors in bulbous helmets had been scratched into the floor. They depicted the helmeted warriors slaying a double-headed eagle, smiting it out of the sky with stylised tongues of fire. Like the machine itself, this circle bore no footprints in its dust rind, although the stone outside its circumference had been worn smooth by pedestrian traffic.

'Someone has to do it,' croaked a toothless elder of the Muru kinship.

'Nay, you are older than I, so the honour is yours!' rebuked another elder.

'Do not be frightened, you are young and vital. You should do it!' another countered.

Soon the congregation were openly shouting and it became clear that no one wanted to touch the machine. No one knew what it would do.

'I'll do it!' shouted a young man as he stepped forwards. 'I'll summon the Godspawn.' The brave's distinctive plaited hair marked him as a brave of the Kosi kinship, reckless riders from the Western Plains. No one argued with him as he pushed his way through the assembly and made his way towards the centre of the temple.

The plainsmen had once worshipped a God-Emperor in the darkest reaches of their dimmest histories. But that had been during the time of the Colonies, a time of dreaming for them. Isolated as it was, Hauts Bassiq suffered many raids from alien invaders and human pirates. For a time, the plainsmen had lived fearful lives, constantly nomadic to avoid conflict. But then the Godspawn came to drive away the xenos. The Godspawn had been their protectors and so it had always been, as far as the plainsmen were concerned.

The Kosi brave took a deep breath and planted a foot inside the carved boundary. The crowd inched back, fearfully expectant, but nothing occurred. Exhaling slowly, the Kosi entered the circle fully and knelt down to inspect the machine.

The machine seemed intuitive enough and there

was nothing for the brave to do but turn the cranking handle. Gingerly gripping it with thumb and forefinger, he started to wind it. To his surprise, it began to turn smoothly despite its considerable age. He began to turn it faster, feeling the gears within the machine tick over, building up momentum as a soft purr began to emit from the tin box.

With a sudden flash, lights within the temple came alive. Some of the elders exclaimed in wonder while others screamed and covered their heads. High up in the vaulted ceiling, light they had never known existed flared after five thousand and seven hundred years of dormancy, lighting the temple with a bright orange radiance.

The brave continued to turn, as if he had known all along what to do. The purr become a loud, steady hum. Acoustic resonance thrummed the air, shivering the skin with its building pressure. In the back of the assembly, someone begged the brave to stop turning the handle but the Kosi could not stop turning even if he had wanted to; the cranking wheel was now spinning on its own, moving so fast the man could not lift his fingers away.

Then it stopped turning with a click. The temperature in the temple plunged. The breath of the elders plumed white as they waited in expectation. Even the alarmed ones who had screamed were now still. Frost did not exist on Hauts Bassiq, except for when mind-witches used their mind powers. But frost now coated the temple, a thin furry sheet that covered the walls and even the wool of the elders' shukas.

But nothing happened. Except for the winking sequence of lights that played across the machine's press pad, nothing happened. The Kosi brave backed out of the circle and the elders leaned forwards, eager to get a closer look now that the work was done.

That was when a seismic rumble flattened the entire congregation. A wall of energy pushed them down and the machine rose up into the air, suspended for a blink before it clattered back down. This time, everyone shouted in fright. The lights winked out and the temple dimmed, as if a shadow had passed overhead. The elders felt exhausted as they tried to claw their way upright, groping lamely in the darkness.

All of them, even the most dim and psychically inert, could instinctively feel what had happened. Although they could not truly understand it, they knew that the power from the little tin machine had been real.

'I think I have summoned them,' the Kosi brave said, staring at his own hands as if they were sacred objects.

THE SLAVE SCRATCHED at the scar on his cheek without thinking. It was a habit he had developed without ever realising. The small incision, shaped like a ringworm, had been cut below his cheekbone. Every slave bore the same mark as a sign of servitude.

Although he had been a slave for many years he had never become accustomed to that scar. It worried him. He could feel a lump in his face, if he dug his fingers in and felt past the skin, fat and flesh. Inside, the Blood Gorgons had buried a small larva, a thread of white worm no bigger than a fingernail.

For now the larva was inert, hibernating within his

flesh. The slave was not sure how it worked, for it was not his place to know such things, but he knew that each larva was genetically coded to a particular Blood Gorgon, so that if a slave ever strayed too far from his master, the larva would hatch.

What occurred thereafter was the stuff of speculation. Slaves did not wish to talk of such unfortunate things.

Their masters told them often that it would take many hours for the larva to reach the pupal stage, but from there, growth to the final stage was instantaneous. Self-destructive death and engorging of human flesh was its final stage of development but by then, as far as any slave was concerned, escape would be impossible.

It meant he was bound to Master Muhr. Even when he was more than a sub-deck away from his master, the beetle often itched, a sign that the creature was waking and growing hungry.

He scratched again and quickened his pace.

The slave climbed the stairs from the *Cauldron Born*'s cavernous lower decks and began the long trek towards the upper galleries. The ship's size was immense and even after nineteen years of servitude, the slave still found himself lost if he did not leave glowing guide markers to retrace his passage. Some of the passages had been disused for so long that they had developed their own ecology. Softly glowing patches of bacterial flora crept up the walls, while shelled molluscs sucked on reefs of neon dendrites. There, the plant life wept a weak organic acid which corroded the metal bulkheads, forming small grottos and burrows for the darting lantern-eels and other flesh-hungry organisms.

It was a dangerous walk for a slave and he thrashed the darkness in front of him with an ore stave in one hand and a phos-light in the other. He found one of his guide markers at every bend in the tunnels: little glow stones that he had put down when he had walked this path the first time. The walk had taken much longer than expected, and he was afraid his master would punish him for his tardiness. He picked up the glow stones and returned them to his satchel as he found them, until finally he reached a clamp shutter at the end of a tunnel, wreathed in gently nodding anemones of pink, purple and electric blue tentacles.

'Catacomb serf Moselle Grae,' the slave said to the brass vox arrays overhead. 'I have the nutrient sacs that Master Muhr requisitioned. Hurry please.'

The clamp shutters shot upwards with a clatter of machine rollers. On the other side were two guards in brass hauberks and black, tightly wound turbans. They too were slaves and their cheeks were scarred by scarabs, but to Grae they were imposing nonetheless. Grae nodded at them briefly and scurried beneath their crossed halberds.

The guards stood at the threshold of Master Muhr's personal chambers, a towering spire that jutted from the upper tiers of the *Cauldron Born*.

The neotropical flora grew less abundantly here, as if the organisms dared not anger the sorcerer. They were tamed to a fluorescent garden that flanked the winding path towards the spire's lower entrance. Thousands of luminous ferns, swaying like synapses, were surrounded by ponds of condensation from the ship's circulation systems. Only the lower portion of the spire was visible, for its height protruded from the ship's hull, rising through the inner mantle, vacuum seals and the hemispheric armour. The strip path led to double doors of old wood, a rarity aboard the ship, and likely plundered as a trophy on some past raid.

'Emperor bless me,' Grae muttered to himself while touching the iron of his slave collar three times.

The spire of Master Muhr had always made him feel a nauseous fear, no matter how many times he had been there before. It was different from the other parts of the ship. The air here seemed sorcerous, alive with a hateful presence. Grae likened it to a feeling of walking through the site of some terrible past massacre or touching the clothes of a murder victim. Things had happened within these walls, horrible blasphemous things that had left a psychic imprint.

As Grae crept down the path, he found the doors to be ajar. He hesitated, unsure of whether to enter, but decided that it would be an evil day if he did not bring his master the nutrient sacs on time. Easing the door open, he crept inside.

'Master Muhr?' he called out.

There was no answer. As his bare feet padded into the antechamber, glow strips reacted to his movement and permeated the area in low green light. The walls were honeycombed with preserved specimens immortalised in amniotic suspension. Grae went about his business quickly, trying to avoid eye contact with the jars and tanks containing Muhr's creations.

It was like a horror house Grae had visited in the travelling rural fairs, when he had been a child growing up in the tableland counties of Orlen. He made sure to scurry past an open display at the entrance to the west corridor. From afar the display looked like thespians frozen mid-scene. Up close, they were taxidermed slaves, posed in a sickening recreation of a scene from the stage theatre *Ransom of Lady Almas*. Thankfully their glass-eyed faces ignored him, their waxy skin frozen permanently in their rigid poses.

Grae began to check all the chambers in the lower levels, working his way from the lower laboratories into the trophy galleries. There, glass display cases housed the relics Master Muhr had collected on his campaigns. Orkoid teeth, rusting blades, eldar jewellery, polearms, xenos attire and ceramics, all neatly labelled and well dusted. Yet Master Muhr was nowhere to be found.

From these galleries a spiralling staircase of black iron led to the upper levels, but Grae had never been that far up before. Briefly he considered leaving the nutrition sacs at the base of the staircase for Master Muhr to find, but he feared such a gesture would be seen as a sign of disrespect. In fact, many of the jarred experiments had been slaves who had shown Master Muhr disrespect. He thought better of the idea and climbed the staircase.

It was the first time he had been up this far, and frightened though he was, it was difficult not to be awed by the view. He stood in a circular observation deck. The heavy drapes had been pulled back and beyond the void glass was a three hundred and sixty degree view of deep space. It was a never-ending darkness, an infinite deepness interrupted by the fizz and pop of billions of stars. Thousands of kilometres away, a pillar of gas was ponderously exhaling, its plume resembling the head of a horse. Grae knew its unfathomable distance, yet it seemed to rise so close, almost eclipsing his vision. It felt as if a horse-headed god was peering into the tiny viewing glass of his interior.

'The void glass will need resurfacing and cleaning,' Grae muttered to himself as he climbed higher up the staircase. He was talking to himself out of fear. Shaking his head, the slave began to climb to the top level.

But that was when all the glow strips faded out.

Grae almost dropped his satchel there and then. Startled, he fumbled to turn on his phos-light but the bulb had fizzed out. It was strange, as he had made certain to place a fresh bulb into the hand light when he set out. Shaking his head, Grae began to grope his way upwards, cautiously tapping the ground before him with the ore stave.

The air was coarse with chill and Grae became acutely aware that he was shivering. The loincloth and studded iron belt he wore afforded no warmth and he wore nothing else, for his masters were wary of concealed weapons. As he ran his hand along a wall panel, it left a furrow in the hoar frost there.

'Witchcraft,' Grae moaned. He felt as if he were going to be sick.

Grae had been a governor's aide before the Blood Gorgons ransacked his world. His daily job had been receipt of aerial parcels and message wafers for the governor's Chamber of Commerce. It was dreary work for the most part, but once Grae had seen an adept of the Astra Telepathica transmitting urgent interstellar messages from the governor's office. The eyeless man had spooked him, and Grae had become withdrawn in his presence, showing more timidity than he would have liked. By the time the adept had finished his work Grae remembered vividly that the room had become freezing and he'd spent considerable time mopping up the after-frost. The adept had wet the parcel shelves and frozen the ink in his typographer.

He was shocked out of his thoughts as something brushed past him. Grae turned around but saw nothing, or rather, could see nothing. It had been astonishingly quick, like a brisk tug of his clothes.

'Master Muhr?'

He climbed the next few levels slowly, calling for his master the entire way. The air grew colder. He almost lost the skin of his left palm when he placed it on the hand rails.

'Master?'

At the upper atrium, Grae froze. He heard voices. Master Muhr was talking to someone. Not daring to interrupt, Grae crept to a standstill at the top of the stairs, glad that he was hidden within the shadow. He stood within the folds of the curtain with his eyes fixed firmly on the floor. In the periphery of his vision, Grae could see the atrium was bathed in a green light. A forest of black curtains as tall as trees hung from the ceiling; beyond that, he could see nothing else.

'Then it is done. The ambush was clean and the dark eldar performed excellently. Gammadin is dead.'

'That's a good start, Muhr, but we need better assurance,' said a voice that Grae could not recognise.

'Only a start,' Muhr rasped. 'The Crow has begun the sowing of Hauts Bassiq.'

'Plague and famine, Muhr – you've promised plague and famine for so long.'

Grae tried not to listen, he even blocked his ears. These were things a slave had no right to know, he was sure of it.

'The Crow will maintain his side of the bargain,' Muhr retorted. 'He needs our hand in this as much as we need his.'

'And what of Sabtah?' the voice inquired.

'I will kill Sabtah myself,' Muhr answered.

Grae squeezed his eyes together and held his breath. Most of what he heard he did not understand, but there were glimmers of things that he knew he should not be hearing.

'Who else knows about this?' asked the voice in the curtains.

Muhr cleared his throat. 'Only you, a handful of unnamed squads in Fourth and Sixth Companies… and a slave named Moselle Grae.'

The reply jolted Grae. Frightened, he looked up and realised Muhr was already looking at him. The witch's eyes sought him out in his hiding place, boring into him.

'Did you think you could hide there, little mouse?' Muhr asked, addressing him directly.

Grae's nerves could not hold out any longer. He was done. He turned and ran, taking the nutrient sacs with him. There was no logic to what he did, but the fear he felt was deeply primal. It was the same flight instinct that early man had relied upon, a thoughtless, baseless need to just run. That voice was too much for him.

He clattered down the spiral stairs but only made it to the third step.

+*Stop*+ commanded Muhr.

Grae's legs instantly seized up, his mind overwhelmed by Muhr's psionic will.

+*Turn around*+

Jerked like a marionette, Grae spun around without consciously doing so. He saw Muhr rise from the ground, utterly naked except for his mask. A grotesque mass of scars ridged the muscles of Muhr's abdomen, long and thin like the deft cuts of a razor. Grae wanted to scream but he no longer had control of his own body.

Muhr hovered over Grae with his towering stature and studied the slave. He inspected his shaven scalp and tested the muscles of his arms like a rancher inspecting stock. Apparently satisfied, Muhr nodded.

'You are a strong slave. We Blood Gorgons do not waste the lives of our slaves needlessly,' Muhr remarked. 'So you will live.'

Grae was so relieved his left eye began to twitch. It was the only part of him that Muhr's psychic paralysis had not affected.

'But we should lobotomise you. I do not want my aspirations undone by gossiping slaves,' Muhr said sagely.

Grae's left eye widened. There was pure terror in his pupils. The veins on his neck bulged visibly as the slave struggled to move. But Muhr would not let him go.

'We have need for workers such as you on Bassiq. Not living like you are, of course, but dead, yet obedient all the same,' Muhr muttered as he parted the curtains and moved out of Grae's paralysed view. He rustled through the atrium, clicking his eyelids rapidly to adjust to the darkness. With a satisfied whistle, Muhr picked up a sliver of long surgical steel from a trestle table – an orbitoclast.

'This is harmless really. I'm going to insert it through your eye socket and puncture the thin wall of bone to reach your frontal lobe. A few medial and lateral swings should separate your thalamus,' Muhr stated. 'You will not feel much after that.'

CHAPTER FOUR

NINE HUNDRED TRAITOR Marines in congress was unsettling. The Temple Heart barely seemed to contain their wild, exuberant ranks. They stamped their feet like bulls and boasted on vox-amp of their scars and trophies. Silence only fell across them when Sabtah ascended the central dais.

'Chapter-strength deployment,' announced Sabtah the Older. The declaration was momentous and all of the Blood Gorgons, all nine hundred of them, roared their approval.

'Hauts Bassiq is an ancestral world. Many of your brothers can trace their blood line to the lineage of the plains people. I'd wager many more of you have infused Bassiq lineage in your veins through the blood bond.'

The gathered Traitor Marines howled in approval. They sat, lounged or crouched about the temple without any particular display of company order. Congregating in six-man squads, each formed by three blood-bound pairs, each of the pairs were attended to by a train of retainers – black turbans, armour serfs, helm bearers and dancers.

'With Gammadin's death there is a void in ruler-ship,' said Captain Hazareth in his deep metallic bass. 'Until such time as a warrior will be chosen to reign, I pledge wardship of my company in your hands. Whoever else may do so is not of my concern. For now, my swordarm is yours.'

Hazareth the Cruel, Captain of 1st Company, was an embodiment of the Blood Gorgons Chapter. Wild and boisterous, he was a violent thing. When he laughed, and he did so often, the humour behind it was black and bitter yet genuinely mirthful. His face had been melted by fire and his cheek pockmarked with bullet scars. Hazareth wore them like laurels of honour, for his men feared him and the gods favoured him well. A tortoise-like shell had solidified around his shoulders and power pack like a hunch-backed mound of bone, a powerful sign of daemonic favour. The shell ended in a short, muscular tail that sprouted from the base of Hazareth's spine and ended in a knot of fibrous growth. So monstrously thick-framed that he resembled a Dreadnought, Haz-areth had his club tail swept low to balance his ponderous steps.

'Hazareth, your words stir this old heart,' said Sab-tah. The verbal dance was almost theatrical, more of a symbolic gesture than any meaningful exchange. Despite their piratical nature, the Blood Gorgons were traditionalists at heart and Sabtah was a piece of their long history. To the assembly, Sabtah was the old grey ring-wolf they had always known. He was carefully presented in his Mark II Crusade armour, the articulated hoops of the relic lending an impressive bulk to his already broad girth. Most impressive was his beard, a tiered cascade of uniform ringlets that reached the bottom of his chest guard, black and well oiled. There was no doubt that Sabtah was venerable, but more than that, he would ensure the proper functioning of the Chapter beyond the death of Gammadin.

'Full Chapter strength deployment,' Sabtah repeated. 'But understand this – I know that there are those of you who do not support my custodial rule of my fellow brothers.' Sabtah paused to let this statement sink in.

There was an uncomfortable silence from the assembled Blood Gorgons. Amongst them were younger squads who showed fealty to the witch-psyker Muhr. Others still gave tacit support to the few rogue captains who were rumoured to harbour aspirations of Championship. It would be a volatile time for the whole Chapter.

'This is not the time for petty conflict and spiteful loyalties,' Sabtah continued. 'An unknown threat has chosen Hauts Bassiq as a target. Whatever is making our world their playground will soon have nine hundred Blood Gorgons crashing down around their ears. This, this will be a good fight. One that will be remembered, as the ancients remember the massacre at Dunefall!'

Hazareth barked hungrily at the thought, a loud war-mongering belch issued from valve amplifiers.

They all cheered, stamping their traction boots in a deep raft of applause.

'That will not be happening,' declared a psych-amped voice. They turned to see Muhr descending the stairs into the pit of the Temple Heart. His long black hair was slightly wild and his eyes were still milky with the aftergleam of recent psychic strain. 'This will not be happening,' Muhr repeated. 'Gammadin has entrusted the Chapter to me. I will not deploy my Chapter blindly into an unknown threat. Certainly you do not mean to commit and risk all of us to save some *nullius* world of primitives?' Muhr asked as he reached the assembly.

'As great as Lord Gammadin was, he did not have the authority to make you our lord,' Sabtah responded. 'That is the way it has always been. If you seek to rule, then declare it openly. I will challenge your title.'

'I declare it!' hissed Muhr.

As he spoke, Sabtah levelled his power trident at Muhr. The three-pronged *trisula* hummed like a tuning fork as the disruption field vibrated up and down its length.

'I accept your challenge,' Muhr shrieked. The witch-psyker was already amping, his eyes and mouth streaming a harshly unnatural light. He screamed to emphasise his potency and vomited a beam of energy into the ceiling. His own battle-brothers backed away and slaves scattered in mobs. Nearby, a dancer collapsed, her brain haemorrhaged by the psychic build up.

In response, Sabtah fired a quick burst from his bolt pistol over their heads. The gatling burp punctured the far wall, pushing deep holes into the basalt veneers. This was ritual posturing amongst the Blood Gorgons, a slow escalation of violence that could either end in death or the submission of one of the challengers.

The Blood Gorgons were cheering hard now. Amongst the chaos of gunfire and confusion, above the screams of slaves and performers, the bond-brothers were shouting the name of Sabtah. There were others amongst them, a minority of Muhr's allies, who drew concealed blades and punch daggers. The atmosphere became volatile. Muhr pressed forwards until he was within arm's reach of Sabtah, putting his skull directly in front of Sabtah's pistol. In the background, an eager bond-brother emptied his bolter clip into the ceiling.

Sabtah aimed his bolt pistol at Muhr, his trident arm poised like a javelin thrower.

Muhr feinted forwards, provoking Sabtah. The old veteran's nerve held steady; he did not fire. The trident darted forwards, calculated to miss Muhr's neck by a razor's breadth.

Muhr flinched.

'Not now!' Hazareth boomed into the squad links. 'We can't afford this now.' The deep bass tones were so loud that they glitched the broadcast with shrill feedback.

'This is not how Gammadin would have led us,' said Hazareth. 'Is this leadership? To divide the Chapter when our ancestral grounds are threatened?'

'Ancestors? Bassiq is nothing more than a harvesting site for genestock. We can find others,' Muhr said dismissively.

'You are a petulant child,' said Sabtah, his trident still rearing. 'Where is your pride?'

'I am a realist. We don't need to risk ourselves at the summons of some distant, half-remembered populace,' Muhr responded.

Sabtah looked clearly disgusted, as if Muhr was speaking about something else entirely. 'This is not about that. Someone has touched my chattel and property. We don't turn a blind eye. We hit them with the weight of our entire arsenal and inject the fear of angry gods into them.'

Hazareth drummed his heavy tail-end against the ground in agreement. 'Without history we are nothing. We are nomads, and history should mean everything to us. Without pride or connection to our roots we are nothing.'

Muhr was not convinced. The psy-fire did not leave his eyes. If he chose to, the rites of challenge allowed him to slay anyone who opposed him. Even Hazareth, but that would not be wise now.

'I propose a scouting deployment. Five squads,' said Sabtah, bristling. 'You cannot deny us that.'

'I will personally answer to that,' Hazareth agreed. 'I will select the squads from my own company.'

There was no more Muhr could say. Hazareth's company was his to command and only Sabtah could countermand such an action. Several dissident Blood Gorgons leapt up and began to voice their protests. Others howled them down. Muhr hissed and recoiled, displaying displeasure by baring his teeth.

Unseen amidst the pandemonium, Sabtah squared up to face the sorcerer. The old warrior was in his face, his jaw set grimly. 'What do you know of brotherhood?' Sabtah growled. 'The witch-psyker takes no bond. You know nothing of brotherhood. Remain with your coven and leave the business of war to us.'

THE CAULDRON BORN prepared for warp jump at first cycle. The reclamation of Hauts Bassiq was under way.

The coven summoned Yetsugei for his blessing. The witch-surgeons sang and chanted to the gods. Gun-servitors were anointed and their nerve receptors plugged to the vessel's lance batteries, ordnance turrets and the hull-bound gun citadels that studded the vessel's orange hull.

The floating fortress shifted on its gravitational axis as its warp drives gathered power. Even in the expanse of space, the space hulk was a leviathan. From a terrestrial telescope, the *Cauldron Born* resembled a blend of paleo-gothic shipcraft and oceanic fish. High exposure to the warp and the Eye of Terror had mutated the vessel's structure. The neo-tropical flora that infested the ship's interior had expressed itself on the ship's exterior, but on a mammoth scale. Barnacles of lamprey lights clustered like eyes on its hammerhead prow. Large sail-like fins edged with delicate, translucent fronds rippled along its flank. Muscular ridges and weeping fungal colonies contrasted with the architecture of its hull.

It entered the warp-sea slowly, laterally decompressing a void into the fabric of the materium. It sent ripples of gas flowing outwards and disturbed the orbit of minor asteroids and moons. Then, with a final, trembling burst of its engines, the warp-sea swallowed the fish whole.

THE MIDDLE-DAY suns of Bassiq seemed to burn the air, boiling it so hot that every breath stung the nostrils. It grew so hot that sleep during these rest hours was impossible.

Roused from a fevered dream, Ashwana woke up feeling ill again. Her armpits and neck were burning with a throbbing, almost rhythmic pain. Rolling over she tried to bury her face in the straw mat but the clattering became persistent. For a while she blinked, angry at her grandmumu for having woken her. A final, loud clatter brought her up and Ashwana snapped back the curtain that separated her sleep nest from their carriage.

'What are you doing?' Ashwana groaned.

'Going hunting,' muttered her grandmumu, rummaging through a barkskin case of tools.

'*Eish*! We've talked about this. It's too dangerous,' Ashwana whispered.

Her grandmumu Abena wasn't listening to her any more. Her old, creased face was stern with determination. She discarded a flint stone from the case, tossing it to the pile of unwanted tools at her feet.

Ashwana tried to stand up but she was too weak and the head rush brought her back down onto her haunches. 'Don't go,' she pleaded.

'You've not eaten in two days,' scolded Mumu Abena. Braced between her stout legs, a recurved bow was being strung. The bow had once belonged to Ashwana's father and it was a beautiful piece. It had an accentuated curvature and was detailed in the ridged horn of a caprid. For years it had resided, unstrung, in the barkskin tool case.

'Mumu, I'm not even hungry,' said Ashwana. She was telling the truth. She could barely sip on water without nausea. The sickness had caught her swiftly, as it had the rest of her kinship. Three weeks past, the hunter Bulguno had been the first to catch the illness upon his return from a hunting trip in the Central Craters. In that time it had spread and almost all of the kin complained of fevers, pains and insomnia. Within days, the kinship had its first death – it had spread from there.

Lying back down, too tired to argue, Ashwana looked about their carriage – the rusting iron walls, the mesh ceiling, the familiar plastek curtains. It was a small space, a mere cubicle within the road train of their kinship. She could not remember how long they had been camped. They moved with their nomadic road trains, the relics of early prospectors. Many of them still had working gas engines that were thousands of years old, retained and cared for by the shamans. The engines failed often, and they camped until the shamans could coax life back into the valves and pistons that were beyond her understanding. She could not remember how long they had been camped there.

Ashwana's aimless gaze fell upon the shrine that hung above the boiler stove at the centre of their cabin. Hanging from a length of rope was a square clay face, framed by charms of squall feathers and the dismembered hoof of a male caprid. The face was of the Godspawn. A tiny wooden dish of acid berries and gourds was placed beneath it as an offering. Despite the fact that their oven had been cold for days, and there was no other food in the carriage, Mumu Abena had spared enough for the Godspawn. It seemed all they did these days was appease the Godspawn, but in return they received nothing but suffering.

Ashwana had lived with her grandmumu for all the twelve years of her life that she could remember. Without her parents, life had been hard within her nomadic kinship. The community moved often, following the migration patterns of the horned caprid, and it was difficult for her mumu to keep up without the help of anyone else. By all rights, Mumu Abena was an elder, and an elder's immediate family had a filial duty to ensure she was well cared for. But Abena had no other family except little Ashwana and she was too young to do much.

Of course, that had not stopped her from trying. Every day, she tried to tend and milk the caprid, but her hands were too small to placate the wild, shaggy-haired animals. She tried to gather sticks for the communal fires, but she had not been strong enough to carry the enormous bales on her head like the other women. Mumu Abena often laughed and told her that she was not yet old enough and she should play clap sticks with the other youths.

'Your skin is not old and dark like mine,' her mumu would say to her, while pointing to the deep, leathery bronze of her own skin. The sun of their land was exceedingly harsh and while bronzed skin was a sign of seniority among elders, tanned children were a sign of impoverishment. It meant the child had to

work, and was a source of great shame. Her mumu
was too proud a woman to live with that.

So it was that Mumu Abena, old yet spry, tended to
their few domestic caprid, cooked, wove and con-
tributed to the kinship in every way she could. It was
a burden she should not have had to bear given her
age.

But in the past season, things had become progressively worse. Since the strange lights in the sky, there
had been little to eat for weeks. Travelling herdsmen
from distant kinships had brought word of a plague
spreading from the Northern Badlands. Ashwana's
kinship had dismissed it as the panic of isolated
northern plainsmen, but they had been wrong to do
so. It was not one plague, but many. A blackening
wilt had destroyed what meagre vegetation the red
plains had offered. Rinderpest killed the caprid
herds, causing the animals to be so fatigued they
could no longer dig up the roots beneath the clay.
Animals died in masses, flocks of birds fluttering
down from the sky to die amongst the droves of
upturned, sun-swollen caprid bodies.

Travellers told tales that the city of Ur, the only city
on the planet of Bassiq, had sealed its great walls for
fear of the black wilt. But that did not matter to Ashwana. She had only ever seen Ur once, and even
then, only from a distance. The denizens of Ur did
not often make contact with the kinships of the
plains. Most plainsmen were not welcome there.

Now, finally, the plague had come south. It started
with an innocuous cough and an inflammation of
the throat. From there, like the others, Ashwana
developed a persistent fever and painful swelling in

her neck and underarms. Some languished for weeks while others began to die in a matter of days. But it was no merciful death. The sick slowly lost their memory, their eyes becoming dull and their minds deteriorating. There seemed to be no cure and even the medicine men were helpless. White stunt grass did nothing to alleviate the pains and even brewing gecko skin and sunberries only brought temporary relief from the joint pain.

Ashwana still hoped that her sickness was not the plague but a simple condition brought about by weeks of malnutrition. It was a forlorn hope, as the buboes in her neck suggested otherwise. Already, she had experienced brief moments where fragments of her mind seemed to slip, a tell-tale sign of the plague. She forgot simple things like whether her mumu had put oil on her mosquito bumps or what time of day it was.

'I don't need food,' Ashwana murmured again.

Her grandmumu shook her head, the tightly beaded coils of her white hair rattling. 'Some roast talon squall,' she suggested, 'or maybe a bush tail soup.'

'It wouldn't matter. I could die soon.' Ashwana said. The words hung in the air. The bar of honeyed sun shone through the roof hatch, holding tiny motes of dust in suspension. Neither said anything else and Ashwana immediately wished she'd never let the words out. She closed her eyes and silently wished her grandmumu had not heard it.

'You'll be better, my little *duumi*,' said her grandmumu finally. She swung the bow over her shoulder and secured a quiver of long arrows across her hip.

Mumu Abena put on a brave face, the same stern face she used when Ashwana refused to drink her bitter bark soup. 'This will pass soon,' she said soothingly.

Overwhelmed by fatigue, Ashwana rolled over. She couldn't remember what they had been talking about. It seemed there was a dark patch in her memory for the past several hours, perhaps even days. Watching with hooded eyes, Ashwana saw her grandmumu step outside their carriage into the white sunlight outside, a bow across her back and a pail in her hands. Try as she might, Ashwana did not know where her grandmumu was going or why.

GRANDMUMU ABENA LEFT the camp at the base of the crater-like cirque and climbed the highlands with the suns at her back. Before her lay endless longitudinal sand dunes interspersed with shining white salt lakes. Chenopods and the salt-tolerant eragrostis grasses dominated the fringes of the basins.

Despite her age, she was surprisingly nimble and her old legs carried her well. She crossed the dry remains of a creek, remembering that just two seasons past, broods of barraguana, with their long fleshy tails and webbed feet, had basked in the shallow waters. It seemed that even before the plague, the climate was becoming harsher and more untenable, or had it always been so?

She was old now, and she could only remember better times and more glorious days. The plainsmen of Bassiq had always been a hardy people and there had been times in her youth, during the harshest season of Fume, when her kinship would scrape the bark from fissure trees. The bitter bark would be boiled into soup so that its numbing qualities could dull the hunger pains, nothing more. Even then, life had been good. She had been allowed to ride talon squalls and help muster the caprid droves, drink from the communal water jug and sleep on the ground when it rained.

Abena could not remember anything as bad as this before. The plague had taken so many of the kinship and already some were whispering that the world would end. It was not a life she had wanted for her children's children.

She left the creek bed and began to cross the Great Northern Plains. Although there were no roads, she navigated a thin track ridge through the clay desert. Such ancient tracks had been made during seismic surveys for gas and fuel deposits by early colonists, or so the tales went.

After several hours of walking and a short water rest in-between, she approached a familiar place. She was in the territory of the Nullabor, a neighbouring kinship. During the cooler seasons, the Zhosa and the Nullabor had feasted together and performed their traditional dances to celebrate the defeat of the double-headed eagle by the Godspawn, as the suns of Swelter were eclipsed by a red gas giant, marking a twilight and celebration that lasted for an entire lunar cycle.

Perhaps they would know of fertile gorges in the region, or even of karst caves with edible rodentia. Better yet, Abena hoped that despite the famine, the kinship would honour their ties and perhaps spare her a cup of fermented milk for Ashwana.

Through the haze of noon dust, she could

recognise the distinctive silver of their long carriages. The road trains, mechanical beasts from a lost age of mining, were drawn like protective wagons in a circle around the settlement, the rusting bulk of their segmented carriages protecting the tents and lean-tos that clung to their bellies from wind and sandstorm. In all, Abena remembered the Nullabor as a generous but poor kinship. They did not own many heads of caprid, and their road trains were in disrepair, the engines temperamental after sixty centuries of maintenance. They owned only early prospector models with loud engines and noisy wide gauge tracks. Some of the corroded carriages had been shored up with hand-painted wood panelling, giving them a roguish, antiquated air. Yet Abena knew the kinship would still share whatever meagre supplies they could.

Drawing a zinc whistle from her belt, Abena blew a long, warbling note. It was to herald the arrival of a peaceful visitor and its sound travelled far across the sandscape. Yet there was no response whistle from the Nullabor.

Unsettled by the silence, Abena shielded her eyes with her hand and tried to search for the tell-tale signs of carrion birds in the sky. If the Nullabor had fallen ill to plague then surely she'd be able to see carrion birds. Yet there were no birds, just a pervasive sense of lifelessness from the clutch of carriages.

She stood for a while, unsure of whether to enter the settlement or turn back. But Ashwana needed the food, and her old painful knees would not allow her to hunt game so late in the day. Easing an arrow out of her quiver, she rested it across the strike plate, ready to loosen. It was the custom for women of the plains to participate in hunting and herding as much as the men engaged in domestic chores, and although she could no longer run or jump like she used to, her arms were strong from carrying pails of water and stone-milling, more than enough to draw the recurve.

The carriages were occupied. Huddled around their protective bulk, light wooden frames had been erected and then draped with heavy cloth to form lean-tos. Plainsmen would take off their red shukas and spread them over the frame of their tents before they entered a home. The purpose was twofold: one was that the red cloth would ward away evil spirits who would see that a house was already occupied, and the second, perhaps more pragmatically, was to prevent dust and dirt from being carried into the home.

The carriages were hoary with a film of red dust. Dust storms were worst during the night and any respectable plainsmen would have beaten the walls with a stick by morning. The fact that the carriages had accumulated so many days of red dirt meant the kinship had not moved for many days, perhaps weeks. As that notion slowly crept into her mind, Abena suddenly became aware that all the Nullabor could have perished.

'I do not wish to harm you. Restless spirits, do not harm me,' she chanted under her breath as she stepped towards the nearest carriage. At that moment, as if roused by her superstition, a brisk south wind picked up, gusting oxide dust in her direction and flapping the cloth draped across the carriage frames. With it came the sudden stink of rot.

Abena held her breath in fright as she recognised the smell. In her younger days as a shepherdess she had come across a caprid that had strayed from the herd and been mauled by some plains predator. The stench of that carcass under the thermal suns had been horrendous, bloated as it was with gas. The smell coming from the carriages was almost the same.

'Ashwana's grandmumu? We must eat soon before the food is cold,' said a voice from behind her. It was a quiet voice, a young voice.

Startled, Abena turned quickly, drawing her bow smoothly. But when she turned there was nobody there. Perhaps the voice had been carried by the wind? She strained her eyes against the gust of wind to look at the other carriages, set in a concentric ring around a communal firepit.

Whip-fast, in the furthest corner of her vision, she sensed movement. She did not quite see it, but felt that sudden absence of stillness.

'*How de body?*' Abena called out in customary greeting. 'I cannot see you.'

The wind gust picked up, drawing a veil of rusty particles across her vision. No more than twenty paces away, she saw a figure stand up from between two carriages. Judging by the raw-boned shoulders and narrow torso it was a young plainsmen of the Nullabor, but she could not see him well.

'What is your name, little son?' Abena asked the man, making known that she was a person of elder seniority.

'I can't remember my name. I remember yours. You

are Abena. We should put out the fire pit so the others can sleep,' said the silhouette.

The man must be so feverish he was talking nonsense, Abena realised. Her grandmotherly instincts wanted her to tell the boy to sit back down until the rust storm had passed, but something cautioned her to keep quiet. The silhouette began to stumble towards her, speaking fragmentary phrases that made no sense.

'Remember to lock the talon squall pens,' he ordered angrily, before lowering his voice and chuckling. 'This is my best and most favourite shuka.'

Abena was wary. She remembered folktales of the dead who returned to their homes with only fragmentary memories of a past life. *Vodou* they had called them, and although they had no minds, they retained enough fragments of their past – things they had said often in life, or certain things people had said to them, and they mimicked the living with their vocal cords, luring out distraught relatives with pleas and familiar phrases. She had never believed in such things – raising Ashwana on her own had required a sturdy head – but now she was not so sure.

'I do not know you,' Abena shouted.

The rust storm died away, leaving the particles to twirl and settle. Like a curtain falling away, Abena saw the corpse that was walking towards her. That was what shocked Abena more than anything, the corpse walked with a loping gait as it had in life. Despite the fur of mould that grew across its pale, bloodless skin, it was walking. It appeared unhurried as it approached her, although its face, bloated by fluid beyond all recognition, was angled away towards the sky. It was as if the man was stuck between life and death, the skin and flesh rotting away while it talked of a past life and moved like the living.

Abena aimed and fired a hunting arrow into its chest. The dead man wheezed painfully as one of its lungs collapsed, but it kept walking. It was close now and Abena found herself paralysed by a mixture of fear and fascination.

It was so near, she could see the man was dressed in a sarong of undyed funeral wool. It meant the man had been buried and sealed in the bole of a boab tree. Somehow, it had clawed its way out and had returned to its home. Perhaps the tales were true.

It reached out a hand towards her and touched her upper arm. The coldness of the palm on her warm skin shocked her into movement. She ran several steps, her bow already drawn before she swung around and released another arrow. The copper head cut deep below the dead man's ribcage and punched out through his back with a dry, meaty thud. Entirely unfazed by the wounds, the man snatched for Abena with stiffened fingers. She wrenched away, frantic with adrenaline. She began to run, racing down the dune slopes.

Wordlessly, the corpse pursued her. She could feel its presence on the nape of her neck. It no longer tried to talk to her, its intent had become singular. It hit her hard from behind, knocking her down the hill, sending her rolling down the rocky slope. She came to a jarring stop as the creature loomed over her. As it reached down to seize her, Abena thought about Ashwana, lying in her hut alone. How long would it be before these ghosts came for her?

CHAPTER FIVE

Barsabbas woke from his sleep to an aching in his left primary lung. Abruptly uncomfortable, he sat up and swung his legs over the edge of his cot. Grimacing, he rubbed his lower ribs slowly. It was not real pain, not real damage, but it seemed real to him nonetheless.

'Your lung is troubling you again?' Barsabbas called out.

Sargaul appeared in the door frame, dressed in a bodyglove for early sparring. 'The same. I feel it most in the mornings. The Chirurgeons were not thorough in purging the residual shrapnel.'

Barsabbas nodded thoughtfully. He was feeling the old wounds of his blood bond, a common experience between pairs. After all, it had been Barsabbas's left primary lung they had excised and transplanted into Sargaul in their rituals of pairing.

Years ago, as a young neophyte, Barsabbas had not

fully understood the rituals performed upon him. He remembered vaguely the surgical pain. The multiple waking horrors as the Chirurgeons sheared his bones for marrow and opened his muscles like the flaps of a book. There were not many memories from that time, but those were the ones he recalled.

Now, as an older, wiser battle-brother, Barsabbas still knew little of the secret bond. The process itself had become blurred with folklore and mysticism, to the point where effect and placebo became one. Paired with the veteran Sargaul, Barsabbas would become strengthened by their shared experience. He would inherit not only Sargaul's genetic memory, but also his bravery and ferocity. There was an element of witchcraft in this, but whenever Barsabbas felt that twinge in his lung, he was convinced there was substance to their ritual.

'How is your knee?' Sargaul asked, flexing his own.

Barsabbas stretched out his right leg, the thick cords of his thigh rippling. 'Better today,' he shrugged.

'I thought so,' nodded Sargaul, flexing his own right leg. 'They were ferocious, those tau. Much better at war-making than I expected.'

Barsabbas had almost repressed the memory of defeat but Sargaul's words invoked the images back to wakefulness. Just ten lunar cycles ago they had deployed on the tau world designated 'Govina' – a planet targeted for its lush natural resources and relatively weak military presence. It should have been a simple plunder raid for Squad Besheba: hit hard and retreat with a mid-grade quota of slaves. But they had underestimated the aliens, and the tau military presence proved entirely capable.

They engaged on the tundra, trading shots between dwarf shrubs and sedges, low grasses and lichens. By the hundreds, the tau had come, their firing lines disciplined and their shots overwhelming in sheer volume. Pulsating blue plasma hammered them so hard their armour systems had been pushed to failure, and Barsabbas's suit had reached seventy per cent damage threshold within the first few volleys.

The squad had fought with customary aggression and speed. They had burst amongst the tau infantry squares, ploughing through their chest-high adversaries, splintering their helmets and bones. They had killed so many.

But it was the tau's home and they did not flee. Squad Besheba had been driven back, overwhelmed by sheer numbers. In the end, they had fled, chased by ground-hugging tau hoverers. They escaped, but without dignity and their wounds were many. Like Barsabbas's disintegrated patella and Sargaul's collapsed lung, the shame had stayed with them, agonising them for the past ten months.

THOUSANDS OF SLAVES woke to the pulsating itch in their left cheekbones, scratching their scarred faces. It was an urgent, pressing discomfort that could not be ignored.

Beneath each scar could be seen the outline of a flesh burrowing thrall-worm. Agitated during sleep cycle, when the slaves were at a distance from their masters, the thrall-worms bulged against their cheeks like distended tumours. With clockwork precision, at the six-hour mark, the parasites would rouse their hosts by feeding on the rich fat beneath their skins.

Sleepy-eyed, fatigued and forlorn, the slaves would wake to their daily work.

The workforce were of all kinds and pasts, both strong and feeble, soldiers and clerics, shift workers or merchants; here an artisan, over there a human Guard colonel, all of them slaves to the bonded brotherhood. Those strong and young set about the tasks of burden, carrying equipment lockers and hefty pallets. The old and feeble, those who had been branded many years ago, fanned out into the corridors to light the upper halls with sconce lanterns. Others fetched haunches of roast for their twin masters, for although the post-humans did not need such food for sustenance, they enjoyed the taste of rare meat.

The most unfortunate of all were those who formed the work teams – the *delvers*. They were given the impossible duty of clearing the encroaching bioflora that threatened to overwhelm the ship. Such teams often disappeared into the forgotten sectors of the ship, which had become a cavernous ecosystem. Those regions became wildernesses and the delvers with their hatchets and chain cutters could do little to stop their spread. Many were lost to the apex predators that flourished in the abyssal depths of the space hulk.

Slaves who had become favourites were allowed to rise one ship's cycle later than the rest. The black-turbaned sentries in their hauberks of brass, the gun ratings, the deckhands and pleasure pets were all among the number who enjoyed relative luxury.

But on this day, all the slaves, regardless of hierarchy, would forgo sleep or food for the Blood Gorgons mobilisation. It was not full Chapter strength deployment, but it would still be a time of solemn ritual and ceremony. The drop chambers would need to be cleaned and the vacuum locks cleared; weapons would be oiled and armour polished. Sacrifices would be made. There was much work to be done.

IT WAS NOT yet dawn cycle, but Barsabbas and Sargaul were already in the Maze of Acts Martial. Squad Besheba had set up a three-point fire pattern in a little-used section of the maze.

The ceiling of the tunnel had collapsed under the bacterial acid, forming a natural cave shelf. The collapse had also breached several water filtration pipes and the resultant fluid had allowed a host of microorganisms to thrive and grow. Through the thermal imaging of his helmet, the interior wilderness appeared to Barsabbas as a low-lying pattern of fronds, reefs and fungal caps. He opened the vents of his armour and allowed the moist, external air to creep into his suit. Tasting with his tongue, he judged seventy-two per cent humidity in the air combined with a high blend of toxic carbon, likely released by the nearby floral growth. There was something else in the air too, the animal scent of sweat or something similar.

There was a flash of thermal colour to his left and Barsabbas turned to meet it, his ocular targeting systems already synchronising with his bolter sights. A human shape rose from behind a mound of viral lichen and opened fire. The first shot went wide, a ranging shot that left the searing after-image of its trajectory across Barsabbas's vision. The next one clipped him on the hip, ricocheting with a whine off the ceramite plate. His armour's daemon spirit groaned sleepily in protest.

Before Barsabbas could return fire, the human was already dead. Sargaul had finished him with a clean chest shot. Bond-Brothers Hadius and Cython shot him repeatedly, tearing him down to constituent fragments.

'Cease fire!' called Sergeant Sica, waving down their violent excess. Hadius and Cython whooped with glee.

'That's it, we're done here,' added the sergeant's blood bond, Bael-Shura. 'Thirty kills. That's the last of them.'

'No,' said Sargaul, holding up the auspex. 'Squad, hold. I'm getting ghost readouts on the auspex.'

A caged pen of thirty Guardsman captives had been released into the maze less than two hours ago. They had been a platoon of Mordians guarding a merchant vessel en route to Cadia. The men had put up a stoic fight, but by Barsabbas's count, they had killed all thirty. There shouldn't be any more targets within this section of the maze. Yet their auspex was pinging.

Barsabbas took the auspex from Sargaul and studied the tracking device. Whatever it was, the target was large and moved with expert stealth. Several times it moved so quietly that the auspex sonar reflection lost track of its movement. It closed in, only to disappear, then reappear, slightly closer than before.

'A maul mouth?' Sargaul suggested. He was referring to the apex predator that had evolved in the confines of the *Cauldron Born*.

Barsabbas shook his head. Maul mouths were light-framed creatures, their slender, hairless bodies suited to hiding within circulation vents and underneath walkways. This was too big.

Abruptly, the auspex began to ping again. 'Fifty metres!' Sergeant Sica hissed urgently. As quickly as the warning came, the auspex settled again.

The squad fell into interlocking arcs of fire. They couldn't see any targets. Except for the bubble of a dimorphic yeast fungus as it corroded the tunnel walls, there was no sound.

'Thirty-six metres,' Sargaul voxed through the squad link as his auspex caught a fleeting glimpse. The target was moving fast, darting between the auspex's blind spots.

'Eighteen metres.'

Barsabbas toggled between thermal imaging and negative illumination. Neither showed a target. He loosened the muscles of his shoulders and placed one hand on the boarding axe sheathed against the small of his back.

'I've lost target,' Sica voxed, his voice laced with frustration.

Without clearance, Hadius and Cython loosed a quick burst of their bolters. The distinct echo of the jackhammer shots signalled they had hit nothing.

'Cease fire, you soft-backs!' Sica barked.

Suddenly, Cython was flying backwards, as if struck heavily. Hadius lumbered to the aid of his blood bond, but he too was sent sprawling. It was happening so fast that Barsabbas cursed as he tore the hand axe from its casing and looped small circles to warm up his wrist.

Sergeant Sica aimed his bolter at a large dark shape that was suddenly in the middle of their position. Sargaul did the same while Bael-Shura brought the squad flamer to bear. The shape was black, its negative luminescence making it appear colder than its thermal surroundings.

'Hold your weapons, Squad Besheba,' came a familiar voice through their squad's direct link.

Sica lowered his weapon hesitantly. 'Captain?'

'Aye, sergeant.'

Spitting in relief, Barsabbas switched off his thermal imaging. It was dark and he blinked several times, rapidly dilating his pupils to increase visual acuity. The formless black shape immediately became that of Captain Argol. Even in the low light, he was unmistakable. Horn plates cauliflowered up his neck and the left side of his face, sprouting, branching and multiplying like saltwater coral. Argol was immensely proud of his gifts and seldom wore a helmet to hide them.

'You caught us,' Sica admitted. As if on cue, Hadius and Cython staggered back to their feet, their earlier bravado neutered by the ease of their dispatching.

'Learn to adapt quickly. Never become comfortable with one kind of enemy,' said Argol.

Barsabbas knew their captain was right. Space Marine armour was an insulated exterior of ceramite and adamantium, almost invisible to thermal or heat detection. Had they relied on their own hypersensitive vision, perhaps they would have spotted their attacker.

'That's what makes us dangerous. We are the symbiosis of war machine and human ability,' Argol continued. 'Do not rely on gears and motors, remember that you have two hands and a brain.'

Sica unlocked his helmet to reveal a face of heavy cheekbones and long matted coils of hair. His heavy brow ridge was pinched in a grimace. The sergeant did not like being made a fool of, even by the venerable captain. 'You didn't come all this way to lecture us on battle theory, my captain. What do you need from us?'

'Sergeant Sica. Your squad's performance was less than notable on Govina.'

The mere mention of it made Barsabbas wince inwardly. He knew Sargaul would feel the same.

'What of it?' Sica snarled.

'I know you fought hard. Post-operation data showed pict evidence of heavy tau casualties. Have you had the pleasure of viewing the aerial surveillance? There is a pict-capture of a rock ridge lined with tau bodies in a neat little line. All of them, gunned down in a straight line just like that. Pop. Pop. Pop.'

Sica was not amused. 'We faced almost five hundred tau foot-soldiers. They are pliable and break open easily, but their guns are difficult to trade shots with. Even their basic infantry rifle cuts through a clear thirty centimetres of brick.'

'The fact remains – you were defeated, beaten, driven back. It's brought shame to your squad and, by extension, my company.'

Barsabbas heard Bael-Shura hiss, as if warming up the Betcher's gland beneath his tongue. For the past ten months, Squad Besheba had become pariahs within the Chapter.

'What do you need from us?' Sica repeated warily.

'I'm giving you a chance to redeem your performance. Five squads from Captain Hazareth's First Company will be deploying to Hauts Bassiq. Sabtah and Muhr have, for once, agreed to this course of action.'

Barsabbas kept quiet, but his breathing quickened with quiet anticipation. Although it was left unsaid, there was no doubt Captain Argol had requested their presence on this mission. It meant the company, despite their misgivings, still believed Squad Besheba was an effective and dependable squad, but they would need an act to redeem their reputation.

'This is your chance. I have petitioned Captain Hazareth to augment his forces with Squad Besheba. Hazareth has accepted,' Argol finished.

Beside Barsabbas, Sargaul slapped his palms in anticipation. A hush fell over the squad.

'Second Company's honour is at stake here, Sergeant Sica. There existed a long and violent history when I inherited this company, a reputation for being monsters in fables. Bastion, Cadia, Armageddon, the Medina Corridor, the actions at Dunefall. I hope these wars mean as much to you as they do to me, but Second Company have never been found wanting. Good, noble men fear us. Soldiers of alien cultures know us by name and know of our brutality. We make their warrior castes feel inferior.'

They all nodded.

'I won't pressure you, Sergeant Sica. But you must know Squad Besheba carries our history on their shoulders.'

*   *   *

THE BLOOD GORGONS were deploying. Despite the nature of a scouting deployment, the entire *Cauldron Born* was thrumming with activity.

Muhr's coven was coaxing the warp drives and daemon spirits. Alarm sirens were blaring, engine slaves were sweating. There was no rest, no pause in labour. Freight docks were ramped, shrines were tended to and everywhere was the synchronised stomp of boots as black turban patrols doubled.

Weaponsmith Linus knew he would not be sleeping for several rotations. The deploying squads had equipment that needed to be repaired and readied for war and already his apprentices were bowed in focussed work. Alcestis was stooped at her work bench, a portly woman in her fifties who had once been a respected dollmaker in her home hive of Delaphina. Her hands worked quickly, darting between whetstone, file and a Traitor Marine's cutlass. At their benches, others were hammering the dents out of water canisters, re-meshing buckle straps or cleaning trophy racks. These were not the sacred power armours or bolters of the Blood Gorgons, for no slaves were allowed to touch, much less be entrusted with, such artefacts. Rather, these were the various tools of the Traitor Marines.

The slaves worked by the light of small gas lamps and candle flame. It was slow, agonising work, but it was better than being a menial. Although their work chamber was a dark box in the ship's dilapidated lower halls, they were allowed to sleep under their work benches after rotation and were rationed one and half standard meals per day. The walls were covered with old sheets and shredded waste to insulate against the sub-zero space climate. Through an ever-present haze, tabac smoke was chain-lit to help them through their work shifts. Despite these conditions, the mending slaves had come to accept the cubic little chamber as their home. They had learned to make the best of what they had become and even named their portion of the ship *the smokehouse*.

An entire half of the smokehouse was cramped with racks of axes, boarding pikes and gaudy blades that had been delivered there since morning cycle. Varied were the weapons in the collection, as no two Traitor Marines possessed the same arsenal. These were personal caches collected by each individual over their decades or centuries of service, a veritable history of their achievements. Each Blood Gorgon took great pride in their exotic collections, and any fleck of dust or slight damage would cost a weapon-smith one finger. Already, Linus, meticulous with his work though he was, had lost a little finger and a ring finger, once for sharpening an axe blade against the grain and another for leaving carbon build-up in the pommel of a sword that he could not reach with his tools.

'There is a boarding axe which needs sharpening and rebinding,' a young apprentice told Linus. 'Would you like me to finish it, boss?'

Linus shook his head. The apprentice was a mere boy. In time he would learn the finer points of regraining and weave binding, but for now he was too clumsy to be entrusted with so dangerous a task. 'Not now, lad,' replied Linus. 'Squad Brigand needs a half-hundred leather pouches to be oiled, you get along with that.'

Picking up the short-handled axe, he ran a palm along its edge. Although the slaves were told nothing about the nature of deployment, Linus had been enslaved for long enough that he could judge, by the tools the Traitor Marines chose, what the nature of their mission would be.

This time, there was a predominance of light and concealable weapons. The absence of heavier weaponry such as halberds or polearms suggested that it would be no quick, frontal assault. There was no preponderance of boarding pikes to be re-toothed as there often would be before a boarding raid. Lighter weapons meant utility.

Perhaps a long-distance campaign? A planet of smouldering fields and ash plains? Linus remembered distant planets, exotic in plant life and fauna. He remembered when he was younger, the fields outside his hab had been covered in green grass and the swaying growth of trees. But try as he might, he could not remember what they smelled like or how they felt to the touch. He knew only the *Cauldron Born* now and nothing else.

Linus sighed. He often wondered where these Traitor Marines went – even if they were horrifying warzones. Surely anything would be better than a lifetime of enslavement, subsisting on gruel and watery yoghurt?

BARSABBAS AND SARGAUL summoned their retinue sometime around mid-cycle.

Situated in the *Cauldron Born's* middle decks the Blood Gorgons' interior citadels rose along the cliffs and numberless ramparts of the ship's interior structure. Turreted proto-fortresses loomed along the dark rises and shelves of the superstructure, each housing one pair of bonded brethren. Lighting their way with lamps, the personal slaves went quickly and urgently, together in a hurried flock.

There were the two black turbans in their brass armour, Ashar and Dao, striding imperiously in their upturned and pointed boots. The helm bearers came next, little more than young boys in stiffly embroidered tabards. A train of munitions and armament servitors clattered behind, guarded by a trio of scale hounds. Behind them, appearing unrushed, came the litter of pleasure pets, collected from a double dozen planets, each of the women chosen on the nine Slaaneshi principles of exotic beauty.

The fortresses remained unconnected; the chain-link walkways that had connected them had been destroyed centuries ago and never rebuilt. The Blood Gorgons had not always been a unified Chapter before the reign of Gammadin. During the early stages of their excommunication, intra-Chapter conflict had reduced them to little more than a band of thieves escaping together for survival. It had been a time of turmoil, during which the Blood Gorgons had turned upon one another and walled themselves up within their drifting fortress. Even after Gammadin united the Chapter after the Reforging, the citadels remained as a memorial of past failings.

The retinue of Barsabbas and Sargaul arrived at a grated walkway. Beyond them, spanning an abyssal drop, the walkway led towards blast shutters set in a wall that dropped away like a cliff edge. Swathes of rust honeycombed the citadel across the pit. Flat and imposing, it swept four hundred metres down into shadows and dim pinpricks of strobe lighting.

By the time the retinue had cleared the muzzled gun servitors at the entry shutters, they were already late. Barsabbas and Sargaul had begun their anointments and the seven rituals of predomination were about to begin.

Barsabbas met them at the draw gates, unarmoured and imposing. 'Do not be late. Tardiness erodes my efficiency. Entirely erodes it. Understand?'

'Yes,' the slaves said, bowing and hurrying to their positions.

Each slave within the retinue had a personal task in the pre-deployment rituals. Gammadin had coined them 'the Sacrifices of War', but Barsabbas had quietly referred to them as 'the Tedium before Battle'.

With a dismissive wave from Sargaul, the sacrifices began without much fanfare. To Barsabbas, it was slightly deflating. The rituals grew tiresome to him. He attributed the tedium to the reverence in which the senior Blood Gorgons held the rituals. The veterans built up such a sense of solemnity and ceremony that when the younger ranks performed it, half-hearted in youth, the sacrifices seemed to lose all meaning.

Barsabbas sighed wearily. First, he and Sargaul reswore their oaths of brotherhood. The Astartes implant known as the omophagea allowed for learning by eating. Through the implant they were able to 'read' or absorb genetic material that they consumed, the omophagea transmitting the gained information to the brain as a set of memories or experiences. The Blood Gorgons remembered a time when they had fought against one another. Although they had always been one Chapter, the Reforging was part of their Chapter history. The oaths reminded them of this, or so the veterans said.

Barsabbas could not remember the Reforging. That was before his time and no more than a curious relic of history.

Barsabbas cut a small piece of flesh from inside his cheek while Sargaul sliced open the meat of his right thumb. A tiny sample of blood and flesh was collected into a brass bowl and the bloody tissue was diluted with an alcohol solution. Apparently, the blood was traditionally mixed with fermented mead. These days, honey was a rarity for the Chapter and it was simply more efficient to manufacture an alcoholic solvent. Perhaps Barsabbas would appreciate these rituals if they were not some mere nuisance to be observed for the sake of tradition. He shrugged and slugged down the caustic mixture.

The Sacrifice of Armament followed. Barsabbas and Sargaul were stripped naked and lowered their bodies into a simmering cauldron. The water was hot enough to par-boil the outermost layers of skin. Once bathed, the inflamed skin was then vigorously rubbed with coarse-grained salts. Lastly a thick white salve of *woad* – a mixture of animal fat, minerals and bio-chemicals – was applied to toughen the skin, numbing it.

Again, Barsabbas found the process unnecessary. The skin was more prone to infection in humid combat zones. Yet they did not argue the procedure. It was something that had always been.

After the skin treatment, the Traitor Marine's suit of

power armour was fitted into place, segment by segment. The plugs, stem cords and synapse wires were connected from the armour to the black carapace. All present began to chant a simple, almost child-like rhyme, in order to placate the armour's spirit as it was coaxed from its sleep.

Fully suited and armoured, Barsabbas could not help but notice the subtle reaction from his servants. They shied away from him, afraid to be close. It happened often. It was as if normal humans had an instinctive fear of Space Marines, a deeply seeded biological aversion to being close to something so dangerous, so powerful.

Finally came the Sacrifice of Smoke. This was the ritual that Barsabbas found most pragmatic, despite its superstitious nature. While in warp transit, objects were likely to go missing. To a warrior-mind, the phenomenon was unexplainable and oddly disturbing – small items left unlocked or unbolted would disappear. Sometimes these could be vital pieces of wargear, or even the firing pin of a bolter. In order to prevent such warp poltergeist activity, most loyalist Chapters prayed and erected gargoyles.

The Blood Gorgons observed this superstition in their own way by discharging firecrackers and parading in their war helms. It was the Blood Gorgons' belief that war helms needed to be terrifying enough to scare even the daemons of Chaos, or ill fortune would be invited. Barsabbas's helmet was terrifying indeed, a screaming bovine sculpt with a narrow slitted vision lens and wide antlers like arms rearing up to frighten away mischievous spirits. He danced a strange, spasmodic dance, executing clumsy movements in his power armour. Their retinue beat drums and cymbals while singing.

With the final sacrifices complete, Barsabbas and Sargaul stood in their full finery of war. He stole a look in the gilded mirror in their chambers. The creature that looked back at him appeared monstrous – a broad framework of engineered bone and muscle. Theatrical yet pugnacious, his mask was strangely emotionless, its exaggerated scream frozen into the rigor mortis of sculpted brass.

He realised he was the most feared fighting unit in the universe. He allowed that thought to settle upon him for a moment. It was intoxicating. They were mobile fortresses, able to bull-charge head first into a storm of enemy munitions unscathed. They were destructive, the firepower at their immediate disposal able to flatten urban blocks. With his bare hands, gloved in ceramite, he could crush and pry open sheets of metal, maybe even the support girders of a building.

'Master,' cried the slaves as the ritual preparations drew to a close. They mewled collectively, scratching pleadingly at their faces as if Barsabbas and Sargaul had forgotten.

Barsabbas watched Sargaul slide a black metal piston from a leather carrier at his thigh plate. The slaves lined up eagerly. One after another, Sargaul viced their jaws in his hand, turning their faces ever so slightly upwards. The piston punched into their cheek scars with a meaty thud. The slaves would wince, flinching away from Sargaul's grasp with a weeping wound in their cheek.

They liberated the slaves in turn, extracting the larvae from their flesh. Sargaul hurried through the process without veneration, his movements deftly practiced, yet rough and bored. A young girl with a graceful neck was next in line. Barsabbas had never learned her name. She was just a menial.

Sargaul trapped her timid face between the vice of his fingers. The black tube slid into her cheek like a monstrous syringe. She remained stoic as it retracted, leaving a neat incision below her cheekbone. A hard tap of the piston dislodged a tiny white larva onto the floor, oozing with fluid and pus. It trembled fitfully upon contact with the air, expanding rapidly, its membranous cocoon stretching and straining. As the egg skin peeled away, a fleshy nub of fingers and teeth emerged. The newly birthed creature resembled an arachnid, with a swell of bone-shearing mandibles above its abdominal sac. Black hair, coarse and wet, sprouted wirily from its throbbing skin.

Sargaul set his heel down and crushed the skittering mess.

'You are all free until our return,' Sargaul said.

The slaves, some amongst them wadding their palms against bleeding faces, stared at them like a lost herd of particularly dull sheep. Most of them knew no other life than servitude. Some had been born into slavery, their ancestors having dwelt in the slave warrens for many generations.

'But if we do not return, then you will all die with us, for this is the way the gods will it. You serve only us, and live by virtue of our existence. Without us, you cannot be allowed to live,' Sargaul announced.

'It may not make sense to you, but it is only our way.'

IN STEAMING CAULDRONS and platters on carts, the food was served in the Hall of Solemn Supper. Teeming like colony ants, scullery slaves toiled, the patter of their steps strident across the ancient floorboards.

The Hall of Solemn Supper was a narrow, antiquated chamber deep within the ship's furnished core, with great wooden beamed ceilings dating from a time when the ship was an abandoned drifter. Arched windows framed with sculpted mer-maidens and harpies were spaced evenly, allowing the hall full view of distant stars and galaxies.

Here the Blood Gorgons came to feast before deployment and, as was customary, receive their pre-mission assembly with the company commander. Although it marked the last stage of squad-level planning and tactics, it was also a sombre time to gather and feast among brothers.

It was only a small deployment, with five squads. Many of the long tables, arrayed in one-hundred-man company lines, were empty, yet the food and wine were nonetheless bountiful. The kitchen crews had been diligent in their preparation of the Traitor Marines' pre-war nutrition. Loaves of fibre-dense wholegrain breads steamed in baskets. Creamed soups from the vessel's fungal colonies were wheeled out in cauldrons. Roast and furnaced meats of all kinds were hauled out in hand wagons.

The five squads sat together at the long table, with Captain Hazareth at their head. Gathered were Squad Besheba, Squad Hastur, Squad Yuggoth,

Squad Brigand and veteran fire-team Shar-Kali.

Barsabbas found himself sitting opposite a brother of Squad Hastur. He gave him a curt nod but nothing more. It was known amongst the company that Squad Hastur were 'Muhrites', supporters of Muhr's ascension. Their sergeant, Brother Kloden, was an ambitious aspirant who hungered for conquest, and that did not sit well with the company.

The squads fell into silence as Captain Hazareth pushed back his granite bench with a scrape.

'I could not be more confident in the destruction you will cause,' Hazareth began.

The squads stamped and clapped clamorously, spilling wine and bashing the basalt table with their fists. Barsabbas was so caught up in the excitement he crushed a brass dining plate in his hands and hurled it across the hall.

Hazareth motioned for quiet. 'Our wards on Hauts Bassiq have signalled for our aid. It is our duty to our slavestock worlds that we answer their calls, so it has always been.'

He brought up a hololithic display from a vertical projector. 'This is an aerial surveillance pict from the last time we harvested genestock. That was close to sixteen cycles ago, or almost eighty years, standard. As you can see, the terrain is largely open, flat country. The Adeptus Mechanicus blasted the land prior to settlement. In doing so, the ensuing firestorm depleted the atmosphere causing atmospheric temperatures to scale intolerable heights within years.'

Barsabbas took a sip of his wine and realised it could be the last time in months that his hydration levels would be optimal. The furious loss of sweat and Hauts Bassiq's scarcity of water had driven the Imperial colonies away and turned the planet into a ghost desert.

Spilling a cartographer's chart over the table and cutlery, Hazareth tapped the map with a blunt, armoured fingertip. 'Of all our sixty-two recruitment worlds, Hauts Bassiq breeds one of the hardiest stock due to its borderline inhospitable climate. Minerally, it is one of the richest in resources–'

Brother-Sergeant Kloden frowned and rapped the table in-between mouthfuls of beef tendon. 'What use do we have of mineral resources? We have never been ones to hoard.'

Sargaul interjected tersely. 'Warp-iron. Kloden, do you know what warp-iron is?' he asked coldly.

Barsabbas nodded to himself knowingly. Although he was too young to have ever visited Hauts Bassiq, he had researched the catacombs for archived intelligence. Due to Hauts Bassiq's proximity to the *Occularis Terribus*, its surface was marked with warp-stone impacts that had compressed over the ages into a compound similar to uranium. This warp-iron was what kept the *Cauldron Born's* fusion reactors running. Ever since the Chapter had claimed the ghost ship as its own, a piece of irradiated warp-iron almost three hundred metres in length had powered the reactor core.

Before Kloden could respond, Captain Hazareth pointed at the map again. 'Enemy threat disposition is unknown.'

'Xenos, Khoitan?' Sergeant Sica asked.

Hazareth shook his head and drained his wine cup before answering. 'Entirely unknown. The signal beacon from Hauts Bassiq relayed no other information.'

'Try not to retreat if shot at again,' Sergeant Kloden snorted.

Sargaul stood up, clattering dishes and spilling a goblet. His naked blade was drawn.

'Brother Sargaul! I will not have blades at my table,' Captain Hazareth shouted, quick to quell the violence.

Slaves frightened by the outburst scurried from the alcoves to refill wine goblets and placate the warriors with loaded plates of cold meat and spiced offal. The squads fell back to eating, shooting hard glares at each other across the table.

Hazareth rotated the hololith and zoomed in close. 'Your main objective is to reach the city of Ur. This is the last bastion of technology on Bassiq. The remaining Imperialists have sequestered themselves there, in a sealed city. They no longer maintain much contact with the nomads who we use as genestock. If any campaign were to be mounted, it would commence here. There are few other strategic targets amongst the major continents. The plainsmen dwell in semi-nomadic bands elsewhere.'

'Why have our brother-ancestors not conquered Ur already? Why leave an Imperial bastion to blight the landscape?' Barsabbas asked.

'Because we pick and choose our fights carefully. There is nothing to be gained from overthrowing the Barons of Ur. They are an isolationist cult. Yet they protect the world from xenos raids and minor threats when we cannot. They do not even know of our existence or our sovereignty over their lands.'

'Also,' Kloden said, sneeringly, 'we would risk too much. Our Chapter would have a difficult time over-whelming even that little dirthole,' he said to Barsabbas. 'They use a fusion reactor much like our own to power void shields thicker than your skull.'

Captain Hazareth remained impassive, but Barsab-bas could sense his Khoitan's seething resentment for the Muhrites.

'What you may not know,' said Captain Hazareth, 'is that Ur sits upon the largest deposit of warp-iron on the planet. There's estimated to be enough warp-iron there to fuel the *Cauldron Born's* fusion plant for no less than six hundred thousand years, standard.'

Nothing in the archives had mentioned this. Barsabbas craned forwards. 'Why have we not claimed this warp-iron as our own?'

Hazareth shrugged dismissively. 'Because, as Sergeant Kloden has said, we are not hoarders. We have all the warp-iron we need to feed the *Cauldron Born's* reactor. We simply do not need more. We are free that way, and untied to the trouble of earthly possession.'

Kloden exhaled derisively. 'We are a poor man's Chapter. Peasant ignorant.'

Finally, Hazareth turned to Kloden. Only then did Barsabbas realise how imposing his Khoitan appeared. At well over two metres eighty, when Haz-areth faced Kloden square on, he cast a shadow over Kloden's face.

'Sergeant Kloden. I will strip you of your rank and the skin from your sword hand if you cross me once more. I consider myself a tempered commander who judges his men not by the candidate of their allegiance, but by their merits as soldiers. If you befoul this mission with politics I swear I will eat your bones. You will go to Ur, you will report your findings, you will return here with all your men alive. Otherwise, Kloden, I sup on your marrow.'

Kloden nodded quietly and slowly, afraid to meet Hazareth's level gaze. He threw down a half-chewed haunch on his plate with a sullen clatter. His appetite, evidently, had gone.

Despite Kloden's chastisement, Barsabbas oddly felt no better. He too put down his eating knife. They were supposed to be Blood Gorgons, joined in feasting, shoulder to shoulder before their battle. It was not meant to be like this. Barsabbas was too young to remember the Chapter wars, but the thought of internecine conflict disturbed him in the most intrusive manner.

CHAPTER SIX

ON THE DAY the Red Gods descended to Hauts Bassiq, the weather was angry.

A high-pitched wind on the lower part of the south continent built up its strength. By the time it jettisoned itself across the North Territories it was a bellowing dust storm. Grit tore the bark off trees and gales uprooted even the hardy dwarf bushes from the sands. The sky darkened so hungrily that it became black at the height of noon and stayed that way for some hours.

In the central interior plains, a plains herdsman fleeing towards shelter saw several lights in the sky. They winked like stars, but they plummeted, moving too fast across the black sky to be distant astral bodies. He saw them break away from each other, like flowers caught in an updraught, and scatter across the horizon. Peering out from beneath the shuka he had drawn around his face as the sand whipped his lashes, he wondered if they were the cause of such portentous weather.

GUIDE LIGHTS WINKING, fluttering blindly in the sky, the drop-pods became trapped in an updraught. Confined within the coffin slabs of bulk plating, Squad Besheba could only watch the topographic monitors overhead as they veered off course. Violent wind patterns shaped like an eye spiralled outwards and pushed the tiny dots of the Blood Gorgons' drop-pods further and further away from Ur.

'Forward venting disabled. Guiding fins are losing drift. Prepare for freefall!' Sergeant Sica shouted above the drop-pod's death rattle.

Their Dreadclaw was plummeting, freefalling as the thrusters grunted with intermittent effort to slow their descent. Arrest sirens. The crash of high-altitude wind. The stink of loose petroleum. The drop-pod became a self-enclosed world of blind confusion.

Barsabbas was pinned against his restraints by g-force as the entire cabin vibrated against the atmospheric friction. In the restraint harness beside him, Sargaul was utterly impassive behind his helmet and entirely motionless. Barsabbas tried to emulate some of the veteran's composure, but the combat stimms he had ingested were agitating him. He was grinding his teeth as the stimms elevated his heart rate. The crushed enamel tasted like wet sand in his mouth.

Barsabbas almost did not feel the crash. The drop-pod collided with the planet's surface at high speed and continued to bounce with a loose, jarring expulsion of force. The impact would have shattered any normal human's skeletal structure. Rolling, tumbling, flipping head over heels, Barsabbas gripped his restraint harness as the drop-pod swept him along. His neck whipped violently against the arrestor cage and his shoulder popped briefly out of joint before clicking back into the socket. Blood, hot and sour, filled his mouth as his teeth sliced clean through his tongue.

'Up! Up! Up!' Sica shouted.

There was no time for quiet. The alarms were still so loud they beat in his eardrums. Barsabbas shook his head to clear the concussive aftershock. His ears were ringing as the dust settled around him.

'Contact! Multiple massive movement.' Someone shouted the warning into the squad's vox-link but the urgency blurred the words into no more than a sharp smear. He was already up and uncaged from his restraint harness. The drop-pod's surveillance systems were baying with alarm. External motion sensors were detecting encroaching movement.

'Bolters up,' Bael-Shura commanded. The squad uncaged their restraints and readied themselves, slamming bolter clips into their guns. A banging came from the outside, a rapid persistent hammering as if a horde were trying to breach the drop-pod's shell.

Barsabbas checked he had a full load in his sickle-pattern bolter clip. His helmet HUD powered up, its ocular targeting syncing with his bolter sights. Slabs of system reports scrolled by his peripheral vision: climate, energy readouts, atmospheric toxicity, all of which Barsabbas ignored as the alarms brayed and amber cabin lights flashed. He signalled to Bael-Shura that he was ready.

Sica stood by with a hand over the release button. The hammering outside grew louder, almost wild.

'Deploy!' Sica roared, punching the release button.

The drop-pod's side hatches unfolded like flower petals. There was an exhalation of pressurised air. The outside rushed in towards them as if a flood gate had burst open.

Barsabbas crouched and shot on instinct. His first shot punched through a human chest. The body had no chance to fall as others pushed in from behind. It remained upright – jammed by the press of people. The freshly killed male seemed to writhe. Barsabbas thought he saw its arms raise, but he dismissed it as a ghost image from his concussion. He took aim for a second shot – and paused.

The body continued to walk towards him, lurching with blind, drunken steps. This time Barsabbas removed its head with a clean shot and it dropped. Only then did he realise that they were surrounded by the dead.

Hundreds of dead. Their arms were outstretched and their faces waxy. Corpses swarmed over the drop-pod, climbing the chassis and being pushed by thousands more from the rear. Barsabbas saw a naked male in an advanced state of decay, his skin hanging like loose latex garments from his glistening muscle. There was a woman with skin so infected it left fist-sized holes in her belly. Another whose face was grey with mould barely resembled a man.

Recoiling in physical disgust, the Blood Gorgons opened fire with a whittling, sustained volley that fanned out in all directions. High-velocity explosive rounds impacted against a dense wall of naked flesh.

Barsabbas's humidity readings reached almost ninety per cent as a mist of blood and fluid rose in a solid, blinding wall.

The fighting became frantic. Hands reached through the muzzle flashes towards him. Something dragged on his ankle and gave way wetly as he crushed his heel into it. A rotting palm clawed at his vision lens.

Crouched low, Bael-Shura released his flamer. An expert pyro gunner, he applied light pressure to the trigger spoon and played a tight, drilling cone of promethium into the wall of walking dead. Several were incinerated by the direct blast, but many simply caught fire and continued to fight. The flaming corpses flailed wildly, spreading the fire until it swirled in the air and churned a rippling backwash of heat into the drop-pod.

Barsabbas grew agitated as black smoke began to clog his filtration vents. Bael-Shura was a calloused warrior, but he was frustratingly obstinate. The flamer fulfilled a devastating anti-infantry role within the squad, but right now its area of effect was causing more tactical complications than necessary. The weapon spewed a promethium jet that incinerated most unarmoured targets upon contact, but it was precisely because of its super-heated temperatures that it caused surrounding fabric and hair to catch fire. The tide of corpses became mobile tinder. Despite this, Bael-Shura continued to fire, trying to play as narrow a flame as he could.

Barsabbas, however, preferred his mighty bolter. A standard Godwyn-pattern with its high-explosive bolt-round was his lifeline. The bolter might have

been heavy, bulky and had a recoil that could dislo-
cate a human shoulder, but it flattened most targets
with one shot. When engaged in a protracted firefight, Barsabbas had learned it was better to shoot a
target and see it fall than have the wounded target
flee and spend the next few hours wondering if it was
now doubling back to ambush him.

'Besheba, switch to melee and fall behind me. We're
going to drive a wedge through them,' Sica voxed into
the squad link.

Barsabbas had been waiting for this command.
Boarding actions had always been Barsabbas's field of
expertise. It was in the dense, mauling scrum of
breach-fighting that Barsabbas, young though he was,
received the greatest respect. His dense, heavy frame
was well suited to the wrestling, grinding melee. Ever
since his bond with Sargaul and induction into Squad
Besheba, Barsabbas had claimed the role of 'fore-
hammer': the lead point of a boarding advance.

'Besheba, form on me,' said Barsabbas, wrenching
his mace from a waist hook. One and a half metres
long, cold-forged from a single rod of iron, the mace
was capped by a knot of fused metal.

Sica nodded, pushing Barsabbas to the front. 'Tur-
tled advance.'

They drove forwards, Sica with a boarding pike,
stoving ribs and skewering the dead with each thrust.
Barsabbas kept his eyes on the sky and cleared the
path with wide arcs of his swinging mace. As sophis-
ticated as his suit's auto-sensors were, they had no
answer for the blood that congealed over his lenses.
Barsabbas tried wiping them with his gloved fingers
but it simply smeared the blood, resigning him to

seeing through a fog of pink. Beside him, Sargaul slipped on the bodies spilled across the ground, crashing down on one knee. Barsabbas was immediately there, standing over Sargaul and tossing aside body after body. The dead buffeted him from all angles, glancing off his armour, dashing their teeth against his ceramite, climbing upon his back. Although he weighed close to three hundred and sixty kilos in armour, the sheer numbers rocked his heels. Unable to see clearly, Barsabbas felt engulfed by an avalanche of body parts.

'Stay tight and follow me,' Sica repeated. His low, steady voice on the vox-link pierced the jostling, teetering confusion.

Looking over the swarm of undead, Barsabbas watched solitary figures crest the sand dunes on a far horizon. They were more walking dead, attracted by the brilliant contrails of their descending drop-pod. Some sprinted, other walked stiffly, others still seemed to follow in confused huddles. Beyond them, the red ferric peaks surrounded them like low-lying mountains, impervious to the furious fight below.

THE STRATOSPHERIC WIND had blown them wide off course. The landing zone of Squad Besheba had been locked for the infected north, just twelve kilometres away from the sealed city of Ur. Instead, they had been inserted deep into the south, beyond the demarcation of infection, where the black wilt, according to reports, had not yet developed into a contagious threat.

It was not a portentous beginning to their deployment.

Barsabbas set himself upon a rock, fanning out the great trunks of his legs. He unlocked his helmet and a trickle of sweat sheeted down from the neck seal. Running his thick metal fingers through his damp locks, he sighed wearily as Sica reported.

'All squads were blown off target by the storm. All of them except Squad Shar-Kali experienced a mass assault by the dead.'

'Maybe these walking corpses were attracted by the falling lights,' Bael-Shura offered. Under the orange light of sunset, Barsabbas could see tiny scratches over the surface of his power armour. The undead had literally clawed their fingers to bloody stumps in an effort to break him open. Barsabbas imagined he looked much the same.

'Or maybe our arrival was anticipated and they were sent to find us,' Cython said in a rare moment of insight. The usually loud, boorish Cython and his bond Hadius were placated for once by the post-adrenal slump. Despite their superhuman metabolism and delayed onset of lactic acid build-up in their muscles, the exhaustion of hand-to-hand fighting could be felt in their bones. Every fibre in Barsabbas's body, particularly his forearms, was sour with strain. Squad Besheba had managed to travel six kilometres from the crash site, pursued by the undead relentlessly. Scattered, broken bodies were left in their wake. Barsabbas counted one hundred and ninety-six kills by hand, bested perhaps only by Sergeant Sica. They had finally been forced to climb the canyon in order to shake off their pursuers.

'We will press on to Ur when the temperature

permits. It is far, but that is our objective and no orders were issued to deviate.'

As Sica spoke, Barsabbas was already analysing their situation. According to tact-maps they were rock-marooned almost eleven hundred kilometres from their intended dropsite. The local geography was predominantly arid with a high density of ferrous metals in the dirt. To their immediate south lay a bee-hived range of sedimentary formations, the sandstone and clay appearing ominously scarlet. Barsabbas chose to interpret the red as a good omen, a sign of angry retribution.

Sargaul was crouched a little further away, his bolter wedged vigilantly against a rock ledge. By the set of his jawline, Sargaul's conscious mind was shut off, stripped bare of thought. For now, his body was reduced to cardiac, respiratory and autonomic functions and he knew nothing except the scope of his weapon and the trigger finger of his right hand.

Barsabbas settled on a rock next to his bond. Sargaul turned his head slowly to regard him, before nestling his face back behind the weapon. Together they sat in silence, watching the suns leapfrog each other as they slunk beneath the horizon. For a while, nothing was said as they seeped in the sticky, chest-heaving glow of post-combat.

Finally Barsabbas turned to Sargaul. 'What were they?'

'They were the dead.'

'But I've never seen corpses do that before. It is... is it common?' Barsabbas asked. He often tried not to ask Sargaul too many questions. Barsabbas was conscious of the fact that he was the youngest and his combat experience had been limited to raids and squad-level deployments. Questions were weak, grasping things and he often avoided them.

Sargaul shook his head. 'Once, I saw dead men possessed by the puppet strings of an alpha-psyker. They were much the same.'

Barsabbas thought about this. Sargaul had seen many things throughout his service, but something about the corpses had put the veteran on edge. He could feel that his bond was agitated, of that he was sure. 'You are disturbed by this?'

Sargaul did not try to hide it. He nodded, almost to himself. 'I have never seen the dead rise of their own accord, have you? I try not think about why the dead would become so angry as to rise from their sleep and walk the earth. What could have wronged them? What influence makes these old ancestors restless? The walking dead are a by-product, an effect of influence. The answers escapes me and I am disturbed.'

'Do you think the enemy will fear us?'

'No, Barsabbas, I don't think they do,' Sargaul replied without taking his eyes off the scope.

'That's a shame,' said Barsabbas matter-of-factly. 'We look terrifying.'

At first, Barsabbas had taken pleasure in the carnage of the fight. After so many months of slithering through the cramped training tunnels of the ship, it felt good to finally be uncaged and administer so much destruction. But now he felt hollow. The walking dead were not living beings who feared him, nor breathing creatures who felt the despair at the sight of a charging Traitor Marine. They were 'the dead', a thoughtless horde no more sentient than a tide or the weather. It was a pointless fight. But there would be something else here. As Sargaul had said, the dead did not rise of their own accord. Something was causing this. Perhaps if Squad Besheba could find that cause, then they could put the fear into them.

MUHR HAD NOT seen the artificial light of the ship in days, only the darkness of his tower and the glow of his scrying lens. Despite the rituals of deployment and warp transit of the *Cauldron Born*, Muhr remained cloistered, refusing any contact beyond his own sanctuary.

His hair, unwashed and long, hung like a greasy mantle from his armoured shoulders. He was sweating fat beads that ran down his neck. His head was throbbing. Yet still he hung on, wringing the last efforts of psychic strength from his mind.

The mirror was set in a heavy frame, a free-standing structure of sculpted white meerschaum. But the frame was not important, for the mirror itself had had many frames throughout its long existence. It had once belonged to a prophet of the eldar race, or so the story went, and had since changed hands. In the hands of the eldar, it was said to have been an oracle, a scryer and a means of entering the webway, but Muhr dismissed these tales as fanciful. He had never been able to use it for anything more than astro-telepathy, and even then, the image was often poor.

As he waved his hand in an arc, the mirror surface became cloudy and changed. Muhr peered deeply.

He saw a settlement in Hauts Bassiq. A colony of wagons and carts tucked beneath the shade of a red, dusty hill. The image was murky, appearing fractured in some places and layered with ghost images. Muhr tapped the mirror and an image of the huts blossomed across the lens. He saw the corpse of an old man, withered and dry, crouched by the wood frame of a caravan. Periodically, the corpse gnawed on a femur before discarding it, as if it couldn't remember what it was doing, before picking it up and repeating the process.

Muhr tapped again. Now he saw a mass exodus of people. Plodding with stiff gaits, they moved in a single direction as if they were a great herd in migration. Flies settled on their slack lips and eyelids and they did not react. These were the walking dead, victims of the black wilt who spread the disease southwards.

Sudden footsteps intruded upon him. Distracted, Muhr shed the psychic link and turned from the mirror.

'My lord.'

It was Nabonidus, one of his coven. Nabonidus, the Chirurgeon and sorcerer attached to 5th Company.

'My lord,' Nabonidus repeated. 'I report that the scouting element has been deployed. They made landfall thirty-one hours ago, but you were not present at the ceremony.'

Muhr smiled. 'I have been reviewing a joint operation.'

Nabonidus paused. He was a direct man, blunt and obtuse, and often did not understand Muhr. Like the smooth, faceless iron mask that Nabonidus wore, he was very straightforward. Although Muhr relied upon him as an enormously powerful psyker who had a natural affinity for daemonology, and a deft Chirugeon, there were some jobs that Muhr did not entrust him with, for Nabonidus lacked cunning. Muhr perceived him as no more than an effective automaton. Had his latent psychic abilities not been discovered during his neophyte induction, Nabonidus could have become a squad sergeant or even company captain. As a sorcerer of the coven, he would always be limited by his lack of guile.

'Come, Nabonidus. See for yourself.'

Muhr tapped the scrying glass. The same image reappeared as before. Nabonidus looked, his iron mask expressionless.

'That is Hauts Bassiq,' Nabonidus announced flatly.

'That is our joint operation. It is partly the fruits of my labour,' Muhr admitted proudly, his eyes glazed with psy-trance.

Nabonidus tilted his head curiously. 'You are the source of the troubles on Bassiq?' His tone was monotonous, devoid of accusation. Nabonidus was linear and so was his question.

'I am not the source, no,' said Muhr. He thought for a while, relishing the act. 'I am more of a facilitator, if you will.'

'You could be seen as a betrayer,' said Nabonidus. Somehow the words were not at all accusatory. If anyone else had uttered such words, Muhr would have slain him outright. But not deadpan Nabonidus.

'Nothing could be further from the truth. I am doing this for the glory of our Chapter,' said Muhr as he stepped away from the mirror. 'Do you see the work I have done there?'

'Perhaps,' Nabonidus replied, choosing his words carefully. Muhr was testing him now and the coven witch sensed it. If he displayed the slightest sign of dissidence, then he would be done.

Rising up, Muhr closed in on Nabonidus. 'My patron is creating a slave force capable of exploiting the warp-iron on Hauts Bassiq. My patron requires this warp-iron to fuel his expanding fleets of conquest, and only I have the wisdom to facilitate this for him.'

The witch sounded delirious, his hands describing grand arcs in the air. Nabonidus tried to step back but his coven master pressed forwards until he was almost standing face to face.

'Do you understand what I do? Why I did this?'

'I do, Muhr,' Nabonidus said cautiously. 'But we are sending our brethren into a trap. Hazareth's company should be told–'

At this Muhr started, grasping Nabonidus's face in his palms and pulling him until they were eye to eye. 'Nobody needs to be told. No one but those that I choose,' he hissed.

Suddenly casting Nabonidus aside, Muhr swung about and manipulated the mirror again. He saw a fleeting glimpse of Ur – a microcosm of civilisation in the wild plains. A dark cloud hung over the city, suffocating its stacked chimneys and settling like fog on its ramparts.

'See this power? The power of my patron? We can share this power. If we give him Bassiq, we can share it. We do not have to be pirates, scavengers, any more. We will all be noble warlords.'

'Blood Gorgons do not have a patron,' Nabonidus ventured.

'We have a pact, Nabonidus. If the Blood Gorgons relinquish Hauts Bassiq to my patron, my patron will strengthen our Chapter. I am a pragmatist, Nabonidus. I know what needs to be done to raise us above our anonymity.'

'I understand,' Nabonidus said, his voice trembling.

Muhr slapped his palm against the scrying mirror. As the images of Hauts Bassiq faded, all that remained on the glass was the ghostly imprint of his hand. 'We need this. I'm not doing this for myself. I do this for the Chapter,' Muhr said with finality. 'Hauts Bassiq is a worthy sacrifice for the prize that awaits us.'

CHAPTER SEVEN

IT WAS NOT yet dawn but Barsabbas did not think today would be any different from the day before that. The squad crossed another empty creek, leaving gridded prints in loose, dusty clay. They had been moving at a ferocious pace for the past four days, even during the heat peak of midday. They had left the rust and sandhill country of the southern tip far behind and, according to the tact-maps, had penetrated thirty-odd kilometres into the central plains. Strangely, it grew more verdant there. Hauts Bassiq was a land without oceans, yet intermittent rainfall drained gullies and creeks into the central dune fields.

Rust-resistant saltbushes flourished alongside weeping acacias in the red, infertile earth. The remnants of palaeodrainage channels became a refuge for relic plants with ancient lineages. Tall trees in dunefields were perhaps the most striking difference between the central and western territories and their eastern and southern cousins. Following the dry channels, Squad Besheba swept north, ghosting in and out of vox range with their brother squads.

Barsabbas plodded along to the rhythmic hiss of his hydraulic knee suspensors. In such monotonous country, it was easy to fall into a catalepsean sleep, purposely inducing partial consciousness. But he remained alert, forcing himself to make periodic environment scans and disseminate the information through the vox-link. His boltgun was strapped like a sash across his chest, his left hand coiled loosely around the trigger. In the past four days, Squad Besheba had learned to avoid the scavenging mobs of walking dead in order to conserve ammunition. Yet aside from wandering corpses and the stray caprid, there were no significant signs of life.

'I can taste a pocket of high atmospheric disturbance. Bacterial organisms,' Barsabbas announced as the line graph in the upper left corner of his vision spiked. A brisk wind had picked up, throwing dust into their faces. 'What say you?'

Although no human disease could penetrate the immune system of a Space Marine, Sargaul vented his helmet. 'I taste it too. Very acidic. Very strong,' he confirmed, spitting saliva out through his helmet's grille.

Cython did the same, but breathed in deeply and immediately coughed, his multi-lung rejecting the airborne substance. 'I can't identify,' he said, his words spurting out between violent hacking. 'This is pure strain.'

The squad halted as Cython continued to hack and gurgle. The fact that the substance could force even a Space Marine's multi-lung to respond so harshly was testament to its lethality. His lung sphincters were constricting as the organ attempted to flood his system with cleansing mucus.

'No more samples,' Sergeant Sica ordered angrily. 'Barsabbas, fade off your environment monitor. You're putting the fear in all of us.'

Barsabbas swore fluently but obeyed. The power plant core of his armour was two thousand years old and its spirit was temperamental if not outright malevolent, but it would not lie to him. He had detected something else on his monitors besides the bacteria. There had been a peripheral spike of detection, an organic pattern that was familiar to Barsabbas.

'Remember what Argol said,' Sica continued. 'Instinct will save your skin where scanners do not. Use your eyes and listen with your ears, and stop distracting yourself.'

With that, the squad peeled off, negotiating their way down the slope of a dry riverbed. But Barsabbas lingered. Argol's words resonated with him.

Suddenly alert, Barsabbas loosened his helmet seal and tested the air with his tongue. It was bitter at first, laced with a ferociously destructive organism that was corrosive to his hyper-sensitive taste glands. But he tasted something else on his palate too, fleeting and subtle. There! Hidden behind the airborne toxins was a familiar taste, a coppery taint that was unmistakable. Fresh blood.

'Blood. Fresh blood.'

'Blood. Blood.' The word echoed amongst the squad with breathless anticipation.

Sergeant Sica waved them to a halt at Barsabbas's warning. Cython tasted again, wary this time. He spat. 'Now that you say it, I can taste it too. You can barely pinpoint it with all the other tox on the wind current.'

'Which direction?' asked Bael-Shura. His augmetic jaw was sutured to much of his upper trachea, destroying the neuroglottis that allowed others to track by taste alone.

'Far from here, at least six kilometres to our north-east,' Barsabbas confirmed.

'We go there,' said Sica. 'Sharp find, Brother Barsabbas.'

The wind gained momentum, forcing the tall acacias to kneel and uprooting the saltbushes in bales. There was something angry and sentient about the viral wind. Barsabbas made sure both atmospheric venting and extraneous seals were entirely locked, a precaution usually reserved for vacuum or space exposure. The wind buffeted and rattled his armour like a cyclone grinding against a bunker.

They turned in defiance of the wind. It punished them with the full force of its gale. Heads low, shoulders set against the rising dust storm, Sergeant Sica led them in pursuit of freshly spilled blood.

ABOARD THE CAULDRON BORN, Sabtah roamed the old corridors. He rolled and unrolled his neck, loosening the muscles and working out the knots with pops and crackles, pacing the halls with a pensive focus. He did so often when things weighed heavily on his mind, such as now.

The shrine was a place where he came to think. These days it seemed like the younger Chaos Space Marines were too martial, too physical. They seldom tended to their war shrines. It was a quiet place and a place where Sabtah came to brood.

He sat before his shrine and retrieved his most precious prize.

The axe was of Fenrisian make, with a richly decorated brass haft-cap secured the trumpet blade. It was one of Sabtah's own trophies and one he kept at all times within his personal shrine.

Lifting the axe, Sabtah slashed the air with clumsy practice swings. It was not his weapon – it had once belonged to a Grey Hunter, one of Leman Russ's cursed children. Sabtah remembered the time when the Blood Gorgons had been declared *Excommunicate Traitoris* by the Inquisition within six decades of Founding. He had been a young neophyte then, not even blooded, yet those had been ignominious days. They had been driven from their home world by Space Wolves, a broken Chapter pursued into the warp by lupine hunters. They became thieves: foraging, hiding, always hunted. The brothers had stayed together only for survival, the Chapter divided by minor war-captains and factions who sealed off entire sections of the *Cauldron Born* as their own fiefdoms and baronies. There was no dignity to their name.

It was to be Gammadin who united the warring companies. It was he who waged an intra-Chapter war that left much of the space hulk in devastation, even to this day. But in the aftermath of fratricide, the Blood Gorgons found cohesion. It had been

Gammadin who devised the rituals of blood-bonding to ensure that his Chapter would never again fight internally, pledging their very co-existence to each other and the powers of Chaos. No Blood Gorgon would ever turn his blades on his brother again.

But Sabtah believed history came and went in cycles. What was due, would be due. The Blood Gorgons' unity had been constructed and could thus be dismantled.

Yet Sabtah also believed he could change it and map the course of his Chapter; it was his duty as Gammadin's blood bond. After all, Sabtah had been there from the beginning. He had been there the very day the Blood Gorgons rose up, seething and angry after decades of shame, to confront their Space Wolf pursuers.

Sabtah could still remember the fury and pent-up anguish that the Blood Gorgons had released against those loyalist Space Marines. Sabtah had never experienced anything like it since. They had engaged the Space Wolves with Lamprey boarding craft simply to inflict damage, a malicious hit-and-run assault that left their pursuers with severe casualties. Feared though the Wolves were in battle, they did not possess the refined boarding tactics of the Blood Gorgons. Although Sabtah had been a fresh-blood then, he slew a Grey Hunter that day. He had even scalped his enemy's long beard and plundered his axe.

He could not bear to see the Blood Gorgons live such shallow, inglorious existences again. They were a free Chapter, free to travel to the edge of the universe. The Blood Gorgons knew nothing of restraint.

Restraint, to Sabtah, was the bane of human existence. He knew that citizens of the Imperium worked their constant shift cycles until they withered and died, never deviating from doorstep to factorum. That was not existence. No, Blood Gorgons were like the sword-bearing generals of Old Terra, conquering and plundering whatever they touched. There was substance to that. It was something Sabtah could be proud of.

Suddenly, Sabtah snapped out of his reverie. He felt a tweak in the base of his neck, and a chill ran across his skin. A flutter of nerves made his abdomen coil and uncoil.

Something was wrong.

Sabtah trusted his instincts without hesitation. The veteran pivoted on his ankle. He glimpsed movement as he spun mid-turn. It was fleeting. A ghostly double image in the corner of his vision, disappearing behind the pillars that framed the temple entrance.

He was old, but his eyes did not lie to him.

Sabtah gave chase, exploding into a flat sprint. He did not know what he had seen. The *Cauldron Born* was old and large. He had seen odd things aboard the vessel before. There were rumours of strange, immaterial things that dwelt in the forgotten catacombs and drainage sumps in the lower levels of the ship. Others spoke of a dark terror that lurked in the collapsed passages beneath the rear boiler decks. Those with no knowledge of the arcane would accuse the ship of being 'haunted'. Sabtah knew it was an inevitable influence of warp travel.

Twice more he caught sight of something large yet frustratingly elusive to his eyes. He pursued doggedly, his heavy legs pounding the ground. It led him further and further away from the serviced areas of the vessel. Sabtah chased hard, refusing to slow. He realised he was being led into the forgotten areas. The corridors became unlit. The ground was uneven, broken by rust and calcification, but Sabtah was consumed by the chase. His hearts pulsated in his eardrums.

The thing, whatever it was that Sabtah saw, appeared once more, like a black sheet caught in the wind, and then vanished.

Sabtah found himself in a cavern. Leakage in the overhead pipes had created a curtain of stalactites, some pencil-thin but others as stout as the trunks of trees. A carpet of mossy fungal growth glowed a cool, pale blue.

His lungs expanding with oxygen, Sabtah realised he was still gripping the Fenrisian axe. In his haste, he had left his bolter behind. Despite its brutish appearance, the axe was gyroscopically balanced – but Sabtah lacked the axe-craft of a Fenrisian. Instead, he would have to rely on brute strength to force its leverage, and Sabtah had plenty of brute strength. Clutching the awkward, top-heavy tool in a double grip, he advanced.

The creature had baited him deep. Sabtah knew that, and part of him enjoyed the thrill of a sentient adversary. By his reckoning, he had grown slow and fat on board the ship. He was a specimen made for war.

Slowly, adrenaline drew his muscles tight, the sheaths of his musculature taut with that familiar feeling of pre-combat. His knees and forearms quavered uncontrollably, every spindle of muscle building up with unspent energy.

He saw movement. This time it appeared and stopped, rising to its height less than thirty metres away: a human shape, clothed in shadow.

For no apparent reason, the Imperial scripture *'and they shall know no fear'* scrolled through his head. Sabtah snorted.

With that, he charged through the stalactite forest. His plate-cased shoulders splintered the drip-rock to powder upon impact. He ploughed through it unarrested, a storm of fragmented stone churned in his wake. Baring fangs through his wild beard, Sabtah howled with joyous aggression. His arms yearned to uncoil and channel all of his strength, all of his momentum and all of his rage through the edge of his axe and into the flesh of his foe.

'Sabtah. Stop!'

Sabtah did not hear anything except the red wash of fury in his ears. He looped the axe in a hammer-thrower's arc, tearing down four or five stalactites in one sweep. The black shadow flickered like a disrupted pict-feed.

'Sabtah!'

Unresponsive, Sabtah drew the axe far back for another swing.

'Muhr is going to kill you. Sabtah! You have to listen to me.'

The axe froze.

Finally, a hint of recognition creased Sabtah's furrowed, animalistic brow. The feral snarl softened behind the beard. The killing rage ebbed. Sabtah lowered his axe cautiously, peering into the dark.

'Nabonidus?'

A figure walked towards the glow-lights of the

ground fungus. It was indeed Nabonidus – chosen of Muhr's coven. The witch-surgeon had shed his power armour and was clad in a hauberk of supple chainmail. His face was painted white and his eyes daubed with ash. The sorcerer clicked his fingers and the shadowy apparition standing before Sabtah dissipated.

Sabtah cursed. 'I could have killed you, Nabonidus. What did you think you were doing?'

Nabonidus pushed a finger to his lips. 'Hush, Sabtah. Please lower your voice.' He ducked his head and peered about the cavern. Finally satisfied that they were alone, Nabonidus whispered, 'I lured you here for a reason.'

Sabtah raised his axe cautiously. Nabonidus was a sorcerer. There was an innate distrust between the coven and their warrior brethren. He watched the witch's hands carefully.

'I lured you here because that is the only way it would be safe. I can't be seen talking to you, Sabtah. It's not safe.'

'Safe for who?' Sabtah asked.

Nabonidus's reply was tinged with a genuine terror. 'For me,' he admitted.

Still unconvinced, Sabtah remained silent. 'I will give you one chance to explain yourself.'

'Muhr is behind this. The Chapter rift. It is part of his power game. The troubles on Hauts Bassiq are his doing. It will cause a Chapter war from which Muhr is positioned to emerge the victor.'

Sabtah shrugged. 'I suspected this. But he has nothing I cannot deal with.'

Nabonidus shook his head. 'It is more than Muhr. There is another force at play here, more powerful than Muhr. There is some sort of pact between them.'

'Who is that patron?'

Nabonidus took a step back. 'I don't know, Sabtah. All I know is that Muhr is a mere minion. This patron is destroying Hauts Bassiq, and in return for Muhr's role, this patron is willing to aid Muhr in his ascension to power. That's all I know.'

'Why are you telling me this, witch?'

'Because I am frightened, Sabtah. I am seven hundred years old and I am frightened, not for myself but for the Chapter. I do not want a Chapter war. It's your duty now, Sabtah. You are his only obstacle.'

THE BLOOD WIND led them north-east, trembling across the lowlands. It led them to a ravine, a shallow cleft that revealed the headframe of an ancient mine. It was partially sealed by the wreckage of a collapsed hoist, like a steel spider web crushed into the entrance.

Such delving was not uncommon. The landscape was porous with such abandonment. Some were large scale constructs, open shelf mines that sliced slabs of the continent away from its crust. Others were smaller shaft mines, long forgotten and extinguished by collapse.

This one – according to the squad's pre-deployment briefing – fell somewhere in-between the two extremes. A perfect circle, jagged with cog's-teeth markings, had been cut into the ravine's coarse-grained sandstone. Wide enough to accommodate seismic earth-tractors, the severed remains of a rail system led directly into the worm's-mouth entrance.

Much of the shaft entrance had become buried beneath thousands of years of sand, dust and clay, forming a natural ramp that descended into the flat, black depths. Lobed spinifex grass lined the natural stairway, covering the flaking fossils of frames and sheave wheels.

There was blood amongst the spinifex too.

Here and there amid the tufts of coarse grass could be seen bright dashes of red. From the pattern and volume, Barsabbas knew this was not the spotted trail of a wounded animal. Strong violence had occurred there.

The squad skirted the ravine warily, appraising the area from a tactical perspective. Below them lay an irregular basin of yellowing grasses and crumbling clay. The rough terrain provided plenty of hiding space for unseen predators, but little meaningful cover for a Chaos Space Marine. Across the basin floor, the mine entrance was an edifice of sagging, oxidised framework, a perfect circle cut into the side-wall of the ravine. Even with his enhanced vision, Barsabbas could not see into the girdered depths.

Sica studied it for a while, not moving, not speaking, simply sitting and watching. After what seemed like an eternity he finally spoke. 'There is no cover. We will cross the basin in pairs. First pair moves across with the others covering: once the first pair reaches the headframe, turn around and provide cover. Clear?'

'Clear,' Barsabbas repeated with his brethren.

THEY ONLY DISCOVERED the carnage once they reached the bottom of the ravine.

The giant spinifex grass was much thicker than Barsabbas realised, dragging at him with thorny burrs. The megaflora formed unusual growth patterns where the inner grass died off and new stems sprouted from the outside forming concentric circles of various sizes.

Barsabbas mowed through the giant spinifex, flattening it with great sweeps of his metal paws. Sargaul prowled at his side, bolter loose but ready. They crunched through the loose threads of ochre grass, stopping sporadically to study the blood that flecked the area. Behind them, the rest of the squad kept an invisible watch.

Sargaul's voice suddenly came over the squad voxlink. 'I found a dead one.'

By his tone, Sargaul was anxious. Moving over to him, Barsabbas parted the grass to see what Sargaul had discovered.

There was a plainsman. Dead. A warrior, judging by the way he wore his red shuka and the quiver resting on his exposed spine. Two parallel impact hits had segmented him and smeared him into the clay. Barsabbas stopped and marvelled at the freshly slain corpse. It always amazed him how soft and easily broken was the normal human body. Mankind was not meant for war – a pouch of soft, vulnerable tissue encased in pain-receptive skin, all reinforced by a skeletal structure no more durable than pottery ceramic. Mankind was too mortal for war.

'The walking dead don't have the combat capacity for that,' Sargaul concluded.

The pair swept the area, realising the full extent of the violence. There had been combat, a fight of some sort. A broken hatchet with its edge blunted by heavy impact. Broken arrows lying in the grass. Pieces of humans thrown far and wide by the tremendous force and violence.

They found another plainsman tossed some distance away, a jumble of filleted flesh and splintered bone barely held together by skin and sinew. Barsabbas knew there were more – he saw enough hands and broken parts to know there were others, but they could no longer be found. Just pieces.

For a moment, Barsabbas was overwhelmed by the urge to spray his bolter wildly, directly into the mine shaft. But the frenzied urge was fleeting and the Chaos Space Marine's discipline held. They reached the sloping wall on the other side and took a knee, covering the area as the next pair made their way across.

A brief, keening cry echoed up from the mine shaft, causing Barsabbas to turn quickly, his bolter heavy in his hands. Despite switching to thermal version, Barsabbas could see nothing down the rocky throat. The angled shaft simply slipped away into lightless, visionless nothing. The scream came again.

'Besheba, move on!'

The last pair, Sica and Bael-Shura, had crossed the basin. It was time to confront.

'Divide into bonds. Sargaul and Barsabbas to head east, Cython and Hadius to the west, we'll spearhead north. Keep constant vox-link at both high and medium frequencies. Explore the facility and report. Stay fluid,' ordered Sica.

With that the six Chaos Space Marines descended the shaft slope at a sprint, their footfalls rumbling like the infant tremors of an earthquake.

* * *

A SHADOW FELL across the wallowing blackness of the entrance shaft. Not a physical shadow, for nothing could be discerned in the pitch dark, but a shadowed presence.

It walked quietly, yet each step crushed calcite into mineral dust. It moved softly in the shadows, gliding and shifting, yet its girth eclipsed almost the entire passage. Its heart did not beat, but it was not dead.

It followed Squad Besheba for a time, stalking warily out of auspex range. As the Blood Gorgons split off to sweep the stope tunnels, it followed too.

CYTHON AND HADIUS followed a railed tunnel for several kilometres. The railway was old, with much of the wood disintegrated and the metal a crisp, flaking shell. Yet amongst the crumbling dust, Cython could see fresh footprints. Fresh humanoid prints, some bare-footed but others in heavy-soled shoes.

It would be eighty-six minutes into their descent before Squad Besheba encountered the enemy on Hauts Bassiq.

The tunnel widened into a large, yet low-ceilinged chamber. Huddles of men and women were digging at the walls with their bare hands, scraping the soft chalk with their nails and scooping the powder into mine carts. There were perhaps two hundred of them, working in unison, yet none of them registered any heat signals under thermal vision. They were already dead.

Standing guard over the work detail was a trio of men. These three were alive, their living signatures throbbing with vital signs in Cython's HUD. Their heads and necks were hooded in loose bags of canvas. Their faces were hidden but for the pair of round vision goggles, wide like the eyes of a monstrous doll. Their bodies were armoured in cheap, mass-moulded segments of rubberised sheathing the grey colour of arsenic – bulky, overlapping and lobster-tailed. None of the men bore any military insignia or heraldry that Cython could recognise.

The three men gave monosyllabic commands to the labouring corpses – carry, retrieve, dig, lift. Already an entire section of the chalk wall had been cleared away to reveal a system of pipes like exposed muscle fibre. It was evident that the dead were re-excavating the ancient mine networks of Hauts Bassiq.

Cython fired a single shot. In the distance, no more than eighty metres down the stope, one of the men spun right around and fell. Hadius felled the other two with such speed that they never uttered a cry. *Bam-Bam-Bam*. Three shots in a semi-second and it was done.

Cython and Hadius pressed on, through the chamber of slave-corpses. These, however, did not attack them. They did not even look up from their work. Without the three men to give them commands, the slaves simply continued to work in their shambling, methodical fashion. The chalk was red with blood as the slaves scraped their fingers down into stumps.

THE MOMENT BEFORE a firefight is an oddly awkward affair. There is a fraction of a second when opposing forces meet and strain to recognise one another. A slight hesitation as the human mind reconciles the concept of shooting down a stranger before actually doing so.

But the Blood Gorgons harboured no such hesitation. Sica opened fire from behind the cover of a gas main.

The procession of hooded men advancing down the tunnel was caught by the ferocity of the sudden ambush. The hooded men fired back. Their shots were surprisingly rapid and precise, solid slugs hammering Sica's chest plate and helmet with percussive shocks, pushing him back. These men were soldiers, or at least fighters of some discipline, Sica could tell. Bael-Shura fell amongst them, an almost platoon-sized element of these cumbersome-looking soldiers. He washed them with his flamer and scattered the survivors with his spiked gauntlet. Although the men were large, imposing things, Bael-Shura made them appear frail and undersized.

The tunnel was large and chaotic. Hundreds of walking corpses were digging, scooping sediments away from the porous shell of an ancient gas main. Hundreds more dragged a monolithic length of plastek piping down the passage, evidently to replace the older, semi-fossilised piece.

Despite the shooting, the walking dead did not seem to notice the Blood Gorgons in their midst. Some looked up almost lazily, like bored grazers, but none reacted. Some were caught in the backwash of Bael-Shura's flamer, but they did not stop work, even as they burned. Their fat boiled and their skin peeled but they continued to drag on the ropes of the replacement pipe. These were obedient workers.

Hooded figures charged down the stope towards

Sica. They were shouting orders, shooting down any corpse who did not move out of their way. Sica made sure to recognise them, blinking his eyes to capture file-picts of the enemy. It would provide valuable reconnaissance should the Blood Gorgons have to deploy in greater force. He zoomed in on their armaments, blunt-muzzled autoguns with trailing belt-fed ammunition; not of Imperial issue, but a distinctly human design nonetheless. They fought in loose platoon formations, but their arsenic-grey armour was too thick for light infantry: a rubberised synthetic moulding that would be simple to manufacture but inferior in quality. It offered no protection against Sica's bolter.

Bael-Shura moved next to him, the tunnel wide enough to allow the Traitor Marines to fight shoulder to shoulder. They laughed as they worked, a dry wicked laughter that was frightening in its intensity. From behind the circular saws of an industrial rock cutter, a hooded man lobbed a rock at Sica. He heard a whistling sound and he turned the slab of his shoulder pad towards the missile. There was a flash of light. Even with his eyes closed, Sica's vision strobed red and bright yellow. It had been a grenade. The explosion pushed Sica slightly and made him grunt with annoyance at his own carelessness. He shot the man off the industrial saw, quickly, as if ashamed.

What seemed like two or three full platoons of the hooded men flooded the tunnel. Perhaps seventy or eighty men, by Sica's estimation. He reported the situation over the squad vox-link in-between shots. It was confirmed without concern. The hulking, rubberised soldiers swarmed over them, firing their underslung autoguns, brass casings flickering rapidly into the air. Sica's armour registered some minor damage in the extremities, particularly the forearms and shoulder regions as bullets chipped the external ceramite and hypodermal mesh.

Laughing, Sica backhanded one of the hooded men with the ridged knuckles of his gauntlet, snapping his neck and throwing two hundred kilos of brutish soldier back into his comrades. Bael-Shura expelled the last of his promethium and did not bother to reload; he crashed into the enemy with his weight, slashing with his studded fists. Bones broke and rubberised armour split like melon rind. There was no stopping them. Panic finally setting in, the hooded men turned and fled.

THE VOX-LINKS WERE dead. Partitioned by solid bedrock, Barsabbas and Sargaul knew nothing of their brethren's conflict. The pair skirted east at Sica's command, following what seemed to be a recent delving. The rock was freshly cut, as if expansion of the ancient mines had began anew.

Barsabbas and Sargaul descended on a chain-belt platform down hundreds of metres. Despite the oxidised state of the iron elevator, the chain belt was of newly galvanised steel and still smelt sweetly of greasing oil. Something had been reconstructing the mine. Perhaps the same things responsible for eviscerating the plainsmen braves above ground.

The elevator came to a clattering halt, fifteen metres above the shaft bottom. They hung there, suspended like a bird cage. Below them, the vault at the pit of the mine was not what they had expected.

There were hundreds of walking dead down there, packed like meat in a storage facility, a dense grid of scalps and jostling shoulders. The cooler temperatures ensured they did not rot or bloat from the surface heat. They did not move and they did not respond. The frigid air rendered them stiff and sluggish. Some moaned and rocked gently on frozen limbs.

'An army of the dead,' Sargaul whistled appreciatively.

'A workforce,' Barsabbas observed.

'But they would make poor slaves. I would not eat food prepared by these creatures.'

'No. I do not think they can do anything except menial labour. No dexterity or cognitive capacity,' Barsabbas suggested.

As if on cue, several of the closest corpses looked up and began to babble nonsense. Their vocal cords had stiffened and gases exhaled from their lungs in a strained, raspy cry.

'But they will work,' said Sargaul.

The walking dead needed no food, no water. They did not suffer under the intolerably harsh climate, and they did not sleep or rest. They would simply work until they rotted apart.

In a way, Barsabbas was awed by the simple logic. It was almost impossible for Hauts Bassiq to host a living workforce – this was the primary reason behind the Imperial exodus. Bassiq lacked water or arable land. The climate could not sustain a proper agriculture. Despite his post-human fortitude, Barsabbas felt the sting of the heat and the fogginess of extreme dehydration – he could not imagine what the conditions were like for natural-born men. In the end, the Adeptus Mechanicus left their great earthmovers and machines to rust and the rich mineral seams unclaimed. It had simply been unworkable.

A standard healthy human forced to toil in the mines or above-ground refineries would not last long. Extreme surface temperatures combined with a lack of available water was a simple yet logistically impossible obstacle. Barsabbas calculated a normal human constitution could withstand no more than an eighteen-hour work shift before death – unless heat stroke, dehydration or muscular contractions put them out of commission first.

'A long time ago, when I was still young, Gammadin had once considered harvesting Bassiq for more than just genestock,' Sargaul said, even as he studied the corpse ranks below them. 'There are enough resources and repairable facilities to equip and power a naval armada, buried just beneath the sand.'

Barsabbas shook his head. 'And Gammadin…'

'And Gammadin was wise enough not to attempt anything so foolish. This world is borderline uninhabitable. Nothing living can really thrive here,' Sargaul said, gesturing at the dead to emphasise his point.

Below them, the dead shuffled on the spot, moaning and occasionally expelling a bellow of bloat gas. There was something developing on a much grander scale, much more than a mere outbreak of pestilence. Of this, Barsabbas was sure.

* * *

THE HOODED MEN thought they had the intruders isolated. These were, after all, their mines and their domain. Slinking within the shadows, they had hunted Cython and Hadius quietly, waiting until they were trapped within the gantry-maze of a bauxite cavern.

But when the fighting erupted in the old mines, the Blood Gorgons did not fall as expected. Instead, the intruders seemed to enjoy the game.

Cython and Hadius, whooping with glee, sprinted down a gantry frame, gunning as they went. They were an old pair, a veteran bond who genuinely enjoyed the business of execution. There was a flippant creativity to their murdercraft and it came as easily to them as walking or sleeping.

Hooded silhouettes rose from the numberless tiers of rock shelves and walkways. The Blood Gorgons blasted them back down, calling out targets to each other in perfect rhythm.

Suddenly Cython barked in laughter. In the upper tiers of the gantry he saw the reflective glint of a gun scope. He turned to warn Hadius, but his bond was already aware. They fired and a grey-clad body plummeted down, bouncing off gantry spurs twice.

'This is bad. I'll wager Sica and Bael are carving up a hellstorm and we're missing out on all the kills,' Hadius said, breathing through his vox-grille.

'They're too afraid to engage!' laughed Cython. He spotted movement to his left and fired on instinct. He worked on drill-conditioned reflex, aiming and shooting before he thought to. Another hooded man died, the bolt-round punching through the metal drum he was cowering behind.

Cython was still laughing when Hadius's helmet exploded in a plume of blood and metal wreckage. It was a definitive kill, the only injury that could truly put down a Traitor Marine. Hadius's body continued to move on muscle memory. He fired twice in a random direction, reloaded his bolter clip in one fluid motion, sank to his knees and died.

Cython stopped running, suddenly mute with shock. He felt the death keenly, as if something had been severed from his physical self. He stood still for one whole second, a momentary lapse in his surgically-enhanced combat discipline, as he looked at his blood bond. It was one whole second he could not afford.

Cython tried to move but he realised something hot was pulsing down his throat and soaking the front of his chest. He put a hand to his throat, trying to stem the flow of blood. Even in the darkness, he could see the arterial sprays spit between his fingers. He aimed his bolter with his free hand but by then he was already falling, the entire left side of his torso, abdomen and arm disintegrating in a blizzard of superheated ash. He hit the bottom after a forty-metre drop and died wordlessly.

Forty metres above him, in the upper crane of the gantry, the stalkers melted away, leaving only the faintest trace of gun smoke in their wake.

A RAPID DATA pulse ran through the squad sensory links. Hadius was dead. His life monitors blanked out with a surge of white noise, then nothing.

A mere moment later, the squad link was disrupted again. Cython was dead. Two dead.

Sergeant Sica had always been in control. It was the only state that he had ever known. Now, crouched in the dark, attempting to re-establish a vox-link, Sica no longer felt in control. The enemy were in the shadows all around him. Shots tested the air, hissing past him and promising more to come.

Slapping the side of his helmet, Sica swore at himself and at everything around him, cursing himself for his lapse in judgement.

Trembling with rage, Sica tore off his helmet. A heavy-calibre round thrummed past his ear with meteoric speed.

'We need to regroup with Sargaul and Barsabbas!' roared Bael-Shura. He was crouched before the bend in the mine shaft, his flamer wedged against the corner. More of the enemy spilled from the surrounding stope tunnels, clattering down staircases with thickly soled boots. Shura forced them backwards with an enormous belch from his flamer. 'We need to regroup,' Bael-Shura repeated urgently.

Sica shook his head. It was too late. 'I don't have coordinates for them. My auspex is jammed with interference.'

Bael-Shura stood up and sprinted over to Sica. He had not taken three steps before his right arm exploded at the elbow. Reeling from the blow, Bael-Shura rocked back on his heels like a teetering fortress. His body was fighting the trauma, flooding him with endorphins as he fell to one knee.

'Not now,' Sica hissed.

A dark shape rose up behind Bael-Shura, engulfing him in its shadow.

It stood head and shoulders taller than either of

them, a monstrous specimen. A great distended gut, studded with barbs, eclipsed Sica's vision. Its power armour was off-white and marbled with fatty threads of lime green. There was a heady aura of disease and the odour of stagnancy. It clutched a leaf-bladed dagger, slick with the blood of Bael-Shura.

'Plague Marine,' spat Sica.

Sica remembered meeting their kind in the Gospar Subsector. Sica had ram-boarded the cargo fleet of a Nurgle warlord, and the bastards were exceedingly difficult to kill. Their plunder had been tainted too – the gold tarnished, their manuscripts rotting and their slaves sickly.

'Pest,' the Plague Marine replied with a shrug of his massive torso.

They clashed then, colliding head to head, shoulder to shoulder. The rotting monster was inhumanly strong and he was larger than any other Chaos Space Marine Sica had ever faced. Tying up the back of the Plague Marine's head with one hand, Sica began to deliver a series of hammer fists with his other. The reinforced, pyramidal studs on his gauntlet cracked his enemy's cyclopean visor. In answer, the Plague Marine hacked with his heavy, chopping knife. The seax slid into the joint between Sica's chest guard and abdominal plates. Roaring, both combatants broke from their clinch with a burst of blood and ceramite fragments. There was a momentary lull in violence as Sica shouldered his bolter and the Plague Marine raised his bolt pistol.

Then they shot at each other repeatedly at point-blank range.

Shots pounded into Sica, crazing his vision,

punching through ceramite, jolting the ground out from beneath him. They exchanged shots on automatic, drilling each other from no more than five paces apart. Seismic vibrations rattled his teeth and dislocated his jaw. Sparks flew and metal fused. Sica's bolter was stronger, larger and its stopping power considerable, popping a trio of gaping holes in the Plague Marine's stomach and tearing a line of ragged shots vertically up into its neck. Simultaneously, the enemy's bolt pistol skipped fat explosive slugs across Sica's groin, chewing the ceramite deeply before penetrating the weaker armour of Sica's upper thigh.

Sica fell to his knee as his femur was shot clean through. The Plague Marine folded, stumbling backwards and recoiling away like a wounded animal.

Bael-Shura, finally seeing a clear shot, enveloped the Plague Marine with a splash of fire. Dying, the monstrous specimen crashed to the flowstone in a mountainous pyre. Even as it fell, another Plague Marine appeared at the end of the tunnel. Then two more appeared in the gantries above them. The Blood Gorgons were surrounded.

Bael-Shura dragged Sica's heavily bleeding form against the rock wall with his remaining arm and crouched next to him.

'I think we're going to die,' Sica said quietly.

'Your leg. It's going to need attention,' Bael-Shura said to Sica as he kicked his own severed arm away to make room.

Sica looked down at his leg and swore. There was a clean hole through his left thigh and the middle section of his femur was no longer there. His entire leg was twisted ninety degrees and attached only by threads of muscle and ceramite plating.

'No time,' Sica said, struggling to sit up.

The Plague Marines began firing. Muzzles flashed in the distance, and nearby rocks and scaffolding crumbled as if scored with an invisible drill. Sica fired two shots and opened the squad vox-channel.

'Sica to Besheba. Threat identified as Chaos Space Marines of Nurgle. We are outnumbered.'

It was the last transmission he would make. As shots barked and snapped around him, Sergeant Sica calmly ejected his spent magazine and clicked a fresh one into place. By his side, Bael-Shura balanced a bolt pistol across the stump of his arm. They began to fire, determined to spend their ammunition while they still could.

EIGHT LEVELS UP, driven into the dead end of a rock grotto, the remnants of Squad Besheba fought. Barsabbas sprinted across a sloping shaft, racing upwards. He fired his bolter to the left as he ran, raking his field of vision. The enemy answered with their own fire, shooting so fiercely that the stalactites trembled from the ceiling. A shot glanced off Sargaul's elbow. Angry, Sargaul risked stopping for a moment and hurled a frag grenade.

The pair were running. What had begun as a coordinated sweep had degenerated into slaughter. The Plague Marines had ensnared them. They had exploited a Traitor Marine's lust for violence by using auxiliary cultists as bait, luring the squad deep.

Barsabbas could barely keep track of enemy positions. They were everywhere. Gunshots exploded

back and forth. They came and went, a rapid barrage
of small-arms fire, sudden and sharp, the whine of
cyclical shots, then the singular shocking roar of
rockets.

'We have to go now,' Barsabbas shouted to Sargaul.
'We have to go.'

'No, we stay,' Sargaul replied.

'They're everywhere,' Barsabbas argued. The violence was overcoming his deference to Sargaul's
seniority. 'We can't do anything here. We need to link
up with another squad.'

The explosions and detonations threatened the
integrity of the tunnel. Drip-rocks above them
rattled, shaking down a raft of dust and loose grit.

'We have to go, brother,' Barsabbas repeated. A missile launcher slid out from behind a support girder,
almost directly in front of him. Barsabbas swung up
his bolter and fired four times. A Plague Marine fell
out from behind cover. The warhead fired and went
wild, detonating overhead.

'Sargaul!'

An overhanging shelf of sandstone weighing at
least twenty tonnes cracked above Sargaul's head.
Oblivious, Sargaul traded shots with their pursuers.
The stone above gave way. There was a whiplash *snap*
as the sandstone split, before it dropped with a tectonic rumble. It missed crushing Sargaul by less than
a metre. Unfazed, Sargaul spared the rock a curious
glance before sprinting behind it for cover.

Fighting the urge to avoid being shot, Barsabbas
waded back out into the open. He was low on
ammunition. He locked onto a Plague Marine and
shot at him, buckling him. In return, a bolter round

exploded against his right chest plate. He felt the lancing pinpricks of shrapnel. The machine spirit of his armour recoiled in seething displeasure.

'I'm getting hit. Absorbing shots and taking hits!' Barsabbas voxed.

Boltguns barked, overlapping shots. Coarse screaming. The stampede of steel-heavy boots. More shots.

'Hold on, brother. Hold on,' Sargaul replied.

Barsabbas saw Sargaul swim through the barrage towards him. His bond-brother was missing a hand. Rounds drilled against his glossy hide. Sargaul ran.

Then the tunnel collapsed.

Creaking girders could no longer support the ancient mine shaft. The entire tunnel buckled, warped, as if the sandstone was momentarily liquefying. Steel girders snapped. The ceiling imploded with a puff.

As the weight of a planet's crust fell upon him, the last thing Barsabbas thought about was the shame he had brought to Squad Besheba.

CHAPTER EIGHT

SABTAH WAS SLEEPING when they came for him.

They dispatched his black turbans quickly and without alarm. One slave-guard was decapitated and hidden in a path of filamentous bacteria, just outside Sabtah's chamber gates. His throat was cut and the blood absorbed into the gossamer hairs, leaving little trace of his murder.

The other sentry was less fortunate still. Standing guard outside Sabtah's vestibule, he found himself unceremoniously rolled down a venting chute. The chopping fans coughed only slightly as his body was fed through them.

Although the iron-bound gates were sealed by sequential trigger locks, the intruders knew the numeric codes and slid them open manually. Once inside, they severed the power cables that veined the ceilings above. Vox-channels, motion sensors and trip lasers were all disconnected. In one quick act, Sabtah's proto-fortress became vulnerable and isolated. Even the phos-lights dimmed to black.

But Sabtah heard it all.

He sat upright in his circadian cradle – a high-backed throne of leather and iron. Spindles of wire sprouted from the cradle and interfaced with the black carapace beneath Sabtah's naked torso. He pretended to be in a drug-induced comatose state. He was unarmoured, wearing nothing but a leather kilt. His chin rested against his chest and his eyes were closed. But in his mind, Sabtah was wide awake.

He kept his eyes closed even as he heard the soft click of his chamber door. In his mind's eye, Sabtah drew a mental map of his vault. The vault was high-ceilinged and circular, a silo of vast but empty proportions. Ringing the walls were racks of disused boarding pikes – hundreds, perhaps thousands of spears, among them Adulasian harpoons, Cestun half-and-halfs and even Persepian marlin-pikes. Dusty and antiquated, the pikes huddled like clusters of old men, their shafts brittle and their tips toothless.

To his right, at the opposite end of the empty chamber, was his MKII power amour. Erect on a dais, the suit watched the vault like an empty sentry. The only other object in the vault was a tiny necklace, a blackened, withered scrap of coarse hair and leather. It was suspended in a glass pillar, floating like a tribal fetish. Sabtah had worn it once when he had been a mere boy, thousands of years ago, in the darkest caves of his memory. Capturing the image behind his eyelids, Sabtah waited.

He allowed the intruders to step closer. He counted

two, judging by their movements. He heard the rasp of metal being unsheathed. It was a good draw, smooth and unhesitant. He restrained his battle instinct and kept his eyes closed.

He heard the final whine of a blade as it cleared the scabbard, so soft it barely disturbed the cool, recycled air.

That was when Sabtah burst into life.

He leapt. His explosiveness was incredible, clearing four metres from a standstill. The spindle wires snapped painfully from his torso plugs but Sabtah didn't feel them.

He seized the knife arm in the dark, wrenching it into a figure-four lock and dislocating the elbow with a wet snap. He judged where the intruder's throat would be in relation to the arm and punched with his fingers, jamming his gnarled digits into the larynx. He was rewarded by a wheeze of pain.

Suddenly an arm seized Sabtah from behind, constricting around his throat. It snapped shut around his carotid arteries like a yoke. The arm was exceedingly strong and corded with smooth slabs of muscle. No normal man could possess such tendon strength; Sabtah knew he was fighting Astartes. It was something he had suspected when they first attacked, but now he was sure. Pivoting his hip, Sabtah tossed the assailant off his back with a smooth shoulder throw. The intruder crunched through his circadian cradle with a clash of sparks and broken circuitry.

Under the fitful, hissing glow of his wrecked sleeping capsule Sabtah caught a brief glimpse of his assassins. They were both Blood Gorgons, and Sabtah knew them well.

Both wore bodygloves of glossy umber; compression suits utilised for rigorous hand-to-hand combat, strength and conditioning drills. Both were young, their faces lacking the mutations of warp-wear. They were newly inducted warriors from Squad Mantica, a unit from the ruthless 5th Company.

'Voldo, Korbaiden, desist!' Sabtah ordered. His voice was sonorous, a blaring wall of sound.

The young warriors faltered, stiffening for a second. But their training, their clinical drive to complete a mission, overtook any fear they held for Sabtah's seniority. They were here to kill Sabtah and they would finish the job.

As Voldo rose from the smoking wreck of the cradle, he lunged at Sabtah with a shard of broken panelling. Sabtah deflected the stab with the palm of his hand, a manoeuvre he had repeated millions of times in the drill halls. The younger warrior's strike was slow in comparison, not yet honed through centuries upon centuries of combat. The trajectory was inefficient by ten degrees to the right and he did not roll his shoulder into the blow. Sabtah was faster and rammed his chin into Voldo's eye. As Voldo reeled from the blow, Sabtah followed up with a rapid flurry of upper-body strikes. An elbow that crunched the orbital bone. A straight punch that dislocated the jaw. A knee that collapsed the sternum. Fists, knees, forearms and elbows, anvil impacts that thrashed Voldo back onto the floor.

'Did Muhr send you?' Sabtah asked forcefully, turning to face Korbaiden.

The younger warrior backed away, his eyes darting left and right for a weapon. As old as Sabtah was, the hoary veteran's body did not show any signs of mortal ageing. His torso was ridged and his legs were deeply striated, quadriceps bulging like hydraulics made flesh. He was short and compact for a Traitor Marine, but he carried the scarred, calloused pride of a weary predator. He could tell Korbaiden was frightened.

'Did Muhr send you here? For me?' Sabtah asked again.

Korbaiden did not answer. He simply closed the distance, stepping to punch with his dislocated arm. Sabtah felt oddly proud of the young Blood Gorgon's determination, but it did not deter him from sidestepping the punch and driving his knee into Korbaiden's liver. Once. Twice. Sabtah wrapped his large, coarse hands behind Korbaiden's head in a tight clinch and continued to knee him over and over again.

He laid out both assassins on the floor. Voldo and Korbaiden were broken. They had suffered massive internal trauma that would have killed any normal human. Bones were split and organs had been ruptured. All of Korbaiden's lungs had collapsed and part of Voldo's face folded inwards.

'Does your squad know of the shame you've brought them?' Sabtah asked, softly this time.

The assassins from Squad Mantica remained silent. Voldo tried to crawl towards a discarded knife, but his broken thigh would not hold him and he slid onto his stomach, eyes wide open as he breathed long, jagged breaths. Sabtah knew there was no sense in interrogating a Traitor Marine. They would not yield.

Crossing over to a wall panel, Sabtah placed his palm on the scanner. The wall emitted an obliging chime and slid open. From the alcove, he retrieved his bolter and a fresh, heavy clip.

As he loaded the weapon and crossed to the two injured Blood Gorgons, Sabtah sighed. He was profoundly sad. He had long feared that history came and went in cycles. The Blood Gorgons looked up at him, eyes wild and face muscles clenched in defiance.

As his bolter banged twice, tremendously loud, it seemed his fears had been proven true.

BARSABBAS REGAINED CONSCIOUSNESS, but it made no difference. He could not move and he could not see. The only thing he could make out was a hairline crack on his otherwise blank, black helmet lens. There were no system reports, squad data-link or auspex monitors. Nothing.

He tried to wriggle his fingers but they were wedged by stone. He tried to turn his neck but that too was viced under the avalanche.

Unable to rely on his machine spirit, Barsabbas closed his eyes to mentally recompose himself. He felt no pain, which meant he was still operational. Except for some minor internal bruising, his major organs and skeleton remained intact. The concussion in his head was already fading, and it seemed his armour sensed his stirring consciousness. Slowly, the armour's power plant roused from dormancy. Systems came online, one after another. His vision flashed, flickered and then became backlit by a luminous green as status updates scrolled across his helmet lens. The power plant would run on standby, slowly regenerating to full power, awaiting Barsabbas's command.

But Barsabbas simply opened his mouth and screamed in rage.

They were defeated. It had never happened before. Barsabbas found it difficult to comprehend.

The retreat on Govina against the tau had been just that: a retreat. It had been shameful, but it was nothing more than a blemish on what should have been an immeasurable history of warfare. But now Squad Besheba would gather no more history. Each warrior had been an invincible, terrifying warmonger. They were the horror stories that quelled unruly children. They were ruthless, clinically developed post-humans.

And now they were all dead.

This concept was something the Chirurgeons had not mentally processed him for. He felt dazed. He had fought Astartes before, both loyalist and renegade. He had repelled a boarding action against Imperial Fists; they had been linear and predictable, tactically sound but uncreative. The Salamanders had possessed heavy, static firepower, but had been susceptible to the Blood Gorgons' guerrilla doctrine. They had even skirmished with the Black Legion – Abaddon's own – over the spoils of a raid and escaped relatively unscathed.

His power armour stirred impatiently, the power-plant surging static into his earpiece. *Sargaul*.

Suddenly Barsabbas jolted. His bond. Where was his bond? Triggering the suit's sensors, Barsabbas attempted to log on to the squad link and search for life signs. His systems were badly damaged. No read-outs or tact-visuals. No squad link. The vox was grainy with static and he had no status monitors on his squad.

Where was Sargaul?

He did not feel the pain of separation experienced by the survivor of a broken bond. The death of a bond brought great mental and physical anguish, but he felt none. Sargaul was still alive, Barsabbas was sure of it.

Again his power armour growled, its power plant surging. The machine spirit of his suit was rousing him to action. He was an operational Traitor Marine. He needed to proceed to Ur, for that was his primary objective. Mental conditioning took over, stabilising his rationality despite the neuro-toxicity of depression and hopelessness. Everything else had become secondary. But first he needed to free himself.

Slowly, millimetre by millimetre, Barsabbas shifted his fingers. Calculating rest periods, it might take days to free himself, but he needed to proceed to Ur. Nothing would stop him while he still lived.

Muscles tensing, suit hydraulics coiling, Barsabbas began the long, agonising process of clawing his way through the avalanche of rock.

MENTAL CONDITIONING WAS the cornerstone of an Astartes warrior. It was not their explosive strength, or the speed of their muscles. What made a Traitor Marine so terrifying a prospect was the conditioning of his mind.

These were the thoughts that Barsabbas focussed on as he worked his way upwards from his burial.

Beneath the suffocating weight of multi-tonne rock, Barsabbas thought of nothing else. He remembered the tale of Bond-Sergeant Ulphrete who fell comatose after a shell-shot to the temple. For ninety-two years, he lay in a coma, unable to be coaxed into wakefulness. Unknown to his brethren, Ulphrete had been awake the entire time. He had simply been unable to control his body. There he lay, trapped inside his own unresponsive form. For almost a century, he was left to his own madness as respirators nurtured his physical frame. The claustrophobia devoured him. What thoughts did one keep to close one's eyes and simply think for one century?

After almost a century, the bond-sergeant finally broke from his coma. To the disbelief of all, Ulphrete had clear memory of the conversations the Chirurgeons had held while they had thought him paralysed and brain dead. He had been awake and he had not gone mad. The mental conditioning of an Astartes had steeled his mind.

For days, Barsabbas thought only of Ulphrete. Sensory deprivation for the first few days was bad. But then afterwards, he became accustomed to the kaleidoscopic scenes behind his eyelids and the utter lack of sound. He wriggled his way, easing out his fingers, creating room for his wrist, slowly pushing and shrugging his shoulders until finally he could move his entire right arm.

He did not know how long it took him. Two days perhaps? Seven? Barsabbas had no way of telling. Painfully, bit by bit, he clawed his way up and out.

* * *

DRAGGING HIS LOWER body free of the rockfall, Barsabbas stood up and stretched his limbs. The sensation of movement felt unnatural to him. Looking around, it took him some time to take in his surroundings. He stood atop the slope of an avalanche, the tunnel collapsed beneath crumbling sandstone. Above him, the upper tiers of the mines had fallen through, the rusting girders finally giving way. Patches of sunlight speared down from the remains of the mine shaft entry.

In the back of his head, Ur still called. Barsabbas knew, if circumstances so required, he could stop thinking altogether and his body would take him to Ur – such was the mental conditioning of the Astartes.

He retraced his steps, clawing his way up the shale slope. Enraged and despondent, the world became disjointed. He followed a trail left by the enemy, a spoor in the dirt. Something was leaking fluid, condensation from the damaged temperature control units of their power armour suit. It was unmistakable. Someone in damaged power armour had walked these same tracks.

Barsabbas followed.

His mind was a blank ocean of fury. Barsabbas's entire world became a thin stream of fluid leakage that he followed. Occasionally, he sniffed the air. He tasted the decaying stink of the Plague Marines. Chasing them like a desperate hound, Barsabbas pushed himself. He crawled on his knees up sand dunes and sprinted where the ground was flat. He was maddened and did not know where he was. He no longer cared. It only mattered that he followed the scent and trail.

When Barsabbas regained his senses he did not know how long he had been walking. The trail petered out, soaking into the sand. He found himself in a field of cenopods. The heat was fading from the day, and the burning light of the sequential twilights had begun, shading through white, red, orange and purple. If he looked to the dune crests behind him he could gauge the hours of remaining light. Already the dune faces were in shadow, the driftwood blue of canegrass contrasting with the sepia of the desert sands.

But he no longer needed light to guide his way. He could see boot prints in the sand, the unmistakable prints of steel-shod boots like small craters made by giant feet. The wind had barely disturbed them yet, tracing fine whorls into the griddled prints, which meant they were fresh.

Squad Shar-Kali did not receive. Squad Yuggoth did not receive. None of the squads responded. Only Squad Brigand made contact with a two-second signal burp. They were ambushed and dying.

Finally, Barsabbas blanked his vox-bead and consigned himself to its soft static. His vox-systems were far too heavily damaged, and even the armour's self-repair systems could only rewire the transmission to other non-damaged but already overloaded data fibres.

As far as Barsabbas knew, he was on his own.

CHAPTER NINE

HEPSHAH WAS A capricious one who did not fear the mon-keigh. He did not even fear the hulking war machines those mon-keigh called the Space Marines. No. Hepshah was too fast, too clever to ever feel the delight of an adrenal dump when confronting the hairy, ponderous anthropoids of humanity.

He certainly did not fear them now, as they ran from him. There was a shocking honesty to a human's terror that Hepshah found strangely endearing. When a man was pushed to the absolute limits of desperation, when the horror of death became impending, a human acted in comical ways. Arched eyebrows, gaping mouth, facial muscles contorted, limbs stiffening as they ran. Hepshah did not laugh often, but their fear was irresistibly amusing.

That was how he came to be hunting humans through the burning settlement, playing with them and extending his victims' misery to the heights of uncontrollable panic. Hepshah even held aloft his aperture, a crystalline shard prized amongst the kabal. Upon exposure to light the warpstone would record sounds and images, so that he could relive this day's festivities in luxury, much later.

He held up his aperture shard, panning it to record a clear panorama of the settlement. There was not much of the settlement left. The road train was upturned and twisted, its silver belly ruptured and spilling bloodied furniture. Its sacred engine was wisping with fire. The tents and lean-tos that cuddled around its protective girth had been flattened into the dirt. The settlement had been camped at the edge of a saltpan and many of the occupants had tried to flee across its basin. Their bodies still lay there now.

Hepshah made sure to catch images of the dead, focussing his warpstone to record close-up shots of their slack faces. Here and there, amongst the live-stock pens, rubble and caravans, survivors still hid. Hepshah caught glimpses of his fellow dark eldar hunting in the ruins. They were dark flashes, quick movements that seemed to elude a clear image.

Hepshah's victim suddenly ran across a caprid pen. He was hunched over and sprinting. His skin was dark and his woollen shawl was bright red. Hepshah had never seen the man before, but he had decided there and then that he was curious to see the man die by his hand.

Hepshah scuttled behind low rubble and ran parallel to the man. His indigo carapace was almost weightless and he easily outpaced the human with long, bouncing strides. As if sensing his danger, the human looked up. He was an older man, his skin prematurely aged by sun. He was crying, his thin shoulders bobbing in the supplicating way that seemed habitually human. Fire burned around him. The bodies of his kin poked out from beneath scattered furnishings and dismantled homes. Hepshah took a moment to savour the carnage.

Suddenly, the man sprinted in the opposite direction. Sensing an end to his pursuit, Hepshah armed his splinter pistol with one hand and held up his aperture for a clear recording. He fired. The splinter barb impacted against a wooden pen-post, punching a nail-sized hole through the wood. The man was still running, weaving between the narrow gap of two punctured train carriages. Laughing, Hepshah pursued.

He only ran five steps before something arrested his momentum hard. His thin neck whiplashed, his laughter choking in his throat, Hepshah's back slammed to the ground. He found himself looking up at a brown, monstrous face, a bovine snarl, branching antlers. A helmet, Hepshah realised.

The warrior towered over him, filling his aperture with images of dark armour, amour like bloodied earth pigment. 'This is my home, little creature. These lands belong to the lineage of the Blood Gorgons.'

Hepshah gave a shrill yelp of surprise. He never realised how tall and thickly built the mon-keigh could become. He had known Space Marines to be cumbersome flocks of tank-like infantry. Now he realised they were not.

As Hepshah struggled to regain his breath, the Chaos Space Marine gripped him firmly by the face, pinning his head with a delicate grip. His other hand darted, whisper quick, tapping him on the temple with a long mace. No more than a light double tap.

Hepshah stopped struggling. The dark eldar was no longer recognisable from the neck up. The encounter took just seconds and by the time Hepshah's body was discovered, Barsabbas was already gone.

MORIBETH FOUND DRAAZ hung from the rafters. She found Fhaisor and Amul-Teth reclining behind a bombed-out dust buggy. In the open, tossed amongst the debris, was a stove boiler that leaked blood. She did not open the coal hatch, but presumed it to contain the remains of Sabhira.

She did not feel fear – only indignity. Snarling, she stalked through the ruins. Occasionally she stopped to crack her whip meaningfully, with a belligerent pop. It was a declaratory snap and most knew to run when they heard it.

'You can't hide from me,' she sang.

She had always been the predator. Ever since her young maiden years, Moribeth had accompanied her cousins on slave raids. This was second nature to her. In her free hand, hidden behind her back, was a neural blade gifted to her by her kabal's mistress. The poison it secreted overloaded the pain nerves in living creatures. She pitied anything that crossed her path.

'Come out, come out,' she cooed.

'Here I am.' The voice sounded like slabs of rockcrete grinding together. A shadow fell across her.

Moribeth turned and her confidence dissipated. She slashed her neural whip low, but the tip snapped listlessly as it connected with ceramite.

With a speed that surprised her, the horned warrior slapped the top of her head with his palm. There was a pop as her spine compressed and vertebrae slipped out of joint. Moribeth died still believing herself a predator.

VHAAL, SECOND-BORN SON of Gil'Ghorad Kabal, heard the death-screams of his fellows. They were loud, even though he was inside the road train's sealed interior. The sound rattled the iron walls, producing an eerie, acoustic vibration. In some parts, the train's ancient glass windows had been replaced by wooden frames with hand-painted paper awnings. The paper fluttered fitfully, the watercoloured scenery shaking ever so slightly.

Vhaal had been skinning trophies with a scalpel when he heard it, but the sound spooked him. Carefully he placed the scalpel on the floor and pulled a blanket over his project.

With a snap of his hands, wrist blades swung out from his vambraces like unfolding guillotines. He retrieved his splinter rifle, propped up against the iron carriage, and hopped down the short rungs. Outside he could see no signs of life. Not his father's soldiers, and no plainsmen.

'Show yourself!' he commanded.

He knew something was out there. He began to fire his splinter rifle. The gun's purr grew into a shrill whine as it spat a tight spread of toxic barbs. It threw up a line of powdered dirt to his front, knocking down the remains of a painted hand cart.

'Come and face me! I am second-born!' he howled.

Pride and familial name were things most fiercely

venerated in his society. Vhaal imagined himself to look quite intimidating. Hooked armour curling on his skeletal frame, swing-blades creaking from his forearms, he was in the full regalia of a dark eldar raider. His hair was brought up into an oiled top-knot, laced through with silver filigree and virgin sinew. He wore a cape of sewn skin fashionably off one shoulder, stitched together from the faces of vanquished foes. He was second-born of Gil'Ghorad.

'Face me!' Vhaal howled, raising his arms into the air in challenge.

A muzzle flashed in the distance. Low and muffled. The bolter's bark.

Vhaal, second son of the kabal, fell unceremoniously through a screen paper window, his feet stiffening awkwardly in the air. He was already dead before he landed, felled by a single shot.

SINDUL HISSED, BARING his teeth. He crouched low on his haunches, his arms spread for balance, lacerator gloves rearing like coiled serpents.

The mon-keigh warrior appeared indifferent to his threats. He walked into and through the caprid fence that separated them, splintering the wood with his shins and thighs.

'Catch me to kill me!' Sindul spat. He leapt up against the sheer rock wall behind him, limbs splayed against the surface, and began to scarper up the vertical drop. He used his lacerator gloves, dragging the hooked claws of his fists for purchase. He shot up the wall like a rodent, scaling twelve metres in a matter of seconds before bounding backwards into the air.

A bolter round missed him as he leapt. He landed behind the mon-keigh, slashing his lacerators as he sailed overhead. But the horned warrior was faster than Sindul had estimated. It was a grave error. The mon-keigh spun with practiced fluidity, pouncing with all the weight and drive of a quarter-tonne primate. Sindul rolled aside, but not fast enough. The mon-keigh snagged him with its paw and dragged him to the ground by his ankles. Sindul tried to regain his gyroscopic balance, but his thin ankle was locked in a hammer grip of ceramite.

'I don't need to kill you yet,' growled the Traitor Marine as Sindul thrashed like a hooked fish.

Dragging his splinter pistol free from its chest holster, the dark eldar began to fire. The first shot hammered a toxic splinter into heavy chest plate. The mon-keigh dodged the second with a little dip of his head.

'Stop, now.'

With that, the mon-keigh backhanded him with steel-bound hands. Sindul's head snapped violently off to the right and he blacked out.

WHEN THE DARK eldar came to, he began to curse in his sepulchral tongue.

He was bound, his wrists anchored by heavy chain that looped up to his neck and head. A muslin bag used to ferment milk curds was wrapped around his face and the chain tightened around it, biting into the flesh of his cheeks and forehead. The bag reeked strongly of sour, human smells that disturbed him.

When the captive tried to move, Barsabbas placed a boot on his chest.

'Tell me your name, darkling.'

The captive tried to writhe. Barsabbas stepped harder. The pressure elicited a mild curse from the struggling captive.

'I am Sindul,' he gasped as the air was pushed from his lungs.

Barsabbas knelt, peering closely at the dark eldar, studying the odd shapes of his insectoid carapace. Everything about the creature was alien, as if the angles and planes of his attire were beyond the conceptual design of a human mind. He did not belong on Hauts Bassiq.

'Why do you trespass, darkling?'

'I will not speak to you,' Sindul replied, his words muffled by the muslin.

'That is not your choice to make.'

'There are others,' Sindul began. 'There are more of us. We will come for you.'

'I've made them all dead, you know,' Barsabbas replied flatly. He stood up and walked to where a row of thin, frail corpses lay amidst the ash and charred earth. The carrion flies were already swarming over their glazed eyes and open mouths. 'I count fourteen. There are no more. Is that true?' Barsabbas asked.

The fact was confirmed by Sindul's silence.

Barsabbas walked back to his captive. 'You will talk,' he said. He released and slid open a hatch on his thigh plate, revealing a half-dozen steel syringes, stacked like rocket pods.

Upon hearing the metallic click, Sindul began to laugh. 'You can try to torture me. But you are truly of diminished wit if you try,' the dark eldar declared in stilted Low Gothic. 'We relish pain.'

Barsabbas already knew this. The dark eldar species was entirely devoted to the cult of pleasure. Psychologically, they were nihilistic, pleasure-driven and irrational. Heightened sensations such as pain would only elevate them to a state of adrenal euphoria. For once, violence would yield nothing.

'Do your worst,' Sindul goaded, almost tauntingly.

Barsabbas extracted a syringe from its sheath. It was a barbarous thing, a pneumatic-gauge needle designed to punch through the thick skin of a Space Marine.

'This is tetrotoxillyn. An anaesthetic, a nerve-killing extract. My constitution inhibits the majority of chemicals from affecting my body. But this...' Barsabbas said, holding up the syringe. 'A dose of one-sixteenth is potent enough to serve as a local anaesthetic for a standard Space Marine. One quarter dose is enough to cause permanent paralysis in a young adult human.'

'We may not be robust in stature, but I assure you, we eldar are very chemically resilient,' Sindul retorted.

He was right, and Barsabbas knew this too. The dark eldar, despite their frail appearance, had a certain tolerance for toxins and chemicals, a tolerance built up through a dark culture of substance abuse. By his calculations, Barsabbas would need to quadruple the human dose.

Without warning, Barsabbas wrenched his captive up by the head, exposing his neck, and drilled the needle deep into the carotid artery. He injected a fractional dose, a mere droplet.

'This is an ion channel blocker. It is not meant for

non-Astartes. It will stop your brain from receiving nerve signals. Can you feel numbness running down your spinal column? It will only be temporary but it signifies the early stages of nerve damage,' Barsabbas said.

Sindul screamed. He began to thrash, his legs windmilling for purchase as Barsabbas restrained him with a knee on his back.

'I could inject you with more. A triple dose and you may begin losing finger dexterity. I'm afraid that would be permanent.' Barsabbas placed the cold steel of the pneumatic needle against Sindul's neck. 'I ask you again – what are you doing here?'

His face pressed into the soupy clay and dung, the dark eldar finally relented. 'Collecting slaves. Nothing more,' Sindul spat.

Barsabbas detected the slightest tremor of panic in his voice, but also defiance. The dark eldar were a notoriously proud race and dignity meant more to them than death.

'There's so much more,' Barsabbas said, injecting him again. 'You are in league with the Death Guard.'

Sindul writhed in numb agony. Although the dose of anaesthetic was considerably less than a Space Marine's standard amount for field application, it was enough to cause him significant nerve trauma. Already Sindul's left arm had begun to twitch involuntarily.

'They allowed us here. They let us take the slaves.'

'Your reward was to plunder the land? Our land? What right have the Death Guard to reward you with property that was not theirs? These slaves are *our* slaves,' Barsabbas barked, withdrawing the needle.

'Mercy. Mercy. Do not inject me any more,' Sindul whimpered.

Barsabbas ignored him, his attention already drifting away from the pathetic thing writhing in his grasp. The notion that the capricious dark eldar raiders would ally with the Sons of Nurgle was monumental. It did not bode well for the Blood Gorgons. He would need answers. Almost carelessly, Barsabbas began to pump anaesthetic into his captive.

The dark eldar's pupils dilated with chemical shock.

'We are mercenaries, no more! We want nothing of the fight between you and your brethren.'

'Why are you here?' Barsabbas roared, suddenly forceful. The needle snapped. He unsheathed a new one.

Sindul shook his head. 'I can't...'

'If I overdose you, it will cause permanent muscular paralysis. You will not feel anything. You will not move anything. You will become a slab of meat. Imprisoned within your own body until you wither away.'

At this, Sindul began to howl, like an animal caged before slaughter.

That was no mere threat for a dark eldar. They were a long-lived race, and that could mean thousands of years, trapped within his own unresponsive body, unable to move or feel. During the Chirurgeon's initial experiments a slave subject had been induced into a paralytic coma for twenty-two years, unable to even open his eyes. The slave had gone mad, of course. But several thousand years of physical and visual deprivation...

A dark eldar could suffer no worse fate than that.

'We were paid by a person called Muhr.'

'Muhr? What does Muhr know of the Plague Marines?'

'I don't know. But they are allies, in league. They paid for the head of Gammadin, they needed a neutral third party to dispose of your Champion. That was us.'

Barsabbas considered injecting the entire tenfold dose into the creature then and there.

'*You* killed Gammadin? How could you kill Gammadin?' Barsabbas asked accusingly. He kicked the dark eldar dismissively, as if disgusted by his lie.

'Not I! Not I! The kabal disposed of him. I know nothing of that! I am only here to claim the kabal's reward. Slavery rights on Bassiq.'

'The right to harvest slaves from *our* territory? You slew Gammadin for that?' Barsabbas was possessed by sudden fury. He punched the needle into the dark eldar's wrist. Sindul would never again feel anything in his right hand. No pain, nor cold, nor heat or any sensation.

'That is my luchin hand! I will never ply my craft again!' shrieked the captive.

'And I will take your other hand for good measure,' Barsabbas stated calmly.

As his captive began to hyperventilate, almost choking in discomfort, Barsabbas sat down and began to think. Muhr, the dark eldar and a cult of Nurgle were in allegiance; they were somehow the source of strife on Hauts Bassiq.

'What did the dark eldar have to gain?'

'As I said. We took slaves. We are not a large kabal.

We only sealed our part of the deal in disposing of Gammadin. Hauts Bassiq means nothing to us, except for raiding rights granted by the Plague Marines.'

'Rights. They have no rights.'

'They say Hauts Bassiq is their world.'

'You must have contact with them then. Where are they?'

'I don't know.'

'Where?' Barsabbas said. He approached Sindul and placed the cold steel of the syringe against the nape of his neck.

He felt Sindul's shoulders slump and his body sag in defeat. 'North. They are gathering for a great war to the north. The native mon-keigh prepare for war against the decaying ones.'

War. That was exactly what Barsabbas needed to hear. War meant the forces of Nurgle would amass. It was not much, but it was better than nothing.

'Good. You will take me there.' With that, Barsabbas hauled on his captive's neck chain, dragging him up like a disobedient dog. 'We go north.'

THE SHAME OF defeat was a heavy mantle and one that Barsabbas could not shake off. He stood in the heat but did not seek shelter. He did not deserve it. The discomfort reminded him of his mistake. Everything he did reminded him of his mistake.

The captive was staked down a distance away, under the shade of a lean-to, a blanket that was secured to a carriage window and pegged to the dirt. As much as Barsabbas would have preferred staking him out under the sun, for now he needed the

creature alive. His leash chain was bound to a
carriage wheel and his head was secured with yet
more chain. Every so often, the captive tested his
patience with whimpers of pain.

Barsabbas ignored the dark eldar's pleas and drew
a long-distance voxsponder, a small, hand-cranked
device, from a flak pouch on his waist. He only
logged several words into the machine, for the
micro-device could not hold much in its memory
and the transmission had to travel far.

'The soldiery of Nurgle has taken Hauts Bassiq,
and Muhr has sold us to them. Muhr has sold Bassiq
to them. He has betrayed us.'

It was a simple message. There could be no mis-
taking it. Even in his desperate state, Barsabbas
remembered to encrypt the message for Sabtah only.
He could not be sure that any other Blood Gorgon
could be trusted.

By nightfall, the tiny voxsponder had received a
return transmission from the orbiting Chapter hulk.
The distance it travelled had been great and interference had robbed the spoken message of much
clarity. Through the garbled static, Barsabbas could
make out the words.

'Return to dropsite. Return to Chapter. Immediate.'

The vox message had been sealed with Sabtah's
personal decryption code.

Barsabbas stared at the voxsponder for a while
before he crushed the device in his palm.

CHAPTER TEN

BEHIND THE MOON of Hauts Bassiq, the *Cauldron Born* remained a lurker, its leviathan bulk anchored behind the rock's spheric shadow. The hour was past end-night and the halls were still but for the tread of sentries. Night menials emerged to prepare the morning gruel and the ship's sleepless maintenance crews worked softly, but it did not dispel the quiet. All the blood brethren had retired for their nightly circadian rest, allowing their bodies to knit and heal for another day's training. All, except a few.

Sabtah awaited the reports of his deployment, poised with the apprehension of a predator in hiding. He knew the Dreadclaws had missed their dropsites by a wide margin. He knew the five squads had engaged enemy combatants: plague victims as the reports confirmed. But then he heard nothing. Sabtah began to fear the worst until Captain Hazareth requested his presence.

In one of the many exterior citadels that studded the ship's upper deck, Hazareth had taken charge of the foreship's amplified vox-transmitter. It was a frontier-grade machine, capable of burst transmissions to surrounding, intra-system receivers.

'We have a long-burst data receipt from Hauts Bassiq, Squad Besheba. It is coded urgent and encrypted to you only, Brother-Master,' Hazareth said, keying the console.

Sabtah ungloved his hand and placed his palm flat across the vox's mainframe panel. There was a compliant click as the vox-transmitter accepted Sabtah's genecode and began to unscramble the data burst.

'I will take my leave,' Hazareth said, bowing.

'No, captain. You can stay for this,' Sabtah said as he adjusted the volume dial on the transmitter. Trust was not much of a concept amongst Chaos Space Marines, for whom abrupt violence was an integral part of their warrior culture. But Sabtah knew Hazareth had principles. He was a soldier who would not fail his brethren.

There was a gurgle of audio, almost completely buried by interference. The *Cauldron Born* lay at high anchor ghosting the orbit of Hauts Bassiq, but the moon they hid behind was causing the transmission to lose clarity.

Sabtah adjusted the volume higher and played the message again. The vox squeaked with feedback.

'The soldiery of Nurgle has taken Hauts Bassiq, and Muhr has sold us to them. Muhr has sold Bassiq to them. He has betrayed us.'

Sabtah punched the metal casing of the trembling vox. He replayed the message, dissecting every word.

Captain Hazareth's face was dark and serious. 'I see why the witch has been so reluctant to deploy on Hauts Bassiq. He has some stake there.'

Sabtah ran a hand through his beard, his eyes closed. He breathed deeply before opening them again. 'Transmit a message back to Bassiq and all units. Tell them to withdraw immediately with all squads. We need more answers.'

Hazareth began to key the sequence from receiving to transmit. He looked up from his work, the sharp quills on his scalp bristling with anger. 'Give me the honour of removing Muhr from our Chapter,' Hazareth growled.

'No.' Sabtah shook his head. 'If we kill Muhr now, there will be intra-Chapter war. I can't allow that to occur under my wardship.'

'Then we will watch him,' Hazareth countered immediately. 'Let me activate Squad Murgash. They are old and will not fail you.'

'Make sure they do not. I always knew those witches were of coward's blood. They are not bonded,' Sabtah said. 'That makes strangers out of them. I'd sooner put my life in the hands of the devious Sons of Alpharius than call a witch my brother.'

SABTAH LOCKED THE doors to his citadel. He shut the double gates of his interior courtyard and posted a double sentry of black turbans outside them. The blast shutters to his central tower and barracks were thrust into emergency lockdown. Finally, the interior wheel locks were turned, sealing the entrance to

Sabtah's bed chambers behind eighty centimetres of psy-dampening plasteel.

Only then did Sabtah listen to the captured transmission.

The transmission from the atmospheric vox-caster was soft and cut with static. Words were clipped, stilted and stuttering, but the gravity of their accusations and the stern deliverance of Bond-Brother Barsabbas was not lost over distance.

'The soldiery of Nurgle has taken Hauts Bassiq, and Muhr has sold us to them. Muhr has sold Bassiq to them. He has betrayed us.'

Sabtah reclined in his throne, resting his back against the solid interior of his power armour and bracing his chin between the fork of his fingers. He thought deeply of Bond-Brother Barsabbas's accusations. It did not surprise him that Hauts Bassiq was the target of foreign conquest. It was a mineral-lush planet and had once been an Imperial mining colony. So close to the Eye, it could serve as a strategic staging post for the first major leg of any campaign, if one were so inclined. The Blood Gorgons had always preferred the freedom of nomadic flight and had never seen the utility of devoting so much infrastructure to the extraction of earthbound resources. But it made sense to Sabtah.

Despite the blunt clarity of Bond-Brother Barsabbas's intelligence, Sabtah could not act hastily. Any provocation of Muhr and his small yet influential faction could spark the tinders of a second Chapter war. The memories of the first fratricidal conflict had faded but never dimmed for Sabtah. He had executed eight of his own brethren in that dark period and still bore the millennia-old scars across his abdomen. He had no wish to fight through another.

Muhr was a cunning creature, and if Sabtah were to confront him, he would need to pick his time judiciously.

Sabtah's ruminations were interrupted. The abrasive howl of a breach siren and the rhythmic pounding of tripwire alarms jolted him. He leapt from his oaken throne and crouched low without thinking. Simultaneously, the phos-lanterns winked out with a crackling hiss of electricity.

The room was dark, but he could still hear the crashing pounding of his alarms. Slipping his war-helm over his face, Sabtah loaded his bolter's underslung flamer with a gilded canister from his oiled leather belt. The world lit up a lambent green behind his visor, his flamer held out before him, like looking through the vision-slit of a tank turret. Beyond his field of vision, pitch-black shadows leaned out across the room like lunging spectres.

Sabtah erased the transmission from the atmospheric caster with a squeal of the turn dial. He slapped a side-mounted magazine into his bolter, made sure the transmission had been cleared, and rose from his seat.

Raising the muzzle of his underslung flamer, Sabtah released the blast seal to his bed chambers. The lighting in the wide, steel corridor outside had been cut. Emergency glo-strips flickered weakly along the mesh decking.

As was his practice, Sabtah hollered for his guard hounds. They were each three hundred kilos of vat-brewed muscle, a mutant species of the bearded crocodilian. Aggressive and unseeing, the guard hounds always answered his calls dutifully but now there was no sign of them.

Edging slowly down the corridor, Sabtah tried to remember the basic foot patterns of silent movement. It had been many thousands of years since he had practised the steps as a neophyte but the neural programming came back to him. Sinking his weight with each step, Sabtah crept softly, although he had not felt the need for stealth in many centuries. As a champion of the Chapter, he could usually afford the luxury of charging from the fore, gladius in one hand and combi-bolter in the other.

But there was an unsettling darkness and quiet that warranted a vigilant approach.

Sabtah swept quickly through the crumbling ruins of his tower's lower levels. Over the years, the plunder and loot of his many campaigns had lain forgotten in his dominion. The hilts of swords and gilded treasures peered from between the cloth-like sheets of spider webs and dust. He swung his weapon at each corner, hunting furtively through the statues and stacked chests for a target.

Sabtah swept out into the interior courtyard. He could smell blood and entrails. His suspicions were confirmed when he saw his gutted sentries, quite dead and sprawled in his garden.

There was a soft ping from his MKII suit's internal auspex.

Sabtah looked up reactively. He spied a large, imposing figure scaling a ceiling cable. It was already disappearing into the smoking, gaseous heights of the *Cauldron Born's* upper ceiling shafts. Guide lights reflecting off the overhead network of pipes turned the deck's upper reaches into an interior atmosphere of smoke clouds and electric stars. Squinting upwards, Sabtah fired a ranging shot with his bolter as the figure was winched up. He fired again, but the figure scrambled onto a nearby gas main and disappeared into a canopy of steam hoses and cables.

Sabtah scanned the courtyard. One of his bearded croc-hounds lay on its side. They had cut the reptile by its throat flaps. One of its clawed hind feet still twitched spasmodically.

His pet's eyes had been cut out and its tongue severed from its gaping maw. The symbolism of the croc-hound's death was not lost on Sabtah. He knew what it meant. The intruders had tried to breach his citadel again but failed, and this time had chosen to leave him a warning.

Sabtah realised Muhr and his patron knew. He did not have time on his side.

ON THE HORIZON of Bassiq, an undulating red plain broken only by occasional boab trees, two figures could be seen. They plodded, slowly and methodically, but forwards, always forwards. One was big and broad. Trailing behind, lashed by a chain, dragged almost on all fours, came a smaller figure bent double. A Blood Gorgon and his dark eldar.

They went north, following the multiple dawns and sunsets on the horizon, always northwards. For five full days Barsabbas walked, leading his captive.

The interior of the central plains was a vast, empty space of bushland and drying river beds where the pockets of wildlife slowly withered to meet the dune systems of the north, the largest longitudinal dune systems on the continent.

The earth had a higher ferric content here, coloured a deep red. Here and there, slivers of water boiled on silty tracts of old waterways. Dunaliella algae lent the lakes a pinkish hue. Barsabbas knew the plainsmen would eat the fish that were preserved in the salt on the river beds, but how he came to know, he could not remember.

Barsabbas and his captive did not talk. They simply plodded along as Sindul pointed the way.

The heat was shocking. Even sealed up in the climate vacuum of his armour, Barsabbas could feel the prickly heat. He made sure to stop and water his captive regularly. When Sindul collapsed from exhaustion, Barsabbas simply draped him across one arm. The dark eldar weighed little more than his bolter.

They did not stop walking, even during the short nights. Barsabbas needed no rest. Inquisitive predators stalked them, but none dared attack.

Soon the land became indistinct and the days merged into one. No matter where he looked, the land stretched outwards and onwards, disappearing eventually into a flat, featureless line. Even the low mountains and dunal corridors that bobbed on the horizon became a regular, rhythmic occurrence, a steady flatness interspersed by humps like the predictable graph of his suit's heart monitor.

Occasionally, in the distance, Barsabbas would spot the silhouette of a lonely wanderer. He knew those to be the dead. No plainsmen would ever be so foolish as to brave the climate alone. Sometimes he encountered larger flocks, but a signal flare in the opposite direction would send the dead sprinting towards the brightness in the sky.

Finally, as they left the interior behind them, Barsabbas heard the bray of war horns. He hoped the battle was nearby.

CHIEF GUMEDE SOUNDED the war horn, rousing his small kinship from their high-noon rest. 'Small' was perhaps an inappropriate term, but Gumede had always considered his family a modestly-sized yet intimate gathering.

Already, the caravan trains were being warmed, the ancient gas engines grumbling as shamans began to rouse the old gears and goad the arthritic pistons to life. At least fifty of Gumede's kin were rising from their makeshift beds under the shade of the wagons and carriages. Another thirty were spreading down to the creek to wash their faces and rinse the sand from their mouths. Outriders, having already mounted their giant bipedal birds, were racing impatiently as the kinship prepared to mount up and move.

Gumede blew his brass war horn again. Although the horn itself had once been the steam valve of a gas engine, it represented his seniority within the kinship. He was the patriarch and his family looked to him for guidance. He was young for such a role, but he was tall and well made and he had a presence that he carried easily with his height and stature.

Amongst the short, wiry plainsmen, Gumede was an imposing figure with a thick neck and a narrow, athletic waist. The kinship had never questioned his leadership, nor his father's before him. Gumede came from a direct lineage of elders, and wisdom was considered his birthright.

Perhaps it would have been safer to flee southwards, away from the troubles. Already the skies to the north had darkened visibly and the horizon appeared as a sick rind of black that settled along the furthest ridges. It would have been safer to travel south, hugging the dust coast, but Gumede knew that it would not be right.

Other kinships were travelling north too. A war host was gathering to repel the spreading evil. They had all heard the echoes of drums and horns and read the plumes of smoke signals from nearby kinships. It was a muster call.

They did not know what evil it was. The simpleminded claimed them to be ghosts, but then again, all disturbances were blamed on restless spirits. Others, more astute, remembered the days of raiders who came from the skies. Gumede was not certain, but he felt compelled to act. It was clear the plainsmen were gathering on the Seamless Plains, the great dividing range that separated the interior from the Northern Reaches. Thousands had already gathered there, to confront the 'evil' with hatchets and shamanic superstition. Now his family would join them.

GUMEDE HAD BARELY saddled his talon squall before his riders came to fetch him.

'Chief! Chief!' they cried, sprinting across the hot sand on their lurching, thudding birds. His braves were in full war regalia. Their red shukas were decorated with squall feathers, braided hair and brooches.

Some preferred breastplates of latticed bark while others preferred salvaged tin. They all balanced recurved bows across their saddles and brandished hatchets overhead. Many brandished las-weapons, traded from distant Ur.

'The Godspawn has come! Quickly, see this!' cried Tanbei, riding at the fore.

Gumede had heard that the Northern Kinships in desperation had summoned the ancestral Godspawn. But he had not believed it. He had not wanted to give himself false hope. But now he was overwhelmed.

'Truly?' asked Gumede, his heart suddenly racing.

But Tanbei had no reason to lie. His face was flushed from a mixture of excitement and awe. 'He comes! He comes!' he shouted.

The commotion stirred the kinship. Children emerged from their household carriages and wagons, throwing aside blankets and creeping out from hiding places. Women and men paused from their task of packing, craning their necks curiously.

'Tanbei.' Gumede's quiet tone commanded silence. 'The Godspawn, Tanbei? Where?'

The young rider reined his bird to a sharp halt, almost startling Gumede's own mount from his hands. Tanbei turned in his saddle and jabbed his finger to the high dunes beyond. Sure enough, Gumede could see a figure cresting the dune spines. Even at a great distance, Gumede could tell that the figure was large, with a long stride that was as sure and as steady as a rising dust tide.

Gumede hurriedly tightened his saddle and vaulted atop his bird. 'Prepare offerings!' he shouted, his tone rising with excitement. 'Gather the shamans! Spread the word to the tribe!'

Wheeling his bird around, Gumede led his flight of outriders to greet the Godspawn.

WHEN THE GODSPAWN came to Gumede's kinship, it was as if the war had been forgotten. All the people gathered in nervous clusters around the road train. They were keen to catch a glimpse but afraid of what they might see. They huddled closely, jostling to be in the middle.

He came to their camp, escorted by Gumede's outriders.

The warrior was so big that a hush fell over the kinship as he approached. The people actually shivered. He resembled a mountain, his armour craggy and pitted, from the solid base of his boots to the sloping swell of his shoulders, all the way up to the branching antlers of his head. Although he was a Godspawn, his armour was not at all like the bright red of their shukas. It was the colour of ferric earth after hard rain – a muddy, burnt orange. Radiant with martial aggression, he appeared to them as an angry golem that had been birthed from a rock womb.

Almost as an afterthought, he dragged a blackened, stick-like captive on a leash. The beast was bound in layers of chain and could barely stand upright.

'I am Barsabbas,' he said. 'The Blood Gorgons have answered your summons.' His first words, loud and metallic, startled the children. But they didn't cry. No one dared to disturb the resonance of his declaration.

Half a dozen shamans, all of them elders of venerable years, hesitantly came forwards. They sacrificed a caprid for him, draining its neck of blood. Another began to pray to him, falling to his knees and touching his forehead to the hot sand.

'My kin are honoured to receive you, Koag Barsabbas,' said Gumede. He rode until he was side on with Barsabbas, reining in his mount a respectful distance away. Tall as Gumede was, and mounted on his talon, Gumede was still barely on eye level with the visitor.

'I've come to find your war. Where is it?' asked the Blood Gorgon. His words were clipped and impatient.

'Over there, beyond those mountains,' Gumede replied. 'You have come to lead our crusade to drive back the evil?' he asked, his face openly honest with hope.

Barsabbas snorted. 'I can lead a mount to a watering hole, but I cannot force it to drink. If you do not want to fight, then I cannot force you to fight well.'

'We are willing,' Gumede replied. 'Many of the kinships of the south and central territories are gathering beyond the Seamless Plains. It is an army that will rid the land of the evil and dead. Can you lead us, great koag?' Gumede asked.

'I will,' answered Barsabbas.

At his words, the kinship erupted into jubilance. The tense mobs dispersed, as if their battle had already been won. Some sprinted down to the creeks to dance in the water or scaled the road train to scream relief to the skies. Those more daring encircled the Blood Gorgon, thrusting offerings towards him – bead quilts, necklaces, empty tins with exotic off-world labels. The shamans cavorted, clapping hand cymbals and tiny percussion drums. All the while, Barsabbas stood immobile amongst them, unable to comprehend their behaviour.

BARSABBAS FELT NOTHING towards these people. They were genestock, they were slavestock. In truth, he loathed them for their ignorance and their dependency. As the plainsmen groped his armour, tapping him for luck and trying to push votive offerings into his hands, Barsabbas curtailed his urge to strike out.

He knew they would all die. He held no illusions about the outcome of a battle between bow-armed plainsmen and Plague Marines of Nurgle. But he could not conceive of a better diversion to allow him to infiltrate into the northern territories. With the war host on the march, Barsabbas would be free to head north, ever deeper into the enemy territory.

They were all expendable if Barsabbas could find Sargaul. He would need them to take him into the deep north. Alone he might fail, but with a mighty war host as a diversion...

THAT NIGHT, BARSABBAS dreamed of Sargaul. A Chaos Space Marine did not often dream. Rather, their catalepsean nodes placed them in a state whereby the resting portions of their brain relived memories throughout the day. Memories of drill, memories of field tactics, memories of war. Decades or centuries of memory that would otherwise be forgotten in the sieve of a human mind.

But that night, Barsabbas dreamed. He dreamed

that he visited Sargaul. His blood bond was tinkering with the wreckage of a Rhino armoured carrier. The desert plains stretched out on every side and the tank was beached in the centre, its paint scorched to cracking by the sun.

Sargaul was muttering softly to himself as he worked on the broken tank. But as Barsabbas approached he saw that there was nothing to fix. The tank was an empty, burnt out shell.

'Brother, what are you doing?' Barsabbas asked as he drew close.

Sargaul looked at him but did not seem to recognise his battle-brother. He started vacantly at Barsabbas before turning his attention back to the wreckage, muttering ceaselessly.

Barsabbas knew his brother was lost. Sargaul was tapping away at a crumpled panel of plating with a tiny work hammer, utterly focussed on the task.

'Brother, where are you going?'

At this Sargaul drowsily raised his hand and pointed to the north without even looking at him. Far away, hazed by the glare of background suns, Ur shone on the horizon.

For a while, Barsabbas attempted to speak to Sargaul, but his bond did not acknowledge him. It was almost as if he did not exist. Only when that seed of doubt was nurtured in Barsabbas's mind, did he think it a dream.

He awoke then.

THE FINAL SUNSET was two hours away when Gumede began the final preparations for departure. The arrival of a Godspawn had been an unexpected delay and the temperamental gas engines of the road train had to be refired. Despite this, he believed the Godspawn was a good portent. As the last of the kinship tied their possessions to the roof and side racks of the convoy, Gumede needed only one more thing before he was ready.

He took from his carriage rack a lasrifle. It was an heirloom, handed down between the elders of the kinship. The gun had always belonged to the family and none knew its precise origins. Some cousins claimed it had been simply traded for two dozen caprid from the city of Ur by a long-lost uncle. But Gumede had also been told by an aunt that it had been given to them by missionaries of the *eagle-headed faith*. Those missionaries did not come to their land any more, but the cells that powered the weapon continued to be recharged by the solar heat of their many suns, even after so many centuries. The use of the lasrifle was a rare skill and something that Gumede had learned from an early age.

He wiped the rifle's metal exterior with a cloth and slotted a rectangular cell into its housing. He chanted a mantra and dialled up the weapon's charge. It hummed softly. He thumbed the well-worn slide down to idle.

'I am ready,' he said to himself. Climbing atop his bird with slow deliberation, he made one last survey of his convoy and began to ride.

CHAPTER ELEVEN

I<small>T WAS JUST</small> a rumour, but Sufjan had learned to take rumours very seriously.

Sufjan Carbo had earned his black turban by keeping a clear head and open ears. Being a slave to the Traitor Marines was usually a short and very brutal existence, but there were those such as he who had learned to thrive in such volatile environments. Men like him had learned to listen and glean every scrap of information to survive. Everything on the *Cauldron Born* happened for a reason, and everything that happened had consequences, even for the lowliest slave.

Things had not always been this way. Sufjan Carbo had been a janitorial factotum for a district scholam. His life had involved distilling the right combination of bleach and water for the cork floors and tightening the scholam's faulty plumbing. Such things were a fading memory. He had come to accept life as a volatile thing, from the moment they took him away from his world, to the dangers of life as an expendable servant of the Chaos powers.

And things, he had learned, had become very volatile lately.

There were rumours amongst galley slaves and the warp engine crews that rival factions were on the verge of intra-Chapter war. The slaves were scared, even more so than usual. They walked timidly, keeping their eyes down, hoping to avoid the attention of their Blood Gorgon masters. Some saw the strife as a good thing, as an opportunity, perhaps, for liberation. But Sufjan knew that nothing good would arise out of it. If the Chapter were to go to war with itself, the slaves would be the first to suffer.

Sufjan did not intend to suffer. He had earned a trusted position standing sentry outside a little-used staircase from strata 23/c that led to the upper spines of the ship. His familiar staircase 23/c, with its rusty spiral stairwell and the globe-lamp larvae that hung in small, grape-like clusters. Compared to other slaves, his job was simple: to keep order amongst the menials and lower caste servants. In doing so, he earned a double ration of protein strands and a billet in the guard barracks. It was not something he intended to relinquish easily.

The vacuum hiss of blast shutters opening woke Sufjan from his fretting.

Suddenly he felt nervous, as he fussed over his orange silks and began to buff the brass etchings on his breastplate. Although the Blood Gorgons were piratical by nature, they enforced uniform infractions amongst the black turbans with a heavy hand.

Thudding footfalls echoed down the corridor. Sufjan bladed his shoulders and stood to attention. His horse-headed halberd was angled in salute, planted forty-five degrees out from his upcurled boot toes.

'None may pass…' Sufjan began to say.

The Blood Gorgon's shadow fell across him. It was Sabtah the Older. The slaves knew him as the *old brown wolf*. Sabtah was followed by a squad of Blood Gorgons that Sufjan did not recognise. They were heavily armed, unusually so. Perhaps the rumours were true.

'Step aside,' Sabtah said in a weary, almost languid tone.

Fighting against his sense of self preservation, Sufjan remained at attention in front of staircase 23/c. 'My apologies, master… but Master Muhr has ordered me to refuse entry at this time.'

'I am countermanding those orders. Step aside.'

Sufjan felt the prick of sweat on his scalp. Master Muhr had been very specific in his instructions that no black turbans were permitted to allow access for anyone to his spire chambers. It had seemed straightforward at the time, but Sufjan had not expected this.

'Master Muhr was very specific,' Sufjan said timidly.

'Why are you even looking at me?' Sabtah asked, his voice remaining even.

Sufjan dropped his gaze to the floor. He realised he was trembling. In his mind, he tried to weigh up the danger of disobeying Master Muhr with the danger of antagonising Master Sabtah, but he could not think properly. All he could think about was the calibre of a boltgun. Zero point seven five. It filled his mind like a void.

'Master Muhr does not wish to be disturbed,' Sufjan murmured into his chest.

'I will kill you, then,' Sabtah said, his hand shooting out to clamp Sufjan's throat. 'Hold still, you won't feel it.'

'No, master, please!'

The bolt pistol swung down to his forehead like an executioner's axe. Cold steel pressed against his skin. He heard the round being chambered. It vibrated through his skull with finality.

'I know things! I've heard things!' Sufjan screamed, his words overlapping each other.

The gun wavered.

'What do you know, slave?'

Sufjan felt weak. He leaned against his halberd for support, his rigid salute collapsing as fear shook his body. 'Muhr, he talks. Other slaves can hear it in the air vents from corridor 25/Upperlevel-32 and in the lavatories of the guard barracks if the warp echo is strong.'

Sabtah seemed interested. He smiled, a flash of curved fangs parting his beard. 'More.'

'Muhr talks constantly with someone he calls *Overlord*. He wishes to merge the Blood Gorgons with his new master. That's all we know!'

Sabtah seemed to ponder that. His eyes took on a

glazed, distant look. But his grip on Sufjan's throat did not loosen and the boltpistol did not waver.

'Slaves heard this?' he said finally.

'I am sure,' Sufjan croaked. 'They listen. Not me personally. But others do.'

Sabtah unlatched his grip from Sufjan's throat. He smoothed the slave's collar with a delicate finger. 'That may be so. But we can't have eavesdropping slaves. You understand?'

The boltpistol clinked. It was the firing pin. Sufjan had never fired a gun before, but somehow he knew it was the firing pin.

THE BLAST SHUTTERS that sealed off Muhr's sanctuary were barred from the inside. Behind Sabtah, the six Blood Gorgons of Squad Pharol wedged their wide shoulders into the cold, wet corridor.

'Sergeant Orchus,' Sabtah said, turning to the squad. 'Breach this door.'

Orchus lumbered his way to the front. 'Milord,' he said, patting his power maul against his palm. The weapon's energy field activated with a crackle of compressed oxygen. The corridor's stale air was cut with the smell of ozone.

Hauling back for a wide backhand, Orchus collided his power maul into the blast shutter. The boarding weapon sank through with a liquid *pop*. Bubbles of molten metal boiled to the surface as the power maul was torn from the shutter. It peeled away a long strip of armoured door, leaving it to slough off like a wilting petal. Orchus struck again, throwing his hips and torso into the swing. Again and again. Droplets of liquefied steel flew.

'That's enough, sergeant,' Sabtah said as the solid steel became doughy, melting in puddles across the decking.

The group entered Muhr's sanctuary proper. They pushed on in a tight formation into Muhr's laboratories. There, the walls were peeling, the cracked paint revealing cryptic designs underneath. Slab-like operating tables lined the wide hall. When Sabtah looked closely, he could see the tables were scarred with irregular human tooth marks. The witch conducted many of his live experiments here, and the pain of his victims had driven them mad.

Four black turbans, unaware of the squad's identity, charged out from behind amniotic tanks and curing shelves with their halberds raised. They realised their mistake too late. Sabtah and his retinue shot them down before they could protest.

Others appeared on the mezzanine steps. Sabtah could not tell whether they were menial servants or armed guards. It did not matter. They shot them all down, chopping down the silhouettes until none appeared above the banisters. The squad stormed up into the unlit upper levels, moving by the muted shades of night vision.

They found Muhr in the upper tip of his tower, a conical chamber with a thin, fluted ceiling. He was stooped over his mirror, his hair matting his face and trailing to the ground like a torn shawl. He stood up quickly, forcefully.

'What is this?' he shrieked.

His outburst stopped even Sabtah in mid-sprint. Muhr had changed. He was unarmoured, but somehow he looked larger. Muhr had always been pallid and thin compared to the others, but now he looked distended, as if his bones, like his nails, had been painfully lengthened.

'Muhr. We have come to detain you,' Sabtah announced from behind the barrel of his bolt pistol.

Muhr laughed aloud. 'On what grounds?'

Sabtah's tone was expressionless. 'You are a traitor, Muhr. Hauts Bassiq, Gammadin's death, it was all your doing, witch. You sold us to Nurgle.'

'I accuse you of the same!' Muhr retorted, his voice rising. 'As do my brothers in arms.'

Above them, high amongst the viewing balconies, warriors of Squad Agamon and two Chirurgeons of 4th and 9th Company emerged. They were resting with their boltguns against the balustrade. Sabtah found himself staring into the barrel of Squad Agamon's autocannon from a second-storey knuckle balcony.

'Brother-Sergeant Phistos. Lower your weapons. I am your superior,' Sabtah commanded. His voice was calm, but inside he seethed. Sabtah knew Phistos as a promising young prospect, a ruthless raider with many years of service to the Chapter. But now he had been led astray by Muhr's promises of change and power, as Sabtah had always feared. The Blood Gorgons were already straining under the first cracks of intra-Chapter war.

Phistos of Agamon hesitated at Sabtah's command. His barrel dipped.

'Weapons trained!' Muhr shouted. 'He is the traitor! Detain him.'

Sabtah knew it was an empty charge, a counter-accusation simply to buy Muhr time.

Muhr knew he had been caught and he was desperate, cornered and crazed. Behind Sabtah, Squad Pharol's guns did not stray from Muhr. Optic scopes chimed and auspexes pinged with feedback as they refused to lock on. To prevent friendly fire in the tight confines of a boarding action, their bolters' machine spirits had been forged to seize up when targeting Blood Gorgon power armour.

There was a brief moment of stillness. The squads were locked, both unable to act, their weapons trained on one another.

Sabtah thought about finishing it. He could kill him now, execute him and be done with it. But such an act would open the floodgates of utter chaos. Muhr's factional supporters would grow uneasy – there would be repercussions. Those rogues who harboured their own ambitions would fear for their own safety. Above all, Sabtah would be viewed as an indiscriminate tyrant. They would never accept him as a rightful Champion. The fabric of Blood Gorgon unity would erode through mistrust and paranoia. Brother would turn against brother, blood bond against blood bond. It would force history to repeat, and that was what Sabtah feared the most.

'All squads, lower your weapons,' Sabtah said quietly. Both squads continued to threaten each other with their guns. 'Now!' Sabtah warned, spiking his vox with amplitude. Once the squads cowled their weapons, he approached Muhr with open palms.

'This can only be resolved by invocation.'

Muhr bared his teeth. 'You dare rouse Yetsugei for this?'

'Why, are you frightened of judgement? The Prince sees all,' Sabtah snorted.

Muhr licked his lips with a serpentine tongue. 'Then we will summon him. The one who survives judgment will stand as ward of this Chapter.'

'You should be dead, Muhr,' Sabtah spat. 'By all rights you should be dead. I should kill you. Now the Prince will have that honour.'

'We shall see, Sabtah. We shall see.'

THE WARP. THE warp was no place to walk barefoot.

There, the sky was constantly expanding, allowing him to glimpse overlapping time loops of the universe's ending. The land curved away from him, never-ending. Crushed stone bit his soles. He could see a citadel. Its towers and parapets sat atop the shell of a turtle like a hive stack. The turtle was ponderous, marching tirelessly across the horizon. How large was it? A thousand kilometres long? Perhaps a million? With each lethargic step, it levelled mountains and bevelled cliffs into biting, crushed stone shards. The scale was hypnotic.

Muhr knew he was dreaming. He was dressed in a cloak of black velvet, but nothing else. At his hip was a sword he did not remember owning.

Sabtah's threats still rang in his ears. Muhr had been thinking about them before he drifted into his psy-trance. Now, even as his spirit waded through the warp, the troubles of the physical world followed him.

He knelt down to pick up a flint. It crumbled at his touch, exploding into powder as if age had stolen its integrity. Muhr stood up quickly, his black cloak snapping. The simple movement caused a rippling wind that puffed a stand of dry, leafless trees into ash. Everything in this world was dead, preserved only by tranquillity.

'Welcome to my home,' said a hollow voice. 'It is as much yours as it is mine.'

'Opsarus! My Overlord!' Muhr gasped. He fell to his knees, pressing his forehead to the powdered stone.

Opsarus appeared to him as old as the world itself. His power armour had a petrified, granular texture, as if a mantle of minerals had risen from the ground to streak it with opaline, jade and sickly lime and white. Its surface was studded with bolts, weeping with rust. Looming over Muhr, Opsarus was a rising ocean wreckage, dragged from the bottom of a powerful sea.

'Get up, Muhr. Act like my lieutenant for once.' The turbines of Opsarus's power pack whirred with a rhythmic hum, constant and powerful. His face was a deathmask of sculpted turquoise, its moulded features noble, almost angelic in bearing and set in the middle of his hulking shoulders. When he spoke, the voice that issued through the metal lips was garbled and distorted.

Muhr got up quickly. 'Why do you bring me here, Overlord?' he asked.

'Be quiet, sorcerer. Listen first, then ask questions,' Opsarus snapped impatiently. 'Too much talking, that's your failing, sorcerer.'

Muhr lowered his head.

'Sabtah seeks to invoke Yetsugei to reveal your true ambitions?' Opsarus chuckled.

Muhr nodded.

Opsarus chuckled again. 'And you are frightened? Yes?'

'Of course, lord. Yetsugei sees all, and the Chapter will listen to the daemon's words. They will discover the truth. It will lay bare our plans.'

'Yetsugei is a jester. A king among men, but a fool among daemonkind.'

'Yet the Chapter heed his words. They will know.'

'Another failing of your Chapter and your gene-seed, sorcerer.'

The words stung, but Muhr knew it was the truth. The Blood Gorgons lacked the favour of the gods. While Opsarus could invoke the power of the Great Unclean One, the Blood Gorgons were left to grovel to some petty daemon prince. It reminded him of their inferiority.

'What can we do, Overlord?'

'All part of the plan,' Opsarus said, laying a hand on Muhr's head. 'I have known this for some time.'

'I'm sure, Overlord. Your wisdom has never led me astray.'

'Take this.'

Opsarus pressed a small, hard object into Muhr's palm. It was a crystal. Unremarkable and entirely mundane. Yet when Muhr peered closer, he saw a scintilla of movement within. When he squinted, Muhr could see a peculiar little thing – a tiny figure was trapped in the fragment. Sure enough, the creature moved again, dancing and prancing inside the crystal. Although Muhr could not see the microscopic expression of the creature inside, there was a malevolence that exuded from it. Muhr was sure the thing was sneering at him.

'Thank you, Overlord. What do you–'

Opsarus cut him off. 'Listen first, Muhr, then questions. Use this shard to disrupt the summoning. Cast it into the wards as you invoke. It will release the daemon within. Yetsugei will not heed the call.'

'Overlord...'

Opsarus turned away. 'Leave.'

Muhr blinked and felt his consciousness resettle in the physical plane. When he opened his eyes, he was in his tower again, surrounded by the familiar pipes and boilers of his laboratory. He rubbed his eyes blearily. As he did so, he realised he clutched something in his palm.

He opened his hand slowly. There, cradled by the folds of his flesh, was a crystal shard.

CHAPTER TWELVE

THE PLAINSMEN TOOK Barsabbas northwards. They left the lowlands to spread out behind them, heading towards the darkening skies and the ruins of the deserted north. Soft sand gave way to a barren, rocky topography. The planet's surface here was scoured dry.

The great muster of kinships was spread beneath the shadow of dormant volcanoes, a range of mountains they called the Weeping Sisters. Acres of tents and shade awnings surrounded the basking silver snakes of various road trains. In the dunes north of the encampment, a kilometre-long stockade of wagons had been drawn up to protect the exposed flank. What few firearms the plainsmen possessed were there, facing the enemy. Flocks of outriders on their birds roamed there, patrolling up into the mountains themselves to crow's-nest the region.

They spotted Barsabbas and his convoy winding their way through the narrow mountain shoulders. A dozen riders were dispatched to meet them. Together they rode down into the encampment.

Barsabbas counted the numbers with a cursory auspex sweep. He calculated the readout in his head, subtracting an estimation of non-combatant families and livestock signatures. The total, even with a generous estimate, would be no more than twenty thousand fighters. It was a gathering of road trains, women and children. A mass exodus, not an army.

He had hoped for more. Twenty thousand men would amount to little more than a speed bump against a well-drilled company of Chaos Space Marines. He needed the plainsmen to occupy the enemy in order for him to infiltrate unnoticed into the deep north. But they would have to do. He would adapt.

The road train pulled to a steaming halt. Barsabbas alighted from the road train's cab, dark eldar in tow. Outriders had ridden in advance to bring news of his arrival. Plainsmen rose to meet him, jostling crowds in bright red shukas. They chanted his name. Children spilled from their parents' tents, eager to claim first sight of the Red God. Women wreathed in brightly coloured neck rings peered sheepishly at him from behind drawn shades. The plainsmen braves, trotting on their predatory birds, came out to regard him with a martial suspicion. They looked like savage men, and Barsabbas understood how his Chapter came to use their ancestors as genestock. Lithe and narrow-waisted, they donned war crests of feather and hauberks of woven bark strips. He recognised the lineage of bronze skin and high cheekbones on many of his fellow brothers. Drovers, hunters, stock tenders, shamans, they all came to see him and exult in his coming.

As they threaded through the throng, Barsabbas could see a massed ring of hand-painted caravans shaded by a large canvas awning. That would no doubt be the command centre. Its conspicuousness annoyed Barsabbas. It was a large, vulnerable and easily identifiable target. The plainsmen may have been brave, but they certainly did not know war.

A procession of chieftains from the gathered kinships rode out to meet him. They were all elders, men with sun-creased faces, long and wizened as if etched from aged wood. Their shukas were freshly re-dyed and left traces of red pigment on their shoulders and arms. At their front, riding several paces ahead upon a black and grey talon squall, was the elder of the entire gathering. Gumede had told Barsabbas of his name, Ngokodjou. Gumede had also warned Barsabbas of his insufferable superiority.

'I am Ngokodjou Akindes, the elder of elders, wisdom of the dunes to the west. You may call me Ngokodjou,' said the elder as he drew closer. He lazily swatted a fly from his face, seemingly unimpressed by the Chaos Space Marine.

Barsabbas did not reply. He studied the haughty chieftain. The elder of elders was a fat man, thick with meat, while those around him were gaunt and emaciated. He was tall too, and carried the arrogance that came to those who were imposingly tall and knew it. Pendant earrings hung like heavy tendrils of gold and onyx from his ears and he carried a recurve bow across his lap. Barsabbas decided he did not like the man. There was a shrewdness to his crescent eyes, an animalistic cunning that told Barsabbas he would be difficult to deal with.

'I have heard of you already,' Barsabbas replied bluntly.

'My reputation precedes me wherever I go,' said Ngokodjou, choosing to take the words as a compliment. 'I too have heard of you. We are equals, you and I, and more similar than you would know.'

Barsabbas snorted. The man had grown accustomed to speaking to his kin as if they were ignorant. 'We are not the same, human. Do not speak to me like that.'

Ngokodjou's eyes flashed with anger. Barsabbas detected a trace of vehemence, fleeting and then gone. But the smile never wavered on Ngokodjou's face. 'Of course, koag.'

In any other place, at any other time, Barsabbas would have shot him through the throat and taken his necklaces as trophies. His trigger finger twitched involuntarily. But he needed the plainsmen. They thought him to be a benevolent and godly spirit, and he needed to exploit that for now.

As if sensing the enmity between them, Gumede stole close to Barsabbas and bowed to Ngokodjou. 'We should bring the koag into the house of elders. Times may be hard but we must not neglect hospitality.'

THEY BROUGHT HIM bowls of gruel. They gave him jugs of curdled caprid milk. A dancing file of children brought them dishes of dried apricots and small, tart berries.

Barsabbas consumed only a small amount of milk to replenish his protein stores.

Wrestlers entered the tent to perform their ritual matches. Young dancers with supple waists danced and chanted in unison.

Barsabbas grew impatient.

He sat awkwardly on a spread of beaded blankets, his hulking form barely contained by the low awnings. The tent was filled with clapping elders. It seemed that the arrival of a 'Red God' was seen as a portent of victory.

'We should plan our attack,' Barsabbas said finally.

'We defend here,' announced one of the chieftains proudly. The others agreed with him by clicking their tongues and nodding sagely.

'No. We need a strategy, supplies, logistics, reports of enemy disposition, structured formations,' Barsabbas said.

Ngokodjou sneered at him, as if he had been waiting for those words. 'But if you are so powerful, then why do we need to do so? With the powers of a god, surely the dead will fall,' said Ngokodjou. It was a direct challenge.

Barsabbas imagined choking the man's jowls with his hands. 'You will face more than just the dead. There will be human fighters with guns. Other threats too, warriors like me, but many times in number.'

The tent grew very quiet. The dancers ran off in a hurry, leaving their hand chimes and tall drums.

'Warriors like you?'

'They follow a different path, but yes.'

'Tell us what to do, koag.'

'Is there disease in the camp?'

'Very little,' said one of the southern chiefs. 'These gathered kinships are mostly from the deep south-lands. When they fall ill, we tie them up.'

'Tie them up?' Barsabbas burst out with deep, bellowing laughter. 'Why do you not just kill them?'

'The families will not allow it,' said another. 'But before the plague takes them, we bind their hands and feet. That way, when they...'

Barsabbas shook his head. He could not under-stand the strange attachments these humans seemed so adamant to cling to. Why risk infecting the entire camp, hundreds of thousands of people in close proximity, when it would be more efficient to leave the infected to die under the sun? There was no logic to it. Why leave someone infected to the care of healthy and vulnerable kin?

A Chaos Space Marine would have been efficient. They would sever an arm before infection set in, and would certainly execute a comrade if sparing him meant compromising the effectiveness of the Chap-ter. Barsabbas was disgusted by the humans' weakness.

'We must preserve our strength. Your army is small and we cannot afford the numbers to dwindle under a plague. We will bring the fight to them. We will push north. The enemy will come, I know how they fight.'

'What about our great conveyors? Or our kin?'

'Take them with us,' Barsabbas said. He did not rel-ish their slaughter. But he needed their diversion, and twenty thousand warriors alone would not be enough, especially with plague slowly but steadily spreading through the camp. It would be a sacrifice, but a necessary one.

THERE HAD BEEN a time when the *Cauldron Born* had been many different ships. There had been a collision of abandoned ghost drifters that had welded the superstructure together by the grinding pressure of mega-tonnes. Gradually, the hulk grew larger, gathering a gravitational pull by virtue of its fattening girth.

Drifting into the Eye of Terror – that legend-haunted region of space – the space hulk began to take form. Daemons and malevolent spirits of the Eye found a home in its cavernous catacombs. There it drifted, a shapeless wreck forced into perpetual motion, gathering size like a ghosting ball of dust.

It was eight thousand years before Gammadin found and tamed this vessel, grafting his own flesh tissue into the drifter's heart and binding it with Chaos witchcraft. From there, the ship grew organically, shaping itself to Gammadin's will. Flesh cauliflowered over the skeletal metal and fused with the dormant engines. It became a living creature, long and lithe. Its daemon spirit made it receptive to the warp, a conduit of energy.

A sacred place to open the warp to the material plane.

IT WOULD TAKE many days for the temple to be prepared for summoning.

First, the temple would need to be swept and cleaned, the wards redrawn and rechecked. Teams of menial slaves climbed scaffolds, using their bare hands and feet to scale sixty metres on yielding wooden supports. The walls were scrubbed clean of psychic residue.

Working vigorously, the slaves did not look at Muhr as he entered the chamber. They did not even dare to acknowledge him. The witch ghosted up the dais's steps and across its marble surface. Set in the centre was a bowl filled with mandrake roots in fresh blood, drowning like swollen dolls. When the warp rift was invoked, the offering would draw daemons like a droplet of blood drew sharks. Every daemon had their own preference. Yetsugei would only answer to a summons of blood and mandrake. Even the slightest change in offerings could result in unwanted visitations.

Muhr cupped the bowl in his hands and began to chant. He was not meant to be here and he rushed the words, almost stumbling over the syllables in his haste.

The bowl contained three large mandrake roots, the roots resembling pudgy human limbs and torsos, sitting in a thin pool of blood from a suffering human. It was a very specific ingredient that could lure many minor warp denizens. This blood had belonged to a slave called Sufjan, or so he had been told. The slave had apparently died an insufferable sort of demise.

Muhr finished his chant and drew the crystal shard. The tiny figure inside, like a painted doll, did not stir. Muhr threw the gem into the bowl. It hit the surface with a guilty plop, before sinking to the bottom.

Hiding his intentions behind an air of solemnity, Muhr descended from the platform, nodding with satisfaction.

CHAPTER THIRTEEN

SABTAH PICKED HIS way through the armoury, shifting apart a quagmire of discarded weaponry. Kicking aside a tower shield, Captain Hazareth stood in agitation, waiting for Sabtah to speak.

'What do you mean, betrayal? Hazareth asked finally.

'Muhr has too much at stake to be undone by this summoning. He will do something to prevent its execution. It's only logical,' Sabtah replied.

Sabtah watched Hazareth's reaction carefully. The captain continued to make his way down the vault, pushing over another shelf of weapons as if to dispel some nervous energy. A wave of short stabbing swords and daggers spilled onto the ground. Hazareth picked through the mess thoughtfully before giving Sabtah a solemn, appraising look.

'What does he stand to gain?'

Sabtah knew the captain had a right to be curious. Feared and accursed, Hazareth was considered neutral. He supported neither Muhr, Sabtah nor the minor factions that struggled for power. Hazareth was the consummate warrior and he cared not for Chapter politics. But Sabtah trusted Hazareth. He knew that the captain valued martial capacity above all else, and Muhr's betrayal would be a direct impediment to the combat abilities of the Chapter. This argument was the only way to get Hazareth on his side.

'Muhr has always advocated a patron. First it was Abaddon, two centuries ago. Muhr had suggested to Gammadin that we pledge our allegiance to the Destroyer. Gammadin would have none of it. He has always been hungry for greater power, greater recognition.'

Hazareth thought judiciously. 'What is wrong with power?'

'It will come at the cost of Blood Gorgon autonomy.'

The captain nudged a pile of swords, but had clearly given up searching for anything.

'It will cost us our identity,' Sabtah continued. 'We may not be a Legion, we may not have a dominion, but we are free. We have always been free. Alliances with any greater force would not bode well for our independence. The Death Guard, the Black Legion, the Renegades Undivided. It would all be the same.'

Sabtah could tell Hazareth was still suspicious. 'But why would he harm Hauts Bassiq?' asked the captain.

'Because his patron wishes to claim Bassiq for himself. Muhr is simply serving a purpose, weakening us from the inside, so that his Overlord can claim the world with minimal losses. In exchange for his aid, his overlord will accept Muhr under his patronage. It is a pact, but not one that I wish this Chapter to fall under.'

Hazareth didn't reply. He had spotted something amongst the disorganised piles. He picked it up. 'Is this it?' he asked.

He held in his hands a dagger. Its handle was polished black wood and its blade was dirty steel. Chipped and worn, the serrated blade was engraved with an arcane script. Sabtah had claimed the weapon six centuries ago from an agent of the hated Ordo Malleus. With its ordinary appearance, Sabtah had initially regarded the piece as nothing more than a trinket. It had taken some four centuries before he ascertained its true nature, and since then it had collected dust in Sabtah's weapon vault, lost between forty-metre-high stacks of plundered weaponry.

'That's what we came here for,' Sabtah said. He kicked his way through the vault and took hold of the knife. Rifles and lasguns scattered like dry leaves before his boots.

'A fine weapon,' Hazareth said, handing it to him.

'A daemon weapon. A she-bitch,' Sabtah said, tossing the knife from palm to palm. The haft vibrated as the daemon within became agitated.

'You think you will need it at the summoning?' Hazareth asked.

'I believe Muhr will show his hand there. Yes.'

Hazareth plucked a warhammer down from a nearby wall mount. 'Then you have First Company's support, Sabtah. You were Gammadin's bond and I uphold my fealty to you.'

Sabtah smiled. 'If something should happen to me, Hazareth, I need you to kill Muhr. The Blood Gorgons must remain as we are and always have been. We are nothing without our history and our tradition. Don't let Muhr change that.'

'I will punish him,' Hazareth promised.

'Good.' Sabtah drew from beneath his nail a sliver of black, no larger than a splinter. 'This is my genecode. It will access most of the vessel's defence systems and security scans. I am bonded to Gammadin and whatever Gammadin can access, you will be able to too.'

Hazareth received it in the tip of his index finger. The splinter curled like a dying earthworm before burrowing beneath his cuticle with a slight sting. 'When will I need this?'

'As long as I live, never,' Sabtah began. He paused, his brows knitting. 'But one day, I have no doubt you will. Keep it close and tell no one.'

THE SHIP'S BAY sirens wailed with the passing of a new cycle. A new day.

Deep in the temple pit, Muhr and his nine were completing the last of their monophonic liturgy. The coven surrounded the wide dais, their vox-speakers generating a constant, steady drone of plainchant. The rims of silver bowls were rubbed, letting their harmonics peal and stretch.

The wards had been drawn by morning. A spider's web of interlocking, overlapping polygons and flat geometry radiated outwards in mutually supporting glyph work. Several external seals, large pentagrammic stars, reinforced the initial containments and spread up into the walls with sharp, linear lines.

Only thirty hand-picked Blood Gorgons and their slave retinues formed a circle around the pit. They each carried a black tapestry. Thirty black tapestries in all, one for each of the warriors lost on Hauts Bassiq.

Slowly, the air grew cold. A wind began to gather as the chants climbed in rhythm. Frost settled down on them like a coarse fog. The wind boomed, thrashing against the interior.

The chanting stopped. The wind stilled abruptly.

Slowly, at the centre of the dais, the air began to bend and tear. It buckled.

Wet frost was coating the dome, running in sheets down the walls and collecting in droplets across the domed ceiling. The coven of Chirurgeon-witches sounded their singing bowls with odd, polyrhythmic melodies. Haunting and drawn, they channelled the psychic focus of the coven.

Slowly and deliberately, Sabtah stepped onto the dais. He was alert, his eyes darting, but his body was fluid and relaxed. He turned and gave the surrounding Blood Gorgons a salute, extending his power trident horizontally before him.

Opposite him, Muhr also stepped onto the dais. The witch's armour was polished clean. New iron studs had been riveted over the polyps that clustered on the shoulders and chest plate. A black cloak poured from his shoulders and a sword that Sabtah had never seen before sat at his hip.

Both were ready for judgement.

Sabtah knelt down, murmured his devotion to the gods and threw fistfuls of rock salt over his

shoulders. The coarse grains cascaded down his back
as he prayed.

'We invoke you for judgement,' intoned one of the
coven. The air continued to distort, warping itself to
bursting point. Patterns solidified in the air as overlapping dimensions within the warp became lucid to
the human mind. The air became so cold, it carried
particles of frost.

Muhr looked at Sabtah, curiously confident despite
his impending judgement.

INSIDE THE SACRIFICE bowl, Muhr's crystal shard rocked
gently as the warp energy was invoked. The creature
within became animated, thrashing its microscopic
arms and dancing with an eerie vigour. As it cavorted,
minute cracks appeared across the tiny shard. The
crystal cracked and began to weep a black fluid. Oozing like treacle, it was pushed outwards from the
crystal shard, discolouring and mingling with the
blood. Bubbling and frothing, it released an absurd
amount of liquid that the tiny crystal could not possibly contain. It filled the bowl until the black fluid
gathered along the edges and poured down in a solid
curtain. With one final shudder, the bowl rocked and
tipped over, spilling a low tide across the marble.

The Blood Gorgons gathered at the edge of the pit
touched their boltguns in trepidation. The invocation was a common ritual but they had never seen
this before.

Sabtah looked up. Across from him, Muhr had
crouched with one knee on the ground. The witch's
head was bowed. His hands were nonchalantly
pressed against the marble. His fingers, subtle and

almost unseen, were scraping away at the painted wards.

Sabtah rose urgently. He opened his mouth to shout a warning. Muhr looked up and smiled at him.

Something was wrong, but it was too late.

Reality began to buckle. The walls of the temple appeared to liquefy, the particles of its structure becoming loose. The floor and ceiling tilted at an angle that was nauseous to the human mind. The three dimensions of the material plane and the numerical perfection of existence was disintegrating as the warp hole began to expand.

And then the world went black.

YETSUGEI WAS AWAKENED. His playthings were pleading for his presence again. The warp was shifting. Beyond any concept of distance or time, a rift was opening. He could sense his invocation. But there was some-thing else there too – a baleful malevolence, strong and reeking. Yetsugei knew better. He curled himself away, folding himself up and squirming into the darkest regions. The presence was too much, even for him. He ignored their call and tried to flee.

THERE WAS AN atom-splitting howl. They all heard it.

It was followed by a sudden and ominous black-out. Every single sconce torch fluttered out.

As a matter of automatic reaction, the Blood Gorgons switched to thermal vision. Nothing. Night reflection. Nothing. Multi-light overlay. Nothing. It was an unnatural darkness flooding in from the warp.

Then the screaming began.

It killed quickly. Brother Talus was disembowelled. Brother-Sergeant Arkum fell in sections, blood drizzling like fine rain. Muzzles flashed.

Inexplicably, the torches fluttered back. A daemon was amongst them. The containment wards had failed. They were scorched into the marble itself, burning like a racing promethium flame.

It towered above them all, thirteen metres tall. Its body was flaccid, covered with sparse, wiry hair. Its eight-dozen arms whipped sickles like a threshing mill. Its maw was ringed by blunt, chiselled teeth.

'Daemon of Nurgle!' shouted one of the coven.

'Basho Eeluk has come for Sabtah,' gurgled the daemon.

Before the coven could banish it, Basho Eeluk shouted a single word, a syllable of power. The warp gate expanded rapidly until it encompassed the entire dais before collapsing with a surge of static. There was a rolling boom like thunder, as air rushed in to fill the vacuum.

The marble dais was gone. The sacrificial bowl lay upturned. Sabtah was gone. Muhr was gone.

SABTAH DID NOT know where he was. His surroundings were dark and insubstantial. The marble dais seemed to be suspended in mid air. He saw only the daemon and moved to flank it. The daemon sensed his intent and swung to meet him. It crashed down onto the dais, splitting the marble, as it bellowed.

Sabtah held his trident in a loose hammer grip, winding his arm back like a javelin thrower. He cast it with all his superhuman strength, pivoting on his toes to wring out every shred of momentum. The weapon punched deep into the daemon's paunch and quivered there like an arrow. Recoiling from the wound, Basho Eeluk began to pull at the protruding weapon shaft even as a conical swarm of bone hornets belched from the daemon's mouth.

Like sharp-edged darts, the swarm richocheted against Sabtah's plate. They slashed his face open, drawing hundreds of tiny, piercing cuts through skin, fat and flesh. Garbling a howl of elation, Basho barged forwards, driving off its powerful legs. Standing his ground, Sabtah sprayed his bolter on automatic. Yet the daemon's multiple hands moved so quickly it seemed as if it fanned out hundreds upon hundreds of arms, catching the bolt-rounds and exploding them in mid-air. His bullets foiled by dark magic, Sabtah pivoted to the side as the daemon pounced. Rolling off his shoulder, Sabtah came up in a crouch, his bolter already tracking.

'Is this what you wanted, Sabtah?' asked a voice from behind his neck.

Spinning quickly, Sabtah saw Muhr. The sorcerer stood at the edge of the marble disc, aiming a bolt pistol. He fired from almost point-blank range.

Sabtah had no choice. He slapped the round away. His left hand exploded in a concentric swirl of blood and armour fragments. Circling away, Sabtah returned with a triple burst of his boltgun. The shots sent Muhr ducking for cover.

And then the daemon was all over him.

Teeth. Fangs. Glistening skin. Sabtah was mauled from all directions at once. He let his boltgun fall on its sling. Basho Eeluk used its bulk, pushing the old warrior to the edge of the marble disc. Solid, black nothingness plummeted away beneath him. Hands slapped at him. Tremendously powerful palm slaps that jostled Sabtah's heavy bones against their ligaments.

Sabtah barely reached the daemon's thigh height, but he clinched up with it. Power armour servos whirring, Sabtah locked up Basho Eeluk's thighs with his arms and began to drive forwards. Blood draining from his severed wrist, Sabtah relied on his arms alone, sucking the daemon's knees towards his chest by tucking his elbows in. Pushing forwards, Sabtah began to lurch the daemon over its centre of gravity, worrying it like a game hound. Basho Eeluk toppled, stretching out a choir of arms to break its fall.

Sabtah muscled the daemon onto the ground and began to climb up its supine form. Basho Eeluk shook its monstrous body, trying to dislodge the old warrior from its torso.

Finally, Sabtah found purchase on the daemon's enormous throat. He wrapped his steel-shod legs around the daemon's neck and constricted his thighs like a lariat. Rearing its greenish bulk, it jerked, suddenly rising. Sabtah dangled off the neck upside down, like an oversized necklace.

With a creak of scraping metal, Basho Eeluk clawed at Sabtah with a forest of hands. Another two-dozen hammered his armoured shell, wrenching him like a struggling crustacean. Sabtah locked his legs tighter and curled his abdomen, pulling himself upright despite the suffocating wave of attacks. He found himself staring directly into the daemon's face. The head was almost as large as Sabtah's torso. Disc-like fish eyes returned his stare with a dull, silver gaze.

A sickle chopped into his side. One of the daemon's many weapons had found a gap in his torso plate. The razor cut deep into his liver, exploding toxins into his bloodstream. Another finally punched through his battered thigh plate.

Gritting his teeth against the accumulating wounds, Sabtah unsheathed the knife. Basho Eeluk rolled, wrenching its body like a surfacing whale. Sabtah swung on the daemon's neck, but his legs only hugged tighter. Reaching up, Sabtah rammed the knife into Basho Eeluk's eye. It scored open like firm fruit.

Basho Eeluk spasmed. It gripped Sabtah with all of its hands, hundreds of clawed fingers grasping and worming away him. Prying and pulling, Basho Eeluk tried to drag Sabtah off its neck like a stubborn leech. Sabtah slashed the knife again, paring away a long strip of daemon flesh. Where the ensorcelled blade made contact, Basho Eeluk corroded, bubbling like acid on metal.

Yet Eeluk refused to die. It reared up and dived back down, head first. There was a sharp, jarring impact. Sabtah's back slammed back into the marble dais. He felt his spine shatter, vertebrae twisting. His legs loosened, flopping aside as his nervous system seized.

Sabtah had one last window of opportunity and he took it. As Eeluk pulled its head free, Sabtah's knife hand followed it.

Basho Eeluk was still bellowing victory as Sabtah blinded its other eye. The daemon reeled. Completely sightless it lurched, limbs awkwardly flailing. Its cry became one of despair. It dragged itself over the edge of the marble dais and slithered over the edge, banishing itself back into the rolling clouds of the warp-sea. It roared one final time, fading cries marking the depth of its descent.

'Muhr,' Sabtah said. He tried to rise, but he no longer had control of his lower body. Given proper clinical treatment and augmentation, the spinal severance would only be a minor injury.

Muhr drifted into view. He stood over Sabtah's splayed body.

'Sabtah. How sad it has come to this,' Muhr said.

'Betrayer,' Sabtah accused hoarsely.

'Not so,' Muhr replied. 'I only have the glory of our warband in mind. I can make the Blood Gorgons a proper Chapter again. Not renegades, but an army.'

'We've always been who we are, Muhr.'

'Vagabonds,' Muhr finished testily.

'We have a name. The Imperium does not wish to fight the Blood Gorgons. We have a history.'

'Under Opsarus and the Legions of Nurgle we will achieve more than we ever could alone. We will raise empires. Empires, Sabtah. Hauts Bassiq is a small price to pay in return for Opsarus's patronage.'

'But we won't be Blood Gorgons any more,' Sabtah concluded bluntly. He was beginning to feel drowsy. His body was fighting the massive trauma he had sustained: a severed hand, a ruptured liver, serious cuts, a broken back. Endorphins flooded his brain as the Larraman cells in his bloodstream coagulated the wounds. His sus-an membrane began to slow the beating of his hearts. His breathing became shallow.

'Nothing you have to worry about, Sabtah.' Muhr

cocked his bolt pistol. 'I never wanted to do this. You are a good warrior and a sound tactician. But our ideologies are irreconcilable.'

Sabtah shook his head as blood bubbled into his beard. A *dowry*. That was what they used to call it.

In order to cement the Blood Gorgons' alliance to greater powers, there needed to be a gift, a token. That was Hauts Bassiq. Mineral-rich, resource-rich, a staging post of conquest that would become the jewel of Opsarus's dominion. In ancient days, humans exchanged livestock, beads, even precious stones. Hauts Bassiq was no different. It was a valuable gem for those who could exploit it.

Meek. That was the accusation Sabtah wanted to use. Muhr was meek. He was selling Sabtah's bond-brothers to the Cult of Rot and Decay merely for the promise of power. Amongst soldiers such as them-selves, the word *meek* was the gravest insult.

But the witch had sold the warband like a bride. There was no allegiance here. Muhr was trying to buy his way into power by offering Nurgle both a Chapter and a world. For a moment, Sabtah was overwhelmed by the hot rush of anger and the contrasting cold of his wounds.

'You are a bondless witch,' Sabtah murmured. He invoked the last of his bleeding strength. 'Muhr the Meek. That is how history will know you.'

Muhr flinched at the accusation. 'I may not have the blood bond but I have devoted myself to this Chapter all the same. You just can't accept it.'

Muhr pressed the pistol against Sabtah's head.

* * *

THE MARBLE DAIS reappeared in the Temple Heart with a clap of expanding gas. The fifty-tonne disc slammed back onto the decking with a force that caused earthquake tremors across a third of the space hulk.

As the dust cloud parted, Muhr was the only one remaining on the dais. Blood and fragments splashed across the white marble. The assembled squads had formed a ring around the dais, weapons primed and aimed. Muhr waved them back.

'The waves and tides of the immaterial realm have cast me in the role of guardian,' he declared.

Some of the Blood Gorgons reacted more slowly than Muhr would have liked, giving him a hesitant salute. There were those among the assembly who did not react at all. Beneath the screaming face-plates of their helmets, there would be surprise and perhaps some measure of fear. Muhr made sure to remember those dissidents who now disrespected his rank; they would need to be quelled soon.

But for now, Muhr had other things to attend to. The air of the warp clung to him and he would need to exorcise his body. Perhaps he would even allow himself some rest. He could afford the time, now he was Chapter Master.

BARSABBAS HAD NOT commanded humans in combat before but if their travel discipline was a measure of their soldiering, then it did not augur well for the campaign. Slow, disorganised and soon needing rest, the humans were incapable of travelling at a competent pace.

The muster travelled for four days and five nights

before reaching the baked clay flats of the north.
Accompanied by the rumble of motors, a line of dust
almost two kilometres in length meandered across
the terrain. Road trains forged the way, escorted by
talon outriders. Herds of caprid straggled behind,
trailing like a spillage of shaggy brown coats in their
wake. The convoy was a mess. It was a wonder that
the enemy did not attack.

Barsabbas rode at the front. His frame was too big
to fit comfortably in the engine cab, so he sat on the
tin roof, surveying the lands with an old retractable
telescope.

Hauts Bassiq had once been an industrial world.
He saw, interspersed between mountains, the artificial outlines of human structures, half buried by sand
and rust. The infrastructure, old as it was, still
remained. There were foundries, gas refineries, open
cut mines and millions of kilometres of pipeline that
had been laid down. They remained like buried mau-
soleums, preserved by the ferric sands.

They encountered the walking dead too, but only
in small, wandering packs. The outriders lured them
away from the main advance and dispatched them
from the saddle with well-placed bowshots.

At one point, during their third day of travel,
mounted scouts returned in a panic. They had spotted a patrol of large men in hoods, shod in bulky
grey: a twenty-man platoon of Septic infantry. It was
a convenient opportunity for Barsabbas to show the
natives what he was capable of. He halted the convoy
and asked the scouts to lead him to where the enemy
were camped. There, from a distance of five hundred
metres, Barsabbas gunned down the entire platoon

of enemy auxiliary as they slept. He slew six before they even realised they were being fired upon. He downed another four more as they struggled to locate his muzzle flashes. By the time the Septic returned feeble, hesitant counter-fire, Barsabbas had put down the rest with precise, clean shots to the chest. The entire engagement took less than a minute and Barsabbas did not even change his thirty-round magazine.

By the time he returned to the convoy, word had already spread about his exploits. Outriders brandished the enemy guns as trophies, even though most did not know how to use them. The plainsmen seemed unduly occupied with deifying him. They truly believed Barsabbas would lead them to victory.

THEY MADE CAMP in the badlands, surrounded by fields of dry organ pipe cactus. Two hundred thousand people spreading out to prepare for the coming war.

While the kinships rested and watered, Barsabbas did not. He debated plans of attack with the chieftains long into the night.

According to the tact-maps and scout reports, they were in the heart of enemy territory. With such a large force, it would only be a matter of time before the enemy responded to their presence.

Barsabbas knew they could do nothing but prepare their defences. He knew they would be overrun, but at least they would cause significant damage to the enemy plans on Hauts Bassiq.

* * *

THE SUNS WERE at their highest ascension. The Celsius gauges peaked at the high fifties. Bare skin seemed to strip and crack upon exposure to the glare.

The camp was alive with the sounds of urgent activity. The cactus fields formed natural fortifications for the camp and the plainsmen went about their daily business of cleaning, washing and cooking. Several of the chieftains attempted to send their closest family members to feed and bathe Barsabbas, perhaps in the hopes of receiving good fortune.

Barsabbas dismissed them all. He gathered Gumede and two-score mounted braves. He ordered them to pack a day's worth of supplies and to travel light. While the camp braced itself for the inevitable assault, Barsabbas intended to ride forth and survey the region.

He also requested a vehicle, something fast that was capable of carrying his significant weight. The braves scattered, eager to be the one to fulfil the Red God's wishes.

Upon their return, a vehicle waited for him, draped under heavy woollen blankets. Underneath was an open frame chassis mounted on four muscular wheels. The rail frame itself formed an integrated roll cage with an exposed gas engine. Barsabbas did not know its age, but he guessed it was pre-colonial, a relic from the planet's prospecting era. Despite the plainsmen's efforts to preserve its condition, the centuries had taken their toll. Much of the roll cage was corroded to a mottled orange, and the exposed engine block was fused together by rust in some parts. Somehow the shamans, with their rote knowledge of machinery and rudimentary repair skills, had managed to keep the engine alive. Rope actually held parts of the vehicle together.

When Barsabbas eased his weight onto the cracked leather seat, the quad groaned under his weight, yet the engine purred responsively to the ignition. Given the situation, Barsabbas considered the quad quite a fortunate find. Nestled within the motored cage, Barsabbas left the camp, a single file of outriders following his dusty plume.

CHAPTER FOURTEEN

THE BADLANDS OF the north appeared as a monotonous, featureless land to Barsabbas, an uninspired painting rendered in a repetitive sequence. But to the plainsmen braves, the terrain was an open book, every tree or stone a page mark for another narrative.

They rode for six kilometres with desperate haste, until they reached the stump of a brittle acacia. The tree looked no different to the sparse, withered things that he had seen standing like lonely fence posts on the horizon. Yet the tree was of some significance to the plainsmen. Barsabbas listened patiently, logging pieces of intelligence into his helmet's data feed.

The tree, he was told, marked a well-known walking path – a line in the sand that was barely visible until they pointed it out to him. Apparently satisfied that neither the walking dead nor the Septic had used the track for some time, they continued on.

As they scouted, the braves, some as young as ten, began to point out the prints of various animals: the splayed bird feet of talon squalls, the crescent prints of the caprid, curving belly marks of a brown-backed serpent. Simply from the depth and size of the tracks, they deduced the animals' gender and age. From this tiny fragment of information, they could tell whether the animals' natural habitat had been disturbed and, if so, in what way.

Two hours into their patrol of their surroundings, Gumede indicated a series of splayed prints in the sand, sprinting in the opposite direction. Judging by the spacing of their strides, Gumede knew many of them were injured by the way some of them left unevenly distributed prints, or dragged the knuckles of their feet.

'Injuries,' Gumede said, running a finger through the prints. 'Many injuries.'

'Tell me what that means,' said Barsabbas, deferring to the plainsman's experience. Barsabbas was an expert tracker. Memo-therapy had imparted into his hippocampus knowledge of wilderness survival across seventy-eight different forms of terrain. This, however, was beyond even his considerable skill.

'Birds are predators. They are rarely injured, and if so, never so many. They were attacked,' said Gumede. 'See here? Running tracks. The birds are running away from something to the north. There are fewer males running with the flock too, far too many chicks and females. It tells me that many of the males were killed protecting the flock.'

'These tracks are fresh?'

'No more than one day old. I would guess whatever attacked the birds is roughly two days' travel from here. Maybe less.'

Barsabbas understood. Out in the badlands, nothing would attack a flock of apex predators, except for something far more dangerous. It was likely something had fired upon the flock, or engaged them in a brief skirmish. The predators, defeated, had fled southwards, away from their attackers.

'Then we do not have much time. The enemy are close,' Barsabbas said.

'We should warn the camp.'

Barsabbas smiled and hefted his boltgun. 'We will return to the muster.'

THE PLAINSMEN WERE ready when they came. Through the low, bulbous fields of cacti the enemy approached. Four thousand Septic infantry, accompanied by light, sand-trawling gun platforms. The keening squeal of hydraulics and the clatter of engines echoed across the badlands. Behind them, with almost no urgency, marched a company of Plague Marines. Twenty-eight warriors in all, a procession that followed the heavy banner of Nurgle.

Barsabbas had brought the road trains into a crescent-shaped wall, a silver ridge of carriages almost one kilometre in length, girded by mountains on either flank and fields of cacti to the fore. Behind them the sprawling tents and lean-tos of the kinships took shelter. Barsabbas did not expect the line to hold. The thin skin of a steel carriage would not resist bolter shot.

Drawn out in front of the camp, standing in a thin

line, came two thousand Bassiq braves. They faced
the enemy, standing against them with bow and
arrow, throwing hatchet and firing their heirloom
rifles. They were crested with massive feathers, quivering fans of squall pinion atop heads and shoulders.
Their faces were painted red, like their brightly
coloured shukas. The red would make them fearless,
or so Barsabbas had been told.

The enemy advanced steadily. Their boots and
tracks crushed the cactus fields. The engines became
a monotone growl.

Anxious and rightfully frightened, the kinships dug
deep within the sheltered encampment. They were
vulnerable. Mothers hid their children under beaded
blankets. The old men sat together and spoke of
younger days and death. Many more – tens of thousands of people – crowded behind the parked road
trains, peering between boarded windows and carriage gaps for a glimpse of the battleline beyond. Far
deeper into the camp, the sickened and infected
began to spasm, as if sensing great evil.

Higher up, on the lower ridges of the mountain,
Barsabbas signalled for Gumede to raise the totem
standard. Each of the waiting flocks returned signal
with their own kinship totems. There were almost
sixteen thousand riders up there. Sixteen thousand
birds clacked and cawed, waiting to stampede down
the slope.

'Weep not. Everything must have its day,' said
Barsabbas, leaning down from his quad-cage to
shout at Gumede above the stormy clash of sound.
'The mettle of your entire culture will be measured in
this one engagement.'

The chief seemed to understand. He raised his lasrifle and lanced the signal upwards. A red beam, straight and true, pierced the sky. With a roar, sixteen thousand voices raised as one, the plainsmen charged down the mountain.

THE SEPTIC INFANTRY began to fire, just three hundred metres distant from the plainsmen. Las-shots and solid slugs came whistling through the organ pipe cactus. They were horrible, rapid fire volleys that cut through the braves in droves. A line of dust plumes kicked up in front of the road trains as dozens upon dozens of unarmoured braves writhed and buckled beneath the firestorm. Support weapons punched clean holes through the carriages behind them, landing ordnance and incendiary directly into the camp itself.

For the first time in his life, Barsabbas felt the fear of facing superior forces. He understood now what his foes had felt when they faced the overwhelming might of an Astartes battle force. Yet he waited, despite the carnage, waiting for the enemy to grow eager, to become lustful in the excitement of slaughter. On the slopes below them, braves continued to die, odd arrows hissing fitfully in reply. Barsabbas waited, waited more, until the enemy drew level in the fields below.

And then they charged.

They charged, and what a stampede it was. Like a rolling avalanche, sixteen thousand talon squalls came. One-tonne beasts, axe-beaks snapping, pumping thighs slamming the dirt with black avian nails. They gathered a wild, heedless momentum.

A rolling tide swallowed the Septic battle line from

the flank. The talon squalls crashed into and over the infantry platoons, rolling, tumbling, thrashing. Bodies were trampled. Shots were fired at close range. Hatchets rose and fell. The men in ghastly hoods fought back with bayonets and pistols, but the crushing juggernaut birds simply ran over them.

Talon squalls sprinted onto the gun platforms. The birds began to peck at the fighting vehicles like shelled prey, clambering atop the chassis to snap at the crew compartments with their long necks and plucking them out like morsels with their clawed feet.

Engaged to the front and suddenly outflanked, the companies of Septic infantry buckled. Their firing lost all focus and coordination. A young brave, no more than sixteen, pounced his bird atop an autocannon trailer, holding two bloodied sacks in one hand as trophies, a slick hatchet whirling in his other.

Surveying the field, Barsabbas dared to think that perhaps the braves might yet send the enemy into retreat.

Then the Plague Marines engaged.

They waded into the fray slowly, as if boredom had finally compelled them to action. They were massive, as tall as a mounted rider and broader than the breast of a talon squall rooster. Incarnations of pestilence, they seemed invincible. Hatchets and arrows skipped off the dirty white surface of their plate, barely scratching the lime green bacterial colonies that beveined the enamel. Helmets with wide, trumpet-like rebreathers and ugly, mismatched goggles encased their heads. They leaked grey and yellow fluid when pierced but showed little reaction to any wounds inflicted.

In their plated gauntlets and thick, rubberised

combat gloves, they fired boltguns. They favoured knives as heavy as short swords; rusted chopping blades that parted flesh crudely. Every stroke of the knife or squeeze of the trigger killed men. Onwards they came, and Barsabbas moved to meet them.

BARSABBAS VAULTED OFF the quad-motor as las-shots raked across its fender. The flimsy vehicle was not fit for a bond-brother. He kicked the roll cage away and began to pick careful shots with his boltgun. His leash chain looped around Barsabbas's wrist, Sindul began to shriek in panic. Hooded and bound, the dark eldar could only squirm in terror as the battle raged blindly around him.

A platoon of Septic infantry appeared out of the rising dust. Thirty or forty soldiers in baggy, hooded masks, advancing in a loose spread. He heard their shouts of alarm as they spotted him.

Barsabbas reacted as he was drilled, pressuring them with a wide spread of automatic fire. The sudden volley of crackling bolt shells cut out in a semicircle. Rounds so heavy that even their passing shockwave haemorrhaged the brains and organs of any target in a one-metre radius. Enemy infantry sprawled, fell and dived under the burst of fire. It was what Barsabbas needed to close the distance.

As the enemy went to ground to escape the initial onslaught, Barsabbas charged and fell amongst them. Now he was in his element and superior enemy numbers did not faze him. At the edge of his visor, he saw a Septic thrust a bayonet towards him. Using his great armspan, Barsabbas lashed his mace over the Septic's rifle and caved in his hooded mask. He fell sideways, lurching into another Septic. Barsabbas killed that one too, breaking his neck with a quick backstroke. So absorbed was he in the practice of death-dealing that Barsabbas had to remind himself that this was not his fight. It was a diversion for him to slip north, past the bulk of the Nurgle armies. He had to keep himself alive. Finding Sargaul was the objective. He had to remind himself of that just to keep his battle rage in check. The nostril-flaring lust to kill almost overwhelmed his logic and conditioning.

'Attack the gaps in his armour!' shouted a Septic officer.

But Barsabbas would not stand still long enough to allow it. Three Septics harried him, surrounding him and trying to slip a bayonet into the gaps of his knee joint. Barsabbas moved faster than they thought he could. Over three hundred kilos of an explosively-moving steel-shod body crushed the nearest Septic. Sindul was dragged along with him, the chain snapping taut and almost decapitating another Septic. Barsabbas felt bayonets snap against his unyielding plate.

Glancing sideways, Barsabbas saw the charge of the mounted braves stalling. They were engaged in a grinding close-quarter melee. Gun shots ruptured the air. Above that could be heard the distinctly hollow chopping of hatchet through bone. Garbled screams rose from both sides and the warm-blooded croak of dying birds floated above the clamour.

It was a messy, discordant battle and Barsabbas allowed himself to indulge slightly, exulting in the violence that he had created.

CHAPTER FIFTEEN

LUREN MENZO LIVED as comfortably as a supply slave could. His quarters in the warrens of the undercellars were exceptionally large, almost three times the cot-space of any other. He had the luxury of curtains that separated his living space from the squalor of the others. Battered cushions, thin blankets, old pict frames and even books littered his den. His possessions were valued amongst slaves, but not stowed securely, for no one would dare to touch them.

Menzo had come through all of this thanks to hard work: hard work in blackmail, extortion and a highly lucrative black market. As a supply overseer, Menzo took charge of a load-bearing team in the ship's cavernous docking hangars. He had a mob of servitors, haulers, riggers and packers who processed and stored the plunder and stock of the Blood Gorgons' raids. Through that, he had built a business of sorts. A cadre of close thugs to do his heavy work, a network of informants and many, many in need of his wares. They called him Mister Menzo and he offered them a service no one else could.

Of course there was no money, but amongst slaves, there was always barter: extra rations for pilfered liquor, a debt to Menzo for a loan, perhaps some information in exchange for a satch of obscura. It was surprising what slaves would do in exchange for a single hit of a narcotic to drown their sorrows.

There came a voice behind his curtain.

'Mister Menzo?'

Menzo drew back the curtain to his den. Bleary from sleep, he rubbed his eyes and checked his chron. It was still four hours until dawn cycle but the slave dens were raucous with activity.

'What? Quickly,' snapped Menzo. He did not like to receive visitors before his shift began.

'Sabtah is dead!' cried the man. Menzo recognised him by his matted hair and the dried, flaking corners of his mouth. It was one of the drug-dependent menials. Culk, or whatever his name was. His eyes were ringed with black from insomnia, the sign of a man who had spent eighteen hours labouring and the following six in a drug-tranced stupor.

'I know that. Quieten your voice,' Menzo said. He threw back his blankets and smoothed down the front of his canvas tunic.

'Will this... this affect your trade?' Culk asked pathetically, wringing his hands with worry.

'Why would it?'

'You always said Gammadin and Sabtah didn't care enough about the slaves to mind what we did with our sleep shift. You said Muhr'd be a hard bastard to try to sneak by.'

'Shut your mouth!' snapped Menzo. He glanced around to make sure no one had heard. Muhr was now the helmsman of the ship, so to speak. Insolence towards any bond-brother was punishable by torture and death, let alone the Witchlord. He could not imagine what harm Muhr would inflict on an insolent slave.

Culk didn't seem to understand the danger of his words. His speech was slurred and his eyelids hooded. Chemicals seemed to have addled his mind. 'But you said that. You said Muhr would be a right stiff pri–'

Menzo cut him off, clapping a palm to Culk's mouth and shoving him against a bulkhead. Culk's glazed eyes suddenly widened. Menzo had stabbed him with a shiv, a screwturner for unpacking sealed crates. He twisted and Culk shuddered all over before falling slack.

As Menzo lowered Culk's body to the floor, he heard footsteps behind him.

It was a trio of slave loaders, judging by the curve of their backs and the slump of their calloused shoulders. The men had just completed a toil shift and were hurrying back to their dens for a flicker of sleep before their labour began anew.

'Long live Lord Muhr!' Menzo shouted to them, his bloodied shiv hidden in his palm.

'Long live Lord Muhr,' they chanted wearily without even acknowledging him with a look.

* * *

POUNDING DRUMS AND the squeal of a viol penetrated the citadel decks of the foreship, a constant babble of sound that suggested relentless energy. It echoed in the abyssal halls with a timbre that did not belong in the pages of man-made music. The citadels themselves were unbarred, their masters and slaves trickling out to cavort on the wide causeways that connected them.

On the stone walkway, Brother Skellion glanded a concoction of industrial chems. The abrasive substance scoured his superhuman fortitude, lapsing him in and out of consciousness. Skellion was naked, except for a loincloth of chain; today was not a day for war. He allowed himself to sink down on his palanquin as menials massaged his keg-like quadriceps. Other menials filed and polished the stubbled horns that grew across his upper back.

Since his ascension, Muhr had declared a day of celebration. For a Blood Gorgon, that meant an orgy of chem-based alcoholics, savage pleasure and pit-fighting. The young warriors of Squad Akkadia indulged themselves. The air was thick with incense, and wine had sluiced in sticky rivers across the floor.

In truth, Skellion did not care whether Sabtah or Muhr ascended. He was a young warrior, inducted two years ago, and he barely remembered Gammadin. Skellion and many other new youngbloods in the Chapter shared the same nonchalance towards the leadership struggle. As long as Muhr promised him plunder and war, Skellion cared nothing for history.

* * *

ABOARD THE CAULDRON BORN, Vigoth locked himself away in his tower, high up in the eastern shelves of the citadel deck. A sagging gambrel roof capped the iron fort that was anchored into the bulkhead, clinging to the wall like a barnacle.

Sheltered within, Chirurgeon Vigoth was left to his brooding. He was not pleased with Muhr's ascension. He was one of the coven, a witch too, but that did not make him one of Muhr's own.

Casting the bones again, he watched the runes tumble in the darkness of his vault. They landed on the sign of the Ophidian – a bad omen.

He feared for the old ways, for Vigoth himself was old. He remembered a time when the Blood Gorgons had roamed freely. There had been no limits, not physically, nor of time in their immortal age, nor of law or code to restrain them. It was precisely that which made them Blood Gorgons. It raised them above the loyalist Slave Marines who were no better than menial servants of the enthroned Emperor.

There were others within the coven who shared his views: Nabonidus, for one. They had scryed. They had cast the bones. They had prayed to the gods.

Picking up the Ophidian tablet, Vigoth traced the rune with his fingers. The serpentine lacuna was a portent of cycles, resembling a snake devouring its own tail. It symbolised destruction and the rebirth of history. Muhr would be a new beginning. But to create anew, Muhr would dismantle the old. Vigoth feared for the old with a deep conviction.

AUTOLOADERS CLICKED ON cyclical. He swivelled, and the paralysed bulk of his lascannon arms tingled gently where machine fibre was sutured to flesh nerves.

His name was Gunner-156X, but the maintenance slave jokingly referred to him as 'Sternface'.

The world outside was boundless and black, impossible for him to understand. Cocooned against the universe, human eyes attuned to nothing but signature scans.

He locked onto a target, a sudden blip on the auspex. He framed it under target lock for a brief second, and then it was gone.

Wires thrummed and electricity coursed through his veins. His focus was singular. In the distance, he heard the deep throb of celebration as the Blood Gorgons revelled. There was the sound of the ship's auspex systems sweeping the regional asteroids, bypassing debris and the looming nearby moons. He heard all these things, but his focus remained singular.

Gunner-156X was a gun servitor. His sole reason for existence was the functioning las blister 156X, a six-stack lascannon turret. A tiny pore on the oceanic hide of the *Cauldron Born*. He was hard-wired, his fleshy torso plugged at the hip into a swivel turret and his arms amputated by the triple pod lascannons affixed to his shoulder sockets.

There. A target again.

Multiple targets. Sizeable threat. Cruiser-sized craft and shoals of escorts. A swarm of unknown predators encircling the leviathan bulk of the *Cauldron Born*.

With a domino effect, defence blisters and lance ports all reported the same active reading. The entire starboard sector came alive with warning.

Gunner-156X suddenly felt alive. This was the only time that he remembered the human concept of excitement. He swivelled his las-stack, locking onto the approaching fleet. They were too far away for him to see, but he could feel them like cold pricks on his skin from the ship's hardplugged monitors.

++All automatic defences stand down. All automatic stand down++

Gunner-156X paused. His muscles twitched. Where the locking clamps of the turret connected to his shoulders he itched. He waited for the override authorization.

++Defence system down. Authorisation: Lord Anko Muhr++

Muhr...

Gunner-156X brought up his memory banks. Muhr was the master now. He knew this had not always been the case. There had been another, but the information had been blanked out. Changed. His machine mind could never bring up that data again.

++Authorisation cleared++

As the unknown fleet lurked closer, Gunner-156X powered down simultaneously alone with all the ship's defences.

THE FLEET OF Opsarus stole upon them suddenly, ambushing them from behind the flare of a gas giant. Skulking cruisers of rusted white, great shambling things, drifting together like listless corpses. They entered the *Cauldron Born's* docking bays without challenge.

No strike fighters were scrambled to intercept the intruders even as eight Light-class cruisers berthed themselves inside the Gorgons' fortress. Neither did the space hulk's lance batteries and gun towers and defence blisters fire upon them. The alarms within the docks did not sound. Void seals did not activate to trap the invaders within the exterior bulkheads.

Most Blood Gorgons, lost within the depths of their delight, did not know what had occurred. Many were still pleasure-drowsed and heavily intoxicated. After all, Lord Muhr had granted them permission– nay, he had encouraged it.

WITHIN EIGHT MINUTES of landing, squads of Plague Marines prowled the lower decks of the floating fortress. The cruisers disgorged almost five full companies of Plague Marines and several regiments of Septic infantry.

Reports were mixed as to what followed; there was considerable confusion. There were a minority of squads who had remained vigilant in the wake of Sabtah's death, Muhr's dissenters. They engaged the invaders in a brief, sporadic firefight in the Maze of Acts Martial and the slave barracks of mid-level 42. Other reports held that armed Blood Gorgons, surprised by the swiftness of the Plague Marine boarding action, could do nothing. Muhr declared on mass broad-speakers that the Nurgle Marines were allies and brothers. In any event, the invaders seized the *Cauldron Born* with minimal resistance and no casualties.

All after-action reports agreed, however, that Muhr welcomed the invaders on the mezzanine level of the ship's helm. In the vast bowels of the armoured prow, the Lord-Sorcerer knelt and greeted the captains of Nurgle. They removed their helmets and clasped forearms.

From around the ship, most of the Blood Gorgons were rounded up and herded into the ship's mezzanine prow. Disorientated and naked, they were forced to obey at gunpoint. The shamed Chaos Space Marines were manhandled, pushed and kicked like animals. The only casualty was Brother-Sergeant Kroder of Squad Zargos, shot through the skull as an example for his squad who assaulted the invaders with their bare hands. A minority managed to flee into the forgotten bowels of the ship, but it was a Pyrrhic victory. The shame was overwhelming.

Under the glittering chandeliers and candle tiers of the mid-prow, Muhr addressed his fallen Chapter, or at least those who had been shepherded there. The Lord Sorcerer pledged his allegiance to the Plague Marines and to Nurgle and grovelled. There was a sickness to his enthusiasm that was utterly at odds with the indignity and fury that raged amongst his Chapter. Even those who had supported his ascension began to doubt the wisdom of their decision.

But it would amount to an impotent rage. There was nothing the Blood Gorgons could do. Two-thirds were unarmoured and shamefully naked. They had been stripped of their weapons. Already, the Plague Marines mocked them, taunting them about desecrating their sacred suits of armour. Surrounded by a thousand Plague Marines, the Blood Gorgons became hostages aboard their own ship.

As a final shame, Opsarus the Crow appeared before them. In his Tactical Dreadnought Armour, he was a living totem of Nurgle's corpulent aesthetics. Hulking and leviathan, his every movement was like the slow grind of a tectonic plate. His head was miniscule in comparison to his mountainous body, a hooded face shaded from light, set in the centre of his torso case. Spores, chittering parasites and entire hives of honeycombed growth glowed an almost lambent green against the ivory surface of his plate. He placed a hand on Muhr's bowed head and raised the other.

'This is my conquest,' Opsarus began. His voice throbbed like a migraine. 'I will carve an empire in the name of Mortarion, and Hauts Bassiq will be the foundation for my fleet. A stepping stone. I thank you for giving me your world, and be assured I will repay you in time. But for now,' he laughed, 'I must subjugate the Blood Gorgons.'

THE PLAGUE MARINES turned the battle into a massacre. A seven-man squad of Plague Marines broke through the main line of fighting and overran into the camp itself. They clambered over the carriages, spilling the heavy steel structures onto their sides, belly-up, tracks whirling. The plainsmen's screams were driven to hysterical heights. Grenades flattened tents and wagons.

Upon hearing the wails of their relatives, a flock of mounted braves broke away from the main battle-line. Barsabbas cursed their lack of discipline. The enemy pushed through the gap that had opened up, punching through the Bassiq muster. Plague Marines spearheaded the rush, tearing braves off their mounts and snapping them with their big, broad hands.

Barsabbas tried to manoeuvre his flanking forces to plug the hole in the line, but his voice was lost under the war clamour. Three squads of Plague Marines, twenty-one warriors, punched through and doubled back to hit the mounted plainsmen from behind.

Shambling, horned, heavy with fur and mould, solid like steel-cased ogres, they tore into the braves. The line threatened to break as the solid phalanx of mounted riders became disjointed, fragmented and slowly isolated.

Frustrated, Barsabbas tried to fight his way towards the gap. A bolt shot smacked off his shoulder pad and a small-calibre round cracked his visor. Ahead, he saw a talon squall rear up and kick a Plague Marine in the pelvis with its powerful legs. It staggered the Traitor Marine. Another talon squall seized the momentary advantage and leapt onto his chest, the one-tonne beast driving the Chaos Space Marine into the ground and worrying his chest plate with a hooked beak. Others piled on, snapping and kicking at the downed enemy. A brave drew his recurve smoothly and unleashed an arrow into the Plague Marine's throat, piercing the rubberised neck seal. The Plague Marine died. It was an island of triumph amidst a rolling ocean of slaughter. Four squads of Plague Marines were too many.

The braves broke. It began at the edges first: a tense, hesitant withdrawal as the screams of the camp became too much. The braves had accounted for themselves longer than Barsabbas had expected. After all, the Plague Marines were gods to them. Malevolent gods, but no less awesome for that. In their retreat, the braves were butchered. Autocannon and heavy bolter fire chased them, chopping them down as they fled.

The camp had been overrun. Plague Marines and their Septic minions were putting the settlement to flame. Hooded men with canister packs and nozzle guns hosed the area with gas. Native kinsmen wandered about, half-dressed and confused. Some did not even try to run, for there was nowhere to go. Clothing and household items were scattered into the dirt. Black smoke and poisonous gas gathered in thick plumes.

The moment had come for Barsabbas to steal away.

He churned across the cactus fields. He stepped amongst the dead and crushed succulents, running ankle-deep through a mire of mud, gore and crushed pulp. Hobbling several paces behind, Sindul was trawled through the fields. He ran several steps and fell, dragged along by his knees, before he regained his footing and tripped again.

A rearguard of Septic infantry spotted the lone Blood Gorgon and his captive. He was a prime target, a proud trophy. They gave chase. It was a stupid thing to do and a trained officer should have known better, perhaps voxed for reinforcements or a gun platform, but their commander was riding the high of a victorious slaughter. They gave chase and Barsabbas shot them all down. He turned and emptied the last of his clip, auto-targetters skipping from one head to the next.

Without turning, Barsabbas set a hard pace up the mountain pass, heading ever north. The sounds of the massacre echoed up the valley, but Barsabbas did not look back.

THE FUNERAL MOUNTAINS were a desolate place. Creosote bushes squirmed from between the cracks of dolomite slabs and pupfish dwelled in the alluvial salt pans. Even the mountains themselves were small and steep, squeezed together to form telescopic peaks that fell away into vertical chasms. The plainsmen interred their ancestors here, marking their resting places with petroglyphs and stick-like carvings.

The rocks were soft and crumbled dangerously beneath his grip. Yet Barsabbas climbed on with an urgent recklessness. He vaulted onto a narrow ledge and dragged Sindul neck-first up the slope after him.

'Please,' choked Sindul. 'Slower.'

Barsabbas ignored him. The enemy were still giving chase. His auspex imprinted the ghostly contrails of their pursuers across his visor.

'Let me free. I can fight. Just let me see the daylight. I can fight,' Sindul wheezed.

Barsabbas tugged the chain leash sharply. 'Be still.'

He settled beyond the ledge, crouching down to minimise his profile. If the enemy insisted on pursuit, then he would give them something to find. He plucked forth one of the frag grenades that hung from chain loops across his left shoulder pad. Stilling his breath, he waited.

Beneath the rock ledge, on the rock-strewn escarpment, a single solitary reading flashed across the auspex. The target was nimble, fast, scaling up the mountain with sure-footed speed.

'Are you stupid? You don't need that,' Sindul murmured from beneath his hood.

'Quiet,' hissed Barsabbas, yanking the chain taut. The target scrambled closer.

'Are you scent blind? That doesn't smell like a cultist of Nurgle. This one stinks of milk curd.'

Barsabbas paused, testing the air with his olfactory glands. Perhaps the dark eldar had a keener sense of smell than he realised. Heightened sensory perception was a trait of the eldar species, but Barsabbas had not expected anything so acute. Although he heard the skitter of pebbles bouncing down the slope, he could smell no distinguishable scent except for the blood and gunsmoke as the updraught carried the stench from the valley below.

'Plainsman!' Sindul shouted out.

Before Barsabbas could silence the dark eldar with a swift repercussive strike, a voice answered from below. '*How de bod, koag!*'

A long-limbed man scuttled up the ledge with his hands and feet gripping the rock with practiced ease. The shredded remains of a feather crest flapped from his head. It was Gumede.

'Why did you follow me?' Barsabbas growled. His hand fell to the mace looped at his hip.

'Why did you abandon us to die?' Gumede asked. His voice cracked. He sounded wounded although he had suffered no physical injury.

'I have plans you would not understand. You have served me well, slavestock, and for that I will give you mercy. But do not seek to follow me. Leave now before I kill you.'

Gumede collapsed onto his knees. 'My people are gone. I have nowhere to go. You may kill me if you wish, Red God.'

Barsabbas began to think tactically, an instinctive cognitive process that was the product of intense psychiatric therapy. He could kill Gumede now and be done with it. It would give him little satisfaction but it would minimise further complications. Or, he could exploit Gumede as his guide. Traversing the northern badlands would be significantly more difficult without the aid of someone who knew the land.

From his brief encounter with the Bassiq, Barsabbas had learned to value their connection with the land. Perhaps this would be the most tactical choice.

'You will come with me, Gumede. I need your knowledge of these lands,' Barsabbas said.

'I will not,' Gumede said, staring vacantly. 'You are a betrayer. You left us to die. I saw you run.'

'I am a god to you,' Barsabbas reminded him, rising to his feet.

'You are a cruel god.'

Barsabbas could not understand the human's misgivings. He knew of them, but he could not understand them. Humans formed emotional connections to things, objects, people, animals. It weakened their minds. Barsabbas knew no bond but the blood bond. The blood bond was a pragmatic thing, a multiplier of combat effectiveness. He felt no love for Sargaul, only a need to recover him, like a swordsman who was missing his swordarm. There was no place in Barsabbas's consciousness for attachment. He did not understand Gumede at all.

'Battles will be won and some will be lost. Today, you lost,' Barsabbas said.

Gumede seemed to wither physically. He shook his head with a grimace. 'I've lost everything.'

'You were born naked and as you are. You have everything. You have simply lost everything you grew attached to,' Barsabbas replied. He crossed over to the rock ledge and surveyed the boiling flames of the camp far, far below.

Gumede's shoulders began to tremble. 'I lost my sons.'

Barsabbas pondered this. Finally he nodded. 'They

have no gene-seed. You can replace them,' he answered, finally enjoying his discourse with the simple-minded human.

When Gumede did not answer, Barsabbas continued. 'You will come with me. I calculate, with your field expertise and knowledge of terrain, you will reduce my travel time by approximately thirty per cent.'

'Leave me be, Red God. There is nothing else you can give me.'

'I have condemned your people. But I can still save your world.'

It was a lie, of course. Barsabbas did not believe that. But lying was another thing that humans did not understand. To lie was to weave reality. Barsabbas did not know what stopped humans from lying – some obscure social contract to their fellow man? Another self-imposed limitation that reduced effectiveness.

'How?' Gumede asked, finally looking up. To see a grown man slack-mouthed from crying disgusted Barsabbas. The Chaos Space Marine was not even sure he possessed tear ducts any more. Hiding his distaste, Barsabbas put a hand on Gumede's shoulder.

'I am a god, remember? I have plans.'

CHAPTER SIXTEEN

AND SO THEY marched together, Gumede of the Plains navigating, the Blood Gorgon striding behind with his chained, captive dark eldar in tow. They followed the trails through the cracked, stony desert. The ground resembled the skin of a blistered heel, dry and flaking. Caprids never grazed here, for the stone wore down their hooves. Between the badlands and Ur, the nomadic kinships were considered poor due to the absence of large herds. But it was also a common tale that the denizens of Ur were shrewd traders and tricked the herdsmen of the north.

There was no trade now.

The days were dark and overcast with clouds of mustard yellow. Humid gases sluiced from the atmosphere, a weak corrosive acid that only scoured the earth. The landscape looked prematurely aged, as if the cycle of seasons, renewal and ecology had ground to a halt. New roots did not sprout from the wilted remains of the old.

During the high noon, when the suns were at their harshest and Gumede and Sindul became fatigued, Barsabbas found shelter in the deathly settlements of the northern plains. The wagons and trailers were empty but stank sour with stale air. Many were marked with the white palm-print of plague. Of the dead, however, there was no sign. It seemed they did not linger in their homes.

Finally, having found some momentary peace, he unhooded the dark eldar. Blinking weakly, Sindul flinched at the sunlight. His weeks of sensory deprivation had left him dazed and psychologically depressed. The chains on his wrists, however, remained, a tightly wound knot of heavy links.

They rested in the settlement for two nights and left on the third dawn. Gumede and Sindul slept in borrowed beds, the sheets still smelling of death and their previous owners. They ate what they could from the abandoned larders, touching only the knots of chewy dried caprid and some dry sugar fruits. Barsabbas did not sleep, nor did he eat anything more than a handful of jerked meat once a day. He spent his hours watching the distance, plotting his course and cleaning, always cleaning his weapons.

As they trekked, Gumede tried to point out the shimmering silver mirages that steamed from the hot clay ground. He gestured at the exposed coal seams that ran like black blood through the gullies and ravines. Barsabbas was unimpressed. He did not even seem to be listening. The plainsman's attachment to his land irritated him and distracted him.

Sometimes, when the march became weary, Gumede even spoke of his kinship. His voice would be heavy with bitterness. He spoke fondly of his kinship and the pain his loss caused him every day.

The Chaos Space Marine simply could not understand how Gumede could come to feel emotionally involved with rocks and soil or other people. Home and family was not a concept his mind could appreciate. His lack of comprehension irritated him. It made him angry, and Barsabbas reacted to anger by killing and breaking.

Everything seemed to matter to these humans. Barsabbas wondered how their fragile intellects could withstand the emotional assault. The Blood Gorgon knew only training and fighting. There were events in-between, but those things did not matter to him. His mind had been sharpened to a singular focus. Barsabbas felt no remorse or guilt at the death of Gumede's people. There was no right or wrong, it had been an act of will in achieving a goal. He simply found no logic in the man's reasoning.

FOUR MORE DAYS in the empty badlands brought them to a broad basin of split clay. The cracked minerals tessellated with regularity like brown tiles. The basin was endorheic, an evaporated ocean floor littered with fossil and coal.

There was a familiarity to the landscape that gave Barsabbas hope. He felt a sense of recollection, and yet he knew he had never seen this place with his own eyes. Without a doubt, Sargaul had been here before, for the feeling of paramnesia was too compelling. Barsabbas remembered the smoke stacks that rose from the hard ground, fluted chimneys that belched smoke. When he peered at the furnaces through his bolter scope, he could see the barbed gravitational tanks of the dark eldar framed within his crosshairs. They were narrow, sword-shaped vehicles that hovered above the ground.

'This is the location?'

Sindul shrugged. 'This is the only place where we strike out on raid, yes. We have herded our captives here.'

Nodding, Barsabbas breathed deep, reliving the sense of familiarity that he had not really experienced firsthand. He felt Sargaul's presence, he was sure of it, as his heart rate began to rise.

'My kabal will still be here,' Sindul said, pointing with his chin.

'Then I will kill more.'

'Give me a blade, let me fight.'

Barsabbas rolled with laughter. 'You think I am stupid? Let you go and you will fight for me?' Barsabbas laughed again.

But Sindul did not. The narrow, slitted features of his face remained gravely serious.

'I cannot allow the kabal to see me captive. I would rather be a traitor.'

'I will not release your chains, eldar. Save your tricks.'

'In my culture, we have a different word for traitor. *Muri'vee*. It means gambler, or opportunist. But its meaning is more subtle than that. It means the "warrior who outplays"'.'

'You wish to be a traitor.'

'Of course. Otherwise I will be a slave in their eyes forever. Even when I am dead I will be remembered as a slave.'

On some level Barsabbas understood. Shame and pride were the foundations of character. Oddly, the dark eldar way of thinking made sense to him. Sindul could not return to his people a captive, a slave or a neutered warrior. The dark eldar would rather be remembered as a traitor. His people valued guile and cunning so at least there was conviction in that.

'Then it will be so,' Barsabbas agreed. Shame was not something that he wished his enemies to feel. He preferred they died fighting him, with a blade in their dead hands.

Barsabbas lunged forwards without warning, seized Sindul and hauled him into his lap by his hair. Sindul squirmed in response, cycling his legs in the air. Pinning Sindul's head with an elbow, Barsabbas began to unscrew the extractor cap hidden inside his mace.

Sindul's legs continued to kick as Barsabbas started to work. It was a long and relatively painful procedure, especially given Sindul's defiant thrashing. By the time Barsabbas had coaxed the larva into the extractor, Sindul's face was slick with blood. A weeping, gaping hole the size of a thumbnail puckered the flesh beneath the dark eldar's cheekbone.

Even as Sindul sulked at the indignity of his manhandling, Barsabbas hauled him up by the arm and yanked at the padlock around his neck, loosening his leash chains.

'Let me make this clear. I do this because I choose to. You present no threat to me, armed or unarmed.

A traitor may be martyred in your culture, but in mine, we punish them severely.'

THE LOWER DUNGEONS of the *Cauldron Born* were honeycombed with oubliettes. They were no more than a maddening burrow of penrose stairs, ascending and descending while never appearing to end, each leading to a dingy grille hatch. The narrow, uneven steps meandered aimlessly, unlit and moist from the coolant leaks.

It was here that heavily armed Plague Marines escorted the Blood Gorgons into the dungeons. The action was executed with a façade of cordiality almost as if the Plague Marines were extending their hand in alliance, and the captivity was only an unfortunate side effect. Yet there was an undertone of veiled aggression. Lord Muhr had assured his brethren it was only a temporary relocation, until order was restored and his new leadership firmly cemented against dissenters.

Resistance was piecemeal, as the squads had quickly been separated upon boarding to prevent any cohesive counter-attack. Many were too drug-fugued to stand. Despite this, many rioted against their captors, fighting back with teeth and fists. But their armouries had been seized and the Plague Marines had the advantage of full combat riggings. Bond-Brothers Gamsis, Paeton and Himerius were shot before order was restored.

Some, including Squad Hezirah, escaped into the uncharted burrows of the space hulk.

Over the coming days, order aboard the *Cauldron Born* continued to deteriorate. Disease spread from the Plague Marines to the sheltered immune systems of the Blood Gorgons' slaves. Within a week, hundreds within the slave warrens, barracks and engine galleys had fallen ill: fevers, dysentery, pneumonic viruses, dermal infections. Even servitors began to glitch as ailments began to affect their biosystems. Without the menials who maintained the inhabited sections of the space hulk, the vessel ceased to function effectively. Circulation systems became blocked as drainage pipes leaked. The lanterns remained unlit and food rotted in storage, untouched.

The touch of Nurgle was everywhere. Like a virus incarnate, the Plague Marine intrusion had weakened the Chapter from within. Rapidly deteriorating, it seemed Sabtah's fears had come true. The Blood Gorgons had become fractured again.

THE UNDERCELLAR WAS dark and cold but this did not matter to Sergeant Krateus, who preferred being cold and free than warm and captive. Squad Hezirah had done well to elude the round-up, processing and lockdown. They had escaped to the infirmary wards during the boarding action and smuggled themselves through a large drainage tunnel during the rioting.

Used to circulate waste, the undercellar was a series of sealed tunnels that laced the lowest sectors of the *Cauldron Born*. They had hidden there for nine days, finding a sanctuary amongst the stinking tubes and low ceilings. Waste matter sluiced through overhead grates, and the ammonia and faecal stink was stinging to their acute senses, but they bided their time.

They were weaponless, but they had escaped fully cased in their power armour. The suits aided them, sealing them against the filth. Rebreathers circulated fresh air. Glucose solutions from med-dispensers fed their bodies. But they could not continue in this way. A Traitor Marine's instinct was to fight and although they had no armaments, they felt compelled to do something.

Nine days after the seizure, Krateus finally decided they could hide no more.

Squad Hezirah headed out, following the disposal tubes. Besides Krateus, there were Brothers Cambysses, Zagros, Magan, Khabur and Ngirsu. Retrieving tact-maps from their suit databanks, they followed the blueprints towards the starboard sub-hangars. They made good progress following a sewage main that ran for almost half the length of the space hulk. In some parts, the partition grates were so thin they could hear the scrape of heavy boots above.

Somewhere between mid-sublevel 12 and some unclaimed corridors, a patrol of Plague Marines strode directly overhead. The squad froze, the shadows of the patrol ghosting across the tops of their helmets. Risking an upwards glance, Krateus counted seven Plague Marines, the sacred number of Nurgle.

They waited until the steps had faded before they began moving again. Krateus thought briefly about moving ahead and ambushing the patrol. They would need the weapons once they reached the docking hangar, but he dismissed the thought. They were too far away and the alarm would be raised too early.

Leaving the sewage main behind, the squad began

to pick their way through the smaller, upward-slanting sluice pipes. It was tough, the drainage systems tight and narrow, and for once their bulk did not aid them.

Krateus led the way, as he would need to disable the high-torque circular saws that lined the tunnels at the entrance. The fan blades shredded organic waste with powerful motors, buzzing to life when their sensor pads came into contact with any material. Being 'disposed' was a common method of culling unwanted slaves through the torque-saws.

Krateus reached out. Sensing movement, the saw began to spasm, oscillating back and forth with jerky, vicious chops. Jamming his fingers into where the blades connected to the motor, Krateus began to fidget the central shaft with his free hand. Sparks hissed like water droplets as the motor began to grind Krateus's armoured fingers. He worked quietly, trying to tear out the wires from the axial casing. The torque-saw squealed as his wedged digits began to give out. Finally, Krateus found the wires and clawed them out with the tips of his fingers, breaking their fibrous bunches.

The torque-saw died. Krateus pulled his hand from the blades. Four of the fingers on his right hand were missing. Blood drooled down his forearm and leaked from his elbow. Proud of his work, the sergeant waved his squad onwards with the stump of his right hand. There would be a time for healing later, perhaps even some augmetic implants, but for now he gave his fingers no second thought. The body was a tool to survive and preservation of non-vital body parts was mere social conditioning.

The Traitor Marine was functional as long as his primary heart still beat. As his wounds began to coagulate, Krateus had already forgotten how many fingers on his right hand he once had. He knew only to keep moving.

IT WAS NOT long before Squad Hezirah reached their intended destination point. Sub-hangar 6 was a minor docking berth. It was essentially a void-shielded garage that held a trio of Hag interceptors and a lone Thunderhawk: the *Sleepwalker*. The armoured compartment was lightly guarded by two Plague Marines, their silhouettes murky and indistinct under the low, red phos-lights.

Hezirah fanned out wide, sprinting behind the heavy fuselage. Keeping to the shadows when they could, shifting their weight lightly despite their size, they crept past the interceptors. The Hags were servitor-crewed, a swarm of vector-thrust light strikers utilised to hunt down incoming space ordnance. These would be of no use to Krateus.

He moved on to the larger *Sleepwalker*, signalling for his squad to remain stationary. The gunship was heavy-muzzled, with a brutishly stubby wingspan and thickly plated fuselage of scratched umber. Using the gunship's pectoral fins for purchase, Krateus pulled himself up by his arms until he was almost chin-level with the cockpit. The gunship squealed softly as he did so, the tiny creak of metal on metal. Krateus held his breath. But the Plague Marines did not seem to notice. Krateus closed his eyes and counted to five before he dared to move again.

Peering into the cockpit bay, he checked the console and almost swore aloud. The fuel gauge sat on empty.

Empty. Krateus felt much the same as he lowered himself down to the decking. Refuelling would be difficult without fuel servitors, and that was assuming the supply lines had not already been locked.

'Empty as we feared?' His bond, Cambysses, appeared next to him.

'Contingency,' Krateus affirmed.

Flexing the piston muscles of his forearms, Krateus with Cambysses at his side rounded the Thunderhawk and stole closer to the Plague Marine sentries. The enemy stood impassive, their backs against the wall, boltguns snug against their chest plates. Auspexes hung from their war belts, the screens greened out on standby.

Krateus knew what to do.

Without warning, he burst into a sprint, darting out from behind the *Sleepwalker*. He rushed for the cover of a Hag interceptor. He felt something clip his shoulder and heard the slamming bark of bolt shot. The Plague Marines gave chase, shouting into their vox-links as they did so. Both sentries ran past the *Sleepwalker* in pursuit.

That was when Cambysses struck. He launched himself out from hiding as the Plague Marines rushed past. He came out low in a wrestler's prowl and tackled the closest sentry into the decking. They were struggling for control of the boltgun before they hit the ground in a crashing roll. Both hands hanging on to the weapon, Cambysses summoned every shred of his upper body strength. But the

Plague Marine held on. They butted heads, grunting with animalistic exertion. Shots went off.

Suddenly, Zagros and Magan were there too. Magan coiled an arm around the Plague Marine's throat from behind and Zagros began to drag on his ankles, sweeping his legs out from underneath him. Khabur and Ngirsu rushed the second sentry. The Plague Marine brought up his weapon but could not shoot before Ngirsu closed the distance and clinched up with him.

There was a brief, intense struggle and loud shouting echoed in the armoured hangar. Another shot rang out. A moment of confusion. Cambysses had shot the Plague Marine. He had finally wrestled the boltgun free. It was more awkward than the Crusade-pattern boltgun Cambysses was familiar with, with pitted wood panelling and an archaic pre-Heresy sliding track mechanism, but it was a boltgun nonetheless. The shot tore a gaping hole in the Plague Marine's neck. Cambysses's next shot killed the Plague Marine who grappled with Ngirsu outright, with a point-blank round to the back of the head.

By then the alarms had began to wail. The low, red phos-lights were strobing to a regular heartbeat. Shot through the neck, the last sentry continued to struggle against Magan and Zagros. Cambysses pushed the stolen boltgun against the bleeding wound on his neck.

'Take him with us,' said Krateus. 'We need him.' The sergeant had retrieved the boltgun from the slain sentry and was checking the magazine.

Magan pulled the wounded Plague Marine to his

feet. The neck wound was bad, a wheezing entry hole that gaped like a skewed mouth. The exit wound was even worse, a fist-sized crater that punched out between the Plague Marine's shoulder blades.

The sentry breathed in short, ragged gasps. The serious wound made him appear slow and lethargic, but he did not seem to be in pain. He even insulted Cambysses's blood lineage as he applied pressure to his neck with his hands. The warriors of Nurgle were notoriously hardy, even by the superhuman standards of the Space Marines. Their corpulent state killed their nervous system, numbed their flesh and thickened their blood. Essentially, they became immune to pain and shock trauma.

Pressing the boltgun to the Plague Marine's head, they marched him on. Moving quickly, at a jog, prodding their hostage with the muzzle of their boltguns, they left sub-hangar 6 behind.

SHIP ALARMS ALL along sub-hangars 6, 12 and their corresponding sub-levels were keening, changing in pitch from long and wailing to short, pulsating howls. Yet on the command deck, all was quiet. Except for the constant throb of air circulators, there was no noise.

Opsarus lounged in the deck's command throne without moving.

Wire spindles and optic thread were interfaced directly into the incisions in his spinal cord. It was a crude surgical method, courtesy of Muhr, which allowed him limited access to the ship's command functions. The spindles squirted visual data into his cerebral cortex, allowing him to view the vessel's many surveillance systems.

But it was precisely the crude nature of the surgery that limited his command. He was not Gammadin, and without Gammadin's genecodes or the ship's proper acquiescence, Opsarus did not have full command of the ship's defence systems. The ship was a predatory steed, but Gammadin's steed. It had a wild sentience, whether artificial or daemonic, that recognised only Gammadin.

Opsarus could observe, but he could not control. His frustration was obvious as his fingers fidgeted, spasming every so often.

He watched impatiently as ghost images flashed behind his eyelids. He saw a rogue squad of Blood Gorgons, mostly unarmed, sprinting down a flashing red corridor. He saw his own, Plague Marines he knew by name, hesitate to shoot. Stalemate.

'This is not right. They need to shoot.'

Opsarus opened his eyes and the images faded. Muhr stood some distance away, watching the console banks that honeycombed the high walls.

'They need to shoot,' Muhr repeated, shaking his head.

'You are a strange soul, sorcerer,' Opsarus chuckled throatily.

Muhr turned away from the consoles, his voice faltering. 'Master?'

'Shooting at your own warriors? I feel no loyalty to your Blood Gorgons, but you should.'

'If we do not shoot, they will escape. We can't afford such mistakes so early. It will weaken us in the eyes of our Chapters. We have to kill them all.'

'That is Brother Hepsamon. Mine. He is a warrior with a good campaign record.'

'Master…'

'We spread lengthy misery, but Grandfather Nurgle is deeply caring towards his mortal and daemonic servants,'

Muhr did not seem to understand.

'That is where you and I differ, Muhr. Your warriors hate you, but they fear you. Mine…' Opsarus did not finish, he simply gestured to the consoles.

On the grainy pict screen, they saw Brother Hepsamon turn on his captors. There was a brief struggle. The hostage threw himself before the flashing bolt-guns of Squad Hezirah. He sacrificed himself, the black and white image falling jerkily to the ground. Waiting Plague Marines swept in for the kill.

'Loyalty. Above the carnage, the slaughter, the violence and the lust, there must exist loyalty. The backbone of a fighting force, tasty marrow. You can't make soup without marrow. Did you know that, Muhr?'

Muhr watched the screen as the last of Squad Hezirah were chopped down by bolter fire. Executed. Had the Plague Marine not given up his life, then the plan might have succeeded.

'If I give an order for my own warriors to kill their brethren, what sort of master would that make me?' Opsarus asked. 'A fat one without trust. No trust. No army,' Opsarus said, blossoming his fingers as if a plume of dust had puffed up.

'That's your flaw, Muhr. You do not know how to foster your brethren,' Opsarus said, chortling with delight.

* * *

MUHR STRODE DOWN the length of the dungeon cells, clattering the cage bars. 'Who here does not swear allegiance to me?'

He pounded the metal grates for emphasis. 'Who?'

Blood Gorgons he had known for decades, some for centuries, stared at him with hatred in their eyes. Muhr knew he was a traitor to them. He was their lord, but they would not follow him.

'Who does not recognise my place within this Chapter? Who?' Muhr repeated. He struck the cage bars with the back of his armoured fist, lashing out in his anger.

None of the Blood Gorgons answered him. They seemed unified by their animosity towards him. The thought made Muhr angrier. Even imprisoned, stripped of their wargear, the Traitor Marines were resolute. They would not give up any ground.

'I do not.'

Muhr turned, finally finding a target for his wrath. It was Captain Zuthau, Commander of 4th Company, a towering giant of a Chaos Space Marine, horned and plated from centuries of warp travel, the skin of his arms and torso pinched and ridged into chitin. Zuthau who had conquered the sea fleets of Shar. Zuthau, the very same who had orchestrated the capture and ransom of a tau caste leader. Zuthau who slew eleven Ultramarines at the Brine Delta Engagement.

Muhr stalked towards Zuthau slowly. The captain stood at the front of his cell. He wore only a breechcloth, yet he stood proud, almost a full head taller than Muhr. Zuthau. A war hero.

Muhr shot him in the belly and then the head. The

gun-shots were so loud and so sudden that Zuthau never reacted. Muhr shot him three more times as he lay in a spreading pool of blood. Zuthau's blood bond, Brother-Sergeant Arkaud, screamed in rage. He threw himself at the cage bars, spittle flying from his mouth. Muhr shot him too, emptying the rest of his bolt pistol.

Arkaud was a veteran, but Muhr reasoned it was a small sacrifice to pay for the greater good of the Chapter.

The dungeons remained quiet. No one shouted from their cells. Even those who could not see what had occurred, knew by the rusty scent of blood and the methane stink of gunsmoke.

CHAPTER SEVENTEEN

As Barsabbas approached the dark eldar encampment, he could hear the bark of warp beasts. The creatures could scent his soul. They were restless, excited, their yaps and wails carrying across the darkness of the night.

But Barsabbas could scent them too.

'Warp hounds,' Barsabbas said softly.

'*Illith-rauch*,' Sindul whispered. 'Hounds of the Arenas. Slave-maulers.'

'Tell me how to get in,' Barsabbas said.

Across the horizon, a field of spined, xerophytic grasses sprawled out for many hundreds of metres, bald patches of clay interspersed with coarse continents of low brush. Beyond that, the chimney stacks of the facility could be seen against a purple sky.

'You can't. My kabal dispatched a large raiding force here to claim our rites of plunder from the

Ner'Gal. Dozens of them. My people are vigilant when slaves are involved.'

Barsabbas narrowed his eyes at the xenos. 'Remember not to run.' The Traitor Marine rubbed his thumb across the scarred bump on Sindul's cheek.

'Watch him,' he told Gumede. Bobbing his head obediently, the chief slid a long arrow from his quiver and notched his recurve bow. Barsabbas doubted the human was any match for the dark eldar in combat, but that didn't matter. Although the dark eldar's capacity for treachery was well known, they were almost painfully predictable.

As Barsabbas turned to go, Sindul seemed to have a change of heart. 'There is one way,' he began.

'Speak. Quickly.'

'Warp beasts are blind. Or at least they do not see in the way that humans see. They sense fear, even the slightest quaver of the heart. My people use them to run down escaped slaves. It doesn't matter when the slave escapes. If you have fear, or doubt, or hesitation, they will find you.'

'So I must not regard them with any measure of emotion.'

'Yes. If you can look upon a warp beast without emotion, then they will not attack you. The warp feeds on emotion.'

Barsabbas was not sure how he could do this. A warp beast was a daemonic creation from another plane of existence. He had never seen one before, but to look upon them and feel nothing seemed an obscure challenge.

'Sindul will guide me in. Gumede, stay here,' Barsabbas ordered.

The plainsman looked hurt, as if his courage had been questioned, but Barsabbas did not care. Humans felt too much emotion, it seemed they were predisposed to hysteria just from being left in the dark. Petty things quailed the human spirit too much. Gumede would definitely be a liability.

'Stay,' he repeated to the plainsman, as if humans were particularly dull.

Barsabbas set off at a low crouch, trying to muffle his heavy footfalls in the clay soil. Sindul ghosted nearby, sliding through dry grass and saltbush without noise. The xenos could move shockingly quietly. Barsabbas had to rely on tactical training: rolling on the soles of his feet, tight control of his muscles, controlled breathing. Sindul seemed effortless. There was a springiness to his movement. The dark eldar was in total control of his body. When he needed to leap from one grass patch to another, he did it, flashing, bobbing and weaving. He moved so effortlessly it was difficult for Barsabbas to understand how it happened. If it were not for the metronome sweep of his auspex, he would have lost the dark eldar in the shadows.

As they neared the facility, Barsabbas pulled them to a halt. Ahead, prowling in front of the power station, were three warp beasts. They circled the perimeter of the main station block, guarding the drawn roller shutters. Another four drifted in and out of the shadows, guarding the fleet of dark eldar grav-tanks parked in the open. They prowled low like dogs, but shared few other canine traits. Their shoulders were thick and almost humanoid, loping arms connected to round deltoids.

'Remember what I said,' Sindul whispered.

'You are distracting me. Be quiet,' Barsabbas said
flatly. He focussed himself. Traitor Marines did not
easily suffer from fear, but they were no emotionless
servitors. The canine creatures made him tense.
Although they posed no physical threat to him, they
could raise the alarm and that gave him doubt.
Breathing deeply, he suppressed it. He felt his heart
rate and pulse dull, drawing out to a slow cadence.

Without hesitation, Barsabbas strode out into the
open.

The warp beasts started and craned their muzzles
skywards, snuffling the air. Barsabbas saw them up
close. They were wet, skinless creatures, pulsating
with exposed arteries and ridged muscle. As he stole
closer, he could smell warp sulphur on their hides.
It reminded him of Yetsugei, and he felt his heart
rate spike. As if catching a sudden scent, the warp
beasts sniffed the air in his direction. Their milk-
white eyes saw nothing but their muzzles curled
back in a growl, unsheathing strong sets of teeth.

Sindul slid past him, shaking his head with a
haughty manner. He walked past the warp beasts,
even putting out a hand to skim the muzzle of one,
almost touching them. The hounds did not react.
Emboldened by Sindul's manner, Barsabbas
reached the armoured shutters without acknowledging them. Once there he turned and saw the
three warp beasts licking their paws and gazing out
across the horizon.

To his fore, the power station seemed empty
beyond its half-drawn shutters. Through the dim
green of his visor display, Barsabbas made out

ancient machinery trapped beneath the woven fabric of thick dust. There were ripples of disturbed dust on the rockcrete ground, kicked-up tufts of floss that showed recent activity. He nodded at Sindul, a meaningful nod that reminded him of their pact.

With a soft click of his boltgun's safety, Barsabbas ducked underneath the shutters. They shuffled through the dust carpet, dragging their feet along the woolly filth to muffle their entrance.

They found themselves in some sort of workshop, dark and cavernous. Cogs, motors, pipes and power blocks were stacked like tetric sculptures, promising dark hiding places for the enemy.

'This way,' Sindul said, flitting up a short flight of metal steps that led into a porthole door. 'The slaves are beyond there.'

Wary of his captive but needing his guidance, Barsabbas rescanned the area with his auspex. Despite the high metal interference in the area, the dark eldar did not seem to be lying. The Blood Gorgon saw the distinct bumps of life signs overlaid with the contoured graphics of crowded machinery.

'Stay within my view, or I will shoot you. Give me any reason to suspect deceit, I will kill all your comrades first and I will bury you alive,' Barsabbas promised.

Sindul did not seem fazed. 'Better a proud traitor than a shameful slave,' he replied.

Barsabbas's knotwork mace flashed in the dark. 'Then go.'

* * *

BARSABBAS CLIMBED A low walkway above furnace vats. Corrugated iron and brittle board shored up gaps in the rusting mesh platform. Below, he could hear the delirious drone of voices, shrill from panic and distress.

Four dark eldar raiders stood guard over the slaves. Close to two hundred prisoners slept on the rockcrete floors, miserable huddles of bodies swathed in rat's-nest clothing. The dark eldar were taking their time to process the slaves, separating any with signs of the black wilt. Three squat furnaces were firing up for the first time in centuries. Barsabbas could imagine what the dark eldar did to dispose of the sick and infected. Further down the power station, separated by a chainlink fence, healthy slaves were being loaded into cubed shipping containers, ready to be shifted off-world.

Barsabbas fired from his vantage point. One of the dark eldar fell away, his torso ruined. Another was chopped down at the shins. In one fluid movement, Barsabbas rolled off the gantry, firing as he went. Sindul followed, landing on his knees and spinning into a forward roll. At the sound of gun-shots, the slaves rose up in one panicked tide. Confused by the sudden chaos, the dark eldar guards fired randomly, spraying splinter fire into the oncoming crowd.

Like a herder, Barsabbas fired his boltgun into the dense, mass of slaves. He switched his vox-casters to maximum amplitude and screamed so loud that the rafters rattled and the dirty-paned windows blew out. Terrified of the braying giant in armour, the captured plainsmen overran their guards. Hundreds of slaves ran amok. People began to shriek in terror.

Barsabbas blasted his voice at Sindul. 'Release the chainlinks, traitor.'

Sindul made his way across the station floor. He knifed any slave that came too close, his pair of hook swords drizzling blood. Crossing over to the holding pens, he struck the greasy padlock with a downward stroke, cutting straight through the soft iron. As the cage door swung open, Sindul had to vault up on top of the chainlink roof in order to avoid the stampede of plainsmen gushing out.

From the side doors and connective rooms, dark eldar raiders emerged from their sleep. Some were half-dressed in kimonos of dark silk. Bleary and dazed, they nonetheless began to lay down indiscriminate splinterfire.

Snatching Sindul by the back of his cuirass, Barsabbas snapped at him, spitting behind his helmet. 'Lead me to him,' he shouted. 'Lead me to him now.'

SARGAUL WAS CLOSE by. Barsabbas could feel the old pains returning, the familiar shared aches and throbs of blood binding. He was sure of it. Sargaul's presence was a tangible thing.

Almost irrational, Barsabbas began to wade through the rush of escaping slaves. Splinter shards drummed off his ceramite plates but he did not care. He fired his boltgun but his mind was not there; the targeting systems locked onto incoming muzzle flashes, framing them with triangular icons, and Barsabbas simply went through the motions. Years of incessant drilling had prepared him for such a moment.

'Where is he?'

Sindul lifted a trembling finger to the metal balconies on the second storey. 'They store personal slaves up there. Hand-picked ones.'

Barsabbas climbed onto a hydraulic elevator and ascended to the mezzanine level. Dark eldar waited for him there in various states of undress, shooting him. The boltgun fired heavy-calibre, self-propelled explosive rounds into their frail naked flesh, a scattering of tiny detonations that misted the air with fine blood. Barsabbas surged past and ran shoulder-first into a locked metal door. It flipped off its hinges, buckled by the impact.

In his rage, he found himself in the generator room. His rush to find Sargaul made him careless. He barely knew where he was. He only noticed fragmentary details, as if his mind was clouded. The room was well-appointed, for the derelict power facility. Dark eldar were purveyors of fine living, and satin sheets lined the wooden floor boards. Incense burned.

He saw warlike dark eldar soldiers, not mere raiders but heavy infantry, in the periphery of his vision but he ignored them. He saw slaves: human females that others would consider facially attractive, robust warriors, a plainsman child with amber eyes. He saw all these, but none of it mattered.

At the far end of the room, chained to the behemoth silos of coal generators, he saw Sargaul.

THE BONE TABLET was small. It was no bigger than a thumb, and upon it was carved a single ophidian coil. Even those within the Chapter who were prophetically obtuse understood the symbolism of the bone.

It was an unsettling portent and one that could have only come from the coven. The bone had been passed through the dungeon cells, slipping into the tiny venting grates at the top of their cubicles.

From there, the tablet had been passed between cells. Each receiver understood full well the meaning of the message. It was a rallying call, a message that reassured the fragmented brothers that there was still cohesion in their ranks.

Reassurance of their cohesion was what the Blood Gorgons needed to spur them into action. Captain Hazareth was of the opinion that he could access the central security block if they could provide some form of distraction to occupy their guards. Baalbek was not sure how Hazareth could break free from his cell, but the captain was adamant he would be able to, and he had never been one to make claims he could not honour.

Baalbek began to push the bone tablet through the venting grate.

A Plague Marine strode past, peering closely through his bulbous goggles at the occupants of each cell. Hearing the rubberised clip of his boots, Baalbek wadded the bone tablet tightly into the meat of his palm.

'What have you got there?' the Plague Marine asked, stopping at the Blood Gorgons' cell.

Before Baalbek could answer, his bond, Brother Hybarus, cut in. 'We're bored, brother. Our bodies should not be bound like this. Let us out to stretch our limbs.'

The Plague Marine ignored Hybarus. 'What's that in his hand?' he asked, pointing at Baalbek.

Baalbek was suddenly very conscious of the tablet clenched in his fist. They had no means of distraction yet, and now the plan would become undone. Baalbek's face remained impassive, but he cursed fluently in his head.

The cell door slid back and the Plague Marine squeezed his bulk through. 'Show me your hand,' he ordered, raising his boltgun.

Stepping in-between them, Hybarus shoved the Plague Marine on the chest. 'You dare threaten us in our own home?' he growled.

The Plague Marine struck Hybarus across the jaw with the pistol grip of his bolter. The clash of metal on bone was clearly audible. Reeling from the blow, Hybarus spat teeth. He could only turtle up, splaying his fingers across his head and keeping his forearms tight to his ribs as the Plague Marine struck him again and again with the pistol grip and solid, reverberating backfists.

In the brief episode of violence, Baalbek slipped the shard under his tongue.

'Show me your hands!' the Plague Marine shouted, snapping his attention back to Baalbek.

Freezing, Baalbek dared not swallow under the Plague Marine's stare. The Plague Marine stood over Hybarus, pressing his boltgun to the back of his skull. Even the bob of Baalbek's throat would likely admit their guilt. Slowly, deliberately he opened his hands and held them out before him.

'Mouth!' shouted the Plague Marine. 'Open your mouth!'

Baalbek hesitated. He opened his mouth slowly.

'Under your tongue!' the Plague Marine shouted.

Baalbek lifted his tongue slowly in defiance. But bared for all to see, there was nothing hidden beneath. Hybarus snorted up at their tormentor through a mouthful of blood.

The Plague Marine pressed the bolter barrel into the hollow of Baalbek's throat. 'You had something,' he said slowly. 'I saw.'

'You saw what you saw,' Baalbek replied unflinchingly.

Behind his goggles, the Plague Marine slitted his eyes. He thumbed the well-worn nub of his bolter's safety.

'Shoot me,' Baalbek dared. 'Execute an unarmed Blood Gorgon without evidence or explanation. Do it and see what riot ensues.'

'Maybe I should. Your mob is nothing more than genetic waste,' the Plague Marine hissed.

But Baalbek knew their jailer wouldn't shoot; such an act would have consequences. Although they were captives, their state of confinement was made under a pretence of eventual allegiance to the Nurgle Legions. Muhr had declared that once his rule was cemented and his dissidents disposed of, the warband would be accepted within the Plague Marine fold. Bond-Brother Baalbek would prefer death than the corpulent existence of a Plague Marine, but for now, that pretence worked in the Blood Gorgon's favour.

'I'll remember you,' the Plague Marine said silkily. 'I have a good mind for faces. You are dead. Nurgle whispers me this.'

The bond-brothers waited until their captor's footsteps drifted off down the corridor. 'Betcher's gland,' Hybarus nodded knowingly. He wormed a finger into his mouth and twisted out a loose incisor.

Swallowing the last remnants of bone, Baalbek ran his tongue along the roof of his mouth. Using the poison glands made his mouth furry and thick with mucus, as if he had eaten something highly acidic. Surgically implanted into their salivary glands, the Betcher could release a limited amount of corrosive and highly toxic venom each day. It was a practice rooted in the traditions of pre-Heresy, when the primarchs' Legions had not only been warriors but crusaders. The Astartes were preachers of the God-Emperor and their words burned with righteousness. Symbolically, they had spat on the heretical texts of old, wiping them blank through the teachings of the Imperium.

The bone tablet had corroded into a fine grit that left Baalbek swallowing saliva gingerly.

Bouncing his tooth off the cell wall, Hybarus stood up as if possessed by a great revelation. 'Our distraction,' he said, crossing over and patting the round gas pipe that provided thermal heat for the cell.

'It will be difficult, those gas mains are reinforced,' Baalbek replied. The volatile gas mains and petro-chemical pipes that carried the ship's interior energy systems were sheathed in rubberised skin almost a quarter-metre thick and laced with steel thread.

'It will take some time, but it can be done,' Hybarus concluded. He laid a hand on the pipe's python-like body, testing the smooth, solid surface. Without warning he spat on it, ejecting another broken tooth.

As Baalbek watched, the streak of clear saliva started to hiss, the chemical reaction beginning to froth the rubber sheathing. It would take some time, but it could be done.

CHAPTER EIGHTEEN

TIME COULD NOT be marked with any regularity in the dungeons. Each day cycle blurred with end-night as the Plague Marines attempted to distort their captives' senses through temporal isolation.

Captain Hazareth no longer knew how long they had been confined. Locked up and separated, he knew very little and as a commander of men, that bothered him. He knew not of the disposition of his men, their general morale or even their exact locations. But he knew they would follow him when the time came, and that was all he needed to be sure of, at least for now.

Hazareth slid the genekey out from beneath the nail of his index finger. The splinter was small and his fingers thick and flesh-bound. It took some time to coax and dig the micro-worm out but with practice, Hazareth could now do it with some ease.

He closed his eyes as he fidgeted with the genekey and resumed his count. There was no chron in his cell and Hazareth had taken to marking the passing of time by the beat of his primary heart. Forty-eight beats was one minute, 2,880 was one hour. Over thirty-four thousand for one ship cycle. Only five ship cycles until the plan was under way.

'You are distressed?' asked Blood-Sergeant Volsinii.

Hazareth opened his eyes. Volsinii was his blood bond; a warrior of four centuries. Grey-skinned and contemplative, there was little that escaped the gaze of his jet-black pupils.

'I am impatient,' Hazareth replied. It had already been two cycles since he had received word, whispered through venting grates from cell-block 22D – Baalbek and Hybarus's cell – that they would provide a diversion. Details were not shared for fear of discovery, only that he would know the diversion when he saw it. Hazareth only had to rely on the word and competence of his men. As their captain, Hazareth knew he owed them that, but it did not placate him. He could not see them, nor could he aid them.

Hazareth, Horned Horror of Medina, sat and waited.

'Do you think the genekey will work?' Volsinii whispered, drumming his fingers on his thighs.

Hazareth slipped the flesh-worm out again. It thrashed its tail like a furious eyelash. 'It is fused with the genetic structures of Gammadin and Sabtah. Of course it will,' Hazareth replied, in low, hushed tones. Volsinii was the only one who knew of his genekey, he was the only one Hazareth trusted with such information.

* * *

THE GAS MAIN was porous with holes along its inside edge. Tiny craters pockmarked a rubbery mass of melted sheathing.

'Is it clear?' Hybarus asked.

Baalbek, crouched near the sliding cage door, pressed his face to the bars and scanned the corridor. He signalled the affirmative.

Working quickly, Hybarus collected the venom from his Betcher's gland beneath his lip. There was not much left. Over the past thirty-six hours, he and Baalbek had been steadily corroding the gas main. Their venom ducts were raw.

A thin trickle of acidic venom hit the pipe with a hiss.

'They're coming!' Baalbek hissed urgently. He lumbered over to the steel bench and sat down, waving Hybarus back to his own.

A pair of Plague Marines swept past. One of them turned to stare directly at Baalbek but they did not stop.

They waited awhile, sitting in dehydrated silence. Slowly, Baalbek got off his bench and crossed to the gas main. Their corrosive fluids had chewed through the sheathing and revealed the chrome metal beneath like bare bone. They were almost through.

Desperate, Baalbek scooped some water from a watering dish their captors had left them. It tasted of bleach and ammonia, but it wet his parched mouth. Rinsing his mouth, Baalbek spat venom, aiming for the exposed metal piping. The venom settled into a pocket crater of melted rubber, sizzling with caustic froth.

With a gaseous pop, the metal disintegrated. It was

only a pinprick hole but it would be enough. Baalbek stabbed his finger into the thick piping in an attempt to crack the corroding metal. There was a metallic click. Eagerly, Baalbek prodded the pipe harder. Thermogas shot up from the breach.

'We're through!' Baalbek roared as he threw himself flat.

Then the world seemed to explode in brilliant, blinding whiteness.

THE EXPLOSION EXPELLED a bow-wave of pressure through the dungeon. Funnels of chemical smoke ripped through the air, rippling and superheated. The eruption shook the squalid cells, loosening brickwork and hatchways with over-pressure.

A squad of Plague Marines clattered down the stairs from the upper levels, issuing commands through vox-grilles. Hazareth was on his feet as soon as the Plague Marines stormed by. He was digging at the gene-worm. Wrenching it out between thumb and forefinger, Hazareth placed the genekey against the cell's gene scanner.

Despite the rusting condition of the hatchway, the gene scanner across the bolt had been meticulously cleaned and oiled. The cogitator scanned the vein structure, layout, and blood flow with an infrared sweep. A layer of light swept up the scanner, passing over the genekey and magnifying its helix structure.

There was a compliant *clunk* as the hatchway's iron bolt retracted.

Out in the corridor itself, a dense cloud of smoke reduced visibility to a pall of featureless grey. Shielding his eyes against the sting, Hazareth sprinted up the nauseating course of stairs. Volsinii followed him, scanning the corridor for signs of their guards. In the confusion, Blood Gorgons began to bray and roar, making as much noise as possible. They pounded on their cell walls as Hazareth made his way towards the guard rooms.

THERE WAS A single Plague Marine patrolling the metal stairs that led up to the central control unit. He was crouched low against the smoke, scanning the corridors in both directions as he stalked with his boltgun.

He approached the blast door of the dungeon warily. It was ajar. The forty-centimetre-thick vault door had been opened, its wheel-lock handle had been unwound, unclamping it from its seal. The Plague Marine opened his vox-link to enquire.

Hazareth got to him first. Appearing out of the smoke, sudden and murderous, Hazareth rammed the Plague Marine against the wall. Steely fingers clamped over the Plague Marine's neck seal, between the underside of his helmet and the protective parapet of his chest plate's gorget. With desperate savagery, Hazareth dashed his enemy's head against the rockcrete. Intense pressure split the ceramite casing, stress fractures spider-webbing the armour immediately. Hazareth tensed. The helmet gave way under the pincer, crunching wetly. Yet even headless, the Plague Marine stumbled, muscles twitching. He brought up his boltgun as if to shoot, stumbled again, lashed out with a desperate fist and then toppled.

'Leave that,' Volsinii urged. 'Follow me and stay close behind.'

They forged their way up the final flight of steps towards the control room. No alarm had been raised yet. Through the glass viewing blister, they could see the control room was empty. The Plague Marines had responded to the diversion as they'd hoped, leaving their posts to deal with the threat of a mass-scale riot.

Hazareth pushed open the ironclad door and stormed inside reaching for the intricate gilded console. He could hear the distant, muffled shouts and hammering in the dungeon cells. He pulled the accordion-lever to unlock the entire cell-block.

Nothing. Not even a click.

'I had no choice,' Volsinii said knowingly from behind Hazareth. 'I had no choice, Captain Hazareth.'

Desperately, Hazareth pulled again but the lever had no resistance, as if connected to nothing. It came away loosely in his hand.

'He apologises profusely, but if he truly meant it, why do it at all?' chortled a low voice.

Opsarus. Hazareth saw him ascend the stairs. His footfalls were death knells upon the metal steps. The deathmask seemed to smile at him with a tranquil serenity. In his left gauntlet, he grasped an autocannon as a man might hold a rifle.

'Why would he warn us of your escape if he is sorry? He's not sorry,' said Opsarus.

Hazareth hammered his claw across the console. Volsinii would not look at him. Staggering back, Hazareth slumped down. Trust was not a concept between the minions of Chaos, but Volsinii had been his blood bond, an extension of himself. It was

the foundation of unity between an otherwise dissident Chapter of raiders. Hazareth bayed like a
wounded bull, shaking his head unsteadily.

'Perhaps the blood bond is a mere placebo. You
give it more meaning than it truly holds,' Opsarus
laughed. It sounded forced, garbled and sudden
behind his reinforced helmet.

Hazareth attacked without warning, spearing
through the air at Opsarus. His claw bounced off the
unyielding plasteel of Crusade-era armour.

Opsarus did not even move. There was a low whir
as the autocannon rose into place, traversing like a
linear siege battery. Hulking down behind the thick
walls of his plating, Opsarus braced himself. He fired.

The blast in the confined space of the console blister was like a firestorm. A wash of flame engulfed the
room. Tearing through the foundations of the room,
the shell blew out the ceiling, disintegrated the cell-
block console and atomised the glass viewing
bubble. The expanding pressure pulled Captain Hazareth apart, and what remained was swept away by
the whirling flame.

Volsinii, too, was caught in the backblast. His
reward, although Opsarus had not intended it, was a
death that would not be remembered. Behind the
external bulwark of his suit, Opsarus breathed
cooled, internal air as ambient temperatures lingered
at the high six hundreds.

The room was now a blackened hole in the high,
vertical bulkhead. Scraps of fire still flickering
against his external layers, Opsarus made his way
down the stairs.

* * *

BARSABBAS CROSSED THE room, emptying two bolt clips within the span of ten seconds. His sole focus was to destroy everything in the room that stood between himself and Sargaul. Everything.

The dark eldar warriors, however, did not give ground. They were different from the raiders: they were incubi, proper soldiers with good firing discipline and martial bearing. They wore heavier form-fitting armour that hugged their slender frames like the black-blue of an angry hornet, and formed a solid protective block around the prize slaves.

Barsabbas had not been hurt in a long time, but his attackers hurt him now. They punished him with electrified halberds, pivoting and striking with precise, practiced strokes. Static shocks wracked his body, threatening to seize his hearts. Warning sigils and power overload warnings flashed across his visor in urgent amber. His blood began to boil. His muscles spasmed.

But his eyes were fixed on Sargaul and his finger glued to the trigger. The bolter bucked like a jackhammer, ripping out the entire clip in one continuous and sudden belch. But the incubi were too many, too hardened. A halberd bounced off Barsabbas's thigh plate, shocking his femoral nerves. Grunting, the bond-brother fell to a knee as his leg cramped and spasmed violently. Another strike chopped into his boltgun, denting its brass finish and almost wrenching the weapon from his grip.

Vomiting into his helmet as his pain receptors fired, Barsabbas raised his head to see Sindul sprint through the door. The dark eldar raider had salvaged a splinter rifle and fired it on automatic, whistling splinter shots into the room.

It was not much, but it gave Barsabbas the brief opportunity he needed. Reeling, he withdrew from the maul of incubi, ejecting his spent clip and slamming home a fresh one. Vomit drooled from his muzzle grille. He cleared his head and unhinged a grenade cluster from his chain loops.

'Down, Sindul, down!'

Tugging out the top pin, he allowed the grenades to cook off for a half count. The delay cost him a splinter shot to the neck seal. Hissing with agony, Barsabbas launched the grenade as a reflex action, skipping it across the rockcrete at an awkward angle. Turning his back to the grenade, he hunched down to make himself a small target.

There was a string of clapping eruptions. It felt like someone had pushed him from behind. He turned into the smoke and began firing. But there was little need. The half-dozen incubi had been crumpled, their bodies contorted on the ground, their limbs rearranged and pockmarked with shrapnel holes.

Above the muffled quiet of the aftershock, Barsabbas heard Sindul stir some distance away, coughing and spitting words in his harsh language. Parting the smoke with his hands, the bond-brother staggered towards his captive. Although he had taken multiple lacerations and some minor internal injuries, Barsabbas felt no pain. He could only concentrate on the pain that ached in his primary left lung – Sargaul's pain. The cold often made it worse. It was a good pain, for without it, there would be no Sargaul.

'Brother Sargaul,' Barsabbas called out.

The solitary figure in the distance raised his head, as if startled from sleep. Even at a distance, Barsabbas could recognise the deep-set eyes, the heavy brow and the missing ear.

'Sargaul,' Barsabbas said, drawing closer. He peeled off his helmet, sucking in deep breaths of dirty, smoky air.

Sargaul looked at him vacantly, expressionless. Finally, he opened his mouth as if finding the right words was an intense focus of will.

'Who are you?' he asked.

SHAFTS OF SUNLIGHT, paper-thin, glowed between the cracks of the boarded windows. They rendered the room in shades of brown, black and a hazy, egg-yolk yellow. The generator silos waited in the back, sleeping giants that had not stirred for centuries, their turbines suffocating under bales of dust. There, chained between two iron cylinders, sitting upon the tiled floor, was Bond-Brother Sargaul.

His armour had been shed in a dismembered heap nearby and a red shuka, salvaged and ill-fitting, was coiled around his waist. Track marks – bruised, ugly holes that scarred his neck, abdomen and wrists – contrasted with his white skin. Parts of him had been surgically tampered with, the sutured slits in his skin still clearly visible. The stitch marks were long and some were infected. Barsabbas could feel his own skin tingle in sympathetic horror.

'Who are you?' Sargaul repeated, words slurred by a swollen, irresponsive tongue.

'It's me, brother,' Barsabbas answered tentatively. 'Barsabbas.'

Sargaul's eyes rolled lazily in his sockets, losing interest in his bond-brother. 'I have to find their gene-seed,' he muttered to himself.

Barsabbas shook his head in disbelief. Sargaul was a veteran Astartes. His mind had been clinically, surgically and chemically conditioned. His mind had been tested through constant, rigorous stress for years before his induction. In fact, most Astartes were, to a minor degree, psychically resistant. Surely, this would be a temporary, a fleeting illness, for nothing could break Sargaul's mental wall for good.

'Reverse it!' Barsabbas shouted, grabbing Sindul by the arm and pulling him close. 'Reverse it!'

'I cannot!' Sindul squealed. 'His mind is ruined. There is nothing I can do.'

'Look at me,' Barsabbas commanded Sargaul, but his bond wasn't listening. Fitful and barely lucid, Sargaul seemed oblivious to his environment. Physically his body was there, but his mind was broken.

'Where is the gene-seed?' said Barsabbas.

Sargaul's eyes widened. 'You found the gene-seed! We can return, then.'

'No, brother. I have not. I need your help.'

Sargaul didn't seem to be listening any more. 'I must find the squad's gene-seed. We need to report back.'

'The haemonculi would have been thorough,' Sindul observed.

Barsabbas punched the ground. 'Impossible. We are Astartes.'

'Especially Astartes. Your pain thresholds are so high, you are every haemonculus's greatest fantasy.'

'What did they do to him?' Barsabbas asked quietly.

'I don't know. It is dependent on the creativeness of the torturer and the hardiness of the recipient,' Sindul said, licking his lips. 'Injecting mercury into the liver, pumping glass filings into the lungs, stimulation of exposed nerves with contact acids, selective lobotomy–'

Barsabbas startled Sindul with a roar, sending the dark eldar scuttling for cover. Enraged, the Blood Gorgon hammered the floor tiles with his fists. The tireless banging split the ceramic and brought down scuds of dust from the rafters. Still howling, Barsabbas rose to his feet and began to beat his own naked face against the generator's iron bearing covers. The ridged metal scored his cheeks and opened up raw, bleeding lines across his forehead. Sargaul began to bawl too, stimulated by the loud noise. His eyes were fixed upon the ceiling and his clumsy tongue worked in a muted, stifled yell.

BARSABBAS RAGED LONG into the night. He did not stop. Seized by an anguish that had no release, he began to tear down the processing facility with his bare hands. Bones splintered wood, boots dented metal. He raged until his fists were black and bleeding and the ceramite of his gauntlets was textured with scratches. Dust clouds fumed as he broke through the walls.

Sindul sheltered behind a storage locker as the world crashed and shook. The Traitor Marine was like an earthquake or a storm. Sindul had little hope of escaping and was helpless to stop it. Instead he hid and hoped it would pass quickly. The noise had promised such fury that even the warp beasts had fled the area, balking at such raw power.

Gumede, hiding far out in the grass fields, prayed. He thought the end of the world had come. He prayed through the night and did not stop until the first sun crested the horizon.

Finally, as the suns reached first dawn, Barsabbas grew tired. By then, he had levelled almost a third of the abandoned facility. He collapsed as the lactic build-up in his muscles reached toxic levels, beyond what even an Astartes could ignore.

Throughout all of this, Sargaul was oblivious. He sat with a look of contentment upon his face as his mind drifted.

SARGAUL LAY SUPINE before Barsabbas. Where once Sargaul had been full of martial vigour, the mindless wreck that shivered on the ground could barely be recognised as him.

'Brother. I have failed.'

Those were the last words Barsabbas said to Sargaul as he stood before him. It was hard to believe there was anything left of Sargaul. Although his body was whole, his mind had been stripped bare.

They had been warriors together. Sargaul who had burned an entire township at Port Veruca just to goad the local garrison into battle. Sargaul who had claimed over a hundred and twenty heads at the Siege of Naraskur. The very same Sargaul who culled slaves unable to lift more than a twenty-kilo standard load.

Barsabbas unchained him and lifted him unsteadily to his feet. He had almost forgotten how much taller Sargaul stood than he, and for some reason that pained him. Tall, venerable Sargaul.

Although Sargaul had no equilibrium to stand on his own, Barsabbas helped the veteran into his salvaged battle dress. He slowly dressed him in his beaten power armour, a painstaking process without the aid of servitor and retinue.

Barsabbas activated Sargaul's armour and as the suit hummed to life, the squad-linked data feed connected between the surviving members of Squad Besheba. Its initial system sweep detected almost no cognitive activity in Sargaul's brain, as if entire portions of it had been excised.

'Gene-seed. I can't go home without the gene-seed.'

It was the same monotone phrase. Barsabbas decided it must have been Sargaul's last lucid thought, the last thing on his mind before the dark eldar took it.

Barsabbas pressed Sargaul's boltgun into his hands and took one step back. In his full battle dress, Sargaul looked whole, if Barsabbas did not look into his eyes. Except that he stood upright only by the power of his armour's servo motors.

'Brother, I have failed.'

Barsabbas unscrewed the hilt of his mace. Holding the pommel he slid a slender metal tube from the shaft of the weapon, a device to extract gene-seed. The removal of the gene-seed was a duty of the Chirurgeon or Apothecary, and so it had been since the early days of the Crusade. But the progenoid gland, as the conduit of genetic data, was held in even greater reverence by the Blood Gorgons. To the bond-brother, the gene-seed was one half of their own lifeblood and each carried the device capable of executing the final duty.

He stabbed the tube into Sargaul, in the pit above the collar bone just over the lip of his neck seal. There was a tearing, agonised shudder. Sargaul's eyes opened, and suddenly they were his again. 'Reclaim our gene-seed, brother,' he said.

There was a flash of lucidity, of consciousness in those eyes. A brief return of Sargaul. For a moment, Barsabbas almost believed he'd needlessly killed his bond. But then Sargaul faded fast, descending into a dazed stupor before expiring quickly, his life signs fading on the squad link.

CHAPTER NINETEEN

THE DECISION HAD been made for Barsabbas. There was no other option but to continue to Ur. Try as he might, he could not turn back. Like the southward bird in winter, Barsabbas was drawn to his objective. It was the behavioural pattern of a Space Marine that he could not have stopped had he wanted to. The impulse to go north lingered over his every thought and action. The original objective was Ur, and until Barsabbas received express orders to desist, his mind would allow him to do nothing else but tread step after step in the direction of that cloistered, faraway place.

Strangely conscious of his mental conditioning, Barsabbas did not resist. The ability to execute their objectives until death made Space Marines the most effective military formation known to man. If Hauts Bassiq had a sea, he would walk along the ocean bed to reach his destination.

Behind him, the power facility burned. A high afternoon wind lifted the flames, taunting them higher and higher. None of that concerned him. In his mind, Barsabbas could only picture the city of Ur – a solid polygon at odds with its environment. Sealed, impervious and smooth-walled, harshly artificial amongst the softly undulating clay plains. A segregated island of man amongst an oceanic spread of feral, uncultivated wilderness.

'What now?' Gumede asked, the roaring fire reflecting off his prominent cheekbones.

'To Ur. It is what Sargaul would have done. Besides, there is little left for me. In Ur, I will find my death or my redemption.'

'You cannot enter Ur. There is no way in,' Gumede replied.

Perhaps not for a plainsman, Barsabbas accepted. Ever since the Blood Gorgons harvested the first plainsman stock to replenish their ranks, they had known of the existence of Ur. But even the Blood Gorgons had never entered the city. It was sealed, a hive world with no entrance nor exit; a ziggurat that could not be entered. In turn, the Blood Gorgons had plundered more vulnerable targets, content to claim the planet of Hauts Bassiq as their own and leave the insulated bastion to itself.

'I have entered Ur,' Sindul proclaimed smugly. Content with himself, the dark eldar lay in the dry grass. He flicked his blades playfully, tossing them and catching them.

Barsabbas remained impassive. 'Tell me how you got in.'

'It is not ruled by the Barons of Ur. The Imperial cult has fallen,' Sindul laughed.

'Don't ignore my question,' Barsabbas growled, shifting his weight menacingly. 'How did you get in?'

'I was in the retinue of my lord's firstborn son. We were guests of the Ner'Gal warlord.'

'Then we will not be welcome. You cannot enter Ur. Not in all of our stories has anyone entered Ur,' Gumede concluded, shaking his head.

'Then you have resigned yourself to following history,' said Barsabbas. 'But I have a plan.'

IT WAS NOT right for an emissary of the kabal to be treated like a pet hound. The humiliation sat like the cold edge of a rock in Sindul's boot. Although the *mon-keigh's* thrall-worm had been excised from his flesh, it would leave a humiliating scar for the rest of his days. Holding a shameful hand to his face, Sindul harboured the resentment deep in his belly.

The three had walked for six kilometres north and made camp in a high cave overlooking the alkali flats. When they looked south, black storm clouds had crept up behind them, promising a heavy afternoon downpour.

Barsabbas departed without explanation, disappearing into the storm as the curtains of rain fell over him.

It was the opportunity that Sindul had been waiting for since his capture. Only Gumede remained to watch over him, an arrow notched loosely inside his bow frame. The plainsman sat cross-legged across from him, watching the sky swirl darker.

But Barsabbas had grown careless. By extracting the slave-seed, he had removed the last reason for Sindul to stay.

The dark eldar was no longer trapped. Barsabbas

had slain the survivors of their raiding party and with it, any trace or evidence of Sindul's disgrace. Alone, Sindul could return home as the sole reminder and the events on Hauts Bassiq would be his words, and only his words. To his great fortune, the Blood Gorgon had, in a fit of human carelessness, even removed his thrall-worm.

Seizing the narrow window of opportunity, Sindul wasted no time. Although Barsabbas had confiscated his hook swords, Sindul knew the plainsman would provide little sport. Every dark eldar, no matter their status, spent considerable hours drilling on the *atami* mats of their kabal's fighting master. Even without weapons, Sindul could use the barbs and edges of his armour to vicious effect.

Sindul coiled himself into a crouch, tentatively watching the slopes for Barsabbas's return. He waited until the rain was thick and nothing could be heard except for the hollow roar of droplets hammering the clay.

That was when he attacked Gumede. The plainsman fought back gamely with clumsy fists and ill-balanced kicks, but Sindul side-sauntered and slipped them almost lazily. He struck Gumede unconscious with a flurry of pinpoint elbow strikes. Briefly, he considered killing the human for sport, but there was no time. Barsabbas could return at any moment.

As the rain began to cease, Sindul skidded down the slope. He knew the location of the kabal's lander was not far. If he recalled correctly, and his memory did not fail him, the vessel would still be docked at the power facility, hidden by now beneath metres of ash and ember.

Retracing the steps he took, slim boots churning in the clay-turned-mud, Sindul fled the way he had come.

A BROKEN NOSE was a painful thing. It obstructed breathing, forcing Gumede to take in jagged mouthfuls of air. Blood and snot simmered in his sinuses, bubbling forth to drool in thick strands down his face. Worst of all was the humiliation, a bleeding, unavoidable token of his failing. An abasement of Chief Gumede's pride.

When he heard Barsabbas crunching up the rock slope, Gumede tried to wipe the blood off his face with his wrists. There were abrasions on his chin and forehead too but his nose was still dribbling blood.

'What happened here?' Barsabbas asked as he ducked underneath the cave entrance.

Gumede backed away, apprehensive of the punishment that would be inflicted upon him. 'He escaped,' the chief admitted.

The Chaos Space Marine stood at the cave mouth, his shoulders barricading the entrance from edge to edge.

'I fought back but I couldn't hit him,' Gumede stammered, reaching for his recurve bow.

Barsabbas seemed to rumble with a throaty hum of satisfaction. 'I know, I saw him run,' he said finally. 'We can follow him now.'

'You let him escape?' Gumede asked, deeply concerned.

'Of course,' said Barsabbas. 'Where would the dark eldar go?'

Gumede shrugged, uncertain of whether it was a trick question. 'I don't know.'

'Sindul came here by ship. It means Sindul must leave the same way,' Barsabbas said, speaking slowly as if the chief were particularly dim. 'When I track him, he will lead me to that ship.'

'You will use it to enter Ur!' Gumede said, his eyes widening with revelation.

'The dark eldar ship. Guests of Ner'Gal,' Barsabbas purred. 'Sindul is a vindictive and deceitful creature, but predictable.'

'Then this was planned,' Gumede said, pinching the bridge of his nose to stem the blood. 'He could have killed me.'

The Chaos Space Marine chortled as he strode out into the rain, already checking the wet clay for prints. 'I'm surprised he didn't,' Barsabbas said.

SINDUL WAS BREATHLESS. He sucked in deep lungfuls of air to introduce some oxygen back into his burning arms. The sprint from the cave had wearied him but he could not afford to rest. Digging with his bare hands, Sindul was frantic, spurred on by the ever-present threat of discovery.

Despite the rain, the ashes were hot. As the water hit the charred framework, it hissed with steam. Sindul scooped with his palms, scraping at the ashes with his fingers. Like coals, it burnt through his kid-skin gloves, but Sindul didn't feel it. He was running out of time.

Pushing aside a burnt sheet of ply-wall, Sindul uncovered a trapdoor in the ground. The metal hatch had withstood the inferno but the lock had warped and buckled in the heat. Tearing at the trapdoor in his haste, Sindul scrambled down below.

He almost fell directly onto the hull of a ship beneath. Scrambling for purchase he swore and then began to laugh.

The *Harvester*.

An Impaler-class assault ship. Thin and spear-shaped, barbed and tapering, the ship could carry an entire crew of raiders through atmospheric entry. The thin, bat-shaped wings were underslung with pods of shardnets and a trio of dark lances jutted pugnaciously from beneath its needle prow.

It would also be Sindul's only way home.

The ship was berthed in a low, underground hangar. It had probably once been the storage cellar for the power facility, centuries ago. Sagging shelves loaded with dusty tools and pipe ends filled the surrounding walls. Empty slave cages were stacked in along the far wall, ready to be loaded into the *Harvester's* yawning rear ramp.

The ship reacted to Sindul's presence, display consoles becoming suffused by soft purple, blue and white lights. Hololithic displays were projected into the air, displaying the ship's status in rolling eldar script.

With deliberate, practiced movements, Sindul delicately placed receptor fibres. The thin threads interfaced directly with his fingertips, trailing translucent optic thread from each of his fingers. He contorted his fingers like an orchestral maestro and the ship responded with an agonisingly slow whine, the Impaler's thrust engines building power.

Then an object whistled past his ear, hard and fluid-quick. Sindul flinched, thinking something on board had malfunctioned. But when he glanced sidelong he realised it was not a malfunction at all. An arrow had thudded into his pilot cradle. A wooden shaft protruded out of the soft polyfibre headrest, a shaft fletched with a red and black feather.

Shrieking with rage, Sindul saw Gumede drop from the hatch and behind him, Barsabbas.

Wretched Barsabbas. The Blood Gorgon crashed through the hatch and landed on the thin prow. His weight made the large ship dip forwards. Steadily, hand-over-hand, Barsabbas began to climb towards the cockpit.

Sliding back the Impaler's windshield like an eyelid, Sindul drew a splinter pistol from beneath the seat. He loosed a volley of choppy shots at the Traitor Marine, the splinter fire dancing off his ceramite like solid rain. He did not manage more than six shots before Barsabbas reached him.

Barsabbas tore away the canopy and his hand shot for Sindul's throat, clamping tight and dragging him out, tearing him out of the seat restraints. He shook the eldar, knocking his limbs loosely about the air, shaking the pistol out of his hand.

'Look how senseless that was!' Barsabbas shouted through his vox-grille.

'Don't kill me!' Sindul managed to gasp in-between his head lashing back and forth upon his neck.

Maintaining the chokehold, Barsabbas unhooked the lotus-head mace from his girdle and he looped it back like a loaded catapult. 'You knew escape would be your death, but you took that choice. I see no other way.'

'You need me to fly the ship!' wailed Sindul.

Barsabbas lowered his mace. 'Why?'

'To take you to Ur.'

Barsabbas let Sindul drop bonelessly back into the pilot seat. 'I'm glad you understand. Fly well, and perhaps next time I will let you escape for real.'

'You allowed me to escape?'

'To lead me to your ship – yes. Ask yourself this, would you have ever told me? No, yours is a patient race. As frail as your physical bodies may be, the eldar have always been patient. You could have waited for years before you tried to escape to this ship. You work differently from the short-lived races.'

The dark eldar allowed himself a gloating smirk.

Barsabbas crouched down and peered closely at Sindul, his helmet almost level with the dark eldar's face. 'I may be of the Chaos flock, but I am not an irrational man. You cannot coerce me through fear alone. Take me to Ur. Do so without delay or deception. In return, when I leave Hauts Bassiq, you will be free to go.'

'*If* you leave Hauts Bassiq,' Sindul corrected.

'If I die, then you die. Can you not see that our fates are intertwined? The gods have made it so.'

THE HARVESTER CLIMBED in altitude rapidly, angled against the land below at a nauseating slant and rapidly leaving it behind. They pierced the atmospheric clouds at mach speeds. Except for the gloss of sun reflecting from the craft's nose, the world around blurred like wet paint: the brown earth, white sky and grey clouds streaking together into a tunnel of streaming colours.

Barsabbas had utilised the most destructive human war machines, but the dark eldar technology left him in a state of jealous awe. The soldier within him could not deny that the vessel was a dangerous beast. It floated, spiralled and levelled out with a dexterity that was weightless. It could change directions without the hauling, air-dragging lunges of an Imperial fighter. Most impressive of all, grav-dampeners seemed to change the interior air pressure and speed. It felt as if they were not moving at all; there was no hint of velocity or momentum. Even standing in the fluted cockpit, unable to fit into any of the seats, Barsabbas did not budge as the Impaler soared.

According to his helmet's onboard display, the craft was travelling at supersonic speeds of Mach four-point-five, but Barsabbas estimated they were going hypersonic; his power armour simply did not register faster momentum.

Gumede, terrified of the ordeal, was splayed out on the decking in the craft's bottom. Face to the padded flooring, nails digging into the soft polyfoam, the chief's eyes were closed. Barsabbas guessed he had never seen an atmospheric flier before, let alone been on board one. His cowardice, in Barsabbas's mind, was distracting and the Chaos Space Marine ignored him.

They crossed the northern badlands and overshot a narrow dust lake. From their vantage point, the pollution of Nurgle was revealed in its fullness. The intruders had poisoned, sickened and befouled everything.

The further northwards they flew, the more jaundiced the sky became. It was thick with a mustard smog that left threads of heavy pigmented vapour in the clouds. Sometimes it rained and when it did, the downpour was brown like water from a disused and rusting tap. Even with the air-vents locked and the internal vacuum of the ship pressurised, Barsabbas could smell the faint odour of ageing, the sepulchral smell of organic matter falling apart prematurely, of rocks and plant life disintegrating to dust.

The ship's hololith projection of the topography showed almost zero plant or animal life. The mass graves of talon squall and caprid were illuminated as ghost images of bones breaking the monotony of the plains. Surface radiation was detected by the ship's atmospheric reports, a steep increase the closer they flew to Ur.

As the presence of the invaders grew stronger, Barsabbas felt increasingly disconnected with himself and his Chapter. He was on his own. The Traitor Marine let that thought seep in. He had hoped to find Sargaul, but with Sargaul gone, Barsabbas was entirely alone. He allowed the feeling to enrage him, to nurture the despondency into a vengeful rage. Gammadin had preached about harnessing emotions as opposed to wasting them. He nurtured his hate and soon he forgot all about the dust and ageing and emptiness of the plains. Thinking only in terms of kill count and ammunition ratio, Barsabbas prepared himself to enter Ur.

THE CAULDRON BORN had been full of life. Its flank had twinkled with the ship lights of activity, from the release of gases, from the over-venting of the engines, the hazard lights of ship dock, The daily test firing of batteries.

But slowly, like an ailing man, the *Cauldron Born* was dying. Section by section, the ship's lights became dark as the vessel trembled. As a living machine, the *Cauldron Born* was suffering. Its ventilation systems were blocked by mucus. The warp engines became weak and lethargic, consuming more and more power just to remain at anchor.

Like the ship, entire galleries of slaves, the backbone of the space hulk, were falling to disease. Their habitation warrens were heady with the muffled heat of illness. Little by little, the lights switched off and the corridors dimmed as sections of the ship fell into disuse. The slaves who lived there were no longer. Nurgle had entered the vessel like a virus, spreading disease and wasting it away.

Many slaves were reduced to eating scraps as the vast food stores rotted supernaturally fast. The ship's hydroponic fungus farms, the mainstay of their diet, mutated, the edible mushrooms becoming pulsating, monstrous things. Stories were told of the vile, psychotropic poisons that affected victims who ate them.

Perhaps the greatest change was the deliberate dismantling of the Blood Gorgons as a functional fighting force. From the dungeons, in slow piecemeal fashion, the Blood Gorgons were released to crew their ship. Unfamiliar with the workings of the ship, Opsarus's Legion allowed the Blood Gorgons back into the fold, not as masters but as crew.

The objective was to divide them, split them: segregate and neuter their ability to communicate, organise and unify. Companies were broken down into lonely squads, dispatched to crew distant peripheries of the ship.

Some squads were relegated to maintain the warp engines, overseen by armed Plague Marines. Many were forced to perform the menial tasks of crewing surveillance systems or maintaining the ship's bridge.

When the Blood Gorgons were not utilising their combat-honed bodies for menial slavery, they attended indoctrination sessions. The high priests of Nurgle delivered fiery rhetoric about the divinity of decay. They forced the Blood Gorgons to kneel and pray for the poxes and plague of the Old Grandfather.

Many outright refused, preferring to die than face the ignominy of slavery. The riots continued. There was an attempt by Squad Archeme to reach the weapon vaults via the air circulation ducts. Several minor resistances were attempted, but without organisational capacity, each was a needless casualty.

The Blood Gorgons were no longer caged, but they were just as imprisoned. Their proud fighting companies fragmented – disarmed, controlled and infiltrated. Under this assault, there were those among the Chapter who openly admitted that the Blood Gorgons were no more.

CHAPTER TWENTY

From orbital surveillance, Ur had never registered as anything more than a rock formation, a mere smudge upon a strata-map.

But as they flew close, dropping in altitude, Barsabbas could see it in detail. From a distance, it had appeared a featureless bubble, merely a contrasting shape on the horizon. Up close it was a marvellous construct with an artistic symmetry that was not lost even on one so militantly linear.

The city seemed entirely constructed of red clay. From the smooth panes of its siege curtains, it rose up and up for eight hundred metres, forming an imposing girdle of interlaced brick art. The wall was so tall it spread out to either side and up, its edges lost to a haze of dust. With such inferior materials, the city stood only by the design of sound engineering. It resembled a termite mound, the top clustered with finger spires and punctuated with mazes of galleries. Its raw size and flat, unyielding facelessness gave it a prominent, intoxicating stature.

The monolithic walls were sealed within a void blister, a hemisphere of shields tessellating from generator pylons at ground level. Amber hexagons overlapped each other in a semi-sphere of paned scales. It was by far the thickest void shield Barsabbas had ever encountered, possibly sturdier than the shield blisters of the Mechanicus Titans. Bronze, amber and tarnished brass, the tessellating pieces reflected the sunlight like tinfoil.

Those shields, Barsabbas reckoned, had been the primary reason that the Blood Gorgons had never taken Ur. It was not that the Blood Gorgons could not break them – they had simply reasoned the costs to outweigh the gains. Ur, in some ways, protected the plainsmen of Bassiq against roving raiders from beyond the stars when the Blood Gorgons could not. Ur had protected Blood Gorgon interests, and in return the Blood Gorgons had chosen to let them live. Fight only when you have to, as Gammadin had always said.

As the *Harvester* levelled out three hundred metres from Ur proper, a vox-signal was received by the ship's tympanum, bringing Barsabbas out of his thoughts.

'Mercenary, this is Green Father. State landing protocol, archon.'

The voice that hailed them came through the *Harvester's* aural fronds. Grating and intrusive, the voice thrummed through the metallic tuning forks set into the console with crystalline audio clarity.

Sindul opened the vox-link on his console by touching the fibres connected to his ring fingers together. 'This is the archon's troupe. Mercenary awaits the Green Father's welcome. Landing protocol sequenced,' he announced loudly into the aural fronds.

Without a second of delay, one of the shield pylons deactivated, winking a hexagonal gap in the city's void blister. They flew in. The city rushed in to swallow them in a haze of sepia. The sudden change in atmospheric light was disorientating. Sunlight filtered through the void shields in honeyed orange. Everything seemed suspended in amber.

The city itself rose in solid tiers. Enormous canvas awnings – perhaps half a kilometre in length – steepled each ziggurat with broad wings. Flat tiled roofs were set with perfect, geometric regularity up the stepped slope. Orthostats, pillars and open courts gave the architecture a palatial bearing.

Barsabbas constructed a mental map of Ur from his briefing, remembering everything to scale and detail. Cross-referencing his coordinates with the dark eldar ship's console display, Barsabbas remembered the ramparts contained narrow docking chutes heavily guarded by aerial defence silos. Measuring trajectory and angles of entry, he began making swift calculations in his head. 'Zoom in there,' he commanded, tapping the hololith display of the city's rampart.

Sindul's fingers danced across his console, nimble and quick, and the image magnified. There amongst the brickwork was an aperture like an archer's slit, a mere crack in the leviathan wall.

'Take us in there,' said Barsabbas.

Sindul banked the Impaler into a lazy roll and dropped level with the rampart wall. Along the port side, they saw multiple box-battery missile systems swivel to track their descent. The accusatory finger of a turbo-laser tracked them, traversing on a railed track.

'It's time, then,' Barsabbas intoned. He stowed his boltgun, mace and falchion in the storage bays and held out his wrists to Gumede. 'Bind me,' he ordered.

The plainsman hesitantly looped one of the dark eldar's barbed slave cuffs around Barsabbas's forearms. His movements were clumsy and fearful, as if he did not want to touch the Godspawn. He cinched the noose tight around both of Barsabbas's hands.

Gumede peered outside the ship's viewing ports as Ur rose above them. 'I am not sure this will work,' he said wearily, with the voice of a man resigned to death.

Barsabbas shook his head. 'It will work, as long as you both play your part.'

The plan was simple. They would enter Ur and tell the truth, or at least a version of the truth. The dark eldar mercenaries had ambushed a lone Blood Gorgon survivor and captured him. Sindul, acting on behalf of the kabal, had come to negotiate a price for their Traitor Marine captive. Gumede, of course, was Sindul's personal slave, a trophy from Hauts Bassiq.

The plan was not without risks, but Barsabbas saw no other way of locating the gene-seeds or any other Blood Gorgon survivors. Ur was vast and to find a prisoner he would have to become one. Once imprisoned, Sindul would have no choice but to find and free him, lest he risk birthing a slave-scarab.

Crossing over to the pilot's seat with his hands bound, Barsabbas slapped the side of Sindul's face. The dark eldar screamed in shock, the craft jinking as he flinched. A flesh scarab latched onto his milky skin and burrowed under the flesh, creating a bulge before disappearing into the muscle layers.

'Why?' Sindul hissed.

'Do you need to ask?'

'How can the plan work if I die? You need me to free you once you are captured,' Sindul shot back.

'That's exactly why I've marked you. To ensure you do come back for me,' Barsabbas replied.

Sindul had nothing else to say. He simply touched his cheek where the flesh scarab had left a neat, red incision in his white skin.

'You are a traitor, like all of your kind,' Barsabbas said flatly. 'You have five hours to come for me. So you best keep alert.'

Those were the last words he said as the Impaler shot into the wall and into the city of Ur itself.

COMPARED TO THE plains of Hauts Bassiq, the city of Ur seemed like a different world. Sealed within its void shields and walls, it existed as a self-contained ecosystem.

Long ago prospectors, those who did not wish to wander the wastelands as nomads, had retreated to this place. They hoarded the last of the industrial engines with them and constructed the ziggurat – an ancestral symbol of human engineering. It was a construct of simple necessity, a sturdy monument of utility that has held a place within human history.

They hid there. Away from the agonising climate, away from their wayward kin. Hiding, even, from the Imperium itself who had long since assigned the status of Hauts Bassiq as 'inhospitable' and tucked the notation away in forgotten archives.

There, left to isolation, the ancestors of Ur devolved. Insular and inbred, her people became sickly and viciously paranoid. They diverged into their own puritan Imperial Cult, believing the preservation of their isolation the key to resisting corruption.

They became obsessed with locking out the exterior. They raised mighty walls and developed stout shields. All their industry, their resources, all of their salvaged technology was devoted to isolation. To them, the world outside Ur was a hellish, primordial place.

They emerged intermittently to trade with the distant nomads, and even then only for necessities which could not be synthetically produced in Ur's industrial mills and foundries. Beyond that, Ur had remained sealed to the outside.

Refineries in the lowest portions of the city-stack fed electricity and fuel into the city above, appropriately serving as its foundations. Pipe systems large enough to convey steam engines coiled around the bottom stacks like a nest of metal pythons. The refineries cooled the city with cyclopean turbines, recycled water and powered the void shields. The columns of smoke stacks coughed exhaust into the atmosphere, steaming the void shields with their pollutant heat.

Above this, the city itself rose in neat, geometric stacks. Brown-, red- and dust-coloured brickwork rose up in tetric tessellation, as if the buildings were blocks that slotted into each other. No bolt, nail or adhesive could be found. Like the sealed city itself, the architecture was raw and unadorned, shocking in its gigantic scale – blunt and imposing and entirely interlocked.

THE HARVESTER LANDED in the open plaza of the apex palace. From within emerged the dark eldar slaver and his servant, a gold-skinned native. The shambling Traitor Marine was dragged out of the ship's hold by means of anchor chains and barb cuffs. It took an entire platoon of Septic infantry to get him out, hauling taut on his collar, wrist and waist chains as he bayed and roared at the indignity.

The interior of the palace was broad and high-ceilinged. Ivory tiles lined every surface, cool and sterile. Some were arranged in concentric spirals while others formed hypnotic helix patterns across the ceiling. It might have once been beautiful, but there was an air of darkness that spoke of its new occupiers. The tall windows were muffled by dark, heavy drapes to seal out the golden light. Septic soldiers patrolled the corridors or stood sentry in the galleries.

The monstrous captive was led to the council chamber, where the barons of Ur had once held court.

Much had changed since the coming of Nurgle. The tiled walls were scummed with gangrenous mould and mildew. Although the High Baron still sat upon his basalt throne, his face was haggard and his hair white. He was only thirty-two years old, but had aged forty years since the invasion. He was surrounded by his subjects – courtiers, advisors and scribes. They were all dead, their skin grey and their eyes white, but some still stood upright, locked in grovelling poses. Others still had been afflicted with the black wilt. Dirty nobles in filthy finery lurked in the corners like rodents, their wrists chained to the walls as they gnashed hungry teeth and wailed from dead lungs.

As a reflection of the city itself, the court still stood as a dead shell of its former self, unchanged from the outside but decaying from within.

Next to the High Baron stood a warrior-captain of Nurgle, a Plague Marine with a rhinocerine helmet and large, swollen hands that could not fit into armoured gloves. He leaned down to whisper into the ear of the High Baron, 'You may speak.'

And so the dark eldar slaver negotiated for the price of his captive. The High Baron responded, but each time at the behest of the Plague Marine. He was a mere meat puppet, his eyes wandering aimlessly as the Plague Marine prompted words into his mouth.

They settled on a sum of two hundred slaves, of which at least one hundred would be strong, human males, to be paid immediately. In addition, two tonnes of high-grade adamantite from the newly reconstructed mines would be paid later, once the infrastructure was completed.

The deal done, the High Baron bowed low and said, 'May the Emperor protect,' with a bored expression that spoke of thoughtless monotony.

His words incurred a slap from the Plague Marine,

his large, black palms knocking the High Baron to the ground.

Without paying any attention, Sindul strode out of the chamber. The belay team of Septic soldiers following him strained against the chains of a raging Blood Gorgon.

A PROCESSION DESCENDED into the hab quarters. The Septic had yoked Barsabbas to a stone chariot, chaining his limbs tightly against the basalt frame and pulling the ponderous platform on grinding stone wheels. The denizens of Ur mobbed the streets to catch a glimpse of him. For hours, the city's address systems had announced the capture of an invader. Horn speakers from the ramparts promised the 'bringing to heel of distant enemies' – in turn, the survivors of Ur, those not too sick to show fealty to their new rulers, came to see him.

They dragged the slow and trundling carriage through the neatly ordered industrial tier with its smoking foundries and running rivers of molten metal. The air there was cooled by turbine fans the size of small hills that whooped with a constant urgency.

Barsabbas was taken up into the residential tiers, past layer upon layer of stacked, multi-storey villas. Although several children picked despondently through the street litter, the tiled streets were dominated by Nurgle infantry who patrolled in squads.

They led him up and up, towards the apex palace and where the chimney columns protruded through the void shields to belch black clouds into the atmosphere. There, the nobles and prestige castes of Ur,

those who had sworn obedience to their Nurgle overlords, now waited to see him: the captured trophy.

Barsabbas had expected more of the barony. But
the denizens of Ur were a sad, sick group, milky-
skinned from the sun protection of their void
shields, their faces wrapped in glare shades. Their
clothes were crumpled and filthy. Their isolationism
was evident amongst their fading finery; the textiles
once rich and well made were now thinning into
thread. The men preferred tabards and cloaks of
coarse hessian for their resilience, while the women
wore shawls of blues, greys and blacks for their ease
of dyeing. It seemed the barony held monopoly of
the planet's resources but had nothing to spend it on.

The isolation had eroded their health too. Even a
visitor such as Barsabbas could plainly see the effects
of inbreeding and an indigenous immune system
which hadn't been in contact with the pathogens of
an outside world. There were not many children, and
many people balanced upon crooked limbs and
crutches. Rarer still were those of an older age, for it
seemed the elderly did not live long in Ur. Barsabbas
imagined that the arrival of Nurgle would have dev-
astated their sheltered existence through mere
contact with bacteria alone.

They stood with the inattentive wistfulness of forlorn prisoners. The fusion reactors had been made to
leak on purpose, allowing Ur to irradiate its surrounding land and slowly kill its inhabitants. The
Plague Marines with their supernatural constitution
and power-armoured containment were immune,
but these people were not.

Nurgle was poisoning them slowly, yet still they

jeered Barsabbas as his open-topped carriage trundled past. They shouted and hurled pebbles although their taunts lacked conviction. Barsabbas had the sense that these people performed their hate simply to curry the favour of Nurgle. Many simply watched him with sullen looks, empathising with his state of captivity.

IN TRUTH, THE decay of Ur had begun long before the coming of Nurgle. It could be said that by some strange, or perhaps divine, consequence, Nurgle had chosen to conquer them and accelerate their process of decline.

Once, the citizens of Ur had been men of a mono-segregationist Imperial cult. They had believed Bassiq was a trial for the colonists and the God-Emperor had wanted them to remain pure, to shore up their city-state as an island of salvation amongst a sea of godless sin. They believed, in short, that Bassiq with its fire and heat were the canonical hells of the warp.

But they had devolved over the centuries. Sealed away in their city, the people had atrophied, withering like an unused muscle. The Barons of Ur, once Imperial cultists, had quickly relinquished rule to Nurgle.

Now the Barons of Ur attended their sumptuous courts, in a dining gallery in the highest tiers of their clay palace. The woven rugs that adorned the walls were threadbare with silverfish. Men roosted on ceremonial tables whose gilt was flaking to show the worn, chipped wood beneath.

High Baron Matheus Toth sat in his fading chiffon.

His ring-clustered fingers darted as he pantomimed
the act of eating. The table was bare but he supped
on a spoon delicately and drew deep breaths from a
hollow goblet.

The full court had been summoned by their Plague
Marine overseers. Some guests were living, while others, quite dead, were dragged unceremoniously from
their coffins. The unliving sat in their high-backed
chairs, their hands curled into stiff fists and their
faces unmoving. Some were bloated with corpse gas
and slumped awkwardly in their seats. The aggressive
ones had to be tied down by rope, their dignity long
faded as they shouted garbled words from black lips.

A full court of dying nobles, eating dust and
attended by the dead. The richly dark humour of
Papa Nurgle was evident in the actions of his followers. A royal guard blew on a horn with flaking lips
and the celebrations began.

SINDUL SCRATCHED HIS cheek, fidgeting incessantly at
the mark. If he probed with his fingertips, he fancied
he could detect the hard lump buried in his flesh. He
was insufferably bored.

The human architecture did not at all interest him.
The walls were too neat, too vertical and bared brick.
Ugly, wrought-iron torch brackets were fixed to the
walls, but their flames had been replaced with phos-
phor lighting. Sindul supposed the sconce fixtures
were meant to complement the dining hall but they
didn't. The placement of the long trestle tables was
not quite symmetrical and everything about the
chamber was linear and claustrophobic. Sindul had
not wanted to accept the barony's invitation to be the

guest of honour at their banquet. He felt like a vulture dining alongside rodents.

For a moment, it seemed as if the barons were watching him. Playing the part of a willing guest, Sindul's hand drifted back to the table and he picked up a fork. But then he cursed himself inwardly for he remembered they were mostly dead. Those sitting around him were mere carrion kings, propped up between living vassals. Among the hundreds of guests, more than half were corpses set into place by their household servants.

Those who were yet living regarded the xenos in their midst with weary resignation. He remembered that these barons had once been puritanical men. Now they were nothing but puppets of Nurgle. They regarded him with suspicion, and rightly so.

One of the barons leaned over and laid a chubby paw on Sindul's shoulders. His nails were yellowed from malnutrition. Sweaty, yet oddly soft with fat, he smiled at the dark eldar. When he did so, a varicose ulcer on his cheek fluttered tentatively like the heartbeat of a tiny bird.

'If you are hungry, feel free to dine on our departed guests,' the baron suggested, handing him a carving knife.

For a second, Sindul contemplated driving the fork in his hand straight into the man's face. He pondered the after-effect of fork against flesh. The baron was a moist, breathy man and Sindul wondered if he might simply deflate with a burp of corpse gas. The concept intrigued him.

But before Sindul could be tempted to respond, a sentry of Ur began to blast discordant, human music from a crude horn. At the summons, Barsabbas was wheeled in on a stone carriage, his limbs bound to the edges of a circular yoke. They had cleaned him and polished him like a trophy, scouring away the dirt to reveal the rich umber ceramite beneath.

Sindul looked away, feigning disinterest, as other nobles rose from their seats and stole closer to the living trophy.

Finally, almost reluctantly, Sindul mopped the corners of his mouth with coarse cloth and pushed his chair back with a squeal. Now was his chance.

Sindul stole close to Barsabbas. He pretended to marvel at the Traitor Marine's power armour, tracing the enamel and filigree with his hands. Deftly, he slipped a filing spike down Barsabbas's elbow joint.

'I'll find you in the asylum,' Sindul whispered.

Barsabbas nodded imperceptibly.

Touching his cheek gingerly, Sindul moved away from Barsabbas as the nobles closed around him, touching, prodding and gasping in fascination.

AFTER THE IGNOMINY of the banquet, Barsabbas was wheeled into a low-ceilinged room. They closed the door behind them with a *krr-chunk* of a wheeled lock, sealing him in a cubicle of stone. Claystone floor, the same ruddy red on the walls. Marks had been made there, the ant-like scrawl of previous prisoners, scratched, chipped and scraped into the clay brick. He could make out Imperial prayers in the mortar, written in a bastardised Low Gothic. Last testimonies, letters to loved ones, lamentations.

It very slowly dawned on him that those words etched in the stone were the scrawls of dead men.

There was a finality to the lines that sat heavily on Barsabbas's heart as he read them. He became convinced, by virtue of those lamentations, that he was now in an execution chamber.

This was where many had spent their last hours.

Renewed with sudden urgency, Barsabbas began to work the file out from his gauntlet. He wriggled his wrists, nudging the blade file out by friction, trying to bend his fingers towards his palm to catch its tip.

It slid out ever so slightly. Barsabbas changed the angle of his wrist, allowing the file to slide further out from the vambrace. It shifted, slipped out of his grasp and, to his sinking horror, fell to the floor. Barsabbas blinked in disbelief, looking at the file. He struggled for a while, straining against the shipping chain, whipping taut the bindings of his wrist. On board the *Cauldron Born*'s palaestras, it was not uncommon for Barsabbas to press three hundred and eighty kilograms of loaded kettles overhead, unarmoured. Yet the chain did not yield in the slightest.

Finally, with a last look of resignation, Barsabbas began to bite at the chains on his wrists. They were thick industrial links. At first the shock of cold metal against his teeth alarmed him, but he worked through the pain and continued to chew at the metal. A Space Marine's teeth, although heavy and calcified in order to chew indigestible proteins and fibre, could not manage iron. But by the time his calcified enamel was beginning to crack, Barsabbas had mostly lost feeling in his mouth anyway. He salivated, allowing his Betcher's gland to drool acidic mucus as he worked. He savaged the links at his wrist.

Finally the metal, softened by acid, gave way with a snap that split all his remaining molars. Spitting out flakes of iron and fragments of his own teeth, Barsabbas tore his way out of his restraints and began to recouple the power cables to his reactor pack.

The throbbing pain of shredded nerves was forgotten as his power armour hummed to life. Suddenly elevated by euphoria and the surging strength in his limbs, Barsabbas ran his tongue along the jagged rubble of his teeth.

SINDUL CLIMBED THE stairs to the palace through the darkest of routes. Humans were hostile to aliens as a rule, and the sight of a dark eldar, especially the mercenary guest of their new overlords, would not invite good intention. He shied away from the lighted puddles of street lanterns and glided along the narrow side lanes. Gumede followed a respectful distance behind, as befitted a slave. He too carried a weighty medallion of Nurgle to display his favour.

With his body swathed in a hooded cloak of steel thread, Sindul passed the palace sentries with a wave of his copper crest of Nurgle.

The servants and house boys averted their gaze as he passed them by, frightened by the spectre that brandished the favour of their Nurgle overlords. They knew of stories, passed through hushed whispers in the kitchens and launderettes, that the dark eldar slaver had single-handedly captured a great beast of Chaos. A Space Marine.

Finally, Sindul came to the asylum of Ur, a fortified wing of the palace itself. It was connected to the spires of the palace by means of a narrow sky bridge, but it seemed distant and forlorn, a finger of clay balanced on a low tier that overlooked the gas and chemical plants of the lower stack. Even from a distance, Sindul could see the asylum had no windows and despite its proportions, the only entrance was a remarkably ordinary door of very ordinary height. It almost seemed like the door had been added as an afterthought, as if the asylum had never been intended to have any windows or entrances.

A pair of sentries stood guard. They were largely ceremonial, if all that Sindul had heard of the asylum were true. The Barons of Ur, paranoid as they were, incarcerated many. Political dissidents, illegitimate noble births, heretics – any who might threaten the stability of their cloistered, pocketed existence.

But the asylum's reputation had been built upon its most dangerous inmates – psykers, mutants and killers of men. Ur was an unwholesome place and it bred strangely unwholesome deviants. If these were to escape, the pair of sentries, Sindul reckoned, could do little. But then, where would the inmates flee? Into the thirsty death of the desert sands?

Sindul waved Gumede ahead and the chief played the part of slave well, bowing subserviently. He scampered forwards and brandished his emblem of Nurgle at the door. Overbright sodium lamps mounted overhead shone directly into his eyes.

The guards studied him before shaking their heads.

'No,' one said shaking his head dismissively. The man was the younger of the pair, with a pugnaciously set jawline.

Gumede thrust the emblem before him again.

'No, the emblem does not allow,' snapped the

sentry in his stilted, idiomatic tongue. His older companion nodded sleepily.

Sindul gritted his teeth. His left hand, hidden within his cloak, closed around the hilt of his needle blade. He stepped out of the shadows and waved Gumede aside. 'I am a guest of Opsarus the Crow. His captains host my stay.'

'Are you stupid?' snapped the sentry. 'Opsarus cannot be pleased by entry here. No one. No one ever enters. If you enter, you do not leave. This is your last home.'

Sindul still held out his hand with the emblem. But he was no longer showing them. He was distracting them. The guards stared at the emblem, then back to Sindul, before returning their gaze to the emblem again.

Suddenly frustrated, the younger sentry tapped Sindul's forehead. 'No access!' he said. He poked Sindul's forehead again. 'No access.'

Upon seeing this, the older sentry took several quick steps backwards. He was wiser with age and did not have the ego of a younger man. He knew when to be quiet.

As the younger sentry continued to harass Sindul, the dark eldar clenched his jaw. The needle blade flicked out four times. It punctured pressure points and the sentries stiffened and died, their hearts stopped by poison, yet they remained standing. The young man died while pointing pugnaciously at Sindul.

The older sentry, for all his wisdom, died with his face to the wall, the dark eldar knife finding his back again and again.

* * *

THEIR VOICES WERE frantic. 'He is out! The monster is out!'

Barsabbas could hear them echo in the corridors. He could hear the clumsy drone of footfalls as the sentries gathered to find him. They would be checking each of the doors along the passage, checking their prisoners were still contained, all of the mutants, the murderers – the high threats. In their voices he heard panic and the slowed vowels of confusion.

Barsabbas knew the sentries were outmatched. This was not their game. Until several months ago, before the taking of Hauts Bassiq, these men served cloistered military tenures. Raised within the sealed city, most of these men had never heard of a Traitor Marine before, and could have no idea of their capabilities.

Barsabbas rounded a corner, looking for a weapon. He almost walked straight into a quartet of sentries. Before they could finish their initial screams of surprise, Barsabbas swept his forearm and pinned the closest against the wall, crushing his spine. The rest backed away, yelling loud, panicked words. One of them began to fumble with a lasrifle, but he was unfamiliar with it beyond ceremonial purpose. He attempted to fire on Barsabbas with the safety still caught.

Like a great fish breaking the surface, Barsabbas tossed a sentry away and flung him down the corridor. Hastily lashed shock mauls bounced off his unyielding hide. The remaining three men were tossed about like bushels of grain. Each surge of Barsabbas's steel-bound limbs threw them from wall to wall, bouncing them, breaking them. The Blood Gorgon was simply playing with them.

Finally tired of his sport, Barsabbas left the four broken sentries and kicked down the nearest door. The asylum inmates were agitated by the commotion and they had begun to keen and howl, making nonsense noise through the tiny slits of their armoured doors.

Within the cell Barsabbas had opened was a bookish-looking man. Slender from malnutrition and pale from confinement, he had a dash of handsome white hair punctuated with almost neon blue eyes.

As Barsabbas lowered his head to peer through the door, the man struck at him, hacking at his neck seal with the snapped handle of a chamber brush. Before his attack landed, Barsabbas pushed him aside contemptuously.

'Do that again and there will be no turning back,' Barsabbas growled. He should have killed the man for his mistake but he had a use for him yet.

'You are free. Go and kill. Now,' Barsabbas commanded.

Go. Kill. The slender man understood him perfectly. Without another word, the man squirmed through the door past Barsabbas and disappeared, screaming in glee down the hall.

By now the asylum was ringing with the shrill bells of disaster. Sentries huddled behind shields and shock mauls advanced in formation down the hall, three abreast. It would not be long before the Plague Marines responded in force. Barsabbas heard the sentries yell warnings. Something about 'priority inmate'. He did not know who the priority inmate was, but he noted the consternation in their tone.

He began to bash through each door he came across, punching the metal plates off their hinges. There were all kinds in there: murderers, lunatics, an ox-necked man with a hammerhead for a hand, an elderly female who appeared entirely harmless. None attacked him, as if they were minor predators cowed by a far greater threat. Some paused to thank him briefly, awed by his physical size and appearance, before sprinting away to wreak havoc on their gaolers.

Barsabbas followed a sandstone drawbridge that extended across to an otherwise inaccessible door high in the wall. The door was almost invisible in the brickwork, placed in the centre of a wall perhaps forty metres high, as if the sentries had wanted to forget about the inmate within. Judging by the hysteria of the sentries that pursued him, Barsabbas guessed the door to be of some significance. The guards tried to retract the drawbridge, grinding the ancient mechanical gears slowly. Barsabbas leapt the gap with ease as the drawbridge continued to edge back. A las-shot sparked over his head and another missed him by a wide berth. Snorting with disdain, Barsabbas ignored the sentries.

Beyond them, the last door was reinforced with thick brass bands. Not a door but a true vault seal much like the one where he himself had been confined. A coiled nest of pipes was funnelled into the door. They writhed with pumped gases, and Barsabbas scented the sugary smell of nitrous oxide and barbitane. Whatever was inside was kept in a state of controlled sedation.

For a moment, he considered the beast that lay within. He was not prone to fanciful thinking, but the occupant must have been a dangerous one, at least the equal of he. Grasping the locking wheel, Barsabbas turned it, retracting the bolts that anchored the vault seal to bolt locks in the walls. The vault popped with a hiss as the sedative gases were expelled.

The explosion caught even Barsabbas off guard.

Barsabbas was blown backwards off his feet immediately and thrown against the far wall by a wave of pressure. Light poured through the opened vault. The clay walls were melting, dripping with condensation and ice crystals. A voice so deep it was slurred issued from the light.

'I am death!'

A toddler emerged, wild-haired and chubby. He had a mole on his left cheek but besides that was unremarkable. Barsabbas rose to his feet and the boy did not reach past his shin.

'Do you know who I am?' asked the boy in fluent Low Gothic. 'I am death!'

Barsabbas smiled. He had not found a Blood Gorgon but the potential for destruction nonetheless excited him. 'I am a god and I have freed you. Go do your work.'

It amused Barsabbas that the young, crazed psyker thought himself to be an incarnation of death. A juvenile imagination combined with limitless destructive potential would always be entertaining. Moreover, the child seemed devoid of any sanity whatsoever.

He could already hear the horrified shrieks of the

sentries across the chasm of the now retracted bridge. The child psyker curled his chubby arms in an upward direction. There was a snapping of chains and the walls shook as if someone had loosed a succession of bombs. The drawbridge slammed back into place as if it were a mere toy. Clapping, the child skipped across the bridge.

The monsters had escaped, cried the sentries. All the monsters had escaped.

CHAPTER TWENTY-ONE

THE MONSTERS LEFT a trail of mangled bodies in their rampage. Even in their execution of violence, there was no order, only pandemonium and a sense of reckless savagery. Dead men lay amongst the rubble of broken walls, askew and half-buried.

A mezzanine of the second gallery had buckled over its support columns. Sentries of Ur sought shelter under the collapsed walkway, holding their shields timidly above their heads as inmates sprinted through the corridors screaming in their delirium. Far away, in the other wings of the asylum, there could be heard a low banging that was jarring in its reverberation.

Sindul danced over the remains of a sentry, delighting in seeing patterns within the blood fall. Several respectful paces behind him, Gumede stepped gingerly around the carnage. For Sindul, the asylum was festive with the sounds of pandemonium and he felt the flush of excitement. He hurried his pace at the jubilant sounds of screaming.

The pulsating beneath his orbital bone had dulled and the searing pain was beginning to numb as the slave scarab grew calm. It meant Barsabbas was nearby. Perhaps the mon-keigh would remove the creature for good once he kept his part of the bargain. Perhaps not. By his adolescence, Sindul had already murdered his own eldest half-brother over a modest gambling debt. To 'promise' was not a concept that Sindul fully understood. He knew of its existence but had never seen a proper use for it.

He followed the banging sounds. Even at a distance, it seemed the very walls were being clapped together. He hugged the walls for cover, a splinter pistol now holstered against his ribs. High overhead, hooded lamps swung fitfully with each tremor. Crushed clay, red and soft, covered the tiled floors. Metal doors and entire sections of wall had been cast to the ground, discarded like wind-torn debris.

Gumede followed behind him, his steps frustratingly loud to Sindul's ears. His bow was notched, his sinewy forearms tensed against the string. Despite the muffled, indistinct sounds of destruction, the air was still and tense. Sindul did not have the firepower to deal with one of the *Ang'mon-keigh*, especially those half-corpse giants of Nurgle. At his side, the high-velocity splinter pistol seemed terribly meagre. As a species the eldar knew no equal – subtle, savant and entirely beyond human in their intelligence and philosophy. The eldar had developed and proven theories of universal creation and expansion before humanity had invented the wheel. But even the fearsome eldar warriors in full battledress had learned to respect the savage rage of humanity's Space Marines. They fought with a fearless ignorance that the eldar could never hope to replicate…

'Sin… dul,' Gumede whispered. The chief's eyes were saucered in consternation. 'Do you feel that?'

Sindul turned on the chief, ready to lash out at him for disrupting his thought process. But he stopped himself short when he felt it too. A continuous tremor in the very walls. He placed a palm to the clay and it vibrated loosely.

'What is that?' Gumede asked.

'I–'

Sindul did not finish his sentence. The hall shook so violently that the lamps shorted out, burying them in darkness. The ground heaved underneath them as if the world had been tilted onto an angle. Sindul could hear tables and other unbolted furnishings slide across the tiles.

'Get away from the walls,' Sindul managed to shout before his voice was lost to a thunderous clash. Covering his head, the dark eldar curled up and let the world rock him back and forth. The sensation continued for some time, a violent shaking that hummed in his skull and loosened his joints.

By the time he opened his eyes, the light had returned. Or rather, light now pierced where none could before. As he opened his eyes and adjusted to the haze of brick dust, he could see that he lay on the broken edge of tiled flooring. The ground plummeted away from him, along with the entire left-hand wall and structure. An entire portion of the asylum had collapsed.

Beyond the rubble of the destroyed wing, he saw a child standing atop a stone plinth, flinging up his arms like an orchestral maestro. With one lift of his left arm, a surge of clay rose like liquid, radiating outwards with seismic tremors. With a sweep of his right wrist, a wall burst into constituent bricks. Up went both his arms in crescendo as a column of spiralling sandstone spiked from the ground to pierce through the skin of the ceiling. From behind the cover of dog-toothed rubble, sentries of Ur as well as a formation of Plague Marines hammered him with volleys of shots. The ammunition sparked harmlessly off a bubble of kinetic force around the child. It was the most terrifying performance of telekinesis Sindul had ever witnessed.

He might have remained there, mesmerised, had a hand not dragged him away from the edge. Sindul turned, expecting to see Gumede, but found himself staring into the face of a stylised gargoyle – Barsabbas.

'It is *ever* glorious to meet you,' Sindul said, scratching his cheek.

'No, it's not,' Barsabbas refuted, entirely ignorant of Sindul's sarcasm. 'You lie too much.'

Behind them all, the wall ruptured, silencing their exchange. They moved then, darting through the open storm of rock shrapnel and stray rounds. Barsabbas only paused to pick up a weapon, a stray bolter lying next to the body of a fallen Plague Marine. While the power armour of the corpse was unmarked, ugly wounds marked the bare flesh at its joints. The 'monsters' had done their work well here.

Weaving through broken remains of masonry, they left the skirmish between the inmates and their keepers behind.

THE CENTRAL BLOCKHOUSE was empty. Without fuss or ceremony Barsabbas, Sindul and Gumede made their way down the three-hundred-metre hall to the one door at its end. They followed a trail of dead and dying sentries and inmates alike.

The final door was high priority indeed. Despite the rumbles of a not-so-distant fight, a phalanx of twenty Urite sentries crouched pensively by the nickel-plated door. Their collective fear became tangible as they spotted Barsabbas approaching, as if each man were literally shaking from fright. The Traitor Marine's horned helm clapped against the ceiling and his massive, plated shoulders chafed the walls. The tiny, flitting black ghost of the dark eldar was barely noticed and Gumede, eager to indicate his apartness from the group, trailed behind nursing his bow.

At first they panicked. Their sergeant, a wilting man of middle years, flapped his arms in some sort of command or pre-drilled order. 'Release our hound!'

The phalanx remained fixed, no one willing to break away from the protective formation as the Traitor Marine drew closer, towering above them. The sergeant executed the same hesitant command signals. 'The hound, damn you. Babalu! Unlock Babalu!'

Willing themselves into action, the soldiers began

to pry open the weighty door, taking two men to haul on the steering lock and three of them to scrape it open against the suspension hinges.

Barsabbas paused. He staggered his stance into a low crouch ready to receive an oncoming charge. The door edged upon. From beyond came a roar, a challenge.

Stepping under the door frame rose the largest non-modified human Barsabbas had ever seen. At first the man seemed naked: so much flesh did he possess that his bib-and-brace did not trail down past the rolls of his knees or cover the fleshy mountains of his breast. He was easily shoulders, traps, neck and head taller than the guards and weighed perhaps in the mid-three hundred kilos. They had housed most of his torso in riveted metal sheets like a submariner's rig and his paws ended in studded spheres of solid black metal – wrecking balls, pitted, spherical and brutally physical. Barsabbas gathered that this was 'Babalu' – the thing responsible for their so-called 'tier market massacres'.

Babalu turned on his gaolers first, crashing his sledgehammer fists into their soft, yielding bodies. It was only then that Barsabbas realised the guards had been terrified not of him, but of their own weapon. Cringing, the Urite sentries pressed themselves against the walls as Babalu crushed his way through them to lunge at Barsabbas. Some Urites drew their knees to their chests and simply lay down, their will to fight having long deserted their hands and hearts.

The killer issued a challenge, unimpressed by Barsabbas's stature. He clashed his kettled hands together, sounding out his strength and stomped his legs to establish his girth. He postured, flexing the rolling orbs of his biceps. He had the gall to roar at Barsabbas with his quivering jowls.

Barsabbas slapped Babalu's head: a casual, insulting blow that bounced his skull against the wall and it cut the killer's raging screams short. Pressing up close, Barsabbas slapped him again, snake fast. The blow broke Babalu's jaw and he fell, his insensate head lolling to the side. His fat bunched obligingly as he dropped, his bulk jammed against the corridor. Dragging him by his belt, Barsabbas hauled the feared killer aside and did not bother looking at him again. He guessed the man was dead, but he did not really care.

Unnerved by Barsabbas's warpath, Gumede and Sindul followed behind, cautious of the Traitor Marine's volatile strength. As they picked their way through the antechamber, the chief stole glances at the cowering sentries and felt a deep understanding of their fear.

Barsabbas was not an enemy, yet Gumede's manner was nonetheless furtive in his monstrous presence. Barsabbas was running roughshod over everything that stood before him.

The room beyond was a cavernous cell plated in sheet alloy. The reflective floor stretched far out into the distance and the inward-slanting walls warped the reflections back and forth in a nauseating mess of images. There were no seams nor rivets to the coppery compound; the chamber appeared as if it had been hollowed out from a monolithic block of metal, and the asylum had simply been built up, brick by brick, around the maddening metal core.

The prisoner, large though he was, was buried in a cocoon of chains. They had bound him from his head to his shins in the centre of the chamber, anchoring him in mid-air with an archaic winch. Glyphs and ward runes radiated out from him in concentric circles and overlapping hexagons, poured onto the floor with red sand. Barsabbas was not well versed in daemonology, but he recognised the runes of binding and psychic dampening directly beneath the oubliette.

+*Who is that? You are familiar. I have met you before, brother*+

The words brushed across Barsabbas's mind in a quietly commanding manner. He felt compelled to answer, but realised the prisoner would not be able to hear him through the solid ball of chains.

Possessed by a sudden conviction he could not rationalise, Barsabbas kicked and brushed through the wards, sweeping the red sand away. He felt the psychic power emanating more strongly from the prisoner.

+*Lower the winch, brother*+

The voice resonated with Barsabbas. He felt compelled to obey, and indeed found himself doing so on muscle impulse. Eagerly, Barsabbas began to unwind the chains.

Outside the chamber, the pandemonium sounded like the roar of ocean waves. The military force of Nurgle would respond soon if they had not already. Barsabbas knew his time was limited.

+*Yes. We do not have long. I can feel the Plague followers coming closer now. Many of them, like a seething tide*+

Barsabbas tore at the chains with his fingers, snapping the links and shredding the metal fragments with his gauntlet tips. An involuntary cry of triumph escaped his lips: beneath was a corpse-white powder that was familiar to him, the very same pigment with which Blood Gorgons dyed their skin.

He tore at the cheeks to unveil kohled eyepits and a high forehead. The brow ridge was scarred and shelf-like, furrowed over a long, battered face. The bare skin was pitted like gravel. Dark eyes squinted at the light, as if breaking the wards had awoken their owner from some deep, dreadful sleep.

'Lord Gammadin,' Barsabbas cried, falling to his knees.

'None of that,' Gammadin intoned. The Ascendant Champion seemed to flex beneath his cocoon as his dampened mind began to rouse. In a rapidly unwinding spool, the chains fell away. Beneath was the leviathan bulk of horn and plate – the hulking body of Lord Gammadin, thick in the shoulder and heavy in the hands, with its ursine profile. The recognition brought a flutter of thrill to Barsabbas's stomach.

'It is I, Bond-Brother Barsabbas,' Gammadin replied in measured tones. 'Lower your weapon.'

Outside the vault, the sound of footfalls became urgently incisive. A great number of hostiles was gathering outside, yet Gammadin was not at all hastened. Sighing slowly, he shook his head. 'Squad Besheba have fallen, then. I do not feel their presence.'

'They have. I carry the name of Besheba on my shoulders.'

'That is a heavy burden, Barsabbas. After the shame of Govina, the other squads already see you as a weaker pack,' Gammadin said, his neutral tone not at all accusatory.

A small detonation shook the adjacent chambers. Shouts and commands, closer now. Barsabbas heard the bellow of Nurgle trumpet voxes, crackling with coordinates and field reports.

Yet still Gammadin seemed unaffected. He shook out his arms, flexing his one hand. 'How did you arrive?'

'By aerial craft. I have memorised the route from the hangar by retina overlay–'

Barsabbas was cut off as a gunshot echoed from the entrance hall. An arm-sized sliver of wall was gouged out by the slashing bolter-round. Sinking to one knee, Barsabbas returned two shots on instinct.

Ponderously, almost like a mountain harassed into motion, Gammadin met the enemy.

When Gammadin moved, he did so with an unstoppable momentum. He housed so much physical power that it took him some time to pick up speed, like a rolling avalanche, but when he began to move he did not seem capable of slowing.

Plague Marines shot at him. Those shots that Gammadin did not slap out of the air, he took against his shoulder plates. Shrapnel puffed against him. He rose in his full armour, for it had become fused to his muscle and bone, the ceramite laced throughout his entire body. Barsabbas could not even tell where Gammadin's armoured suit ended and his own flesh began. According to Barsabbas's thermal imaging, Gammadin simply appeared as a solid block of ceramite with arterial warmth running through the deepest core. The data calculated Gammadin at seventy-six per cent metal density. By his memory, even a standard template Rhino tank stood at only sixty per cent metallic composition.

As Gammadin howled and bolt shot powdered against his thickened hide, Barsabbas realised how truly destructive his lord could be.

Bodies were tossed aside. Flesh impacted violently with stone. Gammadin simply walked into and through the walls. Small-arms fire glanced against him. Contemptuous, Gammadin pushed his hand through the brick walls like damp card. He was entirely fixated upon moving.

'Lord Gammadin,' Barsabbas called. 'I have an escape route prepared in the city's flight docks.'

With grinding deliberation, Gammadin wrenched a vault seal off its hydraulic hinges. 'Go then, brother. I will follow.'

A CHANGING OF heart. Perhaps that was the one true flaw of the dark eldar race.

Try as he might, Sindul knew no other way. Deceit was like a game to him. It was a constant, never-ending puzzle that he constructed in his mind, whenever he felt himself drifting away. As a culture, the eldar saw cunning as a manifestation of culture and intellect. It was a desired trait in any courtship; indeed, an evolutionary aspect of their entire culture.

Those who could not scheme were seen as dull-witted, *pen'shaar'ul*, which meant 'waiting to be murdered'.

Sindul did not consider himself *pen'shaar'ul*. He had been scheming the moment he and Gumede reached the *Harvester*. The vessel was docked in an open courtyard and had been left unguarded. Septic foot squads passed them, too rushed to give Sindul and his slave any notice.

By Sindul's reckoning, Barsabbas was free. His thoughts were confirmed when there was a distant thrum a hundred metres above. Looking up, Sindul saw puffs of gritty smoke drifting from the distant minarets.

'We must stay and wait for de koag,' Gumede declared, as if sensing Sindul's intentions.

Sindul cast him a sidelong glance, smiling softly.

'We wait,' Gumede repeated firmly. 'You will not do to me again what you did last time.'

The chief stepped back and pointed a lasrifle at Sindul.

'This is awkward,' Sindul began. He shot forwards and parried the lasrifle aside with the blade of his hand. His left hand shot out and seized Gumede's throat.

'You made it easier than last time,' the dark eldar hissed through his teeth. He stepped inside and pushed Gumede against the ship's fuselage. With two strokes, fast and deft, Sindul severed the chief's vocal cords and collapsed his lungs.

Turning swiftly from his act, Sindul looked for any witnesses but saw none. The hangar was empty but for his own long shadow.

Satisfied that he was alone, Sindul began to pare off his own right cheek. He placed the blade against his own face and sliced deep. Startling, blinding pain almost blacked him out. The trauma would have sent a human into shock, but the dark eldar was a connoisseur of pain. The sensation, bright and heated, paralysed him temporarily. For a brief second the wound was too much even for Sindul, and he wobbled on his feet before he regained his senses. He forced down the pain and embraced its sensation until adrenaline numbed it.

Stumbling, leaking a trail of blood, Sindul lurched towards his waiting vessel.

THE CITY WAS a vast place of unfamiliar angles and planes. A lesser man would have been disorientated and lost, yet Barsabbas moved with a sure-footed purpose. The broad plazas, walkways and mezzanines were mapped to hololithic precision in his mind. Retracing the route of his stone chariot, Barsabbas drew upon his short-term memory banks and the pict-captures from his iris.

Bullets fragmented the stone around him as the enemy tracked his escape, but he was unfazed. Barsabbas ran point, snapping back shots when it suited him. He depleted the last of his ammunition, draining clip after clip. City wardens and Septic infantry soon discovered that lattice bricks did not stop bolt shells and fled at the accuracy of his fire. Automatic targetters jumped from victim to victim. Barsabbas fluttered the trigger, coaxing a constant burp of bolt-shot into the overhead ramparts and alcoves. The brickwork was chewed up, forcing the enemy deep into cover.

Behind, Gammadin strode through the smoke. His head was lowered, the antlers of his forehead pointed forwards.

'I've seen this before,' Barsabbas said, gesturing at a stone arch that framed a causeway.

They turned a corner and the view opened before them, an open courtyard framed by inverted columns. Several bodies were strewn across the flagstones – among them was a figure swathed in a red shuka.

Barsabbas recognised Gumede. His bolter flashed up immediately, looking for Sindul. Stepping past the plainsman's body, Barsabbas afforded Gumede a brief glance. He felt a curious sensation, like a man who had lost a valuable tool, but he dismissed the thought immediately.

Some metres away, the *Harvester* was already powering up as incandescent light speared from its rearward engine pods. Barsabbas tensed up at the sound. Something was wrong, or so his instincts told him. Running into the open, Barsabbas waved towards the *Harvester's* cockpit.

In response, the ship swivelled to face him, its engines flaring. Behind the glass viewing shields, Barsabbas could see Sindul's face.

The dark eldar actually smiled at him. He smiled through a face slick with blood.

At first, Barsabbas only noticed the stone pillars around him toppling. Only a second later did he hear the *Harvester's* nose-mounted cannons shriek into life.

Barsabbas was already rolling backwards as flagstones around him liquefied, rolled and rippled under the impacts of a hyper-velocity cannon. He banged back three or four shots with his bolter, feeling impotent as he did so.

As he dived for cover, Barsabbas could hear the increasing whine as the ship's vector thrusters built up to full power. The *Harvester* levitated unsteadily as its landing struts folded into its hovering belly. The cannon continued to shred the surrounding area, felling walls and flattening nearby habs.

+*Desist*+

A sudden wrench of neural pain tingled up Barsabbas's spine and into the back of his head. Screaming, Barsabbas fell into a crouch.

Simultaneously, the *Harvester* seemed to lose balance. Its starboard wing listed and tipped, grazing the flagstones. It righted itself then lurched the other way, its portside wing scraping the tiles with a flash of fat orange sparks.

Barsabbas turned around just in time to see Gammadin raise his hands and hurl another mind bolt.

+*Desist*+

This time, Barsabbas tried to duck, but ducking did nothing to protect him. The psychic pain exploded again. The word 'desist' echoed in his brain. Barsabbas almost dropped his boltgun and lost control of his hands as the muscles spasmed. Although Gammadin's will was focussed on Sindul, such was the power of his psychic echoes that Barsabbas was compelled even by their residual fury.

To his front, the *Harvester* tried to thrust up into the air. It rose hesitantly, stalled and then slammed back down. It came down so quickly that the landing struts snapped and there could be heard the bestial friction of forty tonnes of metal squealing against stone.

+*Show yourself*+

The cockpit hatch popped open with a vacuum hiss and Sindul crawled down the ledge. Blood ran down his face, into his chest and down most of his legs. His hands were clawing his head, his topknot frazzled and wild.

Gammadin crossed the courtyard and bodily lifted the dark eldar into the air with one arm, holding him face to face. 'Twice I have been betrayed by the dark eldar. Twice,' Gammadin said with disgust while studying the specimen in his grasp.

Sindul screamed. Gammadin tossed him onto the hard ground. A boot, wrought like a cloven hoof, was brought down onto Sindul's femur, breaking his leg cleanly. Gammadin stomped again and broke the eldar's other leg.

'We still need him,' Barsabbas gasped as he limped across the courtyard. He could already hear the familiar shouts of soldiers being mustered to find them, and the *crump* of approaching footsteps.

'We still need him to fly his ship.'

Gammadin nodded sagely. 'Well, he can fly without the aid of his mischievous little legs.'

At this, Sindul raised his head with a bloodied grin. When he smiled, the missing part of his right cheek twitched with exposed fat and sinew. Blood stained his teeth and drooled from his lips. 'Well, we better go, then. The enemy are coming for you,' he taunted defiantly.

CHAPTER TWENTY-TWO

ANKO MUHR HAD not expected the influence of
Grandfather Nurgle to pervade so quickly. The God
of Decay was generous to those who gave worship.
The *Cauldron Born* was ailing, its ventilation wheezing like great bellows. Even the Witchlord's own
brothers would one day succumb to the persistent
corruption of Nurgle when their wills were suffi-
ciently broken. Muhr, however, had welcomed the
Lord of Decay openly.

Had his hand always been so black? He was certain
it had not.

For as long as he could remember, Muhr's
ungloved hand had been that of a Blood Gorgon:
pale white and deeply striated, with thick bones and
the wiry muscle that bound them. It was not like that
any more.

Muhr's hand, when he held it up to his face, was

entirely black. The skin itself was so dark it was almost waxen, but not the smooth beautiful black of ebony, it was the black of rot. He had not even noticed the change in colour until his fingernails had slid off his fingertips. Now his hand pulsated, the veins engorged with tarrish blood and swelling the walls of his skin. The changes Muhr had undergone were mesmerising. The gifts of Father Nurgle, the beautification of decay, were endlessly fascinating...

'My sorcerer advisor. That has a measure of dignity to it, does it not? Sorcerer. Advisor. The second of the Crow.'

Muhr turned to see Opsarus standing in his chambers without announcement. The Crow had a habit of doing so.

'Nurgle favours you,' Opsarus continued. 'See the attention he invests in you?'

'Yes,' Muhr replied, hypnotised by his own hand.

'Behold the floral magnificence of Nurgle. Budding flowers of flesh growth, the tessellating landscapes of mould spore. There is no beauty to the unadorned,' Opsarus declared. 'Nurgle is first and foremost an artist. Tzeentch, he is a mere mischief-maker, and young Slaanesh no more than a libertine. Let us not even begin with the linear, narrow-minded aggression of Khorne.'

'Nurgle nurtures,' Muhr said. 'But I do not know how openly my bonded brethren will appreciate the artistic mutations of Nurgle.'

Opsarus's delighted tone changed suddenly. His voice lowered. 'What do you mean?'

Muhr shook his head quickly. 'I did not mean anything by it,' he stammered. 'But the Blood Gorgon companies. They may not be impressed by the physical changes that Nurgle has planned for them.'

Opsarus rose to his full height, his voice a slavering growl. 'Of course they will. You would like it. Soon they will become like you. Like me. We are one. Nurgle will take the Blood Gorgons into the fold, whether they choose it or not.'

Muhr nodded. He stared at his black hand. Nurgle was claiming him because he had allowed Nurgle into his soul. But sooner or later, whether the Blood Gorgons wished it or not, the deathly presence of the Plague Marines would change them. The spores would spread into recycled air, the viruses would consume the space hulk. The very presence of Nurgle himself would eventually change them all.

Opsarus appeared to calm down, his breath slowing to a rasp. 'Good,' he said. 'We can be brothers in Nurgle together. You, I and all your brethren. There will be peace then.'

'Of course, lord,' Muhr agreed. 'Of course.'

THE MOONS OF Hauts Bassiq were not distant beasts. They lingered shyly on the fringes of the sky, sulking behind the fiery light of their solar cousins. Small, brown and fretful, the half-dozen moons fussed across the sky, attempting to find any space, any gap that was not dominated by the harsh glare of day just so they could be seen.

It did not take long for the *Harvester* to locate the secondary moon of Hauspax once they left Bassiq's toxic atmosphere behind. The moon was a slow-moving orbiter, a fat disc that crawled across the sky when viewed from below. What could not be seen from below, however, but became clearly visible on the *Harvester's* sensor, was the leviathan bulk of the *Cauldron Born* hiding behind the moon's unseen side. Its massive energy output and warp engines lit up its presence like a miniature star. Even lurking behind the dark side of the moon, its energy signature was so radiant that it could have been picked up almost a subsector away by any armada scan.

It was a slow, steady affair to navigate the vessel by sensor scans alone. The ship's glare shutters and void shields locked them in a cabin of low blue lighting. Cocooned by insulation, it shielded them from the boiling temperature and the retina-scalding brightness of the proximate suns.

Despite their blind flight, Sindul proved to be a pilot of finesse. They circumvented the locust swarms of micrometeors that obstructed them. The xenos ship was light and comparatively fragile. Its void shields were not the thick-skinned energy-draining monsters favoured by human technology. It floated and spiralled away from oncoming high-velocity rock fragments rather than meeting them head-on, its shield shuddering briefly from hypersonic impacts with dust particles.

As they crested the moon's hemisphere, the *Cauldron Born's* shadow eclipsed the sky. Here, even amongst the depthless expanse of space, the term 'space hulk' was entirely apt. Like the hand of a god it reared its fingers across the moon's horizon. Four thousand metres away, the cityscapes of twinkling lance batteries, torpedo banks and gun turrets welcomed them with a taut, breathless tension.

Although the broadsides were capable of

dismantling continents, they were far too ponderous to harm the *Harvester*. Cloaked by refraction, the dark eldar ship pierced the *Cauldron Born's* scans, registering as nothing more than tiny space debris.

As they approached the tectonic flanks of the *Cauldron Born*, Sindul sped up. Launch tubes that clustered the vast underbelly closed rapidly. The raiding craft darted into a tube like a mosquito, swallowed up by the enormous metal hide of the floating fortress.

IT WAS TOO fast to fly by sight.

The inner launch tube of the *Cauldron Born's* flight passages became a blur, interrupted only by the strobe of overhead lights. Constructed to catapult raider craft from within the docking hangars, the tube's guide markers were not clearly visible as the dark eldar vessel reduced speed to subsonic. Sindul navigated only by the sonar projection of his Impaler, guiding the craft with whisper-soft touches.

By Barsabbas's estimate, the *Harvester* was still going too fast. It was not meant to fly at such speeds. The wingtips barely cleared the tight confines of the entry valves. They banked hard, swerving as they flew deeper into the *Cauldron Born's* sealed hangars. A human craft could never have matched the sharp brakes and switches in air pressure.

Impressively, Sindul guided the craft in blind within the pitch-black chute. As Barsabbas watched, he realised that perhaps the folklore was true. Perhaps all eldarkind, to some extent, were possessed of psychic abilities. Even looking two or three seconds into the future would allow Sindul to pre-empt each turn, bend and elevation in their flight.

A gas main flashed over the cockpit. The overhead ceiling skimmed so close that it felt like they had hit an oil slick.

It seemed as if Sindul was fading. The dark eldar was shaking uncontrollably in his pilot's sheath. As a Traitor Marine, Barsabbas had overlooked the physical and psychological ordeal he had forced upon his captive.

Yet still Sindul laboured on.

The *Harvester* finally slowed as it neared the *Cauldron Born's* first atmospheric seal. It crashed then, as if entirely spent. It dropped, steadied and dropped again like an injured bird. Sindul only just managed to level out before the *Harvester* collided belly-down. It bounced once and skidded, wings sheared by a wall as the ship spun axially on its underside.

Finally, with its rearward engines trailing flame, the ship came to a final, shuddering stop.

Barsabbas pushed the side hatch open and manoeuvred his shoulders out from the frame. Gammadin strode out after him, his ceramite-fused body entirely unaffected by the landing. Without a word, the Ascendant Champion disappeared into the darkness of the launch tube's hangar seal.

Pausing briefly, Brother Barsabbas stole one last look into the *Harvester's* interior. Under the flickering cabin glow, he could see Sindul's body slumped in its cradle. As much as the creature had irked him, the dark eldar's instinct to survive had impressed him. The utter lack of social conditioning, much like that of a Traitor Marine, meant the dark eldar could operate ruthlessly and without inhibition. That much at least was to be admired. Giving Sindul an almost imperceptible little nod, Barsabbas left, following Gammadin into the dark.

SINDUL BREATHED UNSTEADILY.

If he could see himself now, Sindul imagined he would not be the handsome creature he had once been. His pared-open face was smeared with a synthetic gel. Dried blood aproned the front of his chest and thighs. His hair framed wiry strands across his shoulders.

He did not want to look down. He already knew his legs were a mess. The grating pain in his femurs had dulled now, one of the last feelings he would remember.

Shaking uncontrollably, Sindul powered down the *Harvester's* systems. Interior lights dimmed. Resting his head against the pilot's cradle, he fought to stay awake.

THE SEPTIC INFANTRY squad clattered down the lightless launch tube, unmasking the shadows with clumsy floodlight. Striding ahead of the human infantry came Brother Pelgan, a shambling, rusting behemoth of Nurgle. Despite the calls and clicks of animals that lurked in the subterranean depths, Pelgan was by far the most fearsome thing in the region.

They made their way down into the abandoned extremities of the floating fortress. It was too dark to see what purpose these corridors once served, or where they led. In many parts the ceiling had collapsed or the mesh decking simply fell away like a cliff-face. Men stumbled often, sometimes a mere step away from some bottomless drop. It was difficult to imagine how large the *Cauldron Born* appeared from orbit, but within, Pelgan had learned to hate the enormity of its landscape. It was so easy to get lost.

It was for that same reason Pelgan had bemoaned his ill-fortune when his squad sergeant forced him to investigate a foreign object that had breached the ship. It was likely no more than a small meteorite, attracted by the gravitational pull of the floating fortress. Nonetheless, the Septic subordinates could not be entrusted to such a task. With the recent riots in the dungeons, Opsarus had become even more wary, ever more alert.

'Bring that floodlight over here,' Pelgan snapped impatiently. The Septic hauled the heavy lamp over to where Pelgan indicated and began to pan the light back and forth.

At first they saw nothing. The walls were caked with a patina of organic decay. Like an ossuary, the oxidised metal was honeycombed with fossilised plant life. Yet if Pelgan looked closely he could see gouges in the walls – high-impact damage to parts of the ceiling where flora and decay had been ripped away to reveal the raw metal of the ship's infrastructure beneath.

'Over there,' Pelgan said, checking his auspex again.

The floodlight captured something reflective in its beam. A long and fluted silhouette three times the length of a battle tank, yet organic in its sweeping pro-file. Its skin was the colour of a fresh bruise, mottled purple and black.

It took Pelgan a moment to recognise the unfamiliar shape of an alien vessel. Lying tilted on its side, exposing its wounded stomach with one snapped wing saluting upwards, the craft looked severely vulnerable.

Pelgan chortled. Finally, he thought, something worthy of investigation. He beckoned for the Septic infantry to follow. 'Hurry now,' he said as he closed in on the stranded craft.

PELGAN ENTERED THE gaping spacecraft slowly and cautiously. Nurgle had a peculiar method of execution in all things, which was evident in Pelgan's approach. The Plague Marines proceeded slowly, creeping through the xenos craft's unlit interior. Entering through the rear cargo ramp, Pelgan sent his Septic infantry ahead to probe for traps.

Judging by the residual stink of excrement and musk, Pelgan guessed that the hold of the craft had once been used to transport prisoners of war, perhaps even slaves.

As Pelgan edged forwards, the interior was rendered by his thermal imaging into unsettling alien shapes. There was an organic feel to the ship, as if its composition had been grown naturally from bone. Sweeping arches, ridged framework and smooth floors. Pelgan saw no sign of the carving, chopping and bolting so unique to human and orkoid construction.

Boots clopping softly, Pelgan entered the cockpit.

'I was counting how long it would take you.'

The voice came from the pilot cradle facing away from Pelgan. His finger hovered over the trigger of his boltgun.

Strapped into what appeared to be a command seat, Pelgan recognised the figure of a dark eldar. But not like any eldar that Pelgan had encountered in the field of war. This one was dishevelled – pale, weak, bloodied. He did not need to know much about xenos physiology to know that the eldar was in significant pain.

'I can't believe you were stupid enough to come in...' the dark eldar wheezed.

Pelgan stepped back. 'Your employment is no longer required, mercenary. Your payment is to be claimed on Hauts Bassiq. Why are you here? Answer me well, or I shall cut you up.'

The dark eldar's head lolled weakly. His chest heaved up and down with each laborious breath. 'You have less time than I...'

Pelgan's honed battle instinct made him take another step back. 'I will shoot now, mercenary. State your business.'

Suddenly, the ship's power systems hummed back into life. Consoles blinked and overhead lights fluttered brightly. Garbled alien words were emitted from the cockpit.

The dark eldar fixed his gaze on Pelgan. His pupils were enlarged, indicating severe concussion or psychic brain trauma. 'Better to die a traitor than die a slave. The Blood Gorgons, I'm sure, share that sentiment with me.'

The realisation startled Pelgan with a jolt. As far as he knew, eldar guarded their technology with a sacred reverence. Many of their machines were inhabited by the spirit stones of ancestors, eternally bound to the machine's circuitry. No eldar would die and leave their ancestors in human hands. There must be a rational reason for the creature to come here and die.

The command console displays changed rapidly. There was a sequential pattern to the display. Numbers. Numbers counting down.

Pelgan turned his enormous bulk to run.

The console's display blanked out. It blinked three times.

THE ENSUING EXPLOSION made the *Cauldron Born* cry in distress. The iron skeleton of its frame gurgled with a sonorous, keening protest. The blood vessels and throbbing capillaries that wound around the cables and pipes squirmed in agony.

On a gangway high up in a venting shaft, Barsabbas looked down. He knew, without any doubt, that the explosion was the *Harvester's* self-destruction. Far below, he saw a tiny ball of flame puff up, brief and exhilarating, before burning down into a tiny, flickering speck.

Sindul had played his part, Barsabbas at least could give him respect for that. As strange as the dark eldar species were, they had principles. Sindul preferred death over the shame of returning home as a scarred, branded slave. There was never hesitation or doubt. Sindul knew he could never escape Barsabbas. In a strange sense, Barsabbas considered Sindul had simply given up hope and preferred suicide.

'These fanatic Templars of Nurgle will respond in full ponderous strength, as they always do,' Gammadin said. 'Our one advantage is terrain and knowledge of our own home. For once, I do not know if that will suffice. '

Barsabbas counted thirteen shots left in his clip and an empty ammunition sling. Sliding out his knotwork mace, Barsabbas climbed the gantry after Gammadin, leaving the twinkling wreckage of the *Harvester* behind.

CHAPTER TWENTY-THREE

LANCE-NAIK DUMOG OF the Third Septic Infantry considered himself a superstitious man, so it was little wonder that he felt ill at ease.

At the first trumpet, Dumog had woken from his sleep, groggy with phlegm, as he did every other day. But upon rising, he saw – curiously – his own uniform folded neatly at the foot of his cot and his helmet placed on top. Dumog shook his head, not remembering folding his uniform. Nor did he remember polishing his helmet. Routine and tidiness were not cultivated amongst Nurgle's followers.

Stranger yet, Dumog remembered a time before his induction into Nurgle's ranks. Of these distant, diminished memories of a previous life, the clearest image Dumog could recall was that of neatly folded clothes and a hat, placed at the foot of his grandfather's deathbed.

Ever since then, Naik Dumog had associated death with that eerie pastiche of clothes pressed on a bed, with a hat placed ever so hauntingly atop.

The unsettling conclusion, which had been intruding upon his baffled and hesitant mind, was that he was going to die.

That deep sense of foreboding burdened his shoulders heavily, even as he attended systems operation on the *Cauldron Born's* command bridge. Although his eyes were fixed upon the console monitors at his bay, his mind was elsewhere.

His paranoia seemed to be confirmed with a final, awful certainty, when alarm sirens began to bray. Slow at first, then loud and urgent – *To arms! Children of Nurgle, to arms!* Dumog had panicked then. None of the ship's command consoles registered enemy activity either externally or on board the vessel. There had been signatures from a small foreign object piercing the vessel's dermal bulkheads, but such was its fractional size that the bridge commanders had dismissed it as nothing more than standard space debris.

Perhaps, Dumog thought with the sinking regret of hindsight, the object had been more.

The alarms continued to sound as the command bridge erupted with frantic action. The sudden surge in activity quietened Dumog's fretful nerves. The security protocols aboard the command bridge were matched by its fearsome troop disposition. Amongst the hundred-odd bridge crew and officers were three platoons of Septic heavy infantry. Overall command, however, rested with Captain Vyxant, a revered veteran who now snapped at his subordinates from a shrine-throne.

When Dumog looked up at the overhead surveillance slates, he espied panic in the decks. Septic heavy infantry were scrambling to respond, yet to what threat, they did not know. The command bridge had no answer. Neither surveillance pict nor auspex could locate any intrusion.

Through watching the hapless preparations on surveillance, the panic began to infect those crewing the bridge by osmosis. Alarms continued, yet the command bridge could give no commands. Crewmen hurried about, attempting to look occupied, but they had no direction.

Suddenly, Dumog heard a rash of gunfire beyond the command deck's blast doors. Feeling the bile rise in his gorge, he scanned through the pict feeds, trying in vain to bring up a view of the confusion outside.

'Gunfire, sir,' announced a Septic officer, stating the obvious. Muffled shots crackled.

Captain Vyxant shouted through his vox-grille for silence. 'Everything is reined in. Maintain control and keep your wits,' he began, relaying information through his squad's external comm-link. 'There has been an explosion in the lower quarters, likely a result of faulty fuel mains. The fires have been contained by control teams.'

As Vyxant spoke, Dumog coughed in relief. Tapping on his porcelain console, he began to relay Captain Vyxant's squad link through the ship's voxcasters.

'This ship is as old as the bottom of Terra's muddy sea and no sturdier. The sooner we abandon this wreck–'

Captain Vyxant did not finish his assessment. The blast doors peeled outwards with a resonant clap of expanding air. A hard wind, frost-churned and biting, slammed into the command bridge, staggering those caught in its ferocity.

What followed sent Naik Dumog diving for cover. He hid, ducking his limbs awkwardly beneath a command console. He drew his limbs in tight and could think only of his uniform, folded at the foot of his bed.

A white-skinned daemon in power armour charged through the entrance. Or rather, it was no true daemon, but a scarred and warp-fused monstrosity, more daemon than Astartes. It bellowed with an anguished, vengeance-hungry howl. It had the bottled rage of a returned king. Indeed, Dumog knew without a doubt that before him rose an ancient, regal monster. He could brand it no other word but *monster*.

The command bridge erupted with the crackle of small arms. There was a ferocity to the counter-fire that spoke of a pressing urgency. It was indiscriminate. As if they were frightened of the warrior in their midst.

And rightly so. The Blood Gorgons patriarch sent out ripples of psychic shock through the atmosphere. Every console screen blew out along the eastern bank. With his spined pincer, he pierced Captain Vyxant's chest and pinned him against the bulk of a cogitator.

Behind him, almost as an afterthought, came a Chaos Space Marine with bolter in hand. Like a retainer to his knight, the bond-brother guarded his lord's back, firing stiff single shots.

Dumog could only hide his face and recite the 'Canticles of Seven Plagues'. He had a laspistol at his hip, but he considered it worthless. There would be no point.

As the pandemonium continued, Dumog's chest became taut with fright. He could only think that Father Nurgle had reached out to warn him, when he had woken up on such a portentous day. Nearer and nearer he could hear the grinding crunch of the Ascendant Champion. Gurgling and abrupt screams of death accompanied his approach. Dumog tried to reach for his laspistol but the resolve melted from his fingertips. He could do nothing but stay hidden.

There was another crunch. Somewhere close by, a Septic soldier fired a single shot before the crunch of bone could be heard. Dumog could almost hear the presence of his killer – a deep bass rasping of his expansive lungs. He could smell his nearness – the ozone stink of psyk-craft and oiled leather.

Suddenly, Dumog was travelling through the air, horizontally at first and then vertically, with a speed that whiplashed his neck.

He could feel the sores on his face open and weep, a natural response. His killer stared at him, face-to-face, pinching him up by his collar.

It spoke with a voice like slow-moving magma. 'Did Muhr deactivate my *Cauldron Born's* defence grid?'

Dumog nodded three times. He was unable to ver-balise, for his tongue was too heavy to obey. So great was the Blood Gorgon's presence that Dumog felt compelled to grovel before one so favoured by the gods. By the time the Arch-Champion released him,

Dumog's hands were trembling too much to even key the proper sequence into the command consoles.

'Lord Opsarus has shut down the defence grids. We could not control the ship's machine spirit. It turned on us,' Dumog gasped.

'I thought so. Faithful hound. This is a part of me, we are bonded, she and I. It almost boils my blood that you would so dismiss the strength of our bindings,' his killer said. He was already lowering himself into the command throne. A net of neural cords slithered up to connect him to the ship.

As Gammadin left him cowering, Naik Dumog saw that he was the only survivor in the command bridge. The bodies of his comrades were discarded across the floor and cogitator bays. Wiping the pus from his weeping sores, the Septic Naik tried not to move, lest he incur his killer's attention again.

'What do we do with this one?'

Dumog started. He realised his killer's retainer, the Space Marine, was indicating towards him. There was an impassive yet menacing air to his voice, as if Dumog did not really exist.

By now, his killer was nestled in his command throne. The neural cords that had attached to him in rubbery tendrils began to writhe, responding in a way that Captain Vyxant or even Opsarus could not replicate. The *Cauldron Born* was trembling, as though waking from slumber.

'Leave him be,' his killer commanded.

Dumog collapsed to his knees in supplication. 'Praise be, great Lord Undivided!'

So preoccupied was Dumog in his displays of appeasement that he never saw the ceiling-mounted bolters perk up with mechanical vigour. He was still on his knees, prostrate, when the sentry guns fired upon him, killing him, as he had feared all along.

THE ALARMS INVOKED Opsarus's uncontrolled temper. Each whoop and bray was like a taunt to him, a personal taunt that burrowed its way deep into his ego and ate away at his ability to contain the anger.

Opsarus did not consider himself a furious being. He had an infectious laugh and a deep sense of glee. He often took pleasure in surprising his followers with small gifts – a curious pox, a rash to scratch or a boil to pop – and chuckling warmly.

But he had a serious side too, a cold anger that possessed him when he was enraged. A silent fury that rendered him dark and mute. He would move then almost at a prowl, entirely focussed on eliminating that dark spot against his mirth.

When the rapid series of alarms and reports flooded the hulk's navigation helm, Opsarus settled quietly into that very same state.

Everywhere, the Blood Gorgons were rising – a broken beast that was gradually rousing, shaking its head against the fog of fear and confusion as it woke. It built momentum rapidly, a swift devolution and breakdown of order. First he heard Gammadin's voice on the vox exhorting the meticulously divided Gorgon companies to retaliate. That alone had caused Opsarus some concern. The division of the Blood Gorgons had been tenuous, relying solely on isolation of communication between the squads and an absence of central leadership.

Soon after there were sporadic vox reports of Blood

Gorgons squads retaliating against their Plague Marine custodians, of older, veteran Blood Gorgons squads rebelling from the slave galleys, lashing out against their captors with chains and tools. The fighting was quickly suppressed by gunfire.

The last report, issued from the diseased and venerable Sergeant Kulpus, was that the sentry force at the mid-decks had been lost and the Blood Gorgons had reclaimed an unsealed weapons vault. The regular patrols had been forced back by heavy Blood Gorgons fire. They were losing ground to the abrupt nature of the uprising.

Opsarus was not pleased. He had almost been driven into a spontaneous and uncharacteristic outburst of rage. Instead, he calmed himself with jags of breathing. His brass respirator tanks throbbed with exhalation from his chest vents.

'Can you account for this? Is this your doing?' he asked Muhr accusingly. The sorcerer, as always, stood by his side and behind him.

'No, my lord,' Muhr answered, startled. 'Never.'

'How did it come to this? This mess. I hate mess. Nurgle is decay, but there is an order to that. A process. A graduation. It is slow and inevitable but never a mess. This,' Opsarus said, gesturing at the stilted surveillance images on the console banks. 'This is a mess.'

'Shall I summon the bearers?' Muhr asked. He had already drawn his bolt pistol from his holster and was checking the clip.

'No,' Opsarus replied, waving him away. 'I'll do it myself.'

With careful deliberation, he unlocked his

gauntlet. The hand within the shell was black and swollen. From the unintrusive shadows, a servitor of melting flesh and rusting metal scuffled forwards and affixed an autocannon over Opsarus's hand like a weaponised glove. Another servitor coupled the dense ammunition belt to the Terminator suit.

'We go then. To fix this mess that you've created,' Opsarus said. 'As a matter of principle, Muhr, you should do this yourself. But Nurgle is generous.'

With that, the Crow and his witch made for the command deck, weapon servitors clattering in tow.

THE WAR HAD begun. The five hundred and fifty Plague Marines and four companies of Septic were recalled to battle formations. They rushed back through the space hulk's labyrinth, collecting in massed, company-strength formations. In congregation, they were a formidable force. Solid phalanxes of fortified armour and massed firepower – the slow, grinding combat doctrine of Nurgle. Boltguns and shoulder-mounted autocannons were brought to the fore.

They beat their pitted gauntlets against their chest plates. They shouted in unison, a mocking bark that was carried by a thousand voices. They thundered their feet against the metal decking, raising a clamour that sounded like the march of legions.

Opsarus the Crow, towering tall in his Terminator plate and shroud of skin-mail, advanced amongst his warriors. They cheered him as he passed. The sorcerer Muhr followed in his wake, his blackened face bearing his allegiance to Nurgle. They cheered him too, for he was now one of them.

Opsarus gave no orders, except to raise his fist. The companies of Nurgle, in reply, held aloft their standards and totems, clinking with skulls, effigy dolls and the fluttering flags of skinned tattoos. Beyond the grotesque savagery of their formations, there was also a tightly ranked discipline. With a final clash of kettle drums, the Plague Marines went forth to crush the Blood Gorgons rebellion.

THE DECKS QUAKED. From the lighted halls to the dimmest marshes of the basement sewers, the ship trembled. The *Cauldron Born's* fusion reactor scaled from standby to its highest output potential. Monstrous turbines spun with cyclonic force as the reactor core expanded with solar heat.

Gammadin's reclamation of the ship's defence grid could be felt everywhere.

Sentry guns, previously limp and toothless, resumed their methodical scanning. Positioned in high ceilings and bottleneck corridors, the twin-linked bolters and scatter lasers fired on anything that was not slave-marked or of the Blood Gorgons gene-code. Septic officers broadcast frantic reports that the walls themselves were attacking, spreading confusion throughout their ranks.

Gun servitors – chem-nourished reptiles of hulking shoulders, piston limbs and arms of reaper cannon – resumed their patrol of the ship's main decks. Eyeless and drooling, the previously placated beasts relied purely on the ship's defence grid to sight their targets and receive patrol orders. Now, packs of gun-servitors engaged Septic heavy infantry at close range. Their sole task was to seek, engage and eliminate.

Throughout the ship's labyrinthine passages, void shields and lock shutters locked into position. The Nurgle forces, already disorientated by the ship's layout, were confronted by road-blocks and impasse at nearly all the major routes.

By itself the *Cauldron Born* could not win the war. Already the sentry guns were low on ammunition; the linear patrol servitors were outmanoeuvred by animalistic cunning. Plague Marines breached the sealed corridors. Yet the ship itself was turning against its oppressors. It gave the Blood Gorgons the respite to regroup, re-establish lines of communication and rearm.

THE SHIP'S RECLAIMED defence systems could not win them the war, but they gave the Blood Gorgons the small respite they needed to cobble together some semblance of an offensive.

Plague Marines were accustomed to fighting wars of attrition where they could use superior combined arms to overwhelm an opponent over a long, protracted campaign, grinding them down with disease, illness and misery. On marshes, mudfields and bloodied beaches, the Plague Marines could use their numbers.

But the cramped confines of ship-to-ship boarding were the domain of the Blood Gorgons. They were used to using their small numbers to maximise effectiveness in boarding raids.

At the Maze of Acts Martial, standing before its sacred gates, Bond-Brother Kasuga fought on his own. He had no guns, only the spears, swords and maces of the armoury, yet he fought with the gate's wooden posts buttressing his flank and the lintel over his head. Denying the packed Plague Marine squads room to use their massed ranged weaponry, Kasuga broke his spears and blunted his swords across their armour. Wound after wound he sustained, yet there was no other recourse. He fought or he died: the instinct of self-preservation had long been expelled from his psyche.

SERGEANT HAKKAD MOVED his squad out of their billet in the first moments of confusion. They were unarmed, but well armoured, but that did not matter to him. Hakkad had killed men with less.

He ordered his squad to stay low, creeping through the quiet, disused corridors and guided only by the lambent glow of bacteria colonies. From the main tunnels and gangways, he could hear the distinct whoop of alarms and the high-pitched squeal of automatic scatter lasers. There came muffled, indistinct shouting and the rumble of movement.

Yet, above it all... Above all the noise and disruption, Hakkad heard the voice of Lord Gammadin. That voice urged him onwards. He was compelled by the familiar, rasping tones. The long, drawn-out vowels of a commander who was entirely in control.

'Brothers, I am Gammadin returned.'

That was all he heard – Gammadin's voice over the ship's vox.

There had been a call to arms somewhere, but Hakkad had not really heard anything else. With those words, the rebellion that had simmered in his blood had been brought to the boil. He no longer cared if the other squads and broken companies would join him. It no longer mattered that his squad might be the only one to attempt a resistance. It did not matter because Gammadin had returned in the treasure vaults of the lower decks.

But the other squads did join him. Four members of Squad Hurrian had overpowered their keepers and found Hakkad and his men. Together, the ten Blood Gorgons had entered the unlocked vault and seized anything that could be used as weapons. Ancient relic swords, ceremonial sceptres plundered from ecclesiastical coffers, the gilded pistols of distant kings. These were no real weapons, but Hakkad was glad they had taken them.

Gammadin's declaration was neither magic nor sorcery. In its most basic terms, Gammadin's call gave them a conviction they had previously not possessed. Until then, there had been doubt amongst the Blood Gorgons – separated, betrayed and infiltrated by the enemy, they had lost their trust. Without that trust, they lost the ability to act cohesively. They had ceased to exist as a functional fighting force.

Plague Marines poured into the lower decks to maintain order. With no more than ten Blood Gorgons, Sergeant Hakkad engaged them. They fought at close quarters, a furious hurricane of muzzle flash and glinting steel. The Plague Marines overwhelmed them, but by then Hakkad did not care.

On the vox-link he could hear the reactivation of multiple squads – Squad Khrom, Squad Lagash, Venerable Nysus. One by one, the Blood Gorgons reunited.

* * *

EVERY SLAVE DREAMS of liberation, but when liberation becomes an impossibility, the human spirit has remarkable ways of adapting. One finds comfort in small things – stability, shelter and a bed to sleep in.

The diseased legions had taken even that small comfort away from the slaves of the *Cauldron Born*. What little the slaves had managed to amass for themselves had wilted under the sickness and neglect visited upon them.

So it was no surprise that when the slaves heard Gammadin's call to arms, they too rose up. There were thousands of slaves in the warrens, engines bays, loading docks and storage vaults. The belay teams, scullery serfs, custodials, black turbans. All of them. Thousands upon thousands, like soldier ants swarming from the darkest crevices.

They came out of the darkness, vengeful and exhilarated. They harboured no love for the Blood Gorgons, but it was the only life they knew. Men, women, families, children, even the elderly. Out they came, clattering tools, utensils and whatever blunt, heavy objects of revolt they could find.

They were cut down in their hundreds, yet still they forced one foot before the other. They threatened to overwhelm several key positions in the primary decks held by Septic guards. Black turbans wielding halberd and crossbow led the assault against automatic guns.

Although the slaves died in great numbers, they delayed and harassed the Nurgle counter-offensive. They blocked off tunnels, barricading corridors with pyres of wreckage and gas fires. Some barricaded the enemy with their own bodies. The ones who were not fighters, those who knew the futility of fighting, linked arms and sat, their voices raised in song. In doing so, they forced the Plague Marines to gun their way through a morass of living bodies. Each sold their life for the price of one bolt shell, but they died with a dignity that would otherwise have eluded them.

BOND-SERGEANT SHARLON FUMBLED through the steaming carcass of a Plague Marine. He found a coil of access keys hooked around the Traitor's war belt.

His squad, only five strong now, settled down in the entrance to the Maze of Acts Martial. They used the cover well, lying belly-down between the frond growths and honeycombed calcium deposits. Each had claimed themselves a bolter from the newly opened vaults on access-level 45. Their ammunition, however, was low and they picked cautious shots.

Across the access corridor, at the top of an iron stairwell, Plague Marine squads hammered them with automatic fire. Spitting bolt shot sparked off the walls and ate hungry mouthfuls of metal from the surfaces. The angle of fire was awkward and the shot inaccurate but the sheer volume of ammunition thrown down from the stairwell caused Bond-Sergeant Sharlon to bend double and sprint across the open, the access keys jingling softly against his wrist. Plumes of dusty shots traced his footsteps.

The enemy had sighted him now, calling out warnings from the upper gallery. From Sharlon's right fist sagged a cluster of melta bombs. The enemy saw this too and began to shoot with urgency. A bolt shot exploded against the bond-sergeant's ceramite neck guard, spreading fragments into his face-plate. Another struck his hip, punching him with hot lancing pain. Sharlon staggered up the stairs, taking one faltering step on his injured hip as another bolt tore through his thigh. The Plague Marines stood resolute at the top of the steps, refusing to give ground. They were no more than twelve metres away.

Sharlon took several more stubborn steps upwards. The clustered bombs swayed precariously around the storm of fire drilling through the bond-sergeant. Trembling, Sharlon rested a hand against the banisters. The upper right of his torso had become a porous mass of chewed ceramite and open bleeding. He climbed one more step, out of spite.

The primed melta bomb ignited. It detonated every grenade in the half-dozen cluster so brightly that Sharlon's squad could see nothing as their visors automatically blacked out to protect their retinas from the flare.

It took exactly two seconds for the flare to settle and the squad's light-sensitive lenses to recalibrate. By then, a perfect sphere had been cut into the partition bulkheads. Of the balustrade and upper gallery, there was no sign, nor any evidence that they had once existed. Almost an entire section of the bulkhead and upper mezzanine level had evaporated. The only evidence of the destruction was the smouldering red glow at the very edges of the blast.

If the Blood Gorgons did not have the *Cauldron Born* then nobody would, this was Sharlon's parting message. The *Cauldron Born* existed only with them, and they could not live without the *Cauldron Born*. There was a symbiosis there.

The bond of the Blood Gorgons went beyond that of blood brother to blood brother, it bound them all as one single organism. A squad was nothing without its company, a company nothing without unity. Even the slaves co-existed in reciprocity with their Blood Gorgon masters. Every aspect of the Chapter existed as a unified whole. They would stand and fight together, or they would die alone.

A SINGLE PLAGUE Marine stood on a dais, overlooking the sleeping dens of over two hundred slaves. The slaves, some so sickened that they could no longer stomach water, lay in lethargic heaps before him.

Yet when Gammadin's declaration broadcast over the vox, the slaves began to stir. As one, they began to move.

The Plague Marine was disquieted. He checked the magazine on his bolter and braced it against his hip. He shouted for the slaves to remain supine, but some, he noticed, did not obey him. They stood up – pale and trembling, yet they defied him.

By the time Gammadin's voice was heard a second time, the slaves surged. Their collective minds had been spurred. They rushed up to overwhelm the Plague Marine.

Determined though the slaves were, the Traitor Marine was a killer. With one shot, he killed. He had calibrated his methods of execution to the heights of efficiency. There was no warrior who could match him. But he could not withstand the combined savagery of two hundred desperate humans with nothing left to lose.

They drowned him with the weight of their bodies,

tearing at his impervious armour. They crushed the Plague Marine, dying as they did so. For the slaves, it was a dignified end. To be slain in that final thrust of valour, to try but to fail nobly – it was a death they clambered to receive.

TIGHTLY CONFINED VIOLENCE bubbled up from the lower levels and onto the command deck.

At the supply vaults, Sergeant Nightgaunt of Squad Hekuba succeeded in retaking the entire complex after finding it lightly defended. Heavy numbers of Plague Marines supported by Septic heavy infantry continued to press upon their position. The Blood Gorgons utilised the tight confines of the corridors to their advantage, repelling enemy attacks through their knowledge of the maze-like halls and their tunnel fighting expertise. Nightgaunt himself was killed approaching the third hour of combat, slain as he covered the approach against enemy advance. Yet the remaining five brothers of the squad secured the complex until fragments of the 9th Company reinforced their position and established a line of supply, including ammunitions and weaponry, to those skirmishing in the lower decks.

Only thirty-six minutes into the uprising, two black turban slaves arrived in the Temple Halls, where the fighting was heaviest. The black turbans advised most senior Captain Zothique that slaves had reclaimed significant portions of the lower slave warrens and basements. They had driven out the Septic overseers through sheer numbers, forcing the enemy to reconsolidate their positions.

Although it provided little strategic advantage, it renewed the Blood Gorgons' fighting vigour.

Bond-Sergeant Severn, leading the remains of 6th Company, brought the fight to the interior citadels. Assuming command in place of his slain Khoitan, Severn led an eighty-strong contingent of bonded brethren into a frontal assault against dug-in Plague Marines. With the aid of a veteran rocket team in the overhead bulkheads, Severn was able to dislodge a company-sized element of Plague Marines from their personal quarters and scatter them into the narrow catacombs that housed the black turban barracks.

Nurgle battle tactics were little-changed despite the unfamiliar terrain – they relied on solid, frontal advances supported by heavy ordnance. They set up road blocks and static gun pits in an attempt to entice the Blood Gorgons into open warfare. But against a mobile Blood Gorgons force that refused to engage, they were frustrated in any attempts to counter-attack meaningfully. Perhaps by fault of their obstinate nature, the static Plague Marine formations endured ceaseless hit and run attacks that eventually drove them lower down the *Cauldron Born's* extremities.

TWO VERY POWERFUL entities were approaching the command deck, beings of raw Chaos power. Gammadin could feel their psychic imprint and sense their approach through the ship's neural link.

'They are coming,' he said. The Ascendant Champion's eyelids flickered open as he severed neural links with the *Cauldron Born*.

'Can you hear that?' Gammadin asked.

There was a low keening in the air. Barsabbas strained to hear. Low on the wind, almost inaudible, he heard the acoustic echoes of an ancient metal fortress, a monolithic megastructure creaking as all the pressures of the universe pushed against its iron flanks.

'The *Cauldron Born* is warning me of their approach,' Gammadin said. He brushed the neural fibres from his temple and stood up from the command throne. His pincer arm began to click involuntarily in slight agitation.

Barsabbas took a deep, steadying breath, expanding his lungs with much-needed oxygen. His pupils dilated. There was a static burst of machine-scream through the vox-link as his armour's spirit responded to the oncoming threat. Scrolling overlays of system reports, core temperature and power output streamed across his visor. The power armour wasn't calmed until Barsabbas loaded his bolter with a salvaged clip and clicked the magazine into position. Only then did the machine spirit settle, minimising its report tabs and replacing the data streams with a single targeting reticule that bounced from periphery to periphery.

The entire wall on Barsabbas's left was pushed in. All of it. A thirty-tonne section of plasteel bulkhead peeled inwards. Metal groaned in discordant protest as it was sheared from its structure. Warping and twisting, it finally folded diagonally, crushing the ancient cogitator banks beneath it.

Through the shorn wall came Muhr and the Nurgle Overlord, Opsarus.

For a brief moment, Barsabbas froze. He was

occupied by the most curious feeling. Almost foreboding, dashed with a fleeting pall of hopelessness. Was this *fear*? Barsabbas could not be sure. Was this what it felt like, to be a pure human, at all times?

Opsarus crunched through the debris on legs like basalt columns. A behemoth, wading through the wreckage, deliberate and unsinkable. Behind him he dragged a wrecking ball of spherical metal, its solid weight keeping the chain taut.

He seemed to ignore Barsabbas entirely, not even dignifying the battle-brother's presence with a glance. Instead, he crashed towards where Gammadin squared up to meet him. Only then did Barsabbas realise that perhaps he did not feel fear of the enemy, merely fear that he would not be able to do his enemy enough harm.

Gammadin, the Arch-Champion of the Blood Gorgons, was physically smaller. Opsarus stood over him, his Tactical Dreadnought Armour almost eclipsing Gammadin from view. Even his cherubic deathmask, set in the centre of his hunchbacked chest, stood at a higher eye level than Gammadin's defiantly raised head.

Muhr glided to circle Gammadin's left. The witch was stalking him and cutting off his angles of manoeuvre. By his movements, Barsabbas could see that they were preparing to execute Gammadin at close quarters. There was no other way. Mere small-arms would be insufficient against constructs of warfare such as these. Such gods of war could not be felled by the cowardly shot of pistol or rifle.

Almost fifty metres away from Barsabbas,

Gammadin adopted a low grappler's crouch, his monstrous pincer raised high like the striking tail of a scorpion. Opsarus circled steadily closer, dragging a wrecking ball on a high-tensile chain with one hand.

Barsabbas knew he could not face Muhr or Opsarus in open combat. His bolter would not fell such flesh of the ancients. But if Barsabbas could not overcome them, he could prevent at least one of them from engaging Gammadin.

Firming his resolve, Barsabbas raised his bolter, took aim and waited.

Ever the aggressor, Lord Gammadin launched himself to meet the Nurgle warlord. There was a brief, glancing impact as Opsarus pivoted, their shoulders colliding. It sounded like a light tank had just collided with a super-heavy on full acceleration. The command bridge reverberated with the transfer of their kinetic force.

Muhr stood aside, his eyes rolling as he began to enter a sorcerous trance. Barsabbas had seen the coven work often enough to know their weakness. The brief seconds before a sorcerer could channel the warp were his most vulnerable. If Barsabbas still had a role to play, his time would be now.

Barsabbas banged off three shots at Muhr. They were straight and true, a tight cluster all connected with the target's centre of mass. Yet, as Barsabbas had dreaded, a shield of force solidified before the bolt slugs made impact. The sorcerer turned, snarling.

His visage almost startled Barsabbas. He could barely recognise the witch-surgeon.

Muhr's skin, once white and taut, had become black and sallow. His rubbery face was framed by a matted shock of white hair. The eyes that transfixed him were yellow, lacking any iris or pupil.

Barsabbas withdrew, hoping to lure the witch into pursuit. He sprinted to a side exit, barging through the carved wood with his shoulder. Shrieking, the witch pursued. Barsabbas dared to turn at the tunnel entrance. Anko Muhr's dead face filled his vision with a maw of long teeth and white hair. Barsabbas fired twice, turned, and without looking back, sprinted off with Muhr on his heels.

GAMMADIN CHANNELLED HIS vengeance. There was a stranger standing in his home, taking his birthright. When he unleashed his psionic fury, it coalesced into a rolling sphere that rippled the air like an expanding ball of water.

The sound could be heard throughout the ship. The psychic resonance was so loud that Blood Gorgon and Plague Marine alike stopped their combat, their mental faculties overwhelmed by the psychic and sorcerous backlash.

Yet it did nothing to Opsarus. The Overlord simply looked at him and laughed. The jade of his deathmask was white hot and trailing smoke, but Opsarus was otherwise unscathed.

'You are not the only one here with tricks,' the Nurgle warrior chortled. 'Sometimes, methods determine the outcome of fights. and my method is better than yours.'

Gammadin staggered, spent by his one furious outburst. It was something he should not have done but his anger had been too great. Now his forearms were loose and trembling and he could not feel his own legs. His head was throbbing as neuro-toxicity in his brain spiked after his psychic manifestation. Gammadin could only growl drunkenly as Opsarus lunged forwards.

Opsarus buried Gammadin under his weight. At three and a half metres tall and weighing close to eight hundred kilograms, Opsarus mauled the Blood Gorgons champion. He backed up Gammadin with his sheer power. He threw a constant barrage of straight punches. Studded knuckles crunched into the crisp enamel shell of Gammadin's external plates. He gave Gammadin no time to recompose.

Pinning Gammadin against a console bank, Opsarus raised his wrecking ball, loaded to swing. Gammadin rolled to his left, crumpling the cast-iron console. The sphere crunched through where Gammadin had been, bounced a crater in the far wall and swung a pendulum arc back to Opsarus.

Gammadin regained his balance. Distorted images crazed his vision. The psychic attack had been too potent, especially for his weakened state. It would take him too long to recover.

A heavy blow suddenly crushed into his side, sending him over.

The Blood Gorgon Ascendant swiped his pincer like a club, weakly. His vision swam. He should have conserved himself, he should have contained his anger.

Another blow crashed down onto Gammadin's chest. Scrambled lights and warning beacons flashed in his eyes. The fused bone and ceramite of his torso cracked.

Bleeding and dazed, Gammadin could only think that he should not have been so wild with fury.

* * *

FROM THE COMMAND bridge, the multiple sealed side entrances led into a warren of disused bulkheads in the ship's prow region. Over time they had fallen into a blackened, rotting disrepair. Moisture collected on the scummed floors, ankle deep in some places. The air was toxic with carbon and mould. Gases steamed around him. There was a pervasive quiet, as if the blind faecal worms and water snakes dared not disturb the peace.

It slowly dawned on Barsabbas that here was where he might die. As a Blood Gorgon, he had never thought about death before. Even when driven to withdrawal by the tau, Barsabbas had been the superior combatant, the more fearsome of any singular foe. He had never been outmatched before, not like this. Again that strange feeling which might have been fear crept into his chest.

Yet the notion of death did not trouble him. If he were to be killed, Barsabbas reflected, then better it were by a fellow Astartes, and a venerable Blood Gorgon at that. There was no shame in confronting Anko Muhr, a villain so feared and dreaded in the annals of Imperial history.

Barsabbas crouched down low behind a pillar of calcite and switched off all non-essential power drains to his armour. He watched his surroundings only by the glow of shelled molluscs that clustered around the base of each pillar.

Grimly, he reflected on tales of slaves who had escaped down here to become lost. Indeed, Barsabbas fancied that he had felt the distinct crunch of bones beneath his boots as he threaded his way through the mire.

Barsabbas did not want to be lost, nor did he mean

to hide. His purpose was to engage Muhr and this he intended to do. As he heard a distant elevator clang into position, Barsabbas began to shout, his voice caught and reflected by the unseen catacombs around him.

Almost immediately, he was rewarded by sloshing footsteps. Not incisive steps, but the sloshing of a large shape through water.

'Come out,' hissed the blackened witch. The voice echoed, masking the whereabouts of its owner.

Barsabbas held his bolter, pleading to calm its temperamental spirit.

Do not fail me now–

He shouldered his weapon with a solemn finality. His two hearts beat faster in a syncopated pattern. Yes, fear, Barsabbas admitted. What he felt must truly be fear.

For they shall know no fear–

The clumsy sloshing of the water grew closer. Then, suddenly, it stopped. The air grew cold; according to Barsabbas's visor data, atmospheric temperatures plummeted almost twenty degrees in an instant. A rime of crystals coated his vision. Barsabbas wiped the frost away from his helmet with his fingertips.

He heard a soft swish like a carp gliding through a creek, a gentle lapping sound as if someone were skimming the surface of the water, ever so gently. Barsabbas wondered if that sound was the witch, gliding across the water. The wafting white hair. That slackened dead face, levitating above the ground. The image chilled him. He shifted his grip on his bolter and held it tight.

* * *

GAMMADIN WHEELED AS the wrecking ball crashed through a set of ornate banisters and into the command throne.

'Come and fight me!' Opsarus called.

The Blood Gorgon Ascendant had regained his bearings. His head still pounded with residual pain but he had enough faculty to invoke his will again.

Opsarus cornered him, forcing him back up against the mono-crystal viewing ports of the bridge. Feigning defensiveness, Gammadin lunged upwards without warning. He struck rapidly with his pincer, the gnarled crescent claw snapping at the Nurgle Champion's Terminator plate, gouging chunks from the ceramite.

Opsarus replied with a backhanded punch that thrust Gammadin several steps back – enough distance for the wrecking ball to be brought to bear. Still lurching on the balls of his feet, the Blood Gorgons Ascendant balanced himself against the viewing glass. Sensing a momentary lapse in his foe's guard, Opsarus surged forwards with his tremendous bulk.

It was exactly where Gammadin wanted him.

The viewing ports detonated, their fragments shooting in straight, linear paths as the vacuum of space stole them away. Gammadin's mind blast was weak, strained from his earlier effort, but he centred the force well, aiming the full psionic focus at the viewing ports themselves.

The sudden vacuum tore out the command bridge. Parchment, data-slates and even the shredded shells of cogitators were ripped outwards and through the shattered ports. Opsarus lunged, overcommitting as the vacuum tugged him. Shooting off his knees,

Gammadin threw his entire weight forwards and collided with the Overlord's shins. Such was the speed and force of their collision that armour plates detached from boltings, visors shattered, ceramite chipped and steel dented steel. Opsarus snarled and staggered. Gammadin twisted his body and ripped Opsarus's base out from underneath him, spilling him over.

The Nurgle lord fell, out of the empty port space and into the void beyond. His mammoth bulk became weightless as he was pushed beyond the *Cauldron Born*'s artificial gravity. His hand shot out and snagged the port frame, digits sinking into the metal as he fought for purchase.

'Go forth! You are not welcome here. Perish in the seas of space so that no trace of you will remain,' Gammadin bellowed.

He raised his pincer and snapped at Opsarus's anchored hand, shearing it off. Globes of blood drifted from Opsarus's forearm, spilling outwards and upwards in a slow, languid dance. Opsarus spiralled away, silent and still. He pointed at Gammadin, almost accusatory, as the void took him out to drift and drift into a slow, suffering death.

His mind imagined the witch's scalpel fingers sliding across his neck. Still he heard that awful swishing through the water. Taut with energy, Barsabbas shifted uneasily in his crouch.

Gravel skittered under his boots, loud and clattering in the darkness.

'Come out...' a soft voice murmured.

Barsabbas spun out from behind the calcite pillar, squeezing the trigger of his bolter. He screamed something just for the sake of making noise. His neck bulged as he roared, his chest puffed as the bolter flashed ferociously.

Muhr reeled back in surprise. His force shield strobed as a rapid series of impacts exploded around him. One shot after another, Barsabbas aimed for the same spot, attempting to weaken and short out the forcefield. Time slowed down. The impacts seemed frustratingly languid.

The force shield fizzed and then popped with a vacuum clap. Barsabbas's bolter coughed dry clicks. Emboldened by breaching the shield, he leapt forwards with his mace.

Muhr lashed out with his hands and drilled the bond-brother in the face with a hammerblow of invisible energy.

The blow rocked Barsabbas so hard he momentarily blacked out. He was compelled by fear and did not feel it. He saw only red. Muscles bunching from frantic tension, he began to swing his mace harder than he had ever struck anything. There was a crazed desperation to his strength: the strength of a madman and the howls of a brain-addled lunatic. The fear Barsabbas felt gave him a primal savagery he had never known.

Muhr's face collapsed under the crunching onslaught. The witch tried to fend off the savage blows with his hands. Undeterred, the lashing mace haft bit off two fingers and slapped meatily into the side of the witch's neck.

Barsabbas revelled in the exhilaration of fear. A

loyalist Astartes knew no fear, but Barsabbas was impassioned by it. He knew the power of fear, how to control it, how to project it and how to become strong from it.

Yielding under the ceaseless torrent of strikes, Muhr reached for his bolt pistol. Despite all his witchcraft and his daemonic power, Muhr wilted under the pure, pressured aggression of a cornered beast. Slipping to the ground, Muhr fired two shots at Barsabbas. The first shot went wide. His orbitals had broken and they jammed his eyeball at an awkward angle. But the witch resighted and fired off twice.

Barsabbas did not even realise he had been shot. He lashed Muhr once more across the face, flattening the witch's jaw. Only then did he see that the bolt pistol had punched two craters in his abdomen. Barsabbas pushed through the pain and brought his mace down hard between Muhr's eyes.

Blind with pain, Muhr fired up from a seated position. He emptied the rest of the clip point-blank into Barsabbas's chest plate.

You are dying–

Barsabbas pushed the thought aside. He sank to his knees slowly, clutching a gauntlet to his chest to stem the bleeding as he had been trained to. But there was too much. The blood pumped around his hand and drained down his front. His visor dimmed as the damaged machine spirit conserved power. The entire chest plate had been shorn away.

His arm came up weakly, the mace trembling in his tenuous grasp. He swung it down again, with his last effort, bringing it down to bounce piteously off

Muhr's armour. The witch lay prostrate, his face no longer recognisable, his white hair drenched dark black and red. He wheezed through his broken mouth.

Dead now–

Barsabbas's vision began to fade. He could no longer feel the mighty beat of his hearts. He eased himself down, leaning his back against the crumbling bulkhead. He became listless as his lips grew cold.

Lying down almost beside him, Muhr stirred slightly, blood bubbling from his mouth.

Barsabbas shook his head. He could not die before Muhr. Straining, Barsabbas dragged himself onto his front and inched his hand towards Muhr's throat. Barsabbas's vision was flickering and fuzzing around the edges, but he kept his focus singular. He reached out and seized Muhr's throat in his grasp.

The witch wheezed and slapped at his hands weakly. Slowly, little by little, Barsabbas squeezed the life out of his enemy.

THE FIGHTING CONTINUED for nine days and nine nights. Deep in the lightless confines, there was no measure of time but the strobe of gunfire. It degenerated into a siege. Bulkhead by bulkhead, corridor by corridor.

Victory would never be an apt word. Gammadin knew that many Blood Gorgons had died. Many more would follow. Whittled down and fragmented since the incursion, the entire Chapter had been weakened. It was a desperate struggle. But the Blood Gorgons maintained that precious advantage of terrain. They were fighting in their home. There was nothing left to do except fight or die, and armed properly or not, a cornered warrior was a dangerous prospect.

Through the command of hidden passageways, the Blood Gorgons shepherded the Plague Marines into the lowest portions of the ship, away from the command decks and, more vitally, from the supply vaults. If they could not drive them from the ship they would starve them.

By the eighth day of fighting, it became clear that the Plague Marines were consolidating their fighting positions towards the docking hangars, as if in preparation for withdrawal. Their leadership had been decapitated, and the Plague Companies fought on despite the wholesale surrender of their cultist infantry.

Having suffered some two hundred and fifty casualties, the Blood Gorgons nonetheless pursued. Of the remaining six hundred warriors, Gammadin committed two full companies for the final offensive. Among the senior captains, there was concern that two companies would not be enough to force the remaining Plague Marines into defeat. Any loss of Blood Gorgons momentum now would embolden the Plague Marines to continue fighting. Although their schemes lay broken, Nurgle's forces would continue to fight on, out of resilient spite, for such was the way of the Lord of Decay.

Gammadin, however, remained confident in his assessment of the enemy disposition. They were leaderless and fought a symbolic resistance. It would not take much more damage to drive them into flight.

On the ninth day, Gammadin established a number of heavily defended positions around the mid-tier decks and docking hangars encircling the main zone of conflict. Once the perimeter was secured, Bond-Sergeant Severn, now elevated to the honorary rank of *Khoitan-in-absence*, brought the two assaulting companies into position.

After an exchange that lasted some six hours, the Plague Marines finally initiated a fighting withdrawal into their Thunderhawks and strike cruisers. Severn voxed that their objective had been achieved – the Plague Marines were routed.

That was when Gammadin gave the order to unleash the Chapter.

He waited until the Plague Marines were partway embarked and vulnerable. Sweeping from their positions, Blood Gorgons attacked the fleeing ships with heavy weaponry. They pursued the fleeing craft with torpedo and rocket.

Long after their withdrawal, the burning wrecks of vessel carcasses and the drifting specks of Plague Marines orbited the *Cauldron Born*. Pulled by the fortress's gravity, they spun, listlessly, some entombed alive in their armoured casing.

He was Bond-Brother Barsabbas and he carried the weight of Besheba on his shoulders.

That much, at least, was still clear to him in his more lucid moments. But these moments were fewer and fewer now and more frequently punctuated by agony.

The only thing that never changed was the cold operating slab against his back. He had felt that cold metal against his spine for months now, maybe even years, for Barsabbas had no way of measuring time.

Muhr had destroyed his secondary heart and most of the organs in his right side. Steadily, piece by piece, the morass fibrillators and valve pumps substituting Barsabbas's organs were replaced and grafted with the organs of Lord Gammadin. The Ascendant Champion owed a debt to Squad Besheba. A bonded debt.

The Chirurgeons drained and refilled his arteries. They removed parts of his flesh, cutting here, scoring and sampling there. Every time he awoke, he did so to the system shock of extreme physical trauma.

But Barsabbas came to dread his dreams so much more.

The daemons would visit him then. The ghosts of the dead clawed their way back from the warp-sea to cavort in his visions. They tried to frighten him with stories of eternal torment and tempt him with the peace of eternal sleep.

At first the torment was ceaseless, but as time wore on, the daemons became wary of him. They bothered him less and less, sometimes fleeing when Barsabbas's consciousness entered their realms. They began to call him Gammadin.

On the five hundred and eighty-ninth day, Barsabbas was animated from his ritual coma. His remade body felt cold, as if he were not quite accustomed to inhabiting it. Rising from the slab to the click of his atrophied ligaments, Barsabbas placed a hand to his chest. He could feel the pulse beneath his sutured muscles.

Bound in flesh, the dormant volcano of Gammadin's heart rumbled.

ABOUT THE AUTHOR

Henry Zou is an Australian writer from Sydney. He has been known to write down ideas whenever they come to him, whether it be on paper, tables and even the walls of his kitchen. His previous landlords were not impressed. Many of these ideas have found their way into his writing, including *Planetkill, Emperor's Mercy* and *Flesh & Iron*.

AARON DEMBSKI-BOWDEN

SOUL HUNTER

A NIGHT LORDS NOVEL

WARHAMMER
40,000

UK ISBN 978-1-84416-810-1
US ISBN 978-1-84416-811-8

AARON DEMBSKI-BOWDEN

THRONE OF LIES

A NIGHT LORDS AUDIO

WARHAMMER
40,000

AUDIO
DRAMA

UK ISBN 978-1-84416-926-9
US ISBN 978-1-84416-927-6

THE NIGHT LORDS
RETURN

AARON DEMBSKI-BOWDEN

MAY 2011

BLOOD REAVER

A NIGHT LORDS NOVEL

WARHAMMER
40,000

UK ISBN 978-1-84970-038-2
US ISBN 978-1-84970-039-9

WARHAMMER
40,000

A SPACE MARINE BATTLES NOVEL

SINCE THE GENESIS of the Astartes, there has been enmity between the Space Wolves and the Thousand Sons. The brutal and honourable Sons of Fenris and the esoteric Legion of Magnus the Red fought as allies for the Emperor, but all that changed when the Space Wolves attacked Prospero. Magnus and his Thousand Sons were forced to flee their home world to escape annihilation.

The Thousands Sons were defeated, but their hatred only grew in the intervening years. The once-loyal Legion soon fell to Chaos, while the Space Wolves fought bravely in stamping out the Heresy of Horus, proving their loyalty and mettle.

Where once stood brothers now stand the bitterest of enemies.

A thousand years on, the time for vengeance has come. The sorcerous Thousand Sons launch the ultimate attack on their nemesis. Their objective – the Fang, the Space Wolves' fortress on Fenris. Now, a millennia old fury will be unleashed, and destruction and madness will reign. With so many of their brothers chasing Magnus's shadow elsewhere in the galaxy, the Sons of Fenris have never been more vulnerable. The Fang's scant defenders must hold off the overwhelming power of the Thousand Sons, or a proud Chapter will be wiped from the stars forever.

BATTLE OF THE FANG
A SPACE MARINE BATTLES NOVEL
COMING JUNE 2011